# Lincoln Marsh

*a novel by*
S%%TEPHEN%% W%%EST%%

Copyright © 2015 Stephen West
Black Cabin Publishing

All rights reserved. No part of this publication may be reproduced, stored in a retrieval system or transmitted in any form or by any means electrical, mechanical, photocopying, recording or otherwise, without the prior permission of the author.

ISBN-13: 978-1517090128
ISBN-10: 1517090121

For Kirsten

LINCOLN MARSH

# PROLOGUE

LINCOLN MARSH couldn't breathe.

Black earth pressed down hard onto his shoulders and back. His head submerged in a foul smelling trench of mud and water. He tried to push up, but the weight above was too heavy. A gagging, choking convulsion took hold of his body. He screamed into the cold, unforgiving earth. His eyes bulging in the blackness. He had no thoughts of death. No images of his past life flashing before him. Just an agonising, all consuming, biological need to breathe. He felt a dizzy swoop of nausea as his body and brain began to shut down. He tried again to push up, but his hands slipped, unable to gain any purchase in the wet, cold earth. He slumped forward. His lungs ached as a desperate pain gripped his chest. He knew he couldn't hold out much longer.

*       *

The Comtoise clock in the Crown Room of the Burgoyne

Club issued a dreary and regretful chime to mark another hour passed since the club's establishment in 1824. Its founder and benefactor, Field Marshall Frederick Burgoyne, initially limited membership to retired military leaders and other heroes of the British Empire, but during the early part of the twentieth century, entrance requirements were relaxed to accommodate those simply possessing the right breeding and enough money. The elegant rooms and corridors, once occasioned by the very best of Victorian society: the soldiers; the engineers; the reformers; the scientists, were now plagued by the ageing heirs of English estates, mouldering in the happenstance of inherited wealth. The noble ambitions of their predecessors replaced by a vague nothing. The ageing and mean-spirited membership, spoke only of finance, business and commerce, anything that could result in more easy money. The members spent hour after hour at the tables and bars of the club, drinking and dealing, sinking forever deeper into their malodorous slough of mendacity and greed.

 The air in the Crown Room was heavy and stagnant. The weighty velvet curtains, pulled together with finality some hours ago, sealed out any light offered by the fading November afternoon. Outside, the Pall Mall traffic wrenched and wrestled its way across the congested streets of London, but inside, all was still. A gentle hum of male voices washed to and fro across the room, interrupted by the occasional soft clink of decanter on crystal. On the right of the fireplace, underneath the club crest emblazoned with the motto *constantia et virtute*, by firmness and courage, basked one of the more fulsome figured members. Having worn out his manly rage by staring bug-eyed at the latest edition of The Times, occasionally growling and shifting uncomfortably in his chair, he had collapsed into a deep slumber, eased towards rest by a full lunch and a half bottle of decent claret. To the left of the fireplace, in a huddle of incontinence, sat a group of ancient Burgoyne Club members, lost within a misty gaze of the past, their timid confused faces betraying their uncertainty of their current whereabouts. In the opposite corner, alone and irritable, sat Anthony Willoughby, the senior figure of the Willoughby dynasty.

He had been just twenty one years old when he had taken over as Head of the Family in 1965. The past fifty years, under his stewardship, had seen the business prosper, adding still further to the vast wealth of his forefathers. His waxen head of hair was now white with age and greased back, tight, against his skull. His dinner jacket hung loosely on his shoulders, but apart from some stubborn extra weight around his girth, he looked in reasonable condition for his 71 years. The corners of his mouth had rarely been troubled by a smile throughout his life and had now relaxed into a miserable and wrinkled droop. His eyes were a soft, pale blue, lifeless in their translucence, but, look close and you would see the same vicious intent for self-preservation you might find in the eyes of a cornered stoat.

His fingers tapped impatiently against the brandy glass. He rarely met Cassidy face-to-face these days, preferring the relative anonymity offered by email and the telephone, but the November meeting had become a custom during the twenty or so years they had worked together. There were only two agenda points: projected year end profits; and proposed cuts for the year ahead. He knew it had been a good year for the Estate, but Cassidy was responsible for the final reconciliations and he was waiting for his loyal foot soldier to deliver the good news in full. He also needed to make clear his position on the ill-fated venture in Germany. The project was over. Salaries, rents and any additional costs needed to be curtailed immediately. In addition, the Breden Strasse office in Bremen should be closed with immediate effect.

'Where is that blasted man?' he muttered, angrily.

The fact that Cassidy was walking through the doors of the Burgoyne Club as he spoke, exactly on time and as punctual as ever, was unlikely to hold any sway with the irascible Mr Anthony Willoughby.

\* \*

Rajendra Kapur had always found this part of the job difficult.

First he removed the clip on the small plastic bag of items that had been sent down from the Garrett Anderson Emergency Ward. Then he reached forward to angle his desk lamp so it would better illuminate his workstation, which was positioned in a particularly gloomy corner of the basement of Ipswich Hospital. Rajendra positioned the items carefully onto his bench. To his left, he placed the torn, bloody strips of clothing that had been cut and removed from the patient as she was lying on the operating table. Amongst the shredded clothes were thin remnants of surgical dressings that had found their way into the bag of personal belongings, bundled up in haste by the charge nurse earlier that day. To his right, Rajendra placed two rings - one a wedding band; a small gold watch with a cracked face; a single brown leather shoe; a silver hair clip; and a set of car keys. Two dark red drops of blood stained the leather on the Honda branded keyring. The items on the left would be sent to the hospital incinerator for disposal. The items on the right would be bagged, labelled and stored for collection by the bereaved relatives.

Rajendra briefly considered the circumstance surrounding this latest fatality. Looking at the shredded clothes of the deceased, she must have experienced significant trauma involving multiple and severe injuries. Most likely a traffic incident of some description. Rajendra wondered if others had been involved or whether the car had swerved off the road having hit some black ice or maybe one of her tyres burst as she negotiated a sharp bend? Perhaps she had taken an unfamiliar shortcut in her impatience to get home from work after a difficult day at the office or maybe she had briefly looked at her phone to see who was calling, just as a deer bolted across the road in front of her? Who knows? Rajendra shook his head, silently admonishing himself for letting his curiosity get the better of him. It did no good and served no purpose.

He took a deep breath and removed a pen from his jacket pocket. Once he had entered the name, date and hospital details he stuck the label on the bag, ready for filing and placed it on the trolley, stationed next to his chair.

# CHAPTER 1

THE day had started badly.

Lincoln checked his watch. He had less than four hours to get to the family home, some one hundred and sixty miles away. Sorrel Cottage was situated in the small village of Skeilton a short distance from the Suffolk coastline, near the market town of Halesworth and if he left immediately, avoiding the early morning traffic, he might just make it in time. He picked up his mobile from where he had thrown it across the room following his brother's call, checking that it was not damaged, and made his way to the shower. Ten minutes later he was in his car driving down the backroads of Twickenham, towards the M3 motorway.

His phone vibrated on the passenger seat. He could see it was a text from his brother. He had no intention of reading it following their acrimonious call earlier. Five o'clock in the morning was never a good time to talk, particularly when the call was to confirm a meeting with the family solicitor which, so his brother informed him, Lincoln would be attending as the sole family representative. Despite Lincoln's protests, his brother would not consider rescheduling as the solicitor was about to start a walking holiday in the Brecon Beacons and would be unavailable for a week if this appointment was missed. The call soon descended into the terse, vicious language that was a feature of their exchanges over the last few years and resulted in the call being terminated abruptly. Although, who actually put their phone down first, was unclear.

The two brothers did not spend much time in each other's company these days. Benjamin Marsh now lived in a modern, lakeside retreat in Sweden, just outside Gothenburg. He had moved there two years ago with his German wife, Astrid, following his appointment as the CEO of Norse Bank, and with his proliferating wealth and enhanced status had come a self-assured hubris that Lincoln found hard to tolerate. His control of family affairs since their mother's death was in keeping with his brother's new way of doing things. Lincoln accepted that Ben's knowledge of financial matters was particularly helpful when dealing with the inevitable legal complications involved in reconciling an estate, but having appointments made on his behalf without any form of discussion, was a step too far. Nevertheless, here he was, pulling into the small gravel drive in front of the familiar façade of Sorrel Cottage, in time to meet the solicitor, Mr Stillman, at the pre-determined hour of nine o'clock.

Three weeks had passed since the Ward Doctor had confirmed, with emotionless certainty, that his mother was unlikely to regain consciousness. By the following morning, the doctor had been proved right and once Lincoln had said his choking and inadequate farewells, he had slipped out of the hospital building to perform the painful duty of informing his only brother of his mother's passing following her heart attack. Ben had come back to England for the funeral that had taken place in the local church. He came alone, Astrid being busy with an exhibition, and made no attempt to engage with the small huddle of local residents who had come to pay their respects. He spoke to the vicar, his one remaining uncle and Lincoln and then gave his excuses and left for the airport, without even attending the small affair of wine and sandwiches that had been arranged back at the cottage. Since then, a series of businesslike emails had arrived in Lincoln's inbox giving various instructions regarding the house and the appointment of the solicitor. This morning was the first time the brothers had spoken on the phone since their mother's funeral.

Lincoln gazed up at the small, wooden-framed windows of the cottage that looked out from his parent's bedroom. The woodwork had become rotten and needed replacing, revealing black indents amidst the peeling, white paint, flaking around the edges of the window panes. His mother had often sat in front of those windows, reading her Austen, Woolf and Lessing or looking out across the two corn fields opposite, that reached down to the river that split the shallow valley of Blyth. A small cluster of trees divided the two fields, their branches now stripped bare of leaves by the flowing, autumnal winds that swept across the Suffolk landscape at this time of year. The resonating ache of loss took hold in Lincoln's heart. This home had meant everything to his parents, it was their absolute pride and joy. He, his brother and this building were all that was left to mark their short time on earth. All else was gone, taking its leave with the last faint beat of his mother's heart  He took a deep breath and ducked through the small front door, into the hall of the cottage.

The portly figure of Mr Stillman was waiting for him in the sitting room. His mother's will rested on the small oak table alongside a bundle of other papers and a plan, drawn up in 1970, when his parents had first bought the house, detailing the layout of the rooms and surrounding gardens.

'Mr Marsh,' Stillman said, reaching out his hand, 'it is good to see you and thank you for coming all the way from London. I do appreciate it, you see, I am about to go on holiday to Wales.'

'Yes, no problem, Mr Stillman. My brother mentioned

your plans. Not particularly convenient, but it can't be helped I suppose. Shall we get on with whatever we need to take care of and then you can be on your way.'

'Very good, Mr Marsh, shall I talk you through the relevant documents,' he said, waving his hand across the paperwork arranged in neat piles on the table, 'I will try and be as brief as professional responsibility allows.'

\*

Three hours later they were still seated. Mr Stillman had never been comfortable with the merits of condensing legal process and took great pride in the care and fastidiousness he applied in all dealings with his clients. Every legal term was required to be read, explained and understood by all parties. "Cutting to the chase", as he had heard it referred to, simply would not do.

'...and that, Mr Marsh, brings me to my last item.' He picked up the one remaining sheet of paper yet to be discussed. 'Your father, when he died last year, passed onto your mother the contents of his study, which houses an archaeological collection of some significance I believe. His intention was to keep the collection in tact so it could be enjoyed by Mrs Marsh and the remaining family members during their lifetime. Later, at a point in time when your mother had also passed away, it would be up to you and your brother to decide which items from the collection you wished to retain and which you wanted to pass on to the East Anglian Archaeological and Treasure Museum. Therefore, for me to progress the winding up of the estate, I will need you, in the absence of your brother, to review and assign each item within your father's collection as soon as is convenient. Preferably today.'

'Today?'

'Yes, today, if at all possible, sir. My colleague, Maureen, will then complete a revised manifest and arrange shipment to the museum in time for my return from Wales.'

A look of pain appeared in Lincoln's eyes as he recalled the last time he had seen inside his father's chaotic and disorganised study. Mr Stillman was waiting for a response or affirmation from his client so he could wrap up the proceedings and start his winter break, but all Lincoln could manage was a hushed and wistful,

'Oh.'

*

Mr Stillman eventually left the cottage just after one o'clock, with a demob happy glint in his eye, leaving Lincoln to begin the review of his father's collection. After fortifying himself with a strong, black coffee, he made his way up the narrow stairs to the back room of the house. It had been several years since he had stepped foot in his father's study. The last time he had been in there it had proved difficult to manoeuvre across the floor without risking serious injury, such was the extent of his father's work. So it was with a sense of trepidation that he turned the key in the creaking lock. The door would barely open, but following a solid shove, he widened the gap just enough for him to squeeze through. He closed the door behind him and then looked, dumbfounded, at the contents he had agreed to catalogue.

Boxes were piled on boxes, from floor to ceiling. Some collapsing with the weight of their contents. His father's old desk was submerged under reams of paper, listing item after item after item of various archaeological finds. In the far corner, in front of the window, there were some metal shelves, with up to a hundred jars filled with grey and black stones of all shapes and sizes. The room was overwhelmed with fossils, shells, coins, fragments of pottery, small glass bottles, the bones of small animals, broken porcelain and various other relics and curiosities. A large map of the Waveney district and coastline was displayed on the ceiling, covered in a barrage of small red crosses and tiny, illegible writing detailing the whereabouts of each of his digs, dating back to

1980 when his father's hobby first developed into a fully fledged obsession. Lincoln heaved a heavy sigh. It would take days to go through all of the items properly. There was no way he had the time or the inclination to spend the next week cooped up in the study sorting through it all. Besides, he knew that, even though there may be some moderately notable items hidden within the collection, the majority would be of little value or interest. His father had told him as much when he was still alive and admitted he just liked collecting "things" and being surrounded by "the shrapnel of past lives" as he called it. He decided to call Stillman's office and let the solicitor's colleague, Maureen, know that the museum could take the lot and that would be the end of it.

    Lincoln gingerly backed out of the room and was about to close the door behind him when he saw something poking out from behind a small wooden stepladder his father had used when climbing up to some of the higher boxes. It was a child's painting. The clumsy brushstrokes betraying an artist of extremely limited potential, but bundles of youthful exuberance. Lincoln moved forward slowly into the room over to the painting, shuffling boxes and artefacts out of his way and creating a narrow pathway across the floor. The colours used by the artist defied any logic. The sky was green. The hands of the four figures were either orange or purple and the dog, a terrier named Gruff, was an eye-catching pink with a yellow collar. The image portrayed a family of four. A mum, a dad and two boys. The taller boy was holding his mother's hand while the younger one was standing in front of the figure of the father with his purple hands aloft. A speech bubble was circled above his head, with the words "Look Dad, Treasure! We're rich!!". The Dad had a large swipe of black paint across his face, depicting a proud smile and was saying "YES! Well done Lincoln! You're the greatest!" In the bottom corner was the artist's signature, Benjamin Marsh, aged 9. Lincoln looked down at the image and smiled. 'Good painting Ben. . . you bastard.'

    The sense of longing, regret, guilt was making him feel

mawkish. He needed a drink. He decided to take the painting with him and began to remove the drawing pins from the four corners. Maybe he would get it framed when he got back to Twickenham? A memento of his childhood. Or a version of it anyway. He reached down to remove the bottom two drawing pins after moving a small, wooden box to one side. Once he had rolled up the painting, he pushed the box back in place when he noticed it had been labelled - *Sorrel Cottage dig. 1985.* He carefully prised off the lid of the box. Inside there was another pile of meaningless objects, including two bits of rusted metal that looked like they formed part of gate hinge, a small glass vial, a broken stirrup and two flints, which could have been from an axe or could have just been two flints.

Right at the bottom of the box, there was a small, dark brown saddlebag of some sort, about six inches in height, wrapped in some grubby muslin. He decided that the box of 'shrapnel' and the painting were fitting epitaphs to his father's life. He gathered them both up and carefully made his way across the floor. He took one last look at the room and pulled the door to. With the painting in his hand and the wooden box under his arm, he made his way back down the narrow stairs to the sitting room in search of a stiff drink.

# CHAPTER 2

THE drinks cabinet proved to be a significant disappointment, offering up nothing more than a bottle of tabasco, some flat tonic water and half-full decanter of cheap whiskey. A glass tumbler and a fresh mug of black coffee sat on the kitchen table amidst the contents of the box he had retrieved from his father's study. He smiled as he looked down on the small collection of metal junk in front of him. The fractured hinges rested on their side, next to the broken stirrup which rolled back and forth, gently rocked by the old kitchen table with its one uneven leg. The rusty collection reminded him of when his father would return home after a dig and present his day's findings to his wife, carefully explaining the origins of each item. Unfortunately, Mrs Marsh could not have been less interested and met his enthusiasm with infinite indifference.

They loved each other dearly, but his mother had never fully come to terms with her husband's love of archaeology since he first announced his career change in 1990. Prior to that, he had worked in Norwich as a middle manager for a large insurance company, where he had spent most of his working

life. It all sounded very dull to the young Lincoln and indeed it was, but the money was reasonable and the work was not particularly taxing so his father had stuck with it, making the thirty mile trip into Norwich every morning in his rusty, brown Volvo estate. Lincoln's mother stayed at home looking after her two young sons and attempting to keep the three hundred year old cottage in a satisfactory state of repair.
Then, out of the blue, on his 55th birthday, his father came home early from work, smiling and perhaps a little worse for wear, announcing that he had taken an unpaid job with Norwich University who were looking for volunteers to assist with an archaeological dig, just south of Lowestoft. Mrs Marsh, who had always been the more grounded, more practical of the two, did not share her husband's wide-eyed enthusiasm, not talking to him for days and having nothing to do with him apart from silently presenting him with an assortment of monthly utility bills as they arrived through the letterbox. In the top right hand corner of each bill she had drawn a large, red question mark, which she had angrily underlined three times. His father, however, was resolute and one Monday, a few weeks later, he got into his car and after more than twenty years of turning left out of the drive towards Norwich, he now turned right, to the east, in the direction of his new workplace. Relationships between his parents remained strained for a considerable time, but eventually they adjusted and between his father's pension and his mother's income from a few odd jobs she did in the village, they just about got by and slowly the house settled back into its familiar rhythm of meal times and homework. Birthday presents were smaller, holidays were fewer, but, fundamentally, family life carried on much as it had done before.

    Lincoln raised his glass in a silent toast to his parents and downed his drink, wincing at the sour, metallic taste of the whiskey.

    He pushed the metal objects to one side and reached for the saddlebag, unwrapping it from the cloth that surrounded it. Inside the bag there was a handwritten note from his father.

*Leather saddlebag - mid 19th century. Hunting knife with sealed handle chamber - late 19th century. Discovered - 24th August, 1985 in disused well in grounds of Sorrel Cottage, Suffolk.*

Lincoln read the note a second time, puzzled. He had no idea that there was or had ever been a well in the garden. He had played in every square inch of grass and surrounding hedgerow when he was a kid, so it seemed unlikely that between him and his brother they had not, inadvertently, come across this hole in the ground. His parents, he presumed, must have covered it or filled it in and decided not to tell the two of them about it, knowing that it would be too big a draw to the inquisitiveness of the young sons. He reached into the saddlebag and pulled out the knife. The heavy blade was blunt and about five or six inches long. Towards the top, near the handle, there was an inscription which he could just about read if he held the knife up to the light.

*STRATHDON IS ALL*
*Joseph Chapman & Sons, St Albans.*
*1892*

The handle was made of bone and, even though his father had cleaned it, there were still specks of black mud ingrained in it from lying beneath the earth for decades. He looked back at his father's note. It said that the knife had a chamber in the handle but he couldn't see where it could be. He turned the handle over and could just make out a thin, black line running down the centre of the bone. He tried to dig his nails into the crevice, but it was stuck fast. He got a thin cooking knife from the cutlery drawer and gently slid the blade into the narrow gap. After several minutes of careful manipulation he managed to force the handle open to reveal two, small, hollowed out chambers, opposite each other. The chamber on the top of the handle was empty, but the one on the underside contained what looked at first glance like an old, hand-rolled cigarette. Lincoln took it out and carefully unrolled the dry, delicate paper onto the desk just as the uneven table jogged to one side, spilling coffee onto the surface, the hot liquid spreading to within an inch of the wafer thin paper.

'Don't you dare,' he said, swiftly wiping the coffee with the cloth that had been wrapped around the saddlebag, which he then shoved under the uneven leg to avoid any further spills. He dug into the pocket of his jeans to get some coins and gently placed them on all four corners of the small note, pinning it out. He could just about make out some writing. Some words had completely faded and what remained was barely legible, but slowly he managed to decipher some of the letters, making a note of them on a page of his mother's kitchen diary.

a _ _ _ _ sga_ _ _ _ ho_ _ _ _ _ _ _
_ _y_ _ 92 dunnings al_ _ _ 9 _ _ _ _ ham
providence at peasenhall
kill them all

He looked down at the letters and words, unable to make any sense of them. The word 'dunnings' meant nothing to him, although it did seem to ring a vague bell in the back of his mind; 'providence' held no special meaning beyond the dictionary definition; however, 'peasenhall' he recognised as the name of a village some eight miles away from Sorrel Cottage. He had driven through it on many occasions with his family on their way to visit relatives in Cambridge. His dad would always slow down as they drove through the main street so they could watch the peacocks that would walk serenely along the high street, pecking at the hollyhocks and foxgloves that bordered the villager's gardens. The birds moved as one, in an unhurried stroll, oblivious to the impatient motorists whose cars were reduced to a sluggish crawl as the peacocks meandered from one side of the road to the other, at a regal pace. The only other time they visited was when his mother used to shop at the Peasenhall butchers, whose name escaped him for the moment, once a year at Christmas time, buying black peppercorn ham and a jar of locally produced whole grain mustard, which she would serve up on Boxing Day, alongside the leftover turkey.

The final sentence of the note was, in itself, easy to understand but kill what, he wondered? The peacocks? The villagers? He looked again at the words. The second line ended with 'ham' and had four letters missing in front of it. Pigs ham maybe? Although that sounded wrong, ham always coming from pigs, but it could explain the last line. He looked down at the knife. It looked like the blade of a working man, a farmer perhaps. Maybe the note was just a list of tasks he had to take care of, an instruction he had been given to slaughter some of the livestock grazing in the nearby fields and get them ready for market. That seemed to make sense, although he knew he was just guessing. His dad would always say when faced with an indecipherable object he had found buried in the earth or washed up on the beach, "The past is full of wonder, but will not give up its secrets cheaply. You need to know where to look and learn how to see." His father would no doubt have concocted a far more extravagant version of the truth than a farm workers checklist and would have spent the rest of the day locked away in his study, elbow deep in reference books and local histories trying to justify his theory.

Lincoln took another drink from his glass, ignoring the coffee, which had now cooled to room temperature. Outside, the sky was already beginning to darken. From where he sat he had a clear view of the narrow garden leading out onto the dark brown earth of the fields beyond, lying frozen in wait for the resuscitating warmth of spring. The clear late November skies of the last week had brought with them a drop in temperature marking the end of autumn and the onset of winter. He made a mental note to check the oil level before he left the house in the morning. The last thing he needed was to find himself having to explain to his brother that the cottage had been flooded following a burst pipe.

Even though it was still quite early, he decided to get some food on the go. He had bought some stuff from the local garage on the way up, just a pizza and some salad, none of which looked particularly appetising, particularly now that he had removed their packaging. He checked his phone while he waited for the old Belling oven to heat up. There was an email from his brother asking for an update, which he immediately deleted and a text from Sarah Gillespie at work, chasing down some fabricated deadline. He would call her later and calm her fears. Lincoln recognised that he had a tendency to leave things to the last minute, but he was proud of the fact that he did always deliver on time in the end. After the many years of working together, Sarah really should have known that by now.

It bothered him that he couldn't remember the name of the butcher his mother used to visit in Peasenhall. The shop had been there for centuries but he just couldn't think what it was called. He entered the name of the village into Google and clicked on the Wikipedia link. Emmett's. That was it. Established in 1820. Known for providing pickled ham for the Queen Mother. He scanned the rest of the short entry, but apart from a picture of the infamous peacocks and the reference to Emmett's, there didn't seem to be a great deal happening in Peasenhall. Towards the bottom of the screen was a further link titled *The Peasenhall Murder.* Intrigued, Lincoln clicked on the link and read the entry.

*The Peasenhall Murder is a notorious unsolved crime committed in Suffolk, England on the night of 31st October 1902. The house where the murder occurred can be found in the centre of the village, on the opposite corner to Emmett's Store. The case is seen by many as a classic unsolved country house murder, committed near midnight, during a thunderstorm.*

*The victim, Reverend George Barkham, was stabbed to*

*death by an unknown assailant. It was alleged that Barkham, who was married with two children, had conducted an affair with a servant girl, Rose Harsent, who was seven months pregnant at the time of the murder. Rose Harsent was employed by William Gardiner who was the foreman at the local seed drill works (Smyth's of Peasenhall). She lived in the Gardiner's cottage, within sight of Providence House where the murder was committed.*

*Following a short police investigation Harsent was quickly arrested, but the jury, presided over by Sir John Compton Lawrence, were unable to reach a verdict. It was said that the jury was split eleven to one in favour of guilty. The prosecution issued a writ of nolle prosequi. This was distinct from the usual process of formal acquittal. The consequence of the writ is that Harsent is one of the few people in English history to have been tried for murder and to have no verdict ever returned.*

*Rose Harsent never recovered from the shame of the trial, despite not being found guilty, and, unable to find work, she took her life and that of her newly born baby in January 1903, drowning herself in the River Yox, near Valley Farm.*

Lincoln looked down at the blunt, dull blade on the table, his eyes darting between the Wikipedia entry on the screen and the words he had written in his mother's diary, his mind joining the facts together into a new truth. The article mentioned Providence House at Peasenhall; both names were included in the saddlebag note from the well. There had been a murder; the saddlebag note included the instruction to 'kill them all'. The murder victim was called Barkham; one of the illegible words ended in 'ham'. Barkham had been stabbed; there was a knife in the saddlebag along with the note.

He picked up the dagger, looking closely at the rusted point of the blade, turning it over in his hands. Could this really be a murder weapon or was he just letting his imagination run away with itself just like his dad would have done, creating connections that did not exist? If it was the weapon used by the murderer back in October, 1902, what was it doing in a disused well located somewhere in his family's back garden? None of it made any sense. If the killer was Rose Harsent, why would a heavily pregnant woman stab her lover and then trek eight miles away, in the pitch black and during a thunderstorm, just to throw the murder weapon down this particular well? No, it had to be someone else, not Rose. He knew from the maps his father kept in his study that, before they had built the road to the east of Sorrel Cottage, which eventually became the A12, a highway had run from the south of the county, passing through Peasenhall and running directly alongside the border of the cottage, splintering into three routes just a mile further to the north in the direction of the villages of Blyth, Halesworth and the coastal town of Southwold. A rider, making their way to the nearest town after the murder, would almost certainly have used this route. Could the murderer have taken the opportunity to dispose of the weapon during their journey north, tossing it and the saddlebag into the disused well where it had remained safely hidden from sight for over a hundred years?

Maybe it was a bid to reconnect with his dad and his love of the past that made him start looking at the house and garden plan Mr Stillman had left behind? Maybe it was the sadness he felt following his mother's death that made him so reckless? Maybe it was an outlet for the frustration and anger he felt towards his brother? Or, maybe it was just the whiskey? Whatever the reason, ten minutes later Lincoln stepped out into the thickening darkness of the night. In his right hand he held a torch, in his left was the plan of Sorrel Cottage, which now had a circle drawn around the words 'disused well' in the far top corner of the garden, next to a space where his father had erected a shed when Lincoln and Ben would have still been toddlers.

A large hawthorn bush blocked his route to the back of the

wooden hut, but buoyed by the whiskey, he pushed past, ignoring the spiteful barbs, dragging into the flesh of his hands and face, and made his way through to a small patch of ground covered with thick, black tarpaulin. The groundsheet was embedded in the frozen earth, but using a spade he took from the shed, it eventually came away and now sat in a crumpled heap next to the hawthorn bush. Three inches below the surface, under mud and stones and covered in bramble roots was a three foot square iron plate. He dug the spade under the edge, but the metal remained frozen in the earth. He tried instead to use the spade as a lever but still the heavy plate would not move. Thinking he might try it from another angle, he edged round to the far side, pushing the undergrowth clear of his face as he did so. Once again, he dug the spade under the iron covering and tried to prise it out of the earth. On his third attempt, the spade slipped, causing him to fall inelegantly onto his backside, his head buried in the frozen brambles. He lay there for a second, looking through the undergrowth at the night sky and listening to the stillness of the countryside, wondering what the hell he was playing at. The fall had sobered him up slightly. He could now feel the chill of the frozen air and the raw scratches on his hands and face. He would give it one last try and then head back into the warmth of the cottage. He pushed down hard. The full force of his weight bearing down on the spade. He felt some movement and pushed harder. Suddenly the ground gave way beneath his feet as the iron plate became dislodged and flipped over onto the opposite bank. He started sliding down into the hole beneath him. He tried to grab the brambles on the surrounding banks, clutching at the thorny stems, but they could not hold his weight, and, uprooted, fell with him into the cold, blackness of the disused well.

# CHAPTER 3

MILTON S. Cassidy left the Burgoyne Club following a three hour meeting with Anthony Willoughby, reviewing the year-end accounts.

Night had fallen and a chill wind stirred through the trees at the top of Carlton Gardens where he was waiting for the Club valet to deliver his black S63 AMG Mercedes Benz. He glanced at his watch. There was just enough time to return to his Kensington office before getting the night train to Edinburgh where he was due to meet with two property agents the following morning.

Somewhere on the other side of Pall Mall, a group of work colleagues stumbled out of a bar in a drunken heap. They took a moment to get their bearings and then piled forward, looking for their next haunt. Despite the weather, the three young men were dressed in t-shirts more suited to a warm July evening, seemingly immune from the biting north wind. Crossing the road, one of the female revellers, solid limbed, big boned, chunky, caught sight of Cassidy, standing, tall and broad, under the lights of the Club entrance. She nudged her friend, pointing and muttering a salacious comment, causing them both to collapse forward in a lustful cackle. Cassidy continued staring ahead, waiting patiently for his car, oblivious to the the sexual arousal he had engendered. A lone pigeon landed clumsily, just in front of him. Deformed and malnourished, the pigeon hobbled back and forth on his gnarled feet, optimistically pecking the ground for food. As it ventured closer, Cassidy caught sight of the diseased bird and, following a brief moment of assessment, clipped the pigeon on the side of the head with his boot, sending it spinning into the the road.

'Oi!' A cry pierced through the night air as the boyfriend of the big boned reveller shouted in Cassidy's direction.

'Oi! You! You can't do that, you twat.' Although now drunk and stupid, he had noticed his girlfriend's eager eye settle on the old geezer over the road. He turned back to his two mates, a look of appalled disbelief on his face. 'Did you see that? That fucker just kicked that bird,' he said, pointing at the dizzied pigeon, still trying to renegotiate the lip of the pavement. 'I'm not having that. No chance.' He began walking aggressively towards the still heedless Cassidy. 'Come on,' he shouted, waving his arm in the direction of the Club and breaking into some kind of uncoordinated trot. His two mates swaggered behind him, although not fully understanding why their buddy was quite so enraged about the wellbeing of a manky pigeon.

'Oi! I'm talking to you, you twat.' He was in front of Cassidy now, pointing an accusing finger in his face, rocking aggressively from side to side. Cassidy was at last cognisant of the impassioned bird lover. He could smell the gassy, bottled lager on his breath. A fleck of warm spit landed on Cassidy's cheek as the screaming tirade continued. 'Are you some sort of moron, you muppet?' As he shouted, the boyfriend darted his eyes to his left, checking that his girl would have a good view of proceedings when he started slapping down this suited, lanky ponce.

'Who the fuck do you think you are? Picking on some

poor defenceless bird. Try some of this, you twat.' He swung a flailing fist in Cassidy's direction. Cassidy swerved out of the way, grabbing his attacker's arm as he flew past in a tipsy spin. Cassidy kept hold of the arm, twisting it as he threw him down to the floor. The assailant screamed as his face hit the frozen pavement with a hard thud. Cassidy moved over the top of him and stamped on his lower back, grinding his heel deep into his sacroiliac joint. One of his mates instinctively moved in to help. Cassidy turned his passionless eyes towards him, raising one solitary finger as a warning.

'Uh, Mr Cassidy. . . your car is ready.' The valet held out the keys, trying to make sense of the jumble of bodies on the pavement.

Cassidy looked down at the bleeding youth, squirming beneath his feet. He twisted the arm one last time and then released it. The assailant was still howling in agony as Cassidy stepped over his bruised body, handing the valet a small tip as he entered his car in one smooth movement before driving off into the night.

*

Cassidy's office was across from St Mary Abbots Church, just off Kensington High Street. He shared the space with his assistant, Sam Wilson, an Oxford graduate who had now been working for Cassidy for three years. Sam was young, hard-working, extremely bright and deeply unemployable having been caught running a website selling fake legal highs to teenagers. The pills were harmless enough, but he had amassed a considerable sum of money by the time he was caught, all of which was acutely embarrassing to the City security firm he was working for at the time. Not only was Sam running the scam during working hours but he had also hosted the site on the company's servers. When the police froze Sam's accounts, they found that all his ill gotten gains were still, more or less, untouched, enabling him to repay the duped teenagers in full. The judge bore this in mind when sentencing and settled on issuing Sam not much more than a slap on the wrists. The probationary sentence, however meant he was unable to find work. Sam's father, Oscar, approached Anthony Willoughby, who owed him a favour following a recent property deal in the Midlands. Willoughby passed the task onto Cassidy who was quick to spot Sam's potential and reorganised his small team to accommodate the young protege.

'The Bremen office needs to be closed as soon as can be arranged. Can you check the contract, Sam, and give me a copy to read on the train,' Cassidy said, closing the outer door of the small office suite behind him.

'I will print it off now, Mr Cassidy, and get a call lined up with the agent tomorrow morning.' Sam already knew the closure would not present a problem. He had checked the penalty clauses some weeks ago when it was clear that the German venture was doomed to failure.

'Fine. Did you look into that chatter?'

'It was nothing. Something about a hotel chain takeover up in Scotland. I've left a summary on your desk.'

On joining the firm, Sam had set up a programme that would automatically scan a multitude of communication channels concurrently. The software monitored social media, online news, television, radio and, importantly, all national and local police channels. At any given time he could check for references about a project or an individual and determine if there was anything Cassidy should be concerned about. In addition to the ad hoc searches, there were certain keywords that remained constantly live on the system. The word 'Strathdon' had always been and would remain, one of these words.

Cassidy closed his office door and sat down at his large, slate black desk. He scanned the Strathdon report. Sam was right. It was nothing. He needed to make a call to Germany before he caught the train to Edinburgh. He had already begun to wind down the project prior to his meeting at the Burgoyne Club, but now had to make sure the withdrawal could be accelerated, in line with Willoughby's wishes. The turnabout would be logistically difficult and complex to manage, but could be achieved within a satisfactory timeline. Cassidy's job was to ensure that whatever the family wanted, they got and he was very, very good at his job.

Milton Cassidy had been brought up at Widford Hall, the Willoughby's family home in rural Hertfordshire, following the early death of both his parents. He did not attend school or university, but was educated at home by a selection of tutors, hand picked by Anthony, the Head of the Family. During his teenage years he was slowly inducted to various aspects of the family business, visiting recently acquired properties and occasionally attending meetings with some of the family's advisors. At eighteen, Anthony appointed Cassidy as Chief Executive of one of their fledgling operations, a private security firm, called Mission. Cassidy made use of Anthony Willoughby's contact list and soon grew a loyal and well-heeled client base, including bankers, politicians and minor aristocracy, all seeking a discreet security service when on business trips or romantic liaisons, either in this country or abroad. The business thrived well beyond Anthony Willoughby's expectations. By his twenty first birthday, Cassidy was firmly established as Willoughby's right hand man, overseeing large swathes of the family's interests.

On the large, meticulously uncluttered desk, there were no photographs of loved ones. In his world, Cassidy was alone. Outside of business dealings, he generally found people difficult to deal with and annoying to be around. Having spent his formative years cloistered within the hushed remoteness of Widford Hall, he had never found the need for friends or acquaintances, thinking the whole ritual of socialising a difficult and unnecessary exercise. Occasionally, a new business contact would try, unwisely, to befriend the athletically built, suave executive, inviting him for a round of golf or a tennis match, but this would lead nowhere, with Cassidy either rejecting the invitation outright or just not turning up. Women would look longingly towards him as he boarded a plane or stepped into a restaurant, wondering what corporeal delights the tall, lean man with the burning brown eyes could offer them. However, when they swooped in to lure and entice they were met with a withering disinterest. When he should have been bewitching, he was awkward; when he should have been flirtatious, he was matter of fact; when he should have seduced, he was elsewhere. None of this bothered Milton Cassidy, it should be said. The one and only time he thought upon his isolation was when he considered his wealth. The Willoughbys had made him a rich man. Far beyond his needs. Each year his bank accounts and portfolios grew. What exactly was he to do with it all? What's more, where would it all go when he was gone? There was nobody to give it to. No son, daughter, lifelong friend, forgotten cousin. Nobody. Would he be forced to just give it back? Tie it up with a big bow and, on his deathbed, hand it over to the Willoughbys, thanking them for the loan?

No, somewhere in his schedule and some time soon he needed to find the time to acquire progeny.

# CHAPTER 4

THE mud at the bottom of the well was still.  The layers of sodden peat and centuries-old rotting vegetation forming a heavy dark blanket over Lincoln's aching body.  He lay smothered and barely breathing, almost ready to submit and be folded into the damp earth, to become part of the endless cycle of growth, death, regeneration.  There was no sound, no light, no warmth, no easy peace as he slipped towards death, no comforting resolution, no equanimity, no hope.  His heartbeat slowed.  At the moment of final acceptance, his body, in some ancient instinctive twitch, summoned one last bid for life.  He jolted against the weight of the fallen earth.  At first there was no movement, then he felt a slight give in the heavy load weighing on top of him.  Sensing release, he pushed up harder towards the surface until the pile of fallen earth broke and crumbled apart.  He pushed again, slowly feeling his coffinless tomb fall away.  He gasped, choking down the stale air in large gulps, not caring about the foul smelling mud he was sucking into his lungs with each breath.

Lincoln collapsed onto the earth and slumped back against

the rounded wall. He looked up towards the patch of distant light at the top of the well, an uneven circle of night sky, speckled with pale and distant stars. A single sob of relief shook through his body, breaking the dense silence. He slowly rose to his feet and rested his bruised hands, now numb with cold, on the earth walls. For a moment he thought about calling out, but his nearest neighbour was over half a mile away. Mrs Stanford was in her eighties now and her hearing was blunted by age. The solicitor had left hours ago. His brother was in Sweden. Nobody else even knew he was here. He looked back up the narrow shaft. The well wasn't deep, having long ago collapsed in on itself, but he was still over twenty feet from the surface. A vague memory of a school trip to the Lake District nudged its way through his consciousness. Overall, it had been a pointless affair. It had rained incessantly for all three days, leaving the class tent-bound throughout most of their stay. On the final day, when, once again, the weather conditions denied them any attempt at scaling the picturesque mountains surrounding the campsite, they had been herded by their desperate geography teacher into the hire van and driven to an indoor school for mountain climbing. The techniques they had been introduced to that day had slipped from Lincoln's mind, but he did vaguely recall attempting a method of scaling a wall using opposable surfaces. He couldn't remember what the technique was called, but thought that, as long as the walls of the well held firm, then he may be able to use the method to manoeuvre his way to the surface.

It was after his third fall that he remembered that the technique was called stemming. He also remembered that he had been terrible at it. He tried to control his growing sense of panic as he pushed his hands once again into the indentations he had formed in the earth. He could feel the muscles in his legs and arms begin to ache as he negotiated his way towards the rim of the well. The mud towards the surface was frozen and dry, making it hard for him to get a foothold. He moved slowly, carefully edging upwards, knowing that falling from this height again could be fatal. He tried to rid his mind of the image of himself, lying at the bottom of the well, his leg broken and contorted, dying a slow and painful death. The fingers of his left hand could feel the lip of the well now. The broken bramble branches, poked out from the surface, their dark silhouettes marked out against the backdrop of the night sky. He steadied himself once more then swung his right hand over to where his left hand was clinging to the firm ground and then pushed off with his right foot until his body was hanging, unsupported, in the air. He could feel the heavy and dense weight of his limbs, pulling on his exhausted and shaking arms. He heaved himself up as if he was climbing out of a deep and empty swimming pool. His neck and shoulder muscles burning with pain. With one final effort, he pulled the top half of his body onto the firm ground outside the well and crawled forward. Slowly he clambered to his feet, stumbling over the torch lying on top of a pile of turned over earth, its fading beam now only giving off a dull, orange smudge of light. He picked himself up from the ground and lurched forward across the garden, towards the warmth and safety of Sorrel Cottage.

# CHAPTER 5

'IS that light still not fixed, Malc?'

PC Malcolm Hardy looked up from the front desk of the Haxford police station. The end of a long shift was in sight and he was looking forward to getting home to his wife, Molly, and his two young children. The last thing he needed was his pedantic Sergeant prancing about the place, stating the bleeding obvious. The fluorescent tube had been pulsing on and off above the counter for the last four hours, incessantly snapping at him as he worked. PC Hardy could sense a nervous twitch beginning to develop under his left eye as he continued entering the last of the day's case files onto his computer screen, ready for a hasty exit, bang on six o'clock.

'Afraid not, Sarge. No spares out back. I'll sort it in the morning even if I have to nip to Coopers and buy a replacement out of my own money. It has been doing my nut in all day.'

Sergeant Minton opened the heavy wooden hatch and moved to the front of the counter, strolling up and down with eagle-eyed intent. He suddenly stopped and looked down, wiping his fingers across the surface. 'What's all this then? Is this mud here on the counter?'

'Last time I looked, Sarge,' replied PC Hardy, regretting his offhand tone before the words had even left his mouth.

'I beg your pardon, PC Hardy,' said the Sergeant, turning his affronted gaze to the constable, who was staring fixedly at his screen, his fingers frozen above the keys. 'I think it might be helpful if you could leave out the sarcasm and just give me a straight answer, don't you lad? So lets try that again shall we? Is this mud here on the counter, PC Hardy?'

'Yes, Sarge, sorry, Sarge. I was just about to clean off the surfaces before heading home. I'm just finishing up my entries and then I will get right to it sir. It shouldn't take more than a minute.'

'Is that right son? Well, if it only takes a minute, then I suggest you get it done now.'

PC Hardy knew the speech that was coming next and inwardly groaned. He could see the Sergeant was moving into autopilot, rocking back and forth on his heels, hands clasped behind his back. 'Your role Constable is an important one. You are responsible for the public's faith and confidence in the Haxford police force and their belief in this team as the trusted custodians of local law and order. You have the privilege of looking after the shop window of this constabulary. Do your job well, and the public will see a well-ordered and disciplined machine, one determined to deliver a first class citizen focused service, but,' Sergeant Minton leaned forward, tapping the top of the muddy counter to emphasise his point. 'Do your job badly and the public will see ill discipline and chaos. The trust we have all worked so hard to gain will vanish in the wind. Am I making myself clear, PC Hardy?'

'Yes, sir, very clear,' Constable Hardy dutifully replied, straightening his shoulders. Indeed, he had been clear the first time his Sergeant had made this very same speech on joining the Haxford station two months ago. In fact, he had been clear on every occasion since. All six of them.

'We all have our roles to play in this team, young Malcolm' said the Sergeant, warming to his task. 'I have to deal with the onerous responsibility of running the whole station, managing operational strategy and keeping the team here focussed and energised, but your role is just as important as mine, in its own way.' Constable Hardy knew that imminently he would be expected to respond to one of his Sergeant's rallying cries and stiffened himself in readiness. 'We all have our part to play, PC Hardy. Me. You. The Chief Constable. We are all members of the same magnificent team, pulling together as one. Serving the community. Defeating crime. Defending our streets. Can I rely on your support, PC Hardy?'

PC Hardy summoned all of the enthusiasm he could muster. 'Yes, sir. You can, sir.'

'Good lad. Now, say we get the counter cleared and the paperwork boxed away. No loose ends, Malcolm. Everything in its place. You know what I expect of you.'

'Yes, sir.'

Sergeant Minton gave his re-motivated officer a reassuring nod and then slowly retreated into the back offices, satisfied that he had inspired the young constable to raise his game. Don't you worry, he thought, that counter would be cleaned and polished before the end of Hardy's shift, he had made sure of it. The people of Haxford would be able to sleep peacefully in their beds that night.

As the door leading into the back office closed, Malcolm Hardy sighed. He sent a text to Molly to let her know that he wouldn't be home for another hour or so. Best put the kids to bed without him. He had only worked with Sergeant Minton for a couple of months, but already knew how his mind worked. Nothing gave him more pleasure than finding a cut corner or some ignored paperwork so he could thoroughly dress down the culprit, ideally when there was an audience at hand. He knew that, not only would he have to clean and polish the countertop, he would also have to complete the forms he was hoping to ignore, relating to the gentleman who had made the mess on the counter in the first place. What a waste of time, thought PC Hardy. Filling out a load of paperwork just because the man with the funny name dumped some dirty knife on top of his workbench. He had tried to make it clear to the chap that they were in the business of solving crimes that were taking place now, this year, not some make-believe incident from a hundred years ago. If you don't want it, he had told him, that's your business. Put it back in the ground where you found it or dump it in a field or in the sea, whatever, just don't leave it here. But the bloke just couldn't get it. Not his fault, thought PC Hardy. Poor chap was from London.

He tried to recall his name so he could fill out the necessary paperwork. He picked up the card that had been left with the knife. 'That's it,' he said, peering at the business card 'Lincoln Marsh, care of Luminosity TV Production Company, Wardour Street, London W1.' He turned to his computer and opened up the incident form on the screen, muttering to himself. 'Well Mr Marsh, your name sounds like a miserable stretch of bog land and I ain't never heard of Luminosity TV so you ain't all that as far as I'm concerned.' He filled in the relevant details as required. When he got to the box asking for any identifying features of the weapon, he flicked back his pad where he had made some notes. Dirty blade. Blunt. Six inches long. Bone handle. Inscription. He entered the details, including the worded inscription, onto his computer and closed the file.

\*   \*

Sam Wilson was working late at the Kensington office, reviewing some legal documents pertaining to some scrubland on the outskirts of Leeds that had been recently acquired by the Willoughby Estate, when an alert appeared on screen. He read the message, reaching for his mobile in his jacket pocket. His call was answered on the second ring.

'Many apologies for disturbing you, Mr Cassidy, but I felt that you would want to be made aware of a Strathdon related incident that has occurred this evening.'

# CHAPTER 6

WHEN Lincoln pressed the button for the third floor, he noticed that he still had some grime from the well underneath the nail of his index finger. As he looked up, he spotted Jilly, the pretty Luminosity receptionist, trotting towards the lift and thrust his arm out to stop the sliding doors from closing on her.
'Shit. Shit. Shit.' Jilly's coffee spilt onto her hand, dripping onto the floor, after being knocked by the door.
'Everything alright, Jilly?' asked Lincoln.
'Oops sorry, Lincoln, you don't need to hear me swearing away like that first thing on a Monday morning,' she said, while looking at his face and wincing. 'My God, you look like shit.' She winced again, immediately regretting her comments. 'Oh bugger, I shouldn't have said that. And I swore again, didn't I? Oh good grief. I give in. Worst day ever.'
The lift door pinged open on the third floor. Jilly disappeared into the kitchen to hang up her coat, wondering what the rest of the day had in store for her. Lincoln followed her out, but

his step was momentarily halted by the sight of the reception. It was the first time he had been at the Luminosity office since the refurbishment and the walls now pulsed with a sepia and maroon palette. A large puce sofa stood defiantly in front of the reception desk, daring any of today's visitors to take a seat. The name of the company was spelt in giant, gold capital letters across the back wall, glinting in the beams being sprayed out by the new spotlights dotted around the ceiling. Lincoln's eyes took shelter for a moment in the reassuring dark blue of the carpet, although, every few feet, the designers had deemed it wise to insert a viciously yellow square amongst the floor tiles, just to keep everybody on their toes.

'So, what do you think, my sweet?'

Lincoln turned to Sarah Gillespie, the Luminosity Chief Executive, who had silently appeared at his side, dressed in an outfit so garish that it looked like it had come as a job lot along with the office design.

He struggled for a response for a moment, settling on, 'It's invigorating.'

'We think so. We are all very pleased. It makes a statement don't you think? Bold. Modern. Strong. Very now,' she said, with large emphasising sweeps of her hands, her jewellery clattering around her wrists and fingers as she did so. 'It says, "we may be a small company, but we pack a mighty big punch"'.

'Well, you certainly floored me, Sarah,' Lincoln said, his eyes bouncing from one electrified colour to the next, unable to settle.

'There you go. Mission accomplished,' she said, proudly.

'Shall we?' He followed her through the open plan office.

Some of the refit had yet to be completed and a handful of desks were turned at skewed angles, waiting to be repositioned in their usual bays. Scattered amongst the desks were three overweight, male members of the IT team, reconnecting printers and rebooting desktops with varying degrees of success. A kaleidoscope of streamed songs buzzed from almost every desk, competing for attention over the sound of the wall heaters, cranked up to full on this cold November morning. In age terms, at 34, Lincoln was very much in the upper quartile compared to the young team at Luminosity. A difference he felt more acutely on some days than on others.

'Coffee? You look like you need one. You look rubbish if you don't mind me saying. What have you done to your eye for goodness sakes?' Sarah asked, as they entered the glass-walled boardroom in the far corner of the building. Born in Bristol, she had lived in London for over twenty years now, but try as she might, there would always be a hint of the West County lurking within her vowels and consonants.

'I had a bit of a tough weekend. Coffee would be good,' he replied, deciding to leave the details of his night in the well for later in the day when Sarah would no doubt be interrupting him with cakes and pastries from one of the host of high end cafes that had emerged, uninvited, in Soho over recent years.

As she grabbed two oversized mugs from the side, each coloured an inexplicable shade of green, Lincoln noticed the giant black and white prints that had recently been installed in the boardroom, each print depicting one of the prime time television shows developed by Sarah and her team. Pride of place, at the end of the room, was the face of Bernard Bolt, the actor who had played lead in all four series of Castle Eden, created and written by the talented but not greatly prolific, Lincoln Marsh.

Lincoln had initially joined Luminosity as a writers assistant ten years ago, which in those days was not much more than a glorified gofer at the beck and call of the small team of needy writers working on Luminosity projects. The pay was meagre, the hours were long, and, for the most part, the work was routinely unchallenging, but Lincoln kept his head down, thankful for the opportunity. Previously, he had spent nearly four years living on his wits in Europe and South America doing whatever jobs he could to pay his way. When his contract, teaching English to Croatian students in Karlovac, came to an end, he decided it was the right time to return home to England and find some sort of stability. Compared to the other applicants for the role, he was woefully under qualified, so had thought himself lucky to have even reached the interview stage. Sarah had quickly warmed to him during their meeting. He was bright, well travelled, interesting to talk to and had so much more to say than the other nervy, pasty-faced graduates whose company she had endured during the previous two days of interviewing. By the time Lincoln had regaled her with his stories of reindeer hunting in Scandinavia and sea diving on the Valdes Peninsula, he had already landed the job.

For eighteen months Lincoln did exactly what was asked of him, making coffee, doing research, transcribing page after page of monotonous, half-baked ideas. He catered to every desperate whim of the writers. Anything to help get the scripts completed. He learnt what he could, when he could and never complained. Sarah observed him with a motherly pride, taking him under her wing, particularly during those first few months. She went out of her way to find time in her busy schedule to offer advice and guidance as to how, if he applied himself, he too may be able to develop a career within the world of television script writing.

'It is all about experience, talent, timing and luck, in that order,' she advised. 'Work hard, be patient and the opportunity may present itself and, if it does, grab it as if your life depended on it, as the chance may not come around again.'

Lincoln continued to watch and learn, occasionally offering a tentative idea at the writer's weekly meetings with Sarah and the rest of the team. Over time, he became increasingly involved in reviewing and editing scripts, most of which betrayed no ambition beyond the routine and formulaic. His understanding of what worked best with viewers grew, so much so, he began pulling together his own ideas under the provisional title of The Vale of Castle Eden. The script centred around the adventures of Augustus Flood, a Humanities Professor from Durham University, during the interwar period. Flood would use his knowledge of human culture and world history to solve the various crimes taking place with absurd frequency within the Vale. Within two months Lincoln had, almost accidentally, pulled together the first draft of a script. There was nothing strikingly original in the premise of the show, but he thought the structure of the story was sound and the twists of the plot reasonably diverting. In his opinion, it was certainly no worse than some of the tosh that had found favour during the monthly Luminosity commissioning meetings.

Fearing his mentor's displeasure in his first-time efforts, he sent his manuscript instead to one of Luminosity competitors, a company called Global Reach. The covering letter dropped just enough names and references to appear professional and hopefully spark some interest, at least enough to prompt a reading. Three weeks later, astounded and delighted, he appeared at the door of Sarah's office waving a provisional acceptance letter only to be met by a frosty glare of disappointment.

'I feel let down Lincoln and not a little betrayed,' said Sarah in a most quiet and fragile voice. 'What I simply cannot understand is why you felt it necessary to deceive me in this way by going behind my back?'

Lincoln did his best to explain, but to no avail. Sarah was crest fallen. She spent the remainder of the afternoon in her office with the door firmly closed, refusing to take any calls and working her way through a large bag of mini Bakewell tarts. Lincoln could see her through the blinds, wiping a rogue crumb from her lips and occasionally picking up his acceptance letter and shaking her head, despairingly.

The following day, before anybody else had arrived at the office, he emailed Global Reach and withdrew the script, leaving a freshly printed copy on Sarah's desk along with an apology note. Sarah appreciated the gesture and said that she would do her very best to find some time to give it "the once-over" but warned Lincoln not to get his hopes up. Later that same evening, amidst a variety of caveats and faint praise,

Sarah informed Lincoln that Luminosity would agree to take on the development of the show and do their best to drum up some interest with the major TV studios. Two months later, the script began its prosaic march towards production. A pilot, featuring a capable but little known cast, was screened by the end of the year, followed by the commissioning of the six further episodes that constituted the first series. Eight years later, the programme, its title now shortened to just Castle Eden, was recognised as Luminosity's most successful project to date, establishing Lincoln as a writer of some low-key notoriety.

*

It was now one o'clock in the afternoon. Lincoln was gazing out of the boardroom window onto the street below, drinking a cup of black coffee. The door swung open and Sarah burst back into the room, brandishing a heavily marked manuscript in front of her.
'Here it is. I knew I was right. The shepherd from Bellows Burn cannot phone the police to let them know about the red Daimler as you killed him off at the end of the second series. Remember? The accident in the hay barn? It was only mentioned as an aside by the Vicar, but, any way you look at it, that shepherd is most definitely dead.'
Lincoln was tired. His body ached from the fall and he had a piercing headache clawing at the back of his right eye. 'Come on, Sarah. Nobody's going to remember that.'
'I did, Lincoln. If I did then others will. No, you will have to change it. You must maintain firm continuity throughout or the whole thing just looks amateurish.'
Lincoln turned back towards the window. A cold and heavy downpour had begun to fall from the thick grey clouds that hovered just above the London skyline. Below, he could see a multi coloured array of umbrellas scuttling along Wardour Street. It looked like London was being invaded by a slightly theatrical battalion of roman soldiers, sheltering under their

colourfully designed shields as they stormed the city. He knew that Sarah was right. She often was when it came to the detail of the script and would frequently highlight inaccuracies and inconsistencies during the final stages of drafting. Being right however, didn't preclude her observations from being insufferably irritating. By the time Lincoln had finished his first draft, he was usually ready to move on to something new, but Sarah would seemingly delight in frustrating him, quietly unclipping the finishing tape and repositioning it further and further down the track.

'Okay, I'll change it, just for you, but I do not believe for one minute that anybody will have even the vaguest recollection that some nonentity snuffed it four years ago or whenever it was. Jesus, I can barely remember what happened in the last episode and I wrote it.'

'Sure. But if you don't have continuity...'

'Yes, I know, Sarah. I heard you the first time. "Amateurish" wasn't it? Thanks for that.' Lincoln put his coffee cup back on the glass table with more force than he had intended, the loud crack making Sarah jump.

He sighed. He was too tired to fall out with his one-time boss. 'I'm sorry, Sarah, I'm knackered. You're right, thanks for spotting the error. I'll fix this but then I think I'll call it a day and get some rest. Okay?'

Sarah pushed her heavy rimmed glasses back up the bridge of her nose and gave him the sympathetic and slightly condescending smile of one who has become accustomed to the occasional flighty and irrational temper tantrum of the creative talent. 'I'll leave you in peace, my sweet,' she said gently closing the door behind her, only to return some five minutes later, a look of puzzled concern on her face.

'Sorry to disturb, Lincoln, but you've got a visitor. The lady at the reception says she's a policewoman, a Detective Sergeant Martha Green.'

# CHAPTER 7

THE rain from the detective's loosely closed umbrella, pooled out onto the glass table, forming a tiny semi-circular puddle. A thoughtless thing to do, Lincoln thought, impolite, careless at best. He knew the meeting was not going to go well right from the off when the policewoman had refused tea, refused coffee and refused to sit down.

'Where exactly is it now, Mr Marsh? I am unclear as to why you have held onto it?'

At first, Lincoln thought it might be some trifling driving offence the authorities had randomly decided to crack down upon, chided by some diktat from the Home Office. Surely it couldn't be anything to do with that episode yesterday with PC Simpleton? Maybe something had happened to his brother, an accident or some rogue dealing he had become embroiled with?

'What do you intend to do with it, Mr Marsh? Is there something you are not telling me?'

Lincoln felt somehow squat and shrunken, almost frog-like, seated in the boardroom chair as the detective towered over him from the other side of the desk. She had made no attempt to remove her dark brown mac, still wet from the downpour outside. Lincoln hoped that this might be an indication that she did not intend to stay long , although she showed little sign of leaving anytime soon.

'I strongly advise you not to obstruct my enquiries. Why are you refusing to cooperate, Mr Marsh?'

'I'm not refusing to cooperate, Sergeant, I just don't have the knife with me at present. I can't give it to you if it is not here, besides, what pisses me off is that I tried to hand it in to you lot yesterday and you told me to sod off.'

'Please mind your language, sir, it's inappropriate.'

'Oh for fuck's sake.'

'Sir. I do not intend to warn you again.'

'Okay, okay but this is a joke. I will get you the knife, will that satisfy you?'

'I see from the report that you spoke of a murder. Whose murder, sir? Were you involved? Did you use your knife?' Her voice an officious rasp. Accusatory. Pinning him in his seat.

'It's not my knife for God's sake. The murder happened a hundred years ago, surely the other officer told you that? This whole episode has nothing to do with me. I was just trying to do the right thing, you know, help out. I wish I hadn't fucking bothered.'

'Right, I have warned you, sir, about your offensive language. Would you like to continue this interview down at the police station?' She gestured towards the door as if it led directly into a waiting police interview room.

'Sorry, no, I just find your whole tone aggressive to be honest, Detective. You need to remember that I have done nothing wrong.'

'So you say.'

'What?'

'I only have your word for that.'

'Jesus.'

The sky outside had slowly darkened as the rain grew

heavier. Lincoln noticed that two of the recently installed spotlights had already blown, leaving one corner of the boardroom in a shadowy gloom. The Detective Sergeant looked down at her notes. A strand of her hair coming lose from her pony tail and falling across her eyes.

'You informed the officer yesterday that the house where you found the knife belonged to your parents,' she said, using her hands to couch the word "found" within a pair of provocative quotation marks. 'Will they be able to verify that?'

'No. They are both dead.'

'I am sorry to hear that, sir.' The automated commiseration was bland and insincere. She flicked over the page of her notebook.

'You also said that you retrieved the knife from your father's belongings. Could he have been the murderer?'

'What, my dad? No, Sergeant. Don't be absurd.'

'I am not being absurd, sir. Do I need to remind you that you have, as yet, failed to provide me with an explanation as to why you and your father have kept the murder weapon hidden away for all of these years.'

'Oh, for God's sake, neither me or my dad are killers. Got it?' Lincoln was on his feet now, exasperated, raising his voice. 'I do not know who the hell you think you are Sergeant, but you cannot come in here and accuse me of things I know nothing about.'

'What like, sir? Being in possession of a dangerous weapon potentially involved in a murder case? Please sit down, Mr Marsh.'

'No. You can't make me,' he said, petulantly.

'I suggest you avoid using confrontational language, Mr Marsh. Sit down sir.'

'No.'

'Sit. Down. Sir.'

Lincoln and the detective were locked in a combative stare as Sarah cautiously pushed open the door.

'Can I get anyone any drinks at all?' she said,

circumspectly, like an obsequious waiter enquiring if sir and madam were ready to order. 'I thought I should just pop in and check you have everything you need.' She had seen the meeting slowly deteriorate through the glass panels surrounding the boardroom and didn't like the sight of her young protege's body language. 'Lincoln? Can I get you a nice cup of tea perhaps? Lincoln?'

The detective replied first. 'No thank you, Miss Gillespie, we are both fine.'

'Is there anything you want to know that I could help you with, Sergeant?' she asked politely, but already knowing the answer to her question.

'No, Miss Gillespie. This matter does not concern you.'

'I see. Well, I will leave you to it.' She half closed the door before turning back. 'Oh, I hope you don't mind Lincoln but I took the liberty of giving Mr Radcombe a call, my lawyer chappie. He said he could pop over later. He is such a dear and usually so good at sorting out complicated things. Goodness knows he's set me straight a few times when I have landed myself in a bit of a muddle.'

'We are done here. I am just leaving,' the detective said with finality, scribbling a line on one of the pages in her notebook before tearing it out and placing it on the table in front of Lincoln.. 'This is my number, Mr Marsh. I will be waiting to hear from you this afternoon to arrange delivery of the knife. Call me. Thank you for your time, Mr Marsh, Miss Gillespie. I will show myself out.'

\*

'Oh you poor sweet thing. No wonder you look so rough.'

Lincoln had just finished telling Sarah his tale. Explaining about his near-death experience down the well and his scrambled escape. Curious faces from the Marketing and Research teams located just outside the boardroom, continued to bob up over their Macs, checking that all was okay. He gave them a cheery wave.

'She really was quite something wasn't she, that detective woman,' said Sarah. 'I thought you were going to hit her at one point. ' She placed both hands on the table and leaned forward in expectation. 'So, are you going to give her the knife?'

'Yes of course, I never wanted the thing in the first place. I will give her a call once I have picked it up from my flat and arrange to meet her whenever she wants. I presume she will want me to go to the station to hand it over. Send out the search parties if you don't hear from me by the weekend.' He started collecting up his laptop and papers. 'Thinking about it, maybe it would be best to take that lawyer of yours along with me to the station. Just in case things get out of hand again.'

'That might be a bit tricky, my sweet,' replied Sarah. 'Poor Mr Radcombe died five years ago. Fell off a ladder while clearing out some gutters. Terrible shame. You would have loved him. Such a sweetie.'

# CHAPTER 8

GEORGE Giltmore, the Member of Parliament for Easton, took another sip from the glass of sparkling water in front of him. He was sure he had asked for still, but had not corrected the mistake when the glass had been placed on the table, grateful for any source of refreshment. He had always found the air in the Burgoyne Club stifling. A cloying, sweet cocktail of roasted meats and furniture polish, mixed with the smell of the aged membership's decaying flesh. The whole place needed a bloody good airing in his opinion.

It was quarter past eight in the evening. His meeting had started thirty minutes ago following the customary delay when he and his assistant, Harriet Blackwood, had been made to wait for over forty minutes in the outer room until Mr Anthony Willoughby was ready to receive them. George Giltmore had been called to the Burgoyne Club at short notice by Mr Willoughby who required an update on the progress of the Homerton project, wanting to know why there had been yet another delay. Giltmore glanced to his side at the perfect profile of Harriet Blackwood who, with confidence and determination, was doing her best to take control of the meeting.

'Mr Willoughby, I take your point on board and note your frustration, but I must inform you Mr Giltmore will not be governed by such a confected argument. You have Mr Giltmore's assurance that all that can be done is being done to progress the project, but, as you are well aware, it is not within the remit of any serving MP to dictate the proceedings of a council body regarding land development. If there are particular issues that you would like to raise, then your concerns should be progressed through the correct channels. Mr Giltmore has, to this point, accommodated the suggestions you have made, but directly influencing the council members purely to further your best interests is a step too far.'

Willoughby's pale, blue eyes washed across the face of the young woman, noting her tight posture, earnest features and scrubbed-clean skin. Just a silly girl, blinded by her youth into thinking she had something useful to contribute to this meeting of men, he thought to himself.

'That you would think I would ask anything untoward of young Mr Giltmore, pains me to the core,' he said, clasping his bloodless hands to his chest with feigned hurt. 'I merely believe it would assist all of our interests if George could find it in himself to exert a bit more leadership over some of the more wayward council members. I am confident that they will be only too happy to hear, first-hand, the wise words and counsel of the MP for Easton. Isn't that right, George?'

Miss Blackwood returned on the offensive, shaping her head to catch Willoughby's gaze. 'Mr Willoughby, and I say this with the very greatest respect, you are not entitled to direct elected Members to do your bidding. Mr Giltmore is accountable to Parliament and to his constituents, not to you.'

George Giltmore looked down at the empty sheet of A4 paper in front of him. A yellow stain from his glass of water had taken shape at the top of the page. He felt so very tired, wearied by the predictability of his own inadequacy. How had he become such a useless and pointless chump? That bloody trip to Bremen. Why had he agreed to go? Stupid. Stupid Stupid. Over the course of the three days he had become intoxicated with the grace and favour showered upon him as a visiting Member of Parliament. It felt good to be treated with respect and courtesy. It felt good to dine with people who appeared genuinely interested in what you had to say. It felt good to be important, for once. It wasn't until the last night that he met Simone. The beautiful and captivating Simone. Their evening, a thrilling cocktail of endless laughter and tumblers of cool, bubbling alcohol. The flirting in the restaurant, slowly less and less discreet, until they retired, drunk and giggling, to his hotel suite. At first it had been almost magical, like nothing he had experienced before, so gentle and loving, so thoughtful, but then as the hours passed, things slowly got out of hand. What had he done to her? What had she done to him? He shifted in his chair as his recollections of their hotel tryst caused his buttocks to clench.

He received the first image on his phone when he stepped off the plane at Heathrow. By the time the Ministry car had deposited him back at his family home in his constituency, two further images had arrived along with a request to trade silence for money. A great deal of money. Far beyond his limited financial resources.

He had been so grateful when he had received the call from the man from the security firm engaged to look after him during his stay in Bremen. Somehow the conversation had turned to the hotel and, before he realised what he was saying, he was explaining about the explicit images and the demands for payment, crying like a child on the phone to the sympathetic stranger. The representative from Mission Security was appalled and promised to ask one his senior colleagues, a Mr Milton Cassidy, to look into it forthwith. Within twenty four hours, George Giltmore had received a call of reassurance from Mr Cassidy telling him that the situation was in hand and would be dealt with. George remembered the elation he felt that afternoon after he had put down the phone and how relieved he was at the restaurant that evening during the surprise meal he had arranged at the last minute with his wife and his two young boys.

And now this.

Anthony Willoughby smiled. 'Do excuse me young lady, but I think I may have forgotten your name. Was it Miss Greenwood?'

'No, Ms Harriet Blackwood. It is on the card I passed to you when we arrived,' she said, pointing to the table.

'Ah yes, so it is,' he said, picking up the card and turning it over, face down, onto the table. 'Firstly, Ms Blackwood, I would like to thank you for clarifying Mr Giltmore's position. It is extremely helpful to have it all laid out, as it were, so even an old fool like me can get to grips with it.' He smiled again, giving a slight bow of the head across the table. 'Thank you, Ms Blackwood.'

Harriet Blackwood nodded back, albeit less assuredly than she would have liked.

'I feel I too need to furnish you with the clarity of my views,' continued Willoughby. 'Reciprocate, if you will. So, Ms Blackwood, and I say this with the very greatest respect, I feel obliged to inform you that I do not care one drunk monk's fuck what you think I am or I am not entitled to. What second-rate harridans Mr Giltmore wants to surround himself with is up to him, but I do not need to listen to your tiresome complaining so please desist. I am sure you are a competent secretary so feel free to take notes, but leave the talking to us men so we can get this little mess sorted out.' Harriet stiffened in her chair. Despite herself, she felt an embarrassed flush rise to the surface of her pale skin. Full of anger and indignation, she was about to launch into a clumsy and enraged response, only to feel the restraining touch of Giltmore's hand on her arm.

'Let it go, Harriet,' he quietly mumbled, without the strength or decency to look her in the eyes as he did so.

'As I was saying,' continued Willoughby, addressing

himself now exclusively to the slumped figure of the MP for Easton. 'I am sure the members of Homerton council will welcome your insight on matters George and can be ushered towards a conclusion that is agreeable for all concerned. After all, the new development will be providing much needed jobs and homes for people within the community. Lets not forget, this is a good news story all round, particularly for your own constituents, eh George.'

George Giltmore MP continued to stare down at the water stain. An almost indiscernible nod of the head indicated his acceptance.

'Good. No more delays. Is that absolutely understood.' The MP nodded a second time. 'Right,' Willoughby said, concluding the meeting by closing his file of papers. 'I think that is everything so if you will excuse me. George, do please keep me updated, there's a good chap and, Miss Blackwood, please feel free to drop into the bar on your way out. You should try our new house chablis. I am told it is proving most popular with the visiting members of the gentler sex.'

# CHAPTER 9

THE rain had slowed to a fine drizzle as Lincoln stepped out of the Oxford Circus tube station. As he climbed the stairs to the surface, he merged with the early morning shoppers who were already laden with more items than he managed to purchase in a month. In his hand, he carried a solitary Waitrose carrier bag in which he had bundled his dad's stuff to hand over to the detective. The Vauxhall train had been held at Green Park following an earlier signal failure so he was already ten minutes late. He turned left off Oxford Street, lengthening his stride. A neutral location, rather than the formality of a police station suited Lincoln, so he was pleased when Detective Sergeant Green suggested Cafe Copenhagen in Great Titchfield Street as the meeting place. She hadn't bothered phoning back until after nine o'clock the previous night. Her clipped telephone manner just as curt and abrasive as she had been earlier in the day. At least she was consistent, he thought. The cafe was a quarter of a mile down the road on the left hand side. Its large red awning jutting out from the side of the building, providing some meagre shelter for a dismal group of ostracised customers, heads bowed, frozen by the wind. Their cigarettes pinched in between their fingers and a look of smoker's regret in their eyes.

The cafe was only half full, although there was a queue of people clustered around the counter trying to order. The clientele was a blend of office workers, shoppers and media types who had made the quick dash round from the BBC building on Regents Street, seeking the comfort of the well stocked smorgasbord of fish and salami. Lincoln scanned the tables. No sign of the detective. Just a half dozen groups in twos and threes, their winter coats slung over the back of their chairs. He breathed a sigh of relief and joined the back of the queue.

The staff were mainly Danish with a few Swedes thrown in for good measure. They were beautiful, friendly and quite hopeless. The queue swelled like an estuary at high tide. The smiling staff seemingly picking out people to serve at random. A pile of dirty plates and cutlery balanced precariously at the end of the counter, destined to fall and smash onto the tiled floor before the lunchtime rush. The coffee maker buzzed and dripped and steamed although, as far as Lincoln could see, nobody actually appeared to be making hot drinks of any description.

'What is it I can get you today?' Inexplicably it was Lincoln's turn to be served, much to the annoyance of the Australian couple in front who were still waiting to place their order.

'Just a coffee please. Americano.'

'No cake?' inquired the waitress, giving him a faultless smile.

'No, thanks. Just the coffee please.'

'We have good cake today.'

'Just coffee is fine.'

'I always like cake on a day like today. It is so grey out there. You must have cake to warm you up. We have some Drommekage fr Brovst...so dreamy.' The pretty girl laughed as did her tall, blonde, male colleague standing next to her.

When her giggles subsided, she sighed, shaking her head. 'Oh dear, I am in a silly mood today.' She looked back up at Marsh, a broad healthy smile still on her face. 'Shall I get you some cake?'

The patience of the Australian boyfriend in front had finally run out. 'Just have some fucking cake will you mate. Give us all some peace.'

'Sure. OK. Give me a slice of cake then. Some Drom… whatever it is you said. That would be great.'

'Yay!' Lincoln watched as the delighted waitress scampered away to the opposite end of the counter from where the cakes were displayed. He mouthed 'sorry' to the Australians who had seen enough and had bolted for the door.

He scanned the cafe again. This time he spotted her on a small table at the back of the cafe, partially obscured by a group of bulky German tourists. He felt a nervous swoop in his stomach. The sort you get before an interview or a driving test. He was not looking forward to meeting the dread woman again. He checked the progress of his cup of coffee, potentially days away, then looked back across at the seated detective. She looked different than before. An untouched glass of water was on the table in front of her. She was sitting loosely in the chair, her arms hanging at her side, slumped forward slightly, like a wound down toy. She looked completely lost in her own world and as he stared at her face, framed by her shoulder length hair, he couldn't help thinking that she looked so alone, so tired and so very sad. Her eyes rose from the table and met Lincoln's. Within an instant she was on her feet, striding towards him.

'What are you doing? You're late. I said ten o'clock.'

'I know. The tube was late and I was just getting some cake.' He knew as soon as he said the words how ridiculous it sounded. Bloody cake. He didn't even want the cake in the first place.

'What? Some cake? I have been sat here waiting for you for twenty minutes now. Do I have to remind you, Mr Marsh, that this is police business?' She raised her voice just enough

55

for it to be heard by the people immediately surrounding Lincoln in the queue.

'And here is your cake and coffee,' announced the waitress as if she had unearthed the elixir of life. Her glee swiftly smothered by the fearful reprimand of the detective's raised right eyebrow. Lincoln scattered some money onto the counter and followed the detective back to her table.

*

'So, apart from the knife, the saddlebag and the bit of paper in the handle, did you find anything else, Mr Marsh?' Detective Green asked.

The Waitrose bag lay open on top of the table. The Detective Sergeant had discreetly pulled out the knife, shielding it from the rest of the cafe with her other hand. She turned it over gently, looking closely at the blade and the inscription. Angling it, so the light revealed the words, just as Lincoln had done.

'No, that was it.'

She asked another question, but Lincoln couldn't hear over the sound of a small baby who had recently entered the cafe with her young father. The change of sounds and temperature alerting the new born to an altered environment, bouncing her from her deep sleep. She was now swiftly moving through the gears from unconscious slumber to full-on screaming frenzy.

'Do you have the note?' she repeated.

'I put it back in the handle,' he said, pointing to the bag. 'But I have written out what was on it.' He unfolded a piece of paper. 'Some sort of message, I think. That's all I could read. The rest of the words are totally illegible.'

'And this "peasenhall" and "providence", this is the murder you told the constable about?'

'Well, there was a murder in Peasenhall, a village up the road. I was just guessing really. Putting two and two together. It may be nothing.'

She looked back down at the words, trying to extract some meaning. Lincoln noticed that she pulled on a loose strand of hair when she concentrated. Twisting it between her fingers, ravelling and unravelling it. The baby continued her agonised scream for attention. The father, sporting an impressively thick beard which his generation thought young and beatnik while the rest of the world wondered at the proliferation of men who looked like their dull uncles wandering the street, was now at the counter explaining that he would like some milk warmed in their microwave. Good luck with that, thought Lincoln.

'And there was nothing else?'

'I've already said. No, there was nothing else. That's it. Glad to see the back of it. Spent the whole trip over here looking over my shoulders expecting to get nabbed. Don't you have sniffer dogs these days, at stations, tracking knives and stuff?'

The detective ignored his question. 'There was no explanation from your father about why he kept hold of the saddlebag?'

'No, but he kept everything. There's boxes of stuff going back centuries piled up in his study. Your welcome to have a look, if it will help.'

'That won't be necessary.' The young father was returning to his table with a defeated look on his face. A bottle of cold milk and an unwanted piece of cake in his hand. 'Do the words mean anything to you, apart from Peasenhall? Do you know who Dunnings is?'

Lincoln shook his head.

'You've never heard of him?'

'No. Means nothing to me.'

She folded the note and and put it into the Waitrose bag, along with the knife and the saddlebag. 'Right, Mr Marsh, that will do for now.' That tone was back. Cold, critical, one step short of a dressing down. 'But I may need to speak to you again. I have your details, your work and home address and will contact you if I need any further information.' The baby continued to scream. The father was on his feet now, manoeuvring through the chairs, politely apologising when he bumped into shoulders and heads, the bundle of blankets cradled in his arms, gently bouncing up and down. A young woman smiled up at him. For God's sake, don't encourage him, thought Lincoln. The man had a sanctimonious look on his face. 'Well, will you look at me,' it screamed. 'A stay at home dad doing my thing, with the baby and the milk and the rocking back to sleep'. Lincoln rolled his eyes. The clue is in the job title, surely it has to be easier to deal with all the troubling trifles of new parenthood at home. Why make yours and everybody else's life more difficult by planting yourself here, in a busy cafe in central London, away from peace, microwaves and cots?

'So we are completely clear, this is a police investigation, Mr Marsh. If there is anything you have concealed, you are bound by law to inform me now.' She left a short pause to drive the point home. 'So I can take it you have told me everything?' Lincoln nodded obediently. 'May I suggest you forget all about this incident and get on doing whatever it is you do. You need to stay out of the way and lets us do our job. I hope that is absolutely clear.'

'Yes Detective, absolutely clear. But look, just to remind you, I am not the guilty party here. I was just trying to....'

'Goodbye, Mr Marsh.' Sergeant Green cut him short and made her way out of the cafe, pushing past the dad, jostling him out of the way so she could leave. A middle aged couple next to him looked up, checking that he was okay. He smiled, shaking his wise head, wondering at the thoughtlessness of the childless. He waved a reassuring hand at the couple. It's okay. Father and baby are doing fine.

\*

Lincoln hadn't told her quite everything

*Dunnings al* wasn't someone's name. It was a place. Dunnings Alley. He knew the word had rung a bell when he had first read it, back at the cottage, but he just couldn't place it. It was only when the detective mentioned it again that he remembered. When he had first taken the job with Luminosity, he was still living at home, finding his feet. His dad had stumped up the money for a monthly train pass into London, just until he sorted out a flat of his own. A mixture of old train stock, lack of capacity and incompetent management meant that the service out of Liverpool Street was pretty woeful, often leaving Lincoln with hours to kill after work. Rather than hang around the station, Lincoln would wander around the old City of London, looking for crumbling traces of the past within the modern architecture of the financial sector. Some of his dad's enthusiasm must have rubbed off on him over the years, he guessed. He traced the curve of the old London Wall, the church courtyards, the maze of pathways, imagining the lives of the wealthy and the poor. On one of his meandering walks he had come across a sign for Dunnings Alley, cowering between two towering buildings on either side.

It was as Detective Sergeant Green slipped into her accusatory tone that Lincoln had decided to take a visit to his old stamping ground and find the sign again.

# CHAPTER 10

CASSIDY'S visit to Scotland had gone well. The Willoughby's had diversified their interests, particularly during the second half of the last century, but property dealings remained their major source of revenue. Anthony Willoughby and his forefathers excelled in buying up land or buildings at a good price and selling it on down the line, securing a sizeable markup. The three new purchases in and around central Glasgow, in Cassidy's shrewd estimation, would deliver significant value in the longer term. He would certainly not expect to see a return within his own lifetime, but the acquisitions would help shore up the Willoughby family, guaranteeing the wealth of future generations.

His satnav informed him that he was less than five miles from his next meeting at a warehouse in Islington. The soft thrum of his ringtone resonated through the car sound system. It was Sam Wilson updating him on the closure of the Bremen office and wanting to confirm what financial treatment the associated costs should receive.

'Separate out any exceptional costs and leave them on my desk. I will allocate them when I get into the office later today,' confirmed Cassidy. 'Include the charge for Mr Hartmann in that. 'Staff restructuring' should cover it. Treat all other costs in the usual way.'

In the background, Sam could hear the sound of the slow moving traffic, competing for lane space with his boss's car. 'Will do, Mr Cassidy.'

'Do you have any further updates on the Strathdon issue you mentioned last night?'

Sam was expecting this question and had jotted down a few notes on his pad in preparation. 'There was a short flurry of activity during the night between London and the Suffolk Coast constabulary between the hours of seven and nine. A PC Hardy and two people calling on mobile phones, both registered with the Met. Just following up on the day before. I have the numbers if you want them but I doubt there is much significance.'

'Just keep monitoring and let me know, Sam'

'Sure. One thing you should be aware of is that one of the Met numbers belonged to our old friend, Detective Sergeant Green. Are you okay with that, sir?'

The sound of scaffolding poles clanking onto the back of a lorry, echoed down the line as Cassidy considered his response.

'Let Green continue for now. I doubt she will get in our way but let me know if you feel we should step in.' Cassidy ended the call and pulled into a car park just off Tolpuddle Street. Under the circumstances, he was surprised that Martha Green had resurfaced so soon. That, at least, demonstrated a bit of admirable fighting spirit.

\*     \*

The sign was set back from the busy main road slightly.

Small and insignificant, nothing more than a historian's afterthought. The paint had begun to peel away from the edges, but the words were still clear enough to read.

*Dunnings Alley.*
*Original site of the Bishopsgate Workhouse.*
*Parish of St Botolph.*
*Private Property. No Trespassing.*

The short, narrow alley led directly to a large brown door. Presumably this was the old workhouse entrance before the buildings were torn down to make way for the banks, conference centres and office blocks that were piled on top of each other along the busy pavements of Bishopsgate. Ignoring the warning, Lincoln snuck down the alley and pushed against the heavy door. It was locked. To the right of the entrance, as the wall tapered away, there was a window, high up off the ground. Broken glass lay on the paving slabs underneath. It would be a tight squeeze, but if he could pull himself up, he should just about fit through. His forearms ached, yet to recover from his escape from the well, as he heaved himself up to the height of the window. A jagged point of glass nicked him on the side of the face as he crawled through the narrow opening, causing a dark, red drop of blood to fall onto the floor below, marking the spot for his landing when he jumped down from the ledge of the window.

Some old cardboard boxes were flattened on the ground of the small lobby area, along with four empty cans of Tennents Super and a half eaten slice of pizza. A damp, feral smell hung in the air, warm and unwelcoming. Looking at the mould on the crust of the pizza, Lincoln tried to comfort himself that the resident had most likely taken flight some time ago. Many years previously, this entrance must have led to the main rooms of the workhouse, but there was now only one set of stairs leading down to the basement. He moved cautiously down the steps, shining the light of his iPhone before him, sliding his hands against the cold, sandstone walls as he went. At the bottom, the stairs opened up onto a large room. Four frosted skylights, cut into the paving slabs above, offered some beams of muted light. Lincoln could see another set of stairs directly opposite, but apart from that the room was completely empty. The only sound he could hear was the incessant rumble of traffic overhead. He made his way over to the large fireplace near to the other exit. Some charred sticks and cigarette butts lay scattered in the grate. On the right side of the wall, barely visible, he noticed some words scratched into the stone, too faint to read with the naked eye. He fumbled in his pocket and pulled out his phone again. The room lit up in a stark sheet of white light when he bent down to take a single photo. He adjusted the sharpness on the screen and zoomed in.

*hush now my little ones, lay still - sleep forever in the black ditch*

He looked at the words, trying to decipher their meaning or a come up with a connection with the note from the saddlebag, when he heard a sound behind him.

'I thought we had an understanding, Mr Marsh.'

That voice. That bloody voice. It was going to haunt him in his dreams.

'I was quite plain earlier on today, yet here you are. As you are no doubt aware, you are on private property. You leave me with no choice but to arrest you for trespass and breaking and entry.'

'The window was already broken, I just climbed in.'

'Save it, Marsh. I could not be less interested in your excuses. You can discuss it all you want when you get down the station.' Lincoln felt the grip of sudden panic at the thought of his imminent arrest. All he could think about was what his brother would say - 'last straw', 'not surprised', 'thank God your mother isn't here to see this'. A torrent of wagging finger censure.

Detective Sergeant Green stood across from him, her

hands resting on her hips to emphasise her authority. Her beauty obscuring the cruelty of her intention.

'Why are you here anyway, Mr Marsh? Explain yourself.'

A shout echoed down the stairs from above ground before Lincoln could answer. 'Police. Is anybody down there? We are entering the building. Make yourself known.'

'Your colleagues I presume, Sergeant?' said Lincoln. The police woman smiled smugly back at him, enjoying the moment and gesturing towards the door.

'Go on. Make your way upstairs, Mr Marsh. You cannot say you were not warned. I will leave you in the reliable hands of my team and we can continue our chat down at the station in a short while.'

'Can't wait,' he replied sarcastically as he stepped across to the stairway, shouting ahead as he climbed the steps. 'Okay, I'm coming out. My name is Lincoln Marsh and this is all just a stupid misunderstanding.'

\*

'How much longer have I got to wait?' He had been cooped up in Interview Room 2 at Shoreditch Police Station for nearly three hours. A stinking, metallic odour, pervaded the building, the casualty of the endless war between cheap deodorant and nervous sweat. There was no daylight in the interview room, just a fluorescent beam hanging overhead providing an eye-straining, brittle glow. Layer upon layer of warm, stale heat filled the room, pumped out in voluminous quantities from two ground-level metal grids. An empty plastic cup was in the middle of the small table, rolled over on its side, a dribble of warm water hanging off its lip. The walls of the room had been recently painted with the durable but unfriendly matt finish only found in various government funded buildings such as hospital wards and refuge houses. Lincoln shifted on the black, plastic chair, trying to find some form of comfort. He tried crossing his legs, his left foot jogging up and down with impatience.

'Not an earthly clue, sir,' replied the disinterested constable. 'Not my decision you see. I just need to check we've got the right address for you. Richmond Road, Twickenham. Flat 4. That right?'

'It's Richmond Avenue, not Road, but when is somebody going to interview me? I've been here all afternoon for Christ's sake.' He was doing his best to control his temper, but felt like he was being goaded, as if they were just waiting for him to snap. 'I presume this is the work of Sergeant Green. She no doubt gets her kicks from all this. Likes flexing her muscle. Makes her feel important or something.' He took a deep breath, waiting for a response from the police constable who was bent over the table making the amendment, ignoring his protestations. The palm of Lincoln's hand slammed down against the desk. 'That woman is psychotic and you can tell her that from me.'

'You can tell her yourself, sir,' the constable replied, placing the address form back into a clear plastic folder, unfazed by the outburst. 'That is, if you can find her. No Sergeant called Green here, sir.'

'Oh really, is that right?' he said, disbelievingly. 'Detective Sergeant Martha sodding Green.'

'Never heard of her. Not at this nick. Here you go, sir.' He looked up, hearing the door of the interview room click open. 'Looks like they're ready for you.'

A distinguished man carrying a black briefcase, entered the room. A pair of gold-framed half-moon glasses perched precariously on the end of his slightly ruby coloured nose, allowing him to look down on all he surveyed. The smell of late summer roses and hot buttered toast wafted from the expensive linen of his Savile Row suit, tightly buttoned over a charcoal waistcoat. His gold watch chain was taut, straining against the rounded paunch of his stomach.

'Good afternoon, Mr Marsh. It seems you have landed yourself in a bit of a pickle.' He thrust out a soft-skinned and neatly manicured hand as he placed his briefcase on the table. With his other hand, he clicked open the two locks of his case and withdrew a buff, cardboard wallet. 'James Marquand. Sit. Sit,' he said, retrieving a typed page of notes and balancing his posterior as best he could on the inadequate plastic chair. They sat in silence for a moment as Marquand reviewed the updated report. 'You read the signs I presume, Mr Marsh, before you catapulted yourself into somebody else's property?'

'Yes, but as I was trying to explain earlier, I was just being nosy,' Lincoln said, relieved that, at last, he could state his side of the story. 'My inquisitiveness got the better of me for a moment, that's all. I know it was thoughtless, but I really don't think I have caused any harm.'

James Marquand made a note in the folder. The nib of his fountain pen sloping and arching in smooth strokes across the page. The weight of the pen chamber, reassuringly heavy in his hand. 'No harm? I see. Even though you were trespassing and therefore wilfully breaking the law?'

'Well, yeah, if you put it like that.'

'There is no other way to put it, Mr Marsh,' Marquand said forcefully, making direct eye contact for the first time since entering the room. 'My client takes all intrusions on his property with the utmost seriousness, I suggest you do the same.'

'Hang on, your "client",' Lincoln said, puzzled. 'What client? Aren't you a police officer? I thought I was due to be interviewed by a police officer. That's what I was told three hours ago.' He looked across at Marquand, reappraising him. 'And if you're not a police officer then who the hell are you?'

Marquand replaced the cap onto his pen and laid it, sideways, on top of the folder. 'I am someone who is here to help you, Mr Marsh. If you have any intention of getting home tonight, then I suggest you calm down and talk to me. My client is a reasonable man and I may be able to persuade him to drop the charges, but only if you tell me what you were doing on his property.'

'I told you, I was just nosing around and I . . '

Marquand raised his hands off the table. 'Let me stop you

there, Mr Marsh. If you intend to waste my time then I will leave and let the police blunder on with their inquiry in their usual hapless fashion. They should be on top of things by Christmas if all goes well. Or we can work together and get you home to. . .' he paused, looking back at the notes, '. . .to Twickenham. It is completely up to you.'

Lincoln thought Christmas sounded slightly optimistic. He slumped back in his chair with a resigned shrug. 'Fine. What do you need to know?'

'That's a good chap.' Marquand removed the lid from his pen once more and turned to a clean sheet in his foolscap notebook. 'Best tell me everything - how you found the property, what led you there in the first place - the whole lot, soup to nuts, Mr Marsh if you don't mind. Take your time. Now, what have you got yourself involved in?'

For fifteen minutes, Marquand listened with forensic interest to every detail of Lincoln's story. Occasionally interrupting, seeking clarity with a question, before making a note and then waving him on. When the account was complete, Marquand read through his notes in silence. His eyebrows undulating as he ingested the circumstances. When he spoke to Lincoln again, it was in a slightly hushed, almost conspiratorial tone. 'Look, Mr Marsh, I can see you are a decent chap and I am confident that, if you give me a minute or two, I can persuade my client to turn a blind eye on this occasion, but,' emphasising his point by dabbing his finger onto his pad. 'I have to be sure that you have learnt your lesson. I do not want to end up back here in this charming room with you at some later date, listening to another plea for leniency.'

'Never again. I promise, Mr Marquand. Never. You have my word.'

Their eyes met for a moment. A gentlemen's agreement was sealed. 'Right, Mr Marsh, I have your word. That will have to be good enough for now. Let me see what I can do. It will take a little while to placate the arresting officer, but leave it with me.'

Relief and euphoria coursed through Lincoln's body as he imagined finally escaping the police station, the comforting, routine journey on the District Line, the familiarity of his flat. All, at last, within his reach.

'Out of interest, who is your client?' asked Lincoln.

'Just a client, nobody you'd know.' He closed and locked the black leather case and turned to leave. 'Oh, just one more thing, Mr Marsh. You mentioned a Detective Sergeant Martha Green in your statement? I think I know who you are talking about, but she is no detective. She's not even a police woman. At least, not any more. A bit of a bad egg all round, by all accounts. I'd give her a very wide berth indeed if I were you.'

# CHAPTER 11

MILTON Cassidy stood in the reception area of Marquand and Feesbury, waiting for the lawyer to complete a call. Despite being at the centre of Mayfair, the only sound to be heard was the gentle tick, tick, ticking of a small gold clock, placed on a dark, wooden cabinet at the back of the room. Two dark red chairs, luxuriating in their pillowed softness, were positioned in opposing corners, bold and magnificent, like two giant sumo wrestlers waiting to contend a bout. Both had a small oak table, trimmed with polished brass legs, at their sides. The dark green of the walls added to the sense of being secluded from the day-to-day, frozen in some distant point of time away from the City. All remnants of the modern day: the phones, the air conditioning, the light dimmers, all secreted away and out of sight. Even the secretary disappeared into a forgotten absence once she had shown Cassidy through to the waiting area.

He stood in front of the fireplace, warming himself against the flickering coals, staring at the large print above the hearth. His head cocked slightly to the right as he peered deeply into the painting of the dying horse, its eyes bulging with terror as it realised its fate. The purposeless strength of its muscle and sinew etched out by the artist, running along the exposed flank of the horse, useless against the might of the tightening hold of the lion's jaw. Two beasts gripped in life's struggle of the weak contesting the strong, one doomed to an ignoble and bloody end.

'I see you are admiring the Stubbs,' said Marquand, entering the reception room from his adjoining office. 'We like to think it sets the stage for some of our more savage legal affrays, good versus evil, beauty versus the beast and all that. Always good to ask the client which one they see themselves as. The slayer or the slayed. So we all know where we stand.'

Cassidy moved through to Marquand's office, sheltered in the same magnificent silence of the outer room and waited to hear the lawyer's summary, following his recent encounter in Shoreditch police station.

'In my view, he's a nobody, Milton. A curious amateur, nothing more than that. Says he just wanted to poke around. He hadn't even realised he had tripped the alarm. Nice chap and all that, but totally clueless.'

'So, I shouldn't waste my time on him?'

'No, I wouldn't old man. I would be more concerned about that police woman. I was a bit surprised she was still on the scene to be honest. Anthony told me earlier in the week that you'd taken care of all that. Not like you to let things get away from you, Milton.'

Cassidy noted the criticism of the lawyer. It wasn't personal. Marquand was paid to do the bidding of his employer, just as he was. Willoughby had probably asked him to "give him a bit of a prod" on his behalf.

'She is proving to be a bit more tenacious than I first thought,' Cassidy conceded. 'I'm keeping an eye on things, but I doubt we will see a great deal more of her.'

'Well, I hope you're right, old chap. She's definitely still sniffing about at the minute.' Marquand wiped a speck of invisible dust off his dark blue tie. 'Although, there's no collusion between her and Marsh to worry about. Far from it,' he said, laughing, 'Marsh can't stand the woman. Became quite animated when talking about her. She certainly has a way of getting under people's skin, I will give her that.' He gave Cassidy a knowing look, but was greeted with an emotionless stare in return. 'Anyway,' he continued. 'I took the precaution of warning him off Detective Green. Told him to keep away if he knew what was good for him, just to be sure.'

*

Cassidy left the lawyer's office some five minutes later, taking a taxi to Piccadilly where he had a meeting with some out-of-town investors at Caprice in Arlington Street. He planned to use the short trip across town to check his messages on his phone. He discarded most of the emails that had landed in his inbox over the last couple of hours, barely having to read more than the message header to deduce their irrelevance. He kept one from the Scottish property agent confirming the sale price of the Glasgow acquisitions and one from Sam, highlighting an issue that had come to light regarding the planned exit from Germany. Felix Hartmann had been in touch and had requested an increase in his final payment. He had tried to spin a sob story to Sam about his reputation being irreparably damaged, which would prevent him finding new work for a considerable time. He was worried that, without an increased payment, he couldn't pay his bills and may even lose his house. In addition, he had mentioned the Bremen assignment. Sam had included Hartmann's exact words in his email to avoid any misinterpretation - 'I did not receive satisfactory compensation for my services and, due to the ongoing interest of the Bremen authorities, I am unable to guarantee that all aspects of the operation will remain concealed.' In other words, thought Cassidy, he wants more money or he will leak the information about the MP to the police.

Cassidy had never liked Hartmann. In fact he had never liked the German project in its entirety and had strongly advised Anthony Willoughby against it, but Willoughby, encouraged by their success in other parts of Europe, saw Germany as too big an opportunity to ignore. Reluctantly Cassidy set the project in motion and began to acquire cheap land, which, once any local difficulties had been overcome, would be sold on at a later stage for a significant profit. As was usual, extra incentives were required to assist in some of the more problematic purchases. If the land was cheap because of contamination from asbestos, chemicals etc, then health and safety operatives and a demolition company would need to be incentivised. If the land was cheap because the current occupants were temporarily suppressing property prices, whether they be illegal immigrants, travellers, drug users or whoever, then a slum clearance outfit and members of the local police authorities would need to be incentivised. In his experience there were always more than enough people who were willing to turn a blind eye if a cash reward was on the table. It was just a matter of knowing who to contact and setting the right price. Cassidy, however, had never been confident that their customary approach would work in Germany. Not because the Germans were immune to corruption or worked to a higher moral code than the rest of Europe, but because the bureaucracy that ran rampant through the German business world would prove to big an obstacle. The Germans as a people enjoyed structure and consistency more than any other European nation. They liked putting rules in place and, once in place, they liked following them. He strongly believed that this culture was not conducive to the Willoughby Estate modus operandi.

It was Felix Hartmann's job to make contact with the right people and, once approved by Cassidy, offer them an appropriate financial imperative to support the Willoughby's objectives. To the untrained eye, the payments for the most part looked legitimate and above board, but on closer inspection, they could be seen as overly inflated or for services never delivered. In short, they were bribes. Initially progress was good and, for a time, it appeared that the new venture would be a success, however, as the months passed, support dissipated and opposition increased. Hartmann, who was full of confidence when the project was being set up, increasingly brought problems and concerns to the attention of Cassidy. "You do not understand Mr Cassidy. It is not the German way of doing things," he would say, as he pleaded for more time or an increased fund. The bribes grew larger and more frequent, but still the situation worsened. An increasing number of official enquiries were being raised, including requests for employee details, signed letters of authority and proof of comprehensive, financial audit trails. After nearly six months, Cassidy caught sight of an official letter from the Federal Ministry of the Interior threatening police involvement if they did not receive an immediate response to all of their outstanding enquires. The following day, Cassidy instructed Hartmann to cease all activities and stand down.

Cassidy explained the situation to Willoughby two weeks before their annual review meeting at the Burgoyne Club. At first, Willoughby had resisted Cassidy's call to cut and run from Germany and demanded he reverse the decision to exit, however, as the risks and potential repercussions were explained in detail, Willoughby acquiesced and agreed to a gradual termination of relations. By the time they met at the Burgoyne Club, and following the increasingly aggressive stance being taken by the German authorities, Willoughby was demanding a full and immediate withdrawal.

It was left to Cassidy to tie up the loose ends and disentangle the family from the property contracts and other arrangements that had been put in place during the previous months. The German venture proved to be a costly mistake for the Willoughbys. In addition to payments to the the property and multiple service agencies, there would also be the cost of terminating Herr Hartmann's services and securing his ongoing discretion. Cassidy was not comfortable with rewarding failure and had little time for the excuse-laden German, however he arranged a generous pay-off, emphasising to Hartmann that the sum was final and non-negotiable. He also made it clear that, if the agreement was broken, then there would be significant and unpleasant consequences.

He replied to Sam, asking him to book a flight to Bremen on Friday morning. The timing was not particularly convenient, but it would be good to catch up with his German colleague once again and see if he could remove any confusion regarding the terms of their agreement.

# CHAPTER 12

OVER six hundred miles of dark, cold water separated the two brothers. Divided from each other by the salty depths of the North Sea, sinking down 2,300 feet below ground at its lowest point where only worms and crustaceans can survive. Too dense for light and sound. The Marsh boys shared a sameness in genetic identity, a similarity in colouring and gait, maybe some mannerisms, a turn of phrase here and there, but they were living different lives, in different rooms, breathing different air. One sleeping. One awake.

The mobile phone rang three times before Lincoln picked it up. He fumbled for the light switch, knocking over a half finished glass of red wine as he did so. It was ten past six in the morning and he was not at his best.

'Who's this?' he said angrily, watching the stain of the wine seep across the beige carpet. 'And why the hell are you waking me up at the crack of dawn? On a Saturday?'

'Lincoln, it's Ben. We need to talk.'

Lincoln let the phone fall onto his bed, disappearing beneath the softness of his sheets. He silently screamed into his pillow. Not again. He rubbed the sleep from his eyes, propping himself up against the cold, wooden bedstead. His brother's voice sounded like a tiny, distant echo on the other end of the line. 'Lincoln? Lincoln, are you there? Lincoln?' Reluctantly, he picked up the phone from the bed and placed it to his ear.

'Yes, I'm here Ben. What the fuck do you want?'

His brother's voice was sharp, alert. As busy as a wasp. Ben had never needed much sleep, even when he was a boy, sitting up all hours of the night reading, finishing homework and irritating his younger brother, who longed for his parents to come upstairs and call order, turning off the light with a firm and ominous warning.

'You were meant to call. Remember? To let me know about the meeting with Stillman. I left three messages for you.'

Lincoln was already on the defensive, his eyes blinking in the half-light. 'I couldn't. I was going to but things have been busy here. It all got a bit chaotic, what with one thing and another. I was going to call you later today.'

'Sure you were, Lincoln,' Ben replied, resignation in his voice. 'You don't change do you? You've always got an excuse.' The balance of power in their relationship, no matter what, was forever weighted towards the eldest brother. Lincoln was permanently outranked by a two year age difference. 'I've got better things to do than spend half my life chasing you up so from now on, if I say call, then call.'

'Piss off, Ben. I'm not in the mood for one of your lectures. It's too early.'

Ben could hear the sound of aspirins being popped from their casings down the other end of the line and rolled his eyes, not that his brother could see him. 'Just sort yourself out, Lincoln.'

'Yeah. Yeah. Give it a rest, Ben. What was so urgent anyway?'

'We need to sell the house...Sorrel Cottage. I tracked down Stillman in Wales and he doesn't see an issue. There is a bit of paperwork to get sorted but all that's straightforward. You just need to sign the deeds and help get it on the market. I have spoken to two estate agents and have settled on an asking price. If we get a move on, it should be up for sale well before Christmas.' Facts and actions trotted out in quick procession from his snapping lips. Each sentence delivered in a tone resounding with certainty.

'Whoa. Hang on, Ben. When did we discuss this?'

'We're discussing it now.'

'Are we? Cool. I'm not selling.'

'Why?'

'It's our family home, for God's sake. Where we grew up, you know. Where our mum and dad lived for most of their lives. Where we went to school, had birthdays, spent school holidays. I'm not selling it overnight just because you tell me to.'

'What are you going to do with it then?'

'I don't know, but I'm not selling it. It's our home.'

Ben raised his eyes to the heavens. It was all so predictable. 'It's not our home, you fucking child. You haven't lived there for years Lincoln, not for years. I knew you'd be like this. You moved out when you were twenty and disappeared round the world, remember, wasting the best years of your life. When you eventually made it back to England, you barely visited Mum and Dad, apart from Christmas and the occasional birthday. You were never there. Now you want to get all sentimental about your home, the "family home". Do me a favour. Isn't it about time you grew up?'

Lincoln could feel his grip on the phone tighten, throttling it in his hand.

'Mum and Dad are gone,' his brother continued. 'They are not coming back. I'm not having the house empty, slowly rotting away, costing us more and more money to maintain. It gets sold and that's that. You need to meet up with Stillman and get things moving. I can't get over to the UK at the moment. Work. Otherwise I would organise it myself. As usual. Get the paperwork sorted, Lincoln, get it valued and get it on the market. Is that clear?'

Five minutes later, Lincoln picked the phone up off the floor from where he had thrown it across the room. No cracks. There had to be a better way of ending calls with his brother.

He stumbled into the open plan kitchen of his Twickenham flat. His head throbbing. A metal tower of take away cartons was piled next to the sink. Two beer cans and an empty bottle of wine were on the table in front of a half filled ashtray. He rarely smoked these days, but last night, coming back from the police station, felt like a special occasion. There was nobody around to celebrate with, so he made a night of it at home, on his own. Sure, it hadn't been a Mandela-like stretch inside but the taste of freedom was just as sweet. After an hour or so of euphoric bingeing, he had fallen asleep in front of Netflix, before waking up with a start and crawling off to sleep in his bed, fully clothed, exhausted from the trauma of his incarceration and release. He didn't imagine that there would be a mad clamour for the film rights

His phone buzzed. Lincoln looked warily down at the screen. Please God, not again.

It was Sarah.

'Hi, my sweet. It's me. Just wanted to check that you are going to make it tonight. Seven thirty okay with you?'

Sarah had invited him to one of her special dinner parties. The theme; "a winter warmer". The menu; a cheese and beef fondue. It was a set up. She had taken it upon herself to find Lincoln a life partner and regularly paraded him in front of various lovelies from the media world.

'I can't come. I just can't. Too tired, Sarah what with the well and yesterday at the police station.' He heard a question forming on Sarah's lips. 'I'll tell you about it later,' he said. 'I just can't do it tonight. Sorry.'

She let out a large dramatic sigh, although she had expected as much. 'Oh well. Tamsin will be so disappointed. You know, Tamsin Hunter, that gorgeous producer from the

Beeb. I know she was so looking forward to meeting you.'

'I'm sure she'll get over it.'

'Oh I am sure she will, given time and a lot of support and help from her caring friends and relatives. Honestly Lincoln, sometimes I don't know why I bother,' she said, trying to sound angry and hurt but not quite pulling it off.

'Next time,' he said.

'Sure. Next time.' Then, in the guise of an afterthought. 'You haven't forgotten about tomorrow have you?'

'How could I?'

'And you'll be there?'

'Yes.'

'And on your best behaviour?'

'Of course.'

'Bless you, you lovely man. I know it's a bit strange, meeting on a Sunday, but these guys are super busy and this is the only time they have before they fly back to the States. I've got some good caterers coming into the office so food should be fine, fingers crossed.'

For several months now Sarah had been banging on about developing a spin off series from Castle Eden. Lincoln thought it was a naff idea, but after much nagging and cajoling, had agreed to at least look at it. Tomorrow was their first meeting with an American outfit, Adventureland TV, who had spoken to Sarah about commissioning a pilot for one of their subscription channels. Sarah was almost giddy with excitement about the prospect of meeting with the Adventureland executive team. Lincoln, less so.

Slowly, after his third coffee, the fuzz in his head began to clear. He wiped down the kitchen. The sheer modern surfaces reflecting in the light of the dimmed spotlights, neatly submerged into the ceiling. The window was wedged open to let the groggy fumes of the cigarette smoke disappear out into Richmond Avenue. Once he had piled the bottles and rubbish in the assortment of recycling bins on the ground floor, the place looked back in reasonable order. He had nothing planned for the rest of the day and was looking forward to putting the nonsense of the last week behind him.

As he boiled the kettle one last time, Lincoln snapped open his laptop. Marquand's comments about the policewoman had intrigued him. He thought he would Google her and see if anything came up that might give him some sort of clue about what he had meant when he said she wasn't a Detective Sergeant. He reached for his toast as the results appeared on the screen.

*Metropolitan Detective in Drug Frenzy*

*Filthy Filth Fired for Fornicating with the Firm*

*Detective Accused of being Very Drunk and Very, Very Disorderly.*

The slice of toast hung in the air. Melted butter and marmalade slipped down his finger, landing with a dollop onto the newly wiped table top.

He skipped down the page, ignoring the titillating gore of the tabloid headlines and found a Guardian article, hoping that it would provide a few facts and a bit of balance.

*High Flying Detective Hits Rock Bottom*

*It was reported today that Detective Sergeant Martha Green had been suspended from the Metropolitan Police. A spokeswoman said "The Metropolitan Police Service remains committed to preserving exceptional standards of honesty and integrity. It is apparent that Detective Sergeant Green has failed to meet these standards and, following her recent arrest, is suspended from duty pending an internal enquiry."*

*Today's statement failed to provide the specific reasons for Green's suspension citing instead "numerous improprieties which are now being investigated". However, it is known that Green was arrested on Friday evening, November 16, having been found slumped over the wheel of her car in the Croydon area. She had been drinking and was more than eight times over the legal limit. Officers found what they believed to be a stash of drugs during a search of the vehicle. Further suspicious substances were found at her home in Paddington. Green was taken to a police station and later released on bail pending forensic tests on the substances seized and the completion of an internal investigation to be conducted by the Directorate of Professional Standards.*

*These latest charges follow a series of photographs that were published earlier in the month allegedly featuring a naked Martha Green in, what one source called a 'passionate embrace' with a well known member of the London drug world. Several further photographs have since surfaced on the internet, featuring the attractive policewoman in what can only be described as a full scale orgy.*

*Martha Green was fast tracked through the service, reaching the position of Detective Sergeant just four years after joining the Metropolitan Police. By all accounts, she was an exceptional policewoman and was tipped to do great things in what is often considered to be a male dominated profession. However, the events of the last two months have seen an abrupt end to her meteoric rise.*

He was re-reading the lead article, trying and failing to process the information, when the phone rang. Distractedly, he licked the marmalade off from his fingers, his eyes fixed onto the screen, and accepted the call.

At the other end of the line, that voice.

'Mr Marsh. Please don't hang up.'

# CHAPTER 13

'WHERE do you want this stuff?' asked Lincoln, carrying two trays of barely touched food.

'Just leave it. I will sort it out You've made it perfectly clear that you don't want to be here. Just go home, Lincoln,' snapped Sarah, tossing some stale avocado sandwiches into the bin. 'You are one of the most intelligent people I know, but sometimes you can behave like a complete . . . well, like a complete prick.' The expletive hung uneasily in the air between them. Sarah froze for a second, momentarily startled by her own language. It was well known in the office, that Sarah Gillespie, no matter the circumstance, did not swear.

The meeting with the Americans had not gone well. Once introductions were completed and coffees, teas and waters had all been passed around, Sarah explained her concept of unhitching two of the regular characters from the main Castle Eden series and giving them their own vehicle. The characters, Hugh Townes, the vet recently moved to the village with his young family, and Ralph Raskin, the sour-tempered, widowed gamekeeper, had proved popular with the

Sunday night audience. According to the research, a series featuring the pair and centred around their exploits saving wildlife from natural disasters, disease and the virulent, local poachers would be greeted warmly.

The Americans were animated from the start, gushing about the beauty of rural England and the opportunity to promote the green agenda within the new scripts. Their audience would simply lap it up, they exclaimed. Lincoln was totally nonplussed by the whole idea, but remained diplomatically silent throughout, nodding and laughing at all the right places. Right up, that is, until the leader of the party, Chuck Sanchez, voiced up a couple of "fun ideas" they had on the way over that they were "super excited about". Firstly, Chuck thought it would be "mind-blowing" if the two characters formed a sexual relationship and came out to the rest of the village in the first episode. Secondly, he went on, to really cement the bond with the US audience, Chuck thought that the "guys" should "reboot" their lifestyle and move to the States. Portland, apparently, would be ideal.

The meeting closed some ten minutes later with the Americans leaving the building at pace. As they made their way to the lift, Sarah weaved in and out of the party of executives, apologising for Lincoln's rudeness and trying to herd them back towards the meeting.

Thinking it best to keep out of Sarah's way for a while and seeing he was already in the office, Lincoln retreated to the boardroom to work on the most recent Castle Eden script. With everything that had been going on, he hadn't had a chance to make the amends Sarah had flagged the other day. He could hear the angry demonstration continuing in the kitchen, the slamming of the dishwasher, the tossing of cutlery into the sink, the slap of the lid of the bin. He would give her a call this evening when she had calmed down and was able to see the crass absurdity of the Adventureland proposition.

The fug of the aborted lunch lay heavy across the boardroom. Apart from Sarah, the office building was empty and quiet, like a deserted theatre, the props from a recent performance left strewn around the desks and the workstations by the absent players. Lincoln's MacBook emitted a gentle purr as the hard drive reignited and the unfinished script fell silently open onto the screen. Slowly the rhythm of concentration took hold as he gradually receded into the text. There was no sound, apart from the occasional soft clatter of fingers on keys, broken up by a hushed pause. The words on the screen shuffled around like a cryptologist's puzzle, fidgeting and adjusting, until they finally settled into place. Around him, the afternoon moved gently into dusk. The natural winter light slowly replaced by the orange, phosphorous glow of the street lamps dotted along Wardour Street. In the silence, he became aware of a gentle rumble of interruption, a tapping of knuckle on glass.

At the door was an indistinct replica of the policewoman who had walked so confidently into this room a few days ago, now disrobed of all her discipline and purpose. Lincoln's mind slowly resurfaced from the Vale of Castle Eden.

'You have got to be kidding me.' He had put the phone down on her when she had called him last night and had blocked her number, presuming that would be the last he would hear of the disgraced detective.

'I appreciate I have some explaining to do, but if you could just give me five minutes of your time, Mr Marsh?' she said, taking a cautious step into the room.

'Haven't you done enough damage, Sergeant? Should I call you Sergeant or is it just plain Ms Green or how about the Foxy Fed. I think that is what the Sun called you, wasn't it?'

The policewoman bit her lip, demurely staring at the floor. 'I appreciate that we may have got off on the wrong foot, but I can explain if you will let me.' Her tone was probing, searching for reconciliation. 'I would like to apologise for my behaviour earlier. At the time I felt it was the right thing to do.'

Lincoln leaned back in his chair, arms crossed with his best 'oh really' face. 'Was it "the right thing to do" to watch me being arrested and marched off to the police station, Ms

Green? Was that the "right thing to do"? You could have at least helped me to explain to your colleagues, but you vanished into thin air, leaving me high and dry.'

The policewoman took another step into the room to better plead her case. 'I had to get away for reasons which I am sure are only too apparent to you now. Believe me, the arresting officer would have taken great pleasure in locking me up for trespass and breaking the conditions of my bail.' She pressed the palms of her hands together in front of her, clasped in humble supplication. 'I can only say again that I am extremely sorry for deceiving you, Mr Marsh.' She paused for a moment, but then, unable to stop herself, she continued, 'I did warn you though, sir. I said not to interfere on more than one occasion. You should have walked away when I told you to.'

'Oh, so now everything is my fault?'

'Well, yes to be honest. I am sorry for lying, but I told you not to get involved.'

He wanted to rail against her, to remonstrate at the top of his voice, but found he could not. In truth, he had to concede that she was right, she had warned him and he had gone ahead with his trip to Dunnings Alley regardless. 'Okay, okay, I admit it might not have been all your fault but still, you could have helped me.'

'There was simply nothing I could do,' she replied in a matter of fact tone.

Lincoln rolled his eyes. Unhappy, but accepting. 'So, Ms Green, If you don't want me to be involved then what are you doing here? And thinking about it, how did you know I would be here anyway?'

'It's not hard to track a mobile phone, sir. Do I need to remind you that I work for the Metropolitan Police Force,' Green patiently explained. 'As for what I am doing here? I think I need your help. I am not altogether sure how you can help me, but I would appreciate it if you could take me through the circumstance in which you found the knife once again.'

'But we've done all that, Sergeant. Twice,' he added, for effect.

'I know and I appreciate your patience, Mr Marsh, but maybe I missed something.'

'Maybe you did, I don't know, but why should I help a corrupt cop? Maybe I should just call the police and report you for harassment?'

'Please don't do that, sir. I'm aware that I am yet to earn your trust, but all those stories you will have read online, well they are not true. I have been set up.'

'That's convenient. Why should I believe you, Ms Green? Why would anybody want to set you up Sergeant?'

Her eyes looked down onto the desk. 'I don't know.'

'I think you are going to have to do a bit better than that, Sergeant,' fired back Lincoln, enjoying the reversal of roles. Outside the boardroom, he could see Sarah surreptitiously look across as she put on her coat to leave. From her doorway the detective would have been obscured from view by one of the large, vibrantly coloured pillars. She left without saying goodbye, still smarting from the meeting earlier.

'Look, I honestly don't know why I have been framed. I wish I did. All I know is that I was looking into a traffic accident when everything blew up in my face. A lone driver, over the limit, crashed headlong into a lorry on the A12. Indirectly my investigation led to a wealthy family called Willoughby. I started making some general enquiries and the next minute my life was turned upside down.'

'But why? People don't resort to such lengths without severe provocation. Were you questioning one of these Willoughbys? Or threatening them?'

'No, nothing like that. I have never even met any members of that family.'

'Then what? You must had done something to anger them. I am going to need more than that if you want me to help you, Ms. Green.'

She gestured towards the chair, seeking permission.

'Sure. Sit,' he said.

Detective Sergeant Green slid off her coat and folded it onto the table. 'Would you mind if I had a glass of water?'

'Of course not, go ahead,' he said, passing her the jug left over from lunchtime. As she raised the glass to her lips, Lincoln noticed a slight tremble in her hand and the same defeated look in her eyes he had seen at the cafe.

'All I can do is tell you what I know, Mr Marsh, but I can't make you believe me. That is up to you.' She took another drink from her cup. 'A lot of things have happened to me that I simply do not understand. Over the past weeks, I have become untethered from all the things that I hold dear: my career; my family; my friends. All because I was following up some leads, just as I would do on any other case. It was just a routine enquiry relating to the traffic accident I mentioned. The driver, a woman aged 63, died on the operating table at Ipswich General without regaining consciousness. She was the only person injured. Following department procedure, I looked into her background, just as a matter of routine. Just general information, place of birth, next of kin etc. It all looked regular. Nothing suspicious. The only thing that was a little bit out of the ordinary was her home, which was owned by a company called Bixford Holdings. Looking at the victim's bank account, there was no money deducted for rent so she was essentially living for free in a house owned by some other party. It struck me as an unusual arrangement, nothing more, but worth following up.

'There was nothing on our files regarding Bixford Holdings and only the sketchiest information on the Companies House website: a telephone number long since disconnected; an email address that bounced back; and a postal address in Hertfordshire where any correspondence could be sent. There was only one director listed, a Mr Anthony Willoughby. I ran his name through the system, but found little apart from another forwarding address for somewhere in Marchmont Street, London which I visited but could get no reply. I was going to leave it there, figuring it was all a bit of a wild goose chase, but in the end, decided to go back to the building in Marchmont Street with a couple of uniforms and have another go. It was the morning of the visit that I was suddenly called into the office and told that a complaint had been raised against me and I was now under investigation for being drunk while on duty. Things happened quickly after that. Later the same day a packet, containing eight grams of cocaine, was found in my locker and I was suspended from work. Further allegations followed including intent to supply drugs and inappropriate relations with known felons. You probably saw the photographs. They were fake, Mr Marsh, good fakes, but fakes nonetheless. It all culminated with me waking up in a Croydon car park with a pounding head and being told I was being taken into custody. I have no recollection of how I got to the car park and no idea who planted the drugs they found in my car and in my flat. I was charged and released on bail and since then I have been trying to figure out what the hell is going on. If I don't resolve things by the time I'm hauled up in front of the DPS then they will sack me and convict me and I will be sent to jail.'

Lincoln watched the pale policewoman as she continued her story. She looked worn out through worry and lack of sleep. He noticed that she was rotating an engagement ring on her finger. Twirling it around and around.

'And this is the truth this time?' he said. 'This is actually what happened?'

'Like I said, Mr Marsh, I cannot make you believe me if you don't want to.' Detective Green reached across the table for another glass of water. 'All I know is that this whole thing has something to do with the Willoughby family. It all started when I looked into them and then yesterday you led me to that building in Dunnings Alley which, when I looked up the lease, I found was originally bought by the Willoughby Estate back in 1891.'

'But where does that leave you?'

'I don't know. Nowhere probably, but something about your visit yesterday set alarm bells ringing. I followed you to

Shoreditch after you were picked up. I was hoping to persuade you to tell me how you found out about Dunnings Alley once they had given you a slap on the wrists and released you. I found a cafe with a view of the front of the police station and waited. Eventually someone I recognised, a lawyer, James Marquand, arrived. I presume that was for you?'

'Yes,' confirmed Marsh. 'He was very helpful to be honest. He was the first person who actually took the time to listen to me properly without accusing me of God knows what. If it hadn't been for him, I would most likely still be there now.'

'Yes. That's what worries me. Marquand is not a run of the mill brief. His speciality is making the problems of the wealthy disappear and is definitely not someone who would usually involve themselves in a straightforward trespassing case. Did he say who he is was working for?

'No.'

'It has to be Anthony Willoughby,' she said with absolute certainty. 'One good thing is that they let you go. I can only presume that they think you don't know anything.'

'Well, they are right there.'

Detective Green looked up. Their eyes met and for the first time Lincoln saw a glimpse of the ruthless determination he had witnessed in their previous encounters.

'But there must be something, Mr Marsh. There has got to be. Please, talk me through it one more time. From the beginning.'

# CHAPTER 14

THREE times a year, the senior members of the Willoughby dynasty would travel to Hertfordshire to meet at Widford Hall, their ancestral home. The large Jacobean mansion had been in the family since the early 17th century and was the place where the Willoughby children had received schooling and had grown up, insulated from the world by the thick walls of the grey ashlar building. A skeleton staff was retained on site to run the household, even during the numerous weeks of the year when the Willoughbys were absent in London or abroad. Additional staff were called in, as required, to assist with family events, including the triannual business lunches. On these occasions, it was customary to serve roast goose or pheasant, accompanied by a variety of seasonal vegetables, all selected from the rolling eighty acres that surrounded Widford Hall. The family meal was held in the large, austere dining room that looked out onto the manicured lawns at the rear of the home, which now softly glowed with a late dusting of golden, fallen leaves. Canted bay windows provided the backdrop for the informal board meeting, allowing Anthony Willoughby, as Head of the Family, the opportunity to update the others on significant progress and future plans.

Willoughby sat in the large oak chair at the head of the dining table. Either side of Anthony, sat his two sisters, Louisa and Elizabeth. Louisa, the eldest sister, had dark hair, pinned back, with soft greying temples. Her refined features and youthful physique, belied her sixty two years. The finest yet most conservative fashions of the day were draped over her lithe limbs arranged in rigid splendour upon the Elizabethan dining chair. Like her elder brother, she was blessed with a keen intellect and the confidence of one who knew herself to be frequently the most intelligent person in the room. Her sister, Elizabeth, inherited the beauty of her mother, but none of the wit. In recent years, and following two failed marriages, her hours of drinking had increased and she spent most of her days in a soft alcoholic haze, happy to let the world pass her by. Now married to an ex Navy man, she spent much of her life on the coast, waiting for her husband to find harbour in one port or other. Seated to the right of Elizabeth, was Andrew. At 56 he was the youngest member of the Willoughby siblings. Unlike his brother and sisters, Andrew had gone to fat over the last ten years and was now heavy-jowled with a porcine pink glow in his cheeks. Although comparatively young, he had established a successful niche within the varied family business portfolio with an operation so lucrative and so darkly specialist that even Anthony thought best to leave well alone. The final guest at the meal was the family lawyer, James Marquand, invited to record the minutes and provide legal advice and general counsel as required. There was little warmth between the brothers and sisters and the meetings were generally unpleasant affairs not looked forward to by any of the attendees. Outright animosity was rarely displayed, the siblings were too well mannered for that, but an air of malevolence and spite permeated the room and settled on proceedings like falling snow.

As the staff prepared the table for dessert, Anthony Willoughby concluded his financial overview and moved on to Any Other Business, peering around the table, hoping to stifle any impotent questioning with a confrontational scowl.

After a short pause, Louisa Willoughby, raised her index finger slightly and put forward a question, 'And what about Mr Cassidy? How is he faring?'

'Cassidy is well, Louisa,' replied Anthony Willoughby. 'He continues to provide an admirable service for the family.' He shuffled the papers that were on the table next to his glass of dessert wine and looked up. 'Anything else?'

There was another pause. Shorter this time. 'And you still feel comfortable with the arrangement with Mr Cassidy?'

'Yes, Louisa. Quite comfortable,' replied Anthony Willoughby decisively, unable to hide his irritation with the questions raised by his eldest sister. Elizabeth and Andrew looked on amused, knowing that Louisa would not allow her brother to close the conversation down quite so abruptly.

'Even in light of recent undertakings?' Louisa continued. 'You do surprise me, Anthony, although I am, to a degree, comforted by your ongoing confidence. You, of course, are closer to the day-to-day than any of us, so I am sure the actions, that appear so reckless from afar, seem much more measured and deliberate from your standpoint.'

Anthony turned a quizzical eye towards Louisa. 'Reckless? What are you referring to that is so reckless, may I ask?'

'Well, firstly, the foolish foray into Germany and that Bremen affair and then more recently, all that horrid business with the policewoman. Was all that really necessary, Anthony?'

'Yes it was, Louisa. Absolutely. As you quite rightly say, you are removed from the detail. You are best leaving these matters with me to deal with.'

'Well, certainly, Anthony. If it is you indeed, who is dealing with them and not Mr Cassidy working independently. I worry, Anthony, that is all. We all do.' She looked round the table at Elizabeth and Andrew for support, but both seemed reluctant to be drawn into this particular squabble. 'I just don't want the situation to be exacerbated in the absence of appropriate management. Mr Cassidy has served the family well, but could easily become a liability and you do insist on parcelling up so much of his least savoury dealings under that dreadful Strathdon banner.' The room was silent as Louisa took the slightest of tastes from the plate of gooseberry fool that had been placed in front of her some five minutes earlier. After which, she placed the spoon gently back on the plate and left the rest of the dessert untouched. 'I just think closer management is required and perhaps Mr Cassidy needs to be reminded as to what is and what is not within his purview, so things don't become confused later on.'

The hollow sound of a peacock's call could be heard from a distant corner of the grounds. The family sat in silence. Anthony was staring fixedly at Louisa, whose eyes had come to rest upon the disappointing dessert in front of her, nestling on the crisp, white table cloth. She was still. Placid. Like a marble statue. Content that her criticism had hit the mark and wounded her poor elder brother. Elizabeth and Andrew looked on, intrigued, delighting in the drama before them. Anthony eventually took a deep breath and relaxed his menacing, yet impotent, stare. He paused and gathered himself.

'Thank you, Louisa, for your comments. Lets hope I can muster up the "appropriate management" in future.' He leaned forward onto the table, crossing his hands in front of him and continued in a restrained tone. 'I have taken control of family matters for over fifty years now. Under my stewardship, the family interests have prospered and your own personal wealth has significantly increased. The property portfolio now extends throughout Europe and beyond. The satellite businesses are performing well and provide a material and ongoing contribution. The Estate remains extremely cash rich and the balance sheet has never looked healthier. Amidst all this industry. All this endeavour. Sit the three of you.' He gazed slowly around the room. 'You don't work. You don't contribute. You sit and you spend. You spend lavishly. You spend foolishly. You spend unrelentingly. I do not encourage you to do so, nor do I chide and scold. I leave you be, to do as you wish. It is disappointing therefore, that you do not afford me the same level of respect and seek to injure me with your barbed words of criticism.' He paused before raising his chilled glass of Chateau d'Yquem and emptying its contents with one mouthful, banging his glass back down onto the table to mark the end of the matter.

Louisa looked up and rolled her eyes, wearied by her brother's melodrama. 'Please don't play the martyr, Anthony. It does not suit. As you know, my questions are designed to elicit comment, not give insult. I, like you I am sure, do not want the inheritance to be held in jeopardy. That is all.'

Her brother squinted back at her across the table. 'Nor do any of us, Louisa. Maybe it would help if I clarified a couple of points regarding Mr Cassidy and Strathdon.' He nodded at the waitress who was uncomfortably hovering in one corner of the room, beckoning her to refill his glass. 'Firstly, let me state for the record that I remain extremely grateful to Cassidy, who has provided me with unstinting support throughout my tenure. His methods can be brutally direct at times but he always conducts himself in the very best interests of the family, however, please do not confuse my gratitude with negligent loyalty. Cassidy is an exceptional associate, but I am only too acutely aware of the accompanying liability if he were to slip up in his endeavours. That, Louisa, is in part, the reason why Strathdon exists and was first established by our ancestor, Hugo Willoughby, back in 1779. I concede that an unhelpful, enigmatic drama has become attached to the name over the years, most notably during the 18th and 19th centuries when it was commonly inscribed by those who saw the name as a badge of honour, onto the swords, muskets and daggers of those tasked to complete the family's bidding. But, it's primary function has always been as a means of providing the Willoughby Estate with some security. It was Hugo's belief that by keeping any of the more dubious actions and misdemeanours in the one pot as it were, it would be easier to disassociate the family from the goings on if the wrongdoings were ever discovered. The family would be able to deny all knowledge and cite Strathdon as a renegade individual or group of miscreants serving their own interests, independent of the Willoughby dynasty. Times change and considerably more rigour is required to ensure that the family is safe from harm these days, but the principle still applies, as I am sure Mr Marquand will be able to confirm. Strathdon now sits as a separate financial enterprise with Cassidy as its sole Director. He arranges all financing and payments as well as receiving regular additional bonus payments himself, via the Strathdon account. A great deal of time and money has been spent to ensure that there is clear blue water between the Willoughby interests and Strathdon. Isn't that correct, James?'

'Indeed it is, sir. All Strathdon actions and expenses are considerably more than once removed from the Estate,' confirmed the lawyer. 'It would of course be foolhardy to think that if, God forfend, Strathdon was exposed, that the Willoughby Estate could simply step aside and avoid some sort of investigation, but I am confident that, from a legal perspective, there is enough substance to obfuscate any enquiry. Cassidy would undoubtedly be dragged under, but not the family. Some time in the years ahead, the family may want to consider the future viability of retaining Strathdon as an enterprise, but for now it remains the most prudent and sagacious way to conduct the family's affairs.'

Anthony Willoughby looked round the room one more time, his eyes settling on Louisa. 'Now, does anybody else have any points they wish to raise.' Louisa looked as if she was going to say something, but thought better of it and shook her head.

'Good.' Anthony said, picking up his papers from the table. 'In that case I would like to draw the meeting to a close. Marquand will issue the minutes as normal, excluding the AOB section. I trust you will all be joining me at our traditional Christmas gathering later in the year and I look forward to seeing you then.' With that, Anthony Willoughby left the room, soon followed by his two sisters and brother. They each left the family residence separately. Silent and alone. No small talk was shared and no thoughts were confided amongst the siblings as they sequestered themselves back into their various bolt holes across the continent.

# CHAPTER 15

CASSIDY reached into the glove compartment of his hire car and pulled out the bag of croissants he had bought when he landed at Bremen airport earlier. There was one left. He felt thirsty, but had finished his bottle of water about an hour ago when the Hartmann family first arrived at the large iron gates at the entrance of Bürgerpark in the centre of the city. A cold front had crossed over northern Germany during the night, covering the town in a white blanket of snow and the young Hartmann family were making the most of the wintry conditions. Cassidy had met Hartmann's wife, Claudia, a teacher at the local Realschule, on two occasions. She was a tall, attractive woman, perhaps slightly overweight, with thick blonde hair, which she kept in a ponytail. From his car he could see her carrying the youngest of her two daughters, Lulu, as they played in the park. Lulu was five years old, two years younger than her sister, Estelle. Both were blue eyed and had hair the colour of their mother's. Herr and Frau Hartmann had large lumps of snow caked onto their thick overcoats following a lengthy family snowball fight, which judging from their coats, they had let their daughters win. Bounding between the two children was a young labrador puppy, called Ufa. The young dog had clearly never seen snow before and was almost besides himself with excitement. As he ran from one member of the family to the other, yapping hysterically, he would occasionally disappear beneath the drifting snow, emerging wide-eyed and startled, much to the delight of the two young children.

Cassidy patiently waited in his car, occasionally turning on the engine to clear the windscreen of condensation and pump warm air around the vehicle. He flicked though his emails while he waited. Sam Wilson had sent across his daily update along with Cassidy's appointments for the week ahead. Everything seemed to be in order. The property interests in Nice and Glasgow were proceeding satisfactorily and, once he had dealt with Hartmann, all ties to the Willoughby family would be removed. That chapter would be closed. Permanently. There was nothing in Sam's update concerning Detective Green or Strathdon, so it looked as if things were calming down on that front. He was not surprised. One of Cassidy's strengths was his ability to utterly ruin people. Sometimes this involved physical violence, sometimes blackmail and sometimes, as in Detective Green's case, it involved destroying credibility and removing any impetus for future enquiry. He was confident that Martha Green's current life was now in chaos and, while he expected her to have a wish for revenge, he felt assured that she was powerless to do so. After all, there is no creature more friendless than a disgraced police officer.

Finally, after a further twenty minutes, Cassidy could see Frau Hartmann calling her children to the family car, a dark blue BMW X3, and, after a few shouts of protest, they packed up and left for home. Their house was a short distance away from the park on Millstatterstrasse where Cassidy pulled over two hundred metres past the family's drive. The Hartmann's lived in a three storey house, set back from the road. The house had been new when the family moved in three years ago and still looked unspoilt by age. An alley ran along the left side of the building connecting Helmer Strasse with the grounds of the University. Cassidy made his way along the alley then climbed over the fence into Hartmann's large back garden. He slowly walked to the end and took up a position behind one of the tall fir trees that backed onto the lawn some twenty metres from the house, from where he could see through the large, full height windows of the family's sitting room and kitchen.

The two children had changed out of their wet clothes and now sat next to a wood burning stove in the corner of the room, watching cartoons on an oversized television. Ufa, the puppy, lay asleep on his back in between the two girls, spread eagled and exhausted. Frau Hartmann was in the kitchen adding marshmallows and whipped cream to two enormous mugs of hot chocolate. On the other side of the kitchen, Herr Hartmann was piling a big bowl of crisps and a plate of toasted sandwiches onto a tray. Once everything was ready, the parents walked together into the sitting room with the drinks and food and settled down on the floor with Estelle and Lulu, watching television and eating sandwiches and crisps.

Cassidy watched and waited.

\*

It was two hours later when Herr Hartmann's phone rang. He recognised the number and answered.

'Hi Milton. Good to hear from you. I was hoping you would call.' Hartmann was in a jovial mood, but was talking at the top of his voice. His English perfect, but with a slight trace of an American accent. 'Can you hear me okay? Sorry Milton, the children are being a bit loud. Let me go to the kitchen. One minute.' Cassidy waited on the line. In the background he could hear the children shouting as they ran around the house. Hartmann closed the kitchen door and the room fell silent.

'Ah, that's better. Sorry about that. We have a new

puppy, Ufa. He keeps hiding around the house.' Hartmann laughed. 'He seems to have learnt how to play hide and seek already.'

'Sounds hectic,' replied Cassidy. 'Puppies can be such fun.'

'It's like having an extra child, Milton.' Hartmann laughed again. 'Anyway, enough of that. I am guessing Sam got in touch about my payment. Is that why you are calling?'

'Yes, that's right,' confirmed Cassidy.

'Great. I am glad we have a chance to talk about it. You know, face to face, as it were. Well not face to face, but you know what I mean.'

'Yes. I know what you mean. It is always good to talk these things through.'

'Yes. Yes. Thanks for getting in touch. I really do not want to be cheeky, Milton, but as I said to Sam, I just need a bit more money. I don't want to take the piss, you know, it's just so expensive living here right now, what with the mortgage and the kids. Sam probably told you, but I can't get a job. Nobody wants to take me on. I am guessing it will pass in time and they will forget about everything that happened, but for now, nobody wants to employ me. I do not need too much, just say another €50,000. Just to help me through the next couple of years. But as I say, I do not want to take the piss.'

'No indeed, Herr Hartmann,' replied Cassidy. 'I can tell you have given this some serious thought.'

'Felix. Call me Felix,' Hartmann said, relieved that the conversation was going well. 'Germany is an expensive place to live you know. But if I can just get a bit extra then everything will be fine. I will forget about it all, including that business with the MP you had me work on.' He took a breath. 'So, will Sam sort out the details? Should I get back in touch with him now to make the arrangements?'

'Sure,' replied Cassidy. 'Just one question if I may, Herr Hartmann.'

'Yeah. Fire away. How can I help?'

'What happens if we decide not to pay, Herr Hartmann? What do you do then?'

'If . . . if you decide not to pay?' Cassidy could hear the sudden anxiety in Hartmann's voice. 'Well, things would be, you know, difficult. I do not want to cause trouble, I really don't. You know me, Milton, I have always tried to do what is best for you and the Willoughbys, but we did get involved in some pretty crazy stuff,' he said, half laughing. 'You know, pretty bad stuff and look, I don't want to blab to anybody about what was going on, but, you know, Milton, a lot of people are really interested in what went on over here. I am not going to tell anybody, not a word, but I do need just a little bit more money to get by. Things have been really difficult for me, Milton.'

There was silence at the other end of the phone.

'Milton? Milton? Are you there?'

Another silence. Then Cassidy spoke, coldly and clearly.

'Yes, I am here, Herr Hartmann. I will always be here.' He paused again. 'You see, Herr Hartmann. That is the thing about me. I do not go away.'

'I don't understand, Milton. What are you saying?'

'You say you are finding it difficult to get by, Herr Hartmann, but from where I am standing you look fine. Nice house. Beautiful wife. Sweet children. You live in a three storey building with a BMW out front. That doesn't sound so bad. You have a brand new 60" inch TV in the sitting room and, unless my eyes are mistaken, is that a Bang and Olufsen BeoSound system there on the side? Very nice. Very nice indeed.'

Hartmann looked around the kitchen. 'Hey, hang on. What is going on here? How do you know this stuff.' There was panic in his voice now. 'Have you been in my house?'

'Do not interrupt, Herr Hartmann. You have had your say and I listened patiently. Now let me speak. You just need to listen.'

'But . . .'

'No. Just listen.' Hartmann bit his tongue and remained

silent. Cassidy could faintly hear the children calling their puppy down the other end of the line.

'So, Herr Hartmann. Let me try and make things clear for you. You need to understand how things will work from here on in. You will not be receiving any more money. You will not ask for any more money. You will not contact me again. You will not contact Sam again. And finally, and you need to be very clear about this, you will not talk to anybody about the assistance you have provided for the Willoughby Estate. Is that clear, Herr Hartmann?'

'Yes, but . . .'

Cassidy ignored the interruption and continued. 'We had an agreement, Herr Hartmann. You are breaking that agreement. That is not polite or good business, but it is your choice. However, it is important to me, Herr Hartmann, that you understand the level of pain I can bring down on you and your loved ones. If you chose to provoke me I will crush you. I will take your life apart and destroy you. I will infect your life like a pernicious virus and leave you with nothing but decay. I can dismantle your existence any time I chose to. I can walk into your home now . . . do you hear me Hartmann? . . . I can walk in right now if I want to. I can walk in to your lovely home and take your precious little Lulu and gut her like a herring at a fish stall. I can split her in two, right there, in front of you and your lovely wife. I can cleave her body apart and then slap her bloody corpse down onto your beautiful walnut dining table, right there in front of you. That is what I can do to you, Herr Hartmann. That is what will happen if you provoke me, you fucking, malicious, odious, German cunt.'

'You can't . . . you can't talk to me like that . . . you bastard . . . you leave my family alone. You can't come into my house, Cassidy.'

'Too late.'

Cassidy stepped out from the tree he was sheltering behind and shone his torch towards the kitchen where Hartmann was standing, still gripping the phone, shell shocked and angry. Hartmann saw the light at the end of the garden and the tall shape of Cassidy appearing from darkness.

'What are you playing at? Get out of my property, Cassidy, before I call the police.'

There was silence at the end of the line. Hartmann watched as the beam of Cassidy's torch swung to the top of the garden, towards a tall silver birch tree positioned in front of the large sitting room windows. The torch light shone on the base of the tree before moving up towards a shape suspended from one of the branches. Hartmann looked on with horror as the light revealed the hanging body of Ufa, the labrador puppy. He was strung up by his neck about six feet above the ground. A dark, open gash ran the full length of his body. The snow beneath was stained blood red. The dog's innards and intestines were lying in a steaming pile on the frozen snow. Ufa was slowly spinning in the torchlight and Hartmann could see the eyes of his daughter's puppy, bulging and still frozen in terror. He dropped the phone and opened the glass door leading from the kitchen to the back garden and ran out towards the tree. The external security light switched on automatically, illuminating the back of the house. Hartmann instinctively grabbed the savaged dog and wrestled it down from the branch. Inside the house, his two daughters stopped their search for their puppy when the light came on in the garden and turned to look out of the window. There in the darkness, they saw the desperate sight of their father, now covered in blood, holding the flat and lifeless body of their puppy in his hands.

Cassidy could hear the horrified screams of the two young girls, as he stepped into his hire car and made his way back towards the airport.

# CHAPTER 16

**BBC Regional News - London**

**Newsreader:** We can go now to David Turner who has been following the story, which centres around funding irregularities within Easton Council. If new funds are not forthcoming, it is feared that the long-awaited project to redevelop the town centre may be put on hold. In an interview recorded earlier this morning, David is putting questions to the chairman of the Homerton Complex Planning Commission, George Giltmore, Member of Parliament for Easton.
**David Turner (BBC)** - Mr Giltmore, the BBC has established today that the grant set aside in support of the development of the Homerton Complex was significantly reduced during the latest round of austerity cuts. Does this mean that this project, which has been repeatedly acclaimed by yourself as a centrepiece of your administration, is at a standstill?
**George Giltmore MP** - No David, of course it does not

mean that. The Homerton Complex will go ahead as planned. The new development, consisting of retail outlets as well as range of accommodation, including a high proportion of social housing, represents a significant investment for my constituency. It is a vital project for our community and, as I have promised previously, will be delivered on time and on budget.

**David Turner (BBC)** - Even though the promised funding has now been rescinded.

**George Giltmore MP -** Yes. Look David, projects of this scale will of course have to contend with the occasional hiccup, but there is nothing here that cannot be resolved.

**David Turner (BBC)** - Having your budget removed from under you sounds like a pretty big hiccup if you don't mind me saying, Mr Giltmore. You need £18.7 million to complete the initial stages of the development and, following the recent cuts, you now only have £15.7 million in the bank. Why has this only now come to light and where is the rest of the money coming from?

**George Giltmore MP -** David, you are making a mountain out of a molehill if you don't mind me saying. The funding of a project of this size is complex and multi-faceted. It is a significant undertaking and relies on the involvement of a range of investors, not just one council grant.

**David Turner (BBC)** - Many investors you say. Like who?

**George Giltmore MP -** There are several investors proving additional funding.

**David Turner (BBC)** - Name one.

**George Giltmore MP -** You cannot expect me to name all of the parties involved, David. Be reasonable.

**David Turner (BBC)** - Fine. Just name one.

**George Giltmore MP -** I do not have the details of the project to hand, David. Let's focus on what is important here. The Homerton Complex will be developed providing much needed regeneration to this area of East London. Jobs will be created and affordable accommodation for hard working families will be built. It is a good news story for Easton.

**David Turner (BBC)** - Are you seriously telling me Mr Giltmore that you are unable to provide the name of any of your investors? You surely will understand why some of our viewers will be sceptical and may chose to believe that the funding you speak of does not exist.

**George Giltmore MP** - Don't be absurd, David. Of course it exists. I can assure you the funding is very real.

**David Turner (BBC)** - Well, just give me the name of one of these investors. Just one name.

**George Giltmore MP** - Fine. Yes . . . well Willoughby Trading have helped establish financial support during this project and, I expect them, amongst others, to continue to be involved in the many months ahead. Now that is all I want to say on the matter.

**David Turner (BBC)** - Thank you for your time, Mr Giltmore.

(to camera)

*So there you have it. It seems that the project will go ahead after all, despite the £3 million shortfall in council funding. Today Mr Giltmore, the MP for Easton, has assured the BBC that funds will be available, although the provenance of the investment still remains unclear. We will continue to monitor the progress of this important regeneration project during the months ahead but for now, back to the studio.*

Lincoln turned off the television. A week had passed since he had spoken to Martha Green and almost despite himself he felt disappointed that the detective had not called. He presumed that she had decided to not involve him any further in her investigations and had cut him adrift. One of the last things she had told him during the fruitless late night session at the Luminosity office, was that she had arranged to meet one of the relatives of the woman who died in the car crash to see what they knew about the victim living in the house owned by the Willoughbys. He would have liked to have heard what they had to say on the subject, but without an excuse to call, presumed he would never know.

He still carried the saddlebag note around with him, occasionally pulling it from his wallet to re-read the words in case a spark of inspiration provided him with the missing letters, but nothing new had come to him until today. He was holding the note in his hand as he dialled the detective's number, the words of the podge faced politician, ringing in his ears.

The detective answered on the second ring, telling him, in her usual business like voice, to hold the line. He could hear the heels of her shoes echoing down a stone corridor and then the sudden burst of traffic as she walked out onto a busy road.

'Apologies, Mr Marsh, I was in the British Library. How can I help you?'

He relayed the news item he had just watched. She had not seen it. He told her about the shifty MP trying to avoid the probing questions of the BBC reporter; about the the funding shortfall that was putting the development work at risk; about the planned retail sites and housing; and finally about the reference to Willoughby Trading.

'Okay, thanks, Mr Marsh,' she said, unsure that this was quite such a breakthrough. It didn't particularly surprise her that the Willoughbys had business interests in the capital. They were clearly big players, otherwise they would not have been able to entrap her with such ease. It was a useful lead, nothing more. She would look into it and see where it took her.

'Hang on,' said Lincoln. 'You don't get it, do you?'

'Get what, Mr Marsh?'

'The name of the development, the Homerton complex. Homerton,' he exclaimed. 'Don't you see? An eight letter word beginning in 'h', 'o'. From the note. What with the link to the Willoughbys mentioned by that MP, it has to be the missing word.'

There was a blank silence down the other end of the

phone. All Lincoln could hear was the drone of the lunchtime traffic in the background.

'Of course, I have no idea what any of it means but I am pretty certain that this is the word,' he said, still waiting for a response. There was another silence, then he heard the detective's voice. She spoke slowly, as though she was trying to think things through.

'Homerton? So it's not Holywell?'

'Holywell? What's Holywell?'

There was another short pause. 'Sorry. Yes. I thought the word was Holywell,' said the detective. 'That's why I was in the library, tracking down a reference, but yes, from what you have said maybe Homerton does make more sense.'

'Why did you think the word was Holywell?' he asked.

'It's a bit complicated to explain over the phone.' There was some uncertainty in her voice, an unusual overtone of doubt in the words. 'We could meet if you like, if you're not too busy that is?' she suggested. 'Besides, there is something else I need to tell you. Something I should have told you some time ago.'

## CHAPTER 17

DETECTIVE Green had suggested a pub near her Paddington flat, down one of the side streets off Edgware Road. The Chapel was steadfastly unpopular. After decades of being untouched by investment, its decor was from another time. A time when the staff were surly, floors weren't cleaned and a pub was where a man went to get drunk. On the plus side, Lincoln found it easy to get a seat. As some sort of retribution for having the nerve to venture into the place and ask for a glass of Merlot, the barman had enacted his revenge by giving him a to-the-brim serving of the house red. After his first drink, Lincoln could feel a stinging sensation on his lips and tongue. He pushed the glass to one side, saving it for later.

    He found that he was strangely nervous about seeing the detective again, although he wasn't sure why. It might have been the prospect of what she was going to confess to him. That had all sounded a bit ominous, he thought, hoping that she was not going to tell him that she was a drug baron after all and all the stories in the papers had been true. For a moment, the image of the photographs came into his mind.

Unthinking, he reached for his glass and took a large gulp.

'Are you okay, you look like you're crying.' The detective had arrived at eight o'clock on the dot. She was no longer wearing formal work clothes and was now in jeans, a dark blue polo neck jumper and brown boots.

'Sorry, no. It's the wine. Don't have the wine, whatever you do,' he choked. He offered to buy her a drink, but she declined, pulling out a bottle of water from her coat pocket. Smart move, he thought.

Pleasantries out of the way, the detective rounded on Lincoln. Her face a picture of stern officialdom.

'Before we start, I want to get one thing absolutely straight.' Here we go again, he thought, his hackles beginning to rise, wondering what wild accusation she was going to fling at him this time around.

'Under no circumstances, Mr Marsh, will I tolerate you calling me "Ms Green". You can call me "Detective Green" if you want, or "Detective Sergeant" or just "Sarge" if you must, but not "Ms Green". Martha is my name and that will do just fine. Understood?'

Lincoln initially unsure, noticed a smile gently lift the corners of her mouth. 'Understood Dete... understood Martha.'

Things felt better after that. He asked her about her flat and how long she had lived there. She asked about the office and how long he had worked there. He asked about her work and what her boss was like. She asked about his family and what his brother did. It was almost like they were meeting for the first time. After a while, he steered the conversation back to the case, wondering what the relative of the traffic victim had told her, but they had not been able to meet yet. The relative was an old lady and had gone down with a heavy cold so had to cancel. A new date had been scheduled for the end of the week. She went on to tell him what she had found out about the Dunnings Alley building, since they last met.

'As you know, the original workhouse building and the surrounding land was acquired by the Willoughbys back in

1891. They sold the majority of the land in 1907, making a reasonable profit. Nothing spectacular. Down the line, this land was sold again to accommodate the expansion of Liverpool Street Station so someone made a packet, but not the Willoughbys. Two small strips of the original site remained unsold, including the workhouse entrance where you got arrested the other day. This had a preservation order slapped on it in the '30s so the Willoughbys can't do a great deal with it now even if they wanted to.'

'So that's the end of that,' said Marsh.

Martha took a drink from her bottle. 'Yes, I'm afraid so. There doesn't seem to be much more to it.' They sat in silence for a moment. A group of woefully ill-informed students bundled into the pub and sat in the corner opposite, spouting words like 'retro' and 'funky', oblivious to the the astonished gaze of the landlord.

'Thinking about it,' said Lincoln. 'You never told me how you knew where Dunnings Alley was. You seemed certain that Dunnings was a person not a place when we spoke in the cafe.'

'I put a track on your phone, remember? Besides, I was just trying to put you off the scent. I always knew Dunnings was a place. My mother told me.'

Lincoln nodded, not properly taking in the words of the detective at first. 'Hang on,' he said, after a moment. 'What did you just say? Your mother told you? With the greatest respect to your mother, who I am sure is a lovely lady, what on earth does any of this have to do with her?'

Martha shifted uncomfortably in her seat. 'Yes, I probably need to explain that.' She brushed away a few strands of auburn hair that had fallen across her eyes. The students had begun playing some sort of inane drinking game involving the repeated phrase "never have I ever" which struck Lincoln as a particularly irritating way to construct a sentence. He leaned forward, so he could hear Martha's explanation over the noise.

'Back in her youth, my mother was a journalist. Just local

papers. She eventually ended up on the East Anglian Daily Times, but gave up when she had me, although she did occasionally do the odd piece if the paper was short of stories or when she had some time on her hands during school terms. When I got the job with the Met, she would sometimes get in touch if she needed some information. Nothing controversial, just hard to find contact details, car registration numbers, very occasionally criminal records of local people the paper was doing an article on. Anyway, during the summer, she started working on a story off her own back rather than something commissioned by the paper and a few weeks ago, she sent me an email asking if I could help. She was after a whole bunch of stuff, but was particularly interested in two places; Dunnings Alley and Holywell Priory.'

'What did you find out?' Lincoln asked, wondering where all this was leading to.

'At the time, nothing. I was heavily involved in an illegal trafficking case in Essex and was working all hours, so didn't get round to looking them up.' Martha took another drink from her bottle. A look of regret in her eyes. 'Selfish really. I should have found the time.'

'But you've looked them up now, so no harm done.'

'Sure. No harm done. Can't be helped now, can it?' Lincoln noticed she was pulling at the engagement ring again, twisting it around her finger. 'Anyway, Dunnings Alley you know about. The other place, Holywell Priory, was demolished in the 16th century during Henry VIII's reign, but there is a Holywell Row that still exists on the same spot. It's got nothing to do with the Willoughbys, but I checked some records in the library earlier and learned that there was a natural spring at the priory. This spring was the original source to one of London's lost rivers, known colloquially as The Black Ditch.'

Lincoln remembered the image on his phone. 'The name etched onto the wall in the basement of the workhouse at Dunnings Alley?'

'Exactly. The river no longer exists, but it used to run

from Holywell Priory in Shoreditch, joining the Thames at Dunbar Wharf at Limehouse.' Martha sat back slightly in her chair. Lincoln looked at her expectantly, waiting for Martha to explain the connection.

'So?' he said. 'What does it all mean?'

'What does it all mean?' she said. 'Yes. Good question. I'm afraid I have no idea.'

'What? No idea?'

'Not a clue.'

'Well what does your mother say? She sounds like she is onto something. Can't you just ask her what she is working on?'

'I would love to, but no.'

'Why not? What's stopping you?' He wagged his finger at her playfully. 'I hope it's not professional pride, Detective Green,' he teased. 'Go on. Just give her a call.'

'As I said, I would love to, Lincoln. But I can't. My mother's dead.'

A raucous laugh erupted from the table of students just as Martha finished her sentence. Lincoln was shocked into silence, staring across the table at the detective. Her eyes fixed on the bottle of water in her hands.

'I'm so sorry, Martha. I had no idea.'

'It's okay, Lincoln. You weren't to know. How could you?' She placed the bottle back on the table. 'You know what. I think I will have that drink now, if you don't mind.'

\*

Lincoln placed the vodka and ice in front of her and sat down. A moment passed before Lincoln broke the silence between them.

'When did she die, if you don't mind me asking. Was it recently?'

Martha leaned forward. 'Yes, well, that is what I wanted to talk to you about. I haven't been altogether straight with you I'm afraid.' She took a sip from her vodka. 'You see, my mother died just a few weeks ago, in a car accident. On the A12.'

She waited a moment for Lincoln to catch up. She could see the slow realisation appear in his eyes as he processed the information.

'You me... Was she ...?'

'Yes. My mother was the woman in the traffic accident. The drunk driver who ran into the oncoming lorry in the middle of the night. The woman whose house is owned by the Willoughbys. Yes, that's my mother.'

Lincoln leaned back in his chair, astounded. 'Why on earth didn't you say anything?' he asked.

'I don't know really. I suppose I thought it was nothing to do with you,' she said coldly. 'That's what I do, Lincoln. I always think I can sort everything out myself. I don't need help, well not normally. Not a great team player I'm afraid. Besides, I didn't know you, didn't know if I could trust you, what with all the other stuff going on.'

They sat in silence for several minutes. He could hear one of the students trying to explain to the barman what Sangria was. It was not going well. It was Martha who talked first.

'That's how I first found out about the house ownership. On top of everything else, I got a call from the solicitor. My father died some time ago and I have no brothers or sisters, so as the executor and only beneficiary, he wanted to update me on the will. There were a few belongings and a bit of cash put aside in a savings account my parents had set up when I was young, but that was it. It was only when I asked what would happen to the house that he explained that it would revert to the owners of the property, Bixford Holdings. I had no idea. My mum and dad had always spoken as if they owned it. I was born and raised there. I wasn't bothered about the value and, to be honest, I could have done without the hassle of putting a house on the market at the time, but it was still a complete shock.'

'I can imagine,' Lincoln said.

'Then I started to think about the crash. Something didn't

feel right. Maybe it wasn't an accident after all?'

Lincoln nodded. He had been thinking the same thing but hadn't the courage to raise the question.

'I pulled up the papers of the team from Traffic Criminal Justice Division to see if anything rang any alarm bells, but nothing. Everything seemed above board. No surprises. Mum was well over the legal limit and veered across the road on a sharp bend. The other driver had no time to get out of the way. He escaped with a few cuts and bruises. My mother died later at Ipswich General. All very straight forward.'

'And did your mother drink a lot?' he said, immediately regretting the question.

'Yes. That's right Lincoln. My mother was a complete lush and was always driving around the countryside in the middle of the night, pissed out of her head.'

'I'm sorry, Martha. That was thoughtless of me.'

She took a deep breath. 'It's okay. The traffic boys asked me the same question. Insensitive shits. She was no alcoholic, but yes, she did like the occasional glass of wine, sometimes a bit too much, particularly since my dad died, but I have never known her to drive after drinking and have no idea why she was driving so late a few miles from where she lived.' The ring continued twirling around her finger. 'But, hey, I have been in the police force long enough to know that these things do happen. People do stupid and selfish things when they have had a few drinks. It happens. I just didn't think it would happen to my mum.' She finished off the vodka in one mouthful. 'I just wished I had replied to her email or called her before . . . before it happened.'

'You weren't to know, Martha. Don't blame yourself.'

She looked back at Lincoln, flicking her hair out of her eyes again. 'Thanks,' she said. 'And sorry for not telling you everything earlier. I know you were just trying to help.' She closed her eyes in frustration. 'This business is driving me mad. I just can't make sense of it. I know, I just know, it all is connected, but I have no idea how and I am running out of time.'

Lincoln tried to comfort her. 'We just need to join up all the facts,' he said. 'I suppose it would help if we knew what your mother was working on at the time. Is there any chance you could find out, do you think? Will there be a record at her house or at the paper?'

Martha gave a slight knowing nod. 'Oh I know what she was working on,' she replied. 'She was looking into a family scandal from many years ago. My great, great grandfather was murdered. His name was Barkham, Reverend Barkham. He lived in Providence House in Peasenhall.'

## CHAPTER 18

THEY travelled out to East Anglia together on the lunch time train from Liverpool Street, heading to two separate locations less than ten miles apart. Martha's solicitor had received a letter from Bixford Holdings, informing him that Martha had until the end of December to empty her old house, Manorview, of her mother's belongings. She planned to visit the house at Yoxford, a small village less than two miles away from Peasenhall and make preparations to move the furniture into storage. Lincoln had reluctantly agreed to meet up with his brother, who was making a flying visit to the UK. Ben was fed up with waiting for Lincoln to sort things out and had arranged for the two of them and Mr Stillman to meet at Sorrel Cottage to sign the necessary paperwork, so the family home could be sold. The similarity of their grim, filial duties did not escape either of them and lent a melancholy air to the first stages of their journey. It was a crisp late November morning. The sky was a radiant blue and the sun shone down with a heatless and disrespectful glow on the two recently bereaved children.

Once they arrived at Colchester, the carriage emptied and after a short but unexplained delay the train continued on it's journey. The only other remaining people left in the carriage were two suited middle-aged men, travelling together to Norwich on business. One was maniacally staring at the iPad on his lap, engrossed in a game designed for ten year olds. The other was asleep. Head back, mouth open, with the crust from his recently consumed prawn sandwich, nestling on his paunch. Lincoln reached into his jacket pocket and retrieved the saddlebag note from his wallet. He had pencilled in 'barkham' and 'homerton', so now had just three words left to find, however, the note still made no sense.

*axxxxsgaxx xx homerton*
*xxyxx 92 dunnings alley 9 barkham*
*providence at peasenhall*
*kill them all*

They travelled on in silence, Lincoln occasionally looking down at the note, while Martha absentmindedly flicked through a copy of the Evening Standard, left on the table opposite by a departed passenger.

'Out of interest, Martha,' Lincoln said after a while. 'Would you ever have told me about your mother if I hadn't called you the other day?'

Martha carried on skimming through the paper. 'Might have. Probably not though. I didn't think there was much point,' she replied with her customary frankness.

Lincoln stared out of the window, a slightly hurt look on his face, as the urban landscape of Essex slowly melted into the brown and golden hues of the autumnal Suffolk countryside. They travelled on in silence, until Lincoln interrupted the detective once more.

'Before we get to your station, can we get one thing straight please, Martha?' he said determinedly. 'It seems to me, whether you like it or not, that I am involved in this case. My dad's study and my drunken exploit down a disused well have provided you with practically your only tangible lead,' he said, holding up the the saddlebag note. 'It also seems to me that, although you have never asked for it, you need help. And lots of it. I am happy and willing to do what I can, but on one condition. There can be no more secrets. If you discover something, you must tell me. Straight away.'

Martha continued flicking through the Standard. 'Sure. No problem,' she replied breezily, making Lincoln's heavy-handed ultimatum seem a bit foolish. 'Although, to be honest, Mr Marsh, you chose not to tell me about Dunnings Alley as I recall, so I suppose it cuts both ways.' She looked across the table dividing them, her stern face relaxing into a warm smile. 'Message received, Lincoln. Don't worry. No more secrets.'

They changed trains at Ipswich and travelled parallel to the coast on a local service for a further twenty minutes until they arrived at the small village station of Darsham, where Martha left the train. Lincoln scribbled down the latest version of the note for her, with the new words now added and said he would give her a call later to check everything had gone okay at her mother's house. He watched from the train as she stepped into a waiting cab and disappeared into the countryside.

\*    \*

The taxi from Halesworth station dropped him off at the front gate of Sorrel Cottage. There were two cars on the small drive, a mud strewn range rover and a clean, new BMW with a sticker advertising the name of a hire car company in the rear window. He walked round to the back door, taking a moment to look at the garden which was bathed in soft, late afternoon sunshine. Inside, his brother and Mr Stillman were in deep conversation in the sitting room, studying the paperwork which was laid out in front of them.

'Hi. Sorry I'm a bit late. Hope I haven't missed anything too exciting,' he said.

'You need to give us a few minutes. There are some bits

and pieces we are still working through,' his brother replied, without looking up from the table.

He walked into the kitchen to grab a glass of water, muttering to himself. The water tasted earthy and was ice cold. He wondered, not for the first time, why he had agreed to the meeting. He dried the glass, put it back in the cupboard and returned to the sitting room. It was only three thirty in the afternoon, but the wall lights were already switched on. His mother had always kept a fire lit in this room during the winter months and without it, there was an unpleasant chill in the air. He noticed the solicitor had sensibly kept his heavy Barbour jacket on. Lincoln sat over on the far side of the room and watched the two men poring over the paperwork. It still puzzled him how two brothers could be so different. While Lincoln had been avoiding home work and dreaming about sailing around the world, his brother had excelled at both school and university. Even though he went down with a bout of glandular fever during his second year, he still left LSE with a first class degree in Accounting and Finance. On leaving university, he was snapped up by PwC, joining their graduate training scheme at their Tooley Street head office. Two years later he started working for them full time and then, every couple of years, would change jobs, working his way through the big four accountancy firms and receiving an ever higher level of remuneration. His first senior position was in Berlin, which he left some 18 months later to become CEO of Norse Bank. He looked like he had lost weight since they had last seen each other at the funeral. His brother had always been thin, but his face now looked slightly gaunt and drained of life. The responsibility of heading up a high profile bank in a foreign territory was clearly taking its toll.

He drifted over to the window and looked out onto the garden. His mind began to wander and he thought of the knife and the note and how it had ended up in the well when a voice interrupted him.

'Hello, Lincoln'. He span round. He had no idea that

there was anybody else in the house apart from Stillman and his brother.

'Hi, Astrid. Sorry, nobody told me you were here,' he said, recovering his composure. 'You made me jump,' he laughed. 'So good to see you. It has been a while. You look great.'

Astrid Siedel, his brother's German wife, looked back at him without smiling, and then suddenly leaned forward, giving him a kiss on each cheek. She seemed even more cold and removed than she did normally, her eyes focussing at some place off in the distance. 'Yes, good to see you too Lincoln. I just wanted to pop down to say hello. I am going to have a lie down upstairs while you guys sort out all this stuff,' she said pointing to the table. 'Lets catch up later.'

'Sure, let's do that. That would be good,' he replied. Astrid nodded and left the room as silently as she had appeared.

Ben and Astrid had met in Berlin when he was first posted out there and had remained inseparable ever since. She was tall, had blue eyes and cropped blonde hair. Incredibly attractive and very intelligent, with degrees from Heidelberg University and ENS Paris as well as being fluent in four languages. Despite being scouted by several top European companies when she had finished her studies in France, she had not gone into business, but instead had concentrated on her art. Two years later, she had some notable success with her Goldenen Kinder collection, featuring bronze sculptures of children caught in extreme emotions of happiness, fear and despair. She was an extraordinarily talented individual and Lincoln could understand completely why his brother was so in love with her. However, truth be told, Astrid had always terrified him. He couldn't put his finger on why, but he found her extremely difficult to be around. When he talked with her it always felt like he was being evaluated and had been found sadly wanting and disappointingly below par. The German people are not particularly renowned for their sense of humour, but he could not remember Astrid ever making a joke or even a humorous comment. She was serious. All of the time. About everything.

It was another half an hour before his brother was finally ready to speak to Lincoln. Stillman talked though a summary of his mother's estate, which consisted of the house and not a great deal else. He went on to explain that the property needed to be conveyed into the names of the two brothers and then the sale could go ahead, which in the current buoyant market, he did not foresee as being a lengthy process, although because of the delay in getting the documents signed, a sale before Christmas was now extremely unlikely. Lincoln could feel his brother's eyes staring at him as the solicitor talked through the delayed timetable. Stillman had laid the necessary paperwork out on the table in front of them. Lincoln noticed that Ben had already signed his name in all the appropriate places.

He straightened the document on the table in front of him and then looked up at his brother. 'Before we do this, Ben, and give away our family home, are you sure we are doing the right thing?'

'Just get on with it, Lincoln. You've wasted enough time already.'

'But it is our home,' pleaded Lincoln. 'Besides, it is not as if you need the money for God's sake. You could probably buy up the whole of Suffolk by now.'

'Christ, don't start that again. Just sign it.' Ben pushed the documents towards him, placing his black Mont Blanc pen on top of the small pile of papers as a prompt.

'Now sign, Lincoln, so we can all get on with our lives.'

The two brothers locked eyes in anger momentarily before Lincoln looked away. 'Great to see you, Ben. It's been special.' He picked up the pen and turned to Stillman. 'Right, lets get this over with. Show me where I have to put my fucking signature.' Stillman indicated the relevant spaces, thanking him softly each time he completed his name.

As soon as the paperwork had been finalised and witnessed, Ben stood up, reaching for his black overcoat which was neatly folded on the armchair next to him. 'Thank you for your time, Mr Stillman. Please send your invoice directly to me and keep me informed of any future interest in the property. I would like the sale to proceed as quickly as possible. I trust I can leave all of the estate agent and surveying requirements in your capable hands?' Stillman nodded and assured them both that he would deal with the house sale as a priority. Ben picked up his pen and placed it in his jacket pocket and then, to nobody in particular, said, 'I need to get off. There is a direct flight from Stansted to Gothenburg that leaves in three hours.'

Within ten minutes Ben and Astrid were reversing their BMW out of the drive and were on their way back to Sweden. Stillman followed shortly after leaving Lincoln sitting alone in the silent and empty house of his childhood.

## CHAPTER 19

'I admit, I did just panic a bit. That's all. And for that I apologise.' George Giltmore, the MP for Easton, was speaking on the phone, trying to appease Milton Cassidy. A still warm pain aux raisin squatted on the mouse mat in front of him, half eaten. Giltmore eyed it covetously and waited for a suitable break in proceedings to stuff the remaining lump of soggy, French pastry into his mouth. 'I cannot help feel that you are over-egging the seriousness of the situation somewhat?' he continued. 'I really do not see that this is quite such a problem. Embarrassing certainly, but not much more than that. I am afraid this is just the cut and thrust of modern day politics, Mr Cassidy. It will all blow over soon enough, I am sure.'

Giltmore was calling from his public funded constituency office in Digby Road, Homerton. A two-room functional, but unimposing affair with poor ventilation, strip lighting and a shared toilet. Close enough to Homerton High Street to be 'part of the community', but remote enough to avoid a stream of visitors on the days of his constituency surgeries.

'I was cornered by that tiresome journalist,' he continued. 'And momentarily lost it. Sure, look, I fucked up but, really, I don't see what all the fuss is about.'

Down the other end of the phone, Cassidy breathed a sigh of exasperation. 'But why mention Willoughby Trading at all? As you well know, Mr Giltmore, we are not providing any investment whatsoever and have no intention of doing so in the future. That is not what we do.'

'Exactly. That's my point, Mr Cassidy,' proclaimed Giltmore. 'I know Willoughby Trading is not putting up the money and I know I shouldn't have said that you were, but unless you have been at the sharp end of political journalism then, with respect, you don't know what it's like. I was cornered and that sodding reporter could smell blood and Willoughby Trading was the first credible name I could think of. Before I knew what I was saying, I had already said it. Anyway, my point is, the journalist, if he is thorough, may look at the accounts, not that anybody is at all interested, and if he does, he will quickly find that Willoughby Trading is not an investor, so what on earth is the problem?'

'Well, I think there are a couple of issues here, George,' replied Cassidy, as though he were a kindly teacher taking a young student through some incorrect maths homework. 'The first issue is one of discretion. In hindsight, I am sure you will agree, that of all names you could have given the journalist, the name of Willoughby is one that should have been avoided. The second issue, George, and the one that is more immediately pressing, is that you will now need to inform the press who the real investors are and, as you know, there are none at this juncture.' Cassidy could almost hear the dimwitted Member of Parliament cerebrally digest the two obvious facts. There was a slight pause down the end of the line as the MP for Easton considered the position he found himself in. A familiar sense of dread eclipsed his heart, followed by a slight but nagging impulse to vomit.

'Yes, when you put it like that I can see what you mean.'

And then, after a thoughtful pause. 'I don't suppose you think I am better off pretending that Willoughby Trading is putting up the money anyway and just hold that line with the reporter for now until we get some more concrete financial backing in place? I know it is not strictly true and all that, but I'm not sure the journalist is going to be particularly impressed with me saying that I lied to him and that there are no investors.'

'Particularly when you assured the public on national television that the project had financial support and was going ahead on time and on budget,' reminded Cassidy. 'But no, you cannot say Willoughby Trading is providing funding, you need to be really clear about that. Is that absolutely understood, George?'

Cassidy could hear a strange squelching sound down the other end of the line. The MP for Easton, despite his increasing nausea, had succumbed to the gooey sweetness of the creme patisserie.

With mouth full, he mumbled, 'But if I can't say that, then what can I say?'

*

Cassidy was relieved that the MP had finally got to the heart of the matter. The whole thing was a complete mess. The arrangement between Cassidy and Giltmore was that the new development would be built on land acquired from the Willoughbys. In return, Giltmore would be seen as the orchestrator of this high profile initiative, creating wealth and housing right at the very heart of his constituency and almost certainly securing his own victory at the next election. For the project to be a success, Cassidy required Giltmore to smooth the way through the planning and building regulations process where they had previously encountered some niggling problems. The land, when originally acquired by the Willoughbys in 1892, included some consecrated ground where it was estimated between thirty and forty bodies were once buried. To build on consecrated land in the United

Kingdom remains a difficult prospect for landowners and developers, requiring any proposal to be reviewed by a QC at the Consistory Court. If the diocesan authorities opposed the new build, then the QC would rule in favour of the status quo, unless there was a proven and overwhelming public benefit. To date, no such benefit had been established and the affected strip of land remained undeveloped. However, Cassidy had enlisted the help of Marquand and Feesbury in establishing an argument that, due to the multiple change of ownership of adjoined land over the centuries, the Willoughby plot could no longer be viewed as consecrated in the legal sense. The deceased would still need to be removed and re-sited, but the church authorities would no longer be able to block the proposed work. Cassidy was confident that, while Marquand's case had yet to be proven, it did create a good degree of ambiguity and, with the help of the MP for Easton who had been chairing the Homerton Complex Planning Commission, he was comfortable that the issue of consecration could be side-stepped and the value of the Homerton land, owned by the Willoughbys for over one hundred years, would finally be realised. Cassidy had no real interest in the development of the land or who was providing the financial backing. That was exclusively a concern for Giltmore and his colleagues on the Commission. Cassidy's interest ended at the point of sale and while the fund had recently been cut there was still plenty of money available to enable the land sale to go ahead. However, following Giltmore's recent television appearance, Cassidy's plans and the prospects of selling the cursed Homerton land now lay in ruins.

Cassidy's early morning summit with Anthony Willoughby at his club had been unpleasant. Willoughby had insisted on a rare, face-to-face meeting where it had been made abundantly clear by his employer that the Willoughby Estate held Cassidy solely to blame for the Homerton situation. As far as Willoughby was concerned it was Cassidy's job to control 'irksome little ticks' like Giltmore and keep them on script, not leave them unattended so they could discuss confidential matters on the BBC, bandying the good name of Willoughby about as they did so. Cassidy had little choice but to accept the verbal onslaught, no matter how unjust, and wait for the anger of his employer to abate.

The name of Willoughby was rarely visible during the great many business transactions the family undertook during the course of a year. It remained in the twilight, off in the distance, set back, just out of view. So for the Willoughby name to have been given such a public airing was unusual and had caused a great deal of consternation amongst the family members, who all soon became aware of Giltmore's tumultuous indiscretion. Cassidy knew that Anthony Willoughby, as Head of the Family, would be under an inordinate amount of pressure from his siblings to rectify the situation, so it was therefore a particular surprise to him when Willoughby rebutted his initial suggestion. Cassidy had proposed that, as was usual when business situations became uncomfortable or politically sensitive, the family would extricate themselves completely from the Homerton project, putting it on ice until a later date, maybe in several years time, when the circumstances were once again amenable and the project could be resurrected.

Anthony Willoughby did not agree.

'Homerton has been hanging round the neck of this fucking family like a rotting albatross for too long. It goes ahead, Mr Cassidy. Fix it.'

All this left Cassidy with a bit of a problem. How could the project go ahead with inadequate funding? Even if the funding was to be secured, the Commission and the media had seen Giltmore for what he was and would no longer support him.

Brute force was unlikely to fix the problem. A more subtle and diplomatic approach was required on this occasion.

*

'I wont do it.'

'I'm afraid you do not have a choice, George.'

'No, I will not do it and that is final.'

'I trust I do not need to remind you about the photographs, Mr Giltmore,' Cassidy said pointedly. 'Look Mr Giltmore . . . George. I know this is difficult, but unfortunately I do not think we have any other option.'

'You cannot expect me to go back onto the BBC and say the Homerton Complex is cancelled. Not after the promises I have given,' the MP for Easton pleaded desperately. All thoughts of French pastries were beyond poor George now. 'It would be career suicide for God's sake. I would be ruined, completely ruined. No, there must be another way. There has to be. Please, Mr Cassidy. Please. I would lose my job, my income. What would I tell my colleagues? Oh God, what would I tell my wife? No. You have got to think of something else.'

'I am sorry, George. I have been though all of the scenarios,' said Cassidy with finality. 'Please ask your Miss Blackwood to contact me and I am sure we can work out some communications that will at least limit the damage. Either way, Mr Giltmore, we need to close the project down.'

\*

It wasn't until the next morning that Harriet Blackwood called Cassidy.

'Miss Blackwood. Thank you for calling. I was expecting you to contact me yesterday afternoon, but no matter. Now, I take it Mr Giltmore has briefed you regarding his unfortunate predicament? I suggest we move quickly, Miss Blackwood, but first, one for you. It is obvious, I am afraid, that George is done for, so in your experience is it best he resigns up front or is he better to keep his powder dry for now and see how the story unfurls? I bow to your experience on this matter . . . Miss Blackwood? . . . Any views?'

The silence at the other end of the line unsettled Cassidy.

'Mr Cassidy. Good morning,' said Harriet, adopting her usual passive-aggressive tone. 'In answer to your first question, yes, Mr Giltmore has briefed me. In answer to your second question relating to the opportune time for announcing his resignation. Neither, in this case. And, finally, to your third question as to whether I have any views, yes I do. Several in fact.'

There was another short silence. Cassidy could hear a number of papers being reorganised at the other end of the line.

'Right, Mr Cassidy, I take it you have a pen to hand. You may wish to make some notes. Firstly, it is important that you and your employer understand that the Homerton Complex is not cancelled and will go ahead as planned, on time and on budget. Secondly, as I explained to Mr Willoughby when we last met, Mr Giltmore is not in office to do the bidding of private individuals. Finally, I do not know, and I do not wish to know, what leverage your employer has over Mr Giltmore, but from this day on you will not seek to exert undue pressure on this Member of Her Majesty's Parliament. If you do, I will call in the police to investigate and, before you interrupt Mr Cassidy, yes, George is aware that I am making this point to you today. Right, can I help you with any questions or are we both clear as to how the land lies?'

Cassidy was taken aback. He knew Miss Blackwood had some pluck, but had not expected quite such a combative response. Unfortunately, for his plan to work, he felt he had to remind her of some harsh realities of the project and help her to understand why it could not go ahead.

'That's all well and good, Miss Blackwood, and I admire your determination, however, there are some fundamental business matters which fatally impede this particular project. Would it be helpful if I shared them with you, Miss Blackwood?'

'Please do, Mr Cassidy. I am all ears.'

'Well, there's the press for starters, David Turner from the BBC in particular. He is hardly likely to let the issue drop and it does not take a particularly experienced political eye to see that Mr Giltmore is a busted flush. Then there is the issue of the Chairmanship of the Homerton Complex Planning Commission. I am sure that George has been judicial enough to surround himself with a good number of obedient toadies, but even the most accommodating council member is not likely to put up with their Chairman naming a fictitious investor on national television. Without the Chairmanship, Mr Giltmore is very unlikely to be able to influence any future planning application with all it's accompanying building regulations. Finally, and perhaps most importantly Miss Blackwood, you have no investors and, with Mr Giltmore's credibility declining by the hour, you are very unlikely to get any.'

Harriet Blackwood had resisted the urge to interrupt on several occasions. When she was sure that Cassidy had finished, she gave her reply.

'Mr Cassidy, I owe you an apology. I should have called you yesterday, as you pointed out at the beginning of our phone call. Unfortunately, I couldn't as I was extremely busy. I spent most of the afternoon and much of the evening reviewing budgets, talking to central office and engaging with a number of investors. Something that you will not know about me is that I spent my formative years working in private equity and, in that world, you have to learn quickly how to secure investment or die. I am pleased to say, that late last night, I signed heads of terms with a cash rich investment company called Kingsholm. I have informed the Commission of this news earlier this morning, explaining to them that Mr Giltmore was bound by a Non Disclosure Agreement so was unable to announce the details the other day when cornered by the BBC. And as for the reporter, David Turner, well please do not give him another thought. David and I were at Cambridge together and I have brought him fully up to speed and he will be nothing but supportive of Mr Giltmore's career going forward. One final thing, Mr Cassidy, if I may,' said Harriet, pausing for effect. 'I trust that you and your employer will learn from this experience. The democratic process that underpins this country cannot be tampered with. You are not entitled, no matter what great wealth is at your disposal, to bludgeon your way past the checks and balances that are in place to keep people like you at bay. Now, I trust the land acquisition will proceed smoothly, but beyond that I do not envisage having to converse with you or Mr Willoughby in the future. Good morning, Mr Cassidy, and thank you for your time.'

Milton Cassidy slowly returned the phone to the receiver. Miss Harriet Blackwood's efficiency and vigour had almost taken his breath away. Sure, she had clearly realised that with Giltmore's career so went her own, but there was more to her than that. Much more. A good figure, pleasant face, firm and resolute. She was an exceptional creature with an outstanding mind. Cassidy had little doubt that she would enjoy a good measure of success in the world of British politics and looked forward to crossing swords on some other, future occasion.

He looked down at the research notes he had made when he had returned to the office following his meeting with Mr Willoughby at the Burgoyne Club yesterday morning. The notes were entitled 'H. Blackwood.'

* Aggrieved at the way her boss (and herself) have been treated by the Willoughby family
* Intellectually capable and extremely career minded
* Strong willed. Able to manipulate Giltmore
* Went to university with journalist, David Turner
* Father owns a venture capitalist company called Kingsholm

He placed a small, tidy tick next to each line and then screwed up the bit of paper, tossing it into the nearby waste paper basket before leaving for a meeting across town.

## CHAPTER 20

LINCOLN had been looking at a rather forlorn and limited Chinese takeaway menu when Martha had called. She had arranged to meet the relative who she hoped could shed some light on the ownership of her mother's house and wondered if he cared to join them. Plat Principal, was a family run restaurant tucked away in the village of Bramfield, roughly halfway between Yoxford and Halesworth. The restaurant was squashed in between the old post office and the village pub, The Pin and Loop, and was a small affair with no more than a dozen tables scattered around the eating area, most of which remained empty on this chill, November night. As he sat down, a young and friendly waitress poured him a glass of red wine from the bottle, already opened, on the table.

'I did get that right, didn't I?' asked Martha. 'It is Merlot you like?'

Lincoln nodded. 'Perfect. Thank you.' He took an appreciative drink from his glass and looked around the restaurant. The lighting was soft, augmented by an assortment of different sized candles that were placed on the tables and on the large wooden shelves that surrounded the main eating area. The shelves also featured numerous old, hard-backed cookery books from around the world along with other cooking paraphernalia. The restaurant gently resonated with the good-humoured murmur of the guests, enjoying their evening in the relaxed, unhurried atmosphere of the local eatery. Marsh took another drink from his wine glass. This was exactly what he needed to wash away the memories of the ugly encounter with his brother earlier in the day.

'Thank you, Martha, for inviting me,' he said. 'This place is quite lovely.'

'It was Mum's favourite restaurant,' replied Martha. 'She would come here on special occasions, birthdays, anniversaries, that kind of thing. I haven't been here for years but it's still exactly the same.'

Marsh noticed the detective turn her gaze towards the door where two people had just entered. One was an elderly lady, dressed in a long grey coat and leaning on a walking stick. Behind her, propping open the door, was a young woman, in her late teens or early twenties. She wore dark blue jeans and a red shirt and carried a large, brown, canvas bag. She looked like a younger version of the detective, but with longer hair. Martha made the introductions, introducing Lincoln as a friend who was helping her with the case she was working on.

'This is Catherine Marchant-Stone, my great aunt,' said Martha. 'And this young lady is one of her many granddaughters, Rosemary or Rosie as we all know her.'

'Pleased to meet you Lincoln,' said Rosie 'Shall we sit down.' It was clearly Rosie's job to make sure her grandmother was looked after and made it safely to and from the restaurant.

'Oh really Rosie, don't fuss my dear. I can sit down without falling over. I have been doing it for years,' said Catherine, playfully scolding her young helper. 'Now, let me look at you,' she said, reaching across the table to hold

Martha's face in her hands. 'Oh, you are so beautiful Martha, my dear. You have your grandmother's eyes. Just the same shade of brown. It is as if Petra is looking back at me.' Lincoln looked on, enjoying the embarrassed blush on the detective's face. 'You have had such a sad time of it haven't you my dear,' said Catherine. 'Your poor mother. Oh, we were so shocked, weren't we Rosie and so sad.'

'It was such horrible news, Martha,' said Rosie 'We have all been thinking of you. We were so pleased when you got back in touch.'

'And then there were all those stories in the paper,' continued Great Aunt Catherine. 'No wonder you look tired Martha. Running a drugs ring and being a police detective at the same time, plus having all of that sex. You must be exhausted, you poor thing.' There was a short moment of awkwardness before the detective burst out laughing.

The starters arrived some ten minutes later. A selection of local fish caught at Aldeburgh earlier that day. Marsh listened as the family members caught up and shared news and gossip concerning their relatives. It wasn't until the main course was served that Catherine Marchant-Stone turned the conversation to Martha's request for information.

'So my dear, I hear that you have some questions about your mother you think I may be able to help you with.'

'Yes, if you don't mind, Aunt Catherine. It's as I said in my letter, I found out recently that the house I grew up in was not owned by my parents, but by a family called Willoughby. Mum and Dad never mentioned anything to me about it, maybe Mum meant to at some later date, I don't know, but I just wondered if you could shed any light on it. Also, I wondered if you knew what my mother was up to, digging into the murder of Reverend Barkham? Any help you can give me would be so appreciated.'

'I will do the best I can to help, my dear, but it was all such a long time ago now,' replied Catherine, dabbing gently at her lips with her napkin. 'I have been thinking about it all since I received your note. Trying to remember details and the order of things. I think I have most of it clear in my mind. Would you mind, my dear, if we deal with your second question first?'

'Reverend Barkham?' asked Martha.

'Yes, Reverend Barkham, my grandfather.' She reached across to pat her granddaughter on the arm. 'Our very own family murder mystery Rosie my dear. Let me know if you get too frightened,' she said, giving her a playful wink. 'We all called him 'The Reverend', everyone did, even my mother. He was such a glorious man with an old fashioned sense of modesty. He would have hated all the fuss that has been made of him over the years. I knew your mother was interested in the stories surrounding the murder. She had called on me about three months before the accident, asking what I knew of the night back in 1902 when it happened. I told her, "Margaret, my dear, I may look as old as the hills, but even I was not alive back then." We did laugh. She was such a lovely woman your mother, Martha. You must have only good thoughts about her.' She reached across the table and clutched the detective's hands in her own. 'Only good thoughts, my dear.'

'But why was she asking questions, Aunt Catherine?' asked Martha. 'What was she looking for?'

'I am coming to that. A little more patience if you don't mind, my dear.'

Martha silently mouthed 'sorry' and sat back in her chair, remembering that her great aunt loved to tell a tale and had terrified them all on many a Christmas Eve with her stories of ghosts and witches.

'It was The Reverend's daughter, my mother, Mildred Stone, who first started looking into the murder' continued Catherine. 'Mildred was only nine when it happened. She absolutely worshipped her father, so it was so hard for her when, out of the blue, he was killed and, to make matters worse, his supposed killer, Rose Harsent, was meant to have have been his lover. His lover, for goodness sakes. He was a Reverend! Well, you can only imagine the scandal.

'At the time, the police did what they did and charged that poor girl and that was that. Everybody just seemed to accept it. Apart from Mildred that is. She was having none of it. She knew the police were wrong and that Rose Harsent was innocent and, therefore the Reverend's real killer was still walking around the county, scot-free. The injustice of it all just burned away within her during all of her teenage years and when she left school, rather than looking for a husband as you did in those days, she spent all of her time delving into the murder, trying to establish the truth. It became an all consuming obsession for her. She tracked down the Harsent family, she wrote to the police officers who made the arrest back in 1902, she talked to anybody she thought had anything to do with the murder, studiously noting it all down along the way. Sadly, despite all of her efforts, I don't think she ever got to the bottom of it all. Besides, it was still the early 1900s. Nobody was prepared to listen to a young woman raving on about a murder that happened ten years previously.' Catherine paused briefly, looking back down at the table, checking that she had the attention of her audience. 'Then in 1914, when Mildred was twenty one, war broke out and she put her research to one side and threw herself into helping at the auxiliary hospital at Ampton Hall, near Ingham. Following the war, she briefly began looking into the murder again, but by then she had met my father and had fallen in love. It was my father who eventually persuaded her to let matters drop so she could devote more time to looking after her own young family, me and my sister. She would still talk about it on occasion, particularly when my father was not around. As we grew up she spoke about it less and less, but she made damn sure we knew that our grandfather, Reverend Barkham, was a good man, a decent man and not some wild adulterer trapped in some tawdry love triangle.'

Martha leaned forward slightly and cautiously asked, 'But do you know what Mildred thought happened to her father? She must have formed a view on it over the years surely?'

'Your mother wanted to know the same thing, my dear.

My sister and I would listen to Mildred go over the case. She would speak to us about it even though we were too young to be of any help. I think she just wanted to talk through her ideas out loud, to see if they hung together. To my shame, I don't think I was very attentive I'm afraid, but I do remember that it all hinged on a family who had fallen on hard times, called Nicholls. They were a young family with four children, two girls, Rosa and Anne and twin boys, Arthur and George. The father and The Reverend knew each other well as Mr Nicholls tended the grounds of Peasenhall church, unpaid, cutting hedges and keeping the graveyard neat and in order. The Nicholls family lived in a small holding, over on Willow Marsh Lane, north of Sibton. They were decent people, dutiful and hard working and lived a good life. Right up until 1902, when it was decided that a road was needed to connect nearby villages to the main thoroughfare that joined Ipswich to Lowestoft. The new road ran right through their property. In those days tenants had very few rights and so, overnight, the Nicholls family lost their home and their livelihood. Once their house was pulled down, they had little choice but to report to the local workhouse, or House of Industry as it was then known, a few miles away at Blyth.

'The workhouse was a large red brick set of buildings, run by the Master and Matron, Alfred and Jane Caton. It had been operating as a workhouse for over a hundred years, but had a particularly poor reputation by the turn of the century. On arriving the Nicholls' children were immediately moved into a separate ward, away from their parents, who were themselves rested apart into male and female quarters. The Reverend would undertake regular visits to the workhouse as part of his parish duties to keep in touch with members of his congregation who had fallen on hard times or lost their way in life. He would always make a special effort to look in on the Nicholls family and check that the four children were in reasonable health.

'It was some three months later that it was announced that the Blyth workhouse was to close and all inmates were to be moved to alternative accommodation in Suffolk and Norfolk. The Nicholls family were scheduled to be relocated to the new workhouse thirty miles up the coast, at Great Yarmouth, as soon as space allowed. The transfer of the Blyth residents began in July and by the beginning of September the workhouse was empty. The Reverend promised Mr Nicholls that he would continue to visit when he could, despite the distance, and, true to his word, come September, he set off on the sixty mile round trip. When he arrived on site, weary from his journey, he could find no trace of the Nicholls family. The Master of the workhouse, a Mr Mutford, proved to be very accommodating and allowed the Reverend to conduct his own search of the premises in case the family had been recorded incorrectly under a different name, but to no joy. On his return back to his parish he made enquiries of Alfred Canton at Blyth and was presented with a manifest clearly indicating that the family, along with a eighteen other inmates, were in the last group to make the journey up to Great Yarmouth. The paperwork all seemed to be in order, but it was as if the whole family had just vanished into the air.

'The Reverend was not a man to let things go and he spent the following weeks writing to the authorities and harassing Canton for more information, urging him to use his resources to find out what happened to the Nicholls family. Apparently he made quite a nuisance of himself, but to no avail. Canton was totally unhelpful and disinterested. Eventually The Reverend unearthed the name of the owners of the Blyth workhouse, which had been sold by the parish some years before and had subsequently moved into private hands. He hoped to appeal to the owners to support him in tracking down the missing family and perhaps give Canton a boot up the backside at the same time. Unfortunately, the owners were even less keen to help, writing a warning letter to The Reverend as well as enlisting the local police constable to take him to one side, encouraging him to let things drop. We will never know if The Reverend heeded the constable's advice as, by the end of October, my grandfather was lying dead in the drawing room at Providence House with a dagger wound in his back.'

'Are you okay, Grandma? Please, don't upset yourself,' said Rosie refilling her glass. 'Here, have a drink of water.'

'Thank you my dear, but I think I will stick with wine if you don't mind,' Catherine said, regaining her composure and gently tapping the half-filled glass in front of her. 'It's strange talking about it again after all these years. It's as if I can hear my mother's voice telling me the story as she used to do when I was just a young girl.'

'Do you think Mildred ever figured out who killed The Reverend, if it wasn't Rose Harsent?' Lincoln asked.

'No, I don't think so. I don't know, maybe she had her suspicions, but she never said a name, at least, not to me. She was just sure that it wasn't that unfortunate girl.' Catherine shook her head slowly. 'Poor thing.'

'Why were the owners so uncooperative?' Martha asked. 'You would have thought it would have been in their interest to help.'

Catherine reached into a small black handbag she had resting beside her on her chair. 'Yes, I thought the same thing, Martha. I have the note they sent to The Reverend here. There was a box of papers up in the attic from Mildred's investigations. A lot of it has been thrown away over the years, but I knew I had kept hold of some of the correspondence. I had poor Rosie, bless her, scrambling up ladders this afternoon so I could have a quick look through, as something was bothering me. They were really not keen to help though, not keen at all.' Catherine unfolded an old and yellowed sheet of paper. 'Now where is it? Ah yes, here we are, "you are not authorised to enter the Blyth properties or converse with any individuals who are currently or were previously in the employ of the Blyth House of Industry. If you fail to to comply with the above notifications the judicial power of the Suffolk Constabulary and County Council will be brought to bear on you and any party who provides you with assistance in your misguided enquiries."'

'That does seem a bit heavy-handed. Could I take a look?' said Martha, reaching across the table.

'Of course my dear. I thought you should see this particular letter. That's why I asked Rosie to bring the papers along this evening.'

Lincoln leaned towards Martha so they could both look at the rather formal communication, written on stiff parchment, in an ornate and slanted cursive script prevalent at the time. At the bottom of the letter, written in bold, black ink, was the signature of the owner of the Blyth Workhouse, a Mr Norris Willoughby.

## CHAPTER 21

CATHERINE had suggested moving into the small bar area to have their coffee. They had decided to forgo the delights of the dessert menu, apart from Rosie, who still had the nagging appetite of youth and had ordered some chocolate cheesecake accompanied by some salted caramel ice cream. The room was small, with just enough space to accommodate a sofa and two old, but comfortable armchairs. An arch window looked out onto the main road. A thin layer of snow had fallen during their meal, leaving a layer of soft sludge, spraying the narrow pavements as the cars drove cautiously through the village.

    Martha was still thinking about the warning note written to The Reverend.

    'Do you know anything else about the Willoughbys, Aunt Catherine?' she asked.

    Catherine took a sip of her coffee before resting it carefully back onto the saucer. 'No, my dear. When you wrote to me about your house, the name rang a bell. My mother mentioned them when talking about the Nicholls family, but apart from that I have never heard of them. I certainly had no idea that they owned your parents house.'

'You and me both, Catherine,' replied Martha, wondering at the absurdity of the situation regarding her family home. 'It seems none of us knew that Mum didn't own Manorview. It is a strange feeling to think that the house you grew up in, your home, actually belonged to someone else all this time. I don't know why it bothers me, but it does. It just feels wrong.'

Catherine looked up, gently raising her hand, 'Oh no, my dear. That is not what I said. I knew your mother didn't own Manorview, I just didn't know the Willoughbys were involved. I always thought there was quite another arrangement in place.'

Martha had raised her coffee to her lips, but her hand had momentarily frozen, with the cup below her chin. 'You knew?' she said, with surprise almost anger in her voice, replacing the cup back down on the table, ignoring the saucer altogether.

'Yes, I knew, my dear. It is all a bit complicated I'm afraid, but please, do not get angry with your mother. There is no need. She was only trying to do what was right and I am sure she would have told you all about it in time. Yes, I am sure of it.'

'Well that's something we will never know, will we,' Martha replied, petulantly.

'Come now, Martha. How about we order some more coffee and I will tell you what I know?' She looked towards her granddaughter sitting next to her on the sofa. 'Rosie, is there anything further the kitchen can rustle up for you? I am sure they can lay their hands on a side of beef or a joint of gammon if we ask?' Rosie looked up, startled, her mouth full of cheesecake. A crumb of pastry resting on her lower lip. She shook her head, blushing as she did so. Catherine met the detective's eyes, who couldn't help but smile at their young, beautiful and voraciously hungry relative.

'So why did my mum live in a house she did not own?'

143

asked Martha, some moments later when their coffee had been refreshed.

'My sister, Petra, your grandmother, originally lived in Manorview, my dear and had done for a number of years until 1972 when she went to live in France. When she moved abroad she left the house to your mother, who was twenty at the time and had just started working for the East Anglian Times at their offices in Bury St Edmunds. Your mother stayed living in Manorview the rest of her life, making it her home and raising you there.'

'But what have the Willoughbys got to do with it? I know my mother was not paying a mortgage or rent so why would the Willoughbys, of all people give my mother a house to live in for free?'

'They didn't give the house to Margaret, your mother, they gave the house to Petra.'

'But why the Willoughbys?' asked Martha again, exasperation creeping into her voice.

'That I don't know. As I said, I thought the property was given to Petra by someone else. A man named Buller. Edmund Buller.

Martha looked towards Lincoln, seeking reassurance that they had not come across the name before. Lincoln shrugged his shoulders. 'Who on earth is Edmund Buller?' she asked.

Catherine had one of those easy, playful faces, full of intelligence and joy, that always seemed to be on the verge of a smile, but Martha could see the sadness in her eyes as she thought back to a time long ago.

'Edmund Buller was a vile man. Evil and cruel. He brought so much pain into my sister's life, so much unnecessary misery.' Catherine paused, clutching her hands together. 'Oh dear, it always manages to upset me when I think back to those times and my poor sister.'

'Are you sure you are up to this, Grandmother? We could always meet up with Martha again tomorrow if you want. It has been quite an evening already,' said Rosie, looking towards Martha for support.

144

'Rosie is right, Aunt Catherine. The last thing I want to do is upset you.'

'No, no my dears. I am fine. Honestly. I hate all these silly family secrets. They are not good for anyone, besides, you have a right to know Martha.'

'Well, only if you are sure, Catherine.'

'I am sure. Thank you my dear. Although maybe a small brandy might help, if it is not too much trouble.'

The waitress returned with two glasses of brandy, a glass of port and a diet coke five minutes later. Lincoln passed the drinks around, placing the brandy in front of Catherine, the port in front of Martha and handing the diet coke to Rosie.

'I always find the warmth given up by a glass of brandy so invigorating,' said Catherine, replacing her glass back onto the table after taking a modest sip. 'Who said only heroes drink brandy? Somebody very wise, I'm sure.'

'Samuel Johnson, I think, Catherine,' replied Lincoln. '"Claret is the liquor for boys, port for men; but he who aspires to be a hero must drink brandy." I don't think the great man had a great deal to say about diet coke I'm afraid, Rosie.'

'That's it. Johnson,' said Catherine, turning to the detective. 'Not bad Martha, brains as well as looks. You've got a bit of a catch here, my dear,' she said, winking.

'Lets move on, if you don't mind. I don't want to keep you up all night Catherine.' said Martha, clearly not enjoying the inference.

'Oh yes, quite right my dear. Quite right. Let's get on shall we?' She took one more sip of brandy and then leaned forward towards the table. 'My sister and I had always been close, both geographically and emotionally, if you will. We didn't live in each other's pockets but we were always there for each other when needed , but I knew nothing about the house and all the other business until she turned up, unannounced, at our home, Spring Cottage, over in Framlingham. It was in the summer of 1970. It had been one of those beautiful English summer days and we had just finished eating our supper out on the lawn, enjoying the warm evening air. My husband had put the children to bed and had returned with a bottle of chilled chablis and we were both ready to enjoy what was left of the summer's night, when the doorbell rang. It was getting late and I felt strangely anxious when I went back into the house to answer the door, wondering who would be calling at this hour. I remember that I couldn't see anybody through the frosted glass of the door's upper panel, so thought it might be some of the local children messing around or playing dares. However, when I opened the door, I found my sister, sobbing like a child in a crumpled heap on the doorstep. I called my husband and we got her inside. I kept asking her what was wrong, but she wasn't making any sense, just kept saying "My boy. My darling boy." There was nothing to do but try and get her to bed. I made her drink a brandy and then put her in the spare room. I stayed with her all night, holding her and trying to comfort her the best I could. I have never seen anybody so sad, so heartbroken in all my life. My poor darling sister.'

'Where was Grandfather?' Martha asked. 'Had they divorced by then?'

'No, they divorced some time later. He called me the next day, wanting to know if I had seen Petra. Once I told him she was with me, he seemed to lose interest and just told me to keep an eye on her and that was it.'

'So had they had an argument?'

'Sort of my dear. I'm afraid things were a bit more complicated than that. Sam and Petra's marriage you see, was not a bad one as such but it was not a particularly happy one either. That much was obvious. Their relationship had begun while they were still quite young and they were well matched in many ways, similar upbringing, both were gifted musicians, good looking, but there always seemed to be something missing. It all seemed a bit lack lustre. There was never any real spark between them, well, not that I could see anyway. However, after several years of trying, Petra finally got pregnant in 1952, with your mother. I can honestly say that I have never seen such a transformation. Suddenly their marriage was reborn. Sam lost weight and cut down on his drinking, which had started to become a problem in recent years. He even gave up smoking for a short time, although that didn't stick. Petra looked wonderful. She was always a beautiful woman. She had this lovely rich, auburn hair, like yours Martha. Her relationship with Sam seemed to improve. All the restraint that had been there between them, just melted away. They were almost like newlyweds.

'They both adored Margaret, their baby, completely doted on her, but as time passed the relationship between Petra and Sam faded again, returning to how it was before. From the outside they appeared more as good friends than lovers. The marriage drifted on, bound together by their love of Margaret, but there was little passion between them. Then suddenly, in the summer of 1964, completely out of the blue, I received a phone call from Petra telling me that she was pregnant again and the baby was due in February. I was, of course, delighted for her, but a little surprised. By this time Petra was thirty seven years old, which even these days is quite late for a pregnancy, but back in the '60s it was almost unheard of.

'I didn't hear much from Petra during the pregnancy. She seemed to want to keep herself to herself. Then, on the first Saturday in February, I received a call from Sam. He was ringing from the Ipswich Maternity Ward and was in a very bad way. The baby had been still born earlier that morning. He sounded devastated and was so worried about going home and telling Margaret.'

'That's terrible, Catherine. I had no idea,' said Martha. 'That's so sad. Poor Gran and Grandfather. I hate to think of them both being so unhappy. Was it the death of the baby that brought everything to a head do you think? Is that why they ended up getting divorced? They just couldn't live with the sadness of losing their child?'

'Well, unfortunately there was more to it than that my dear,' said Catherine. 'Not that I knew anything about that at the time. It was only when Petra arrived on my doorstep, that summer some five years later that it all came out. By this time Margaret was eighteen and had started going out, having boyfriends, as girls do and I think it was the thought that Margaret was growing up and would inevitably leave home at some point, that had caused Petra to break down all of a sudden. She had bottled it all up inside her for so long, but it became too much for her and it all came flooding out.

'It wasn't until late the following afternoon that my sister was ready to talk. I remember her sitting on the wicker chair, beneath the window that looked out onto the back garden. She looked so fragile, so helpless. I had lent her one of my night gowns. We had always been the same dress size, but she had lost so much weight by then that the gown was literally hanging off her. She didn't look at me when she told me what had happened to her five years ago, she just stared at the floor, speaking in a quiet, monotone voice, without emotion or inflection, almost like she was reading from a script. She spoke of her marriage and how her feelings for Sam had changed following Margaret's birth. Apparently they had taken to sleeping in separate rooms and had rarely been intimate in recent years. She said she was still fond of Sam, but found that now she appreciated him more than loved him. It always struck me a such a damning phrase for her feelings towards the man she was married to, "appreciated him", like you might appreciate a good book or a warm fire on a winter's day.

'In 1963, Sam had taken up an advisory position on the Aldeburgh Music Festival panel and threw himself into his new post, working all hours, coordinating the autumn and spring programmes of classical and choral music. Petra helped out where she could and became particularly adept at managing the visiting artists on festival nights, making sure they had what they needed and were in the right place at the right time. It was during the final week of the Spring festival, in late April, that she met Edmund Buller. Petra described him as a tall, handsome and powerful looking man. Confident and with the air of one who was used to getting his way. She had noticed him as soon as he had appeared at the pre concert drinks in the VIP area, adjacent to the main concert hall at Snape Maltings. He was entertaining a group of suited businessmen that had arrived together on a corporate ticket. Their eyes met and she felt her heart bump, like she had been brought back to life. She tried busying herself, walking around the bar and the auditorium, checking that everything was in order before the evening programme started, but all the time she felt his eyes on her body, following her around the room. When the performance began she positioned herself to the side of the stage and tried to discreetly search for him in the audience. She spotted him in the fourth row from the front, on the far side of the auditorium. He was completely ignoring the string section on stage as it worked it's way through the opening movement of Pachelbel's Canon, instead his gaze was locked onto Petra. They continued looking deep into each others eyes across the darkened auditorium all the way through to the end of the piece, when one of the production crew tapped Petra's shoulder, looking for some guidance regarding the evening's running order.

'Petra said that everything after that felt inevitable, pre-ordained and somehow completely natural. She didn't question the morality of her actions and gave no thought to any future consequence. They met after the recital had finished, talked briefly and then slipped away to his suite at the Seckford Hall hotel. The festival continued all week and they met every night in his rooms, Petra disappearing each evening just as the concert started, returning in time for the encore when she would meet up with the artists as they came off stage, congratulating them on their performance, even though she had not heard a single note. She was consumed with love or lust or whatever you want to call it. During those nights in the hotel, she was able to shake free from the drudgery of her relationship with Sam and step into a world brilliantly alive with sensuous pleasure. She believed she had discovered her perfect man. The soul mate she had longed for when she was younger, but had never found.

Once the festival was over, Edmund had to go abroad for a few months, setting up some new business venture in Europe for his employer. He gave no address, explaining that he would be moving from one hotel to the next so there was no point writing to him. He scribbled down a London telephone number, telling her to call it only if there was an emergency. The people there would know how to contact him. He promised Petra he would call her when he returned to England on the first day of July which, to his credit, he did. By this time Petra knew she was pregnant with his child. She remembered Buller's matter of fact tone when she told him the news, sobbing down the line from a phone box in a lay-by near Saxmundham. He seemed so clear about what to do next. She was not to have an abortion as it carried too many health risks, remembering that in 1965 abortions were still illegal in the UK. Running away together was out of the question. He could not let Petra suffer the guilt of breaking up her family and perhaps losing Margaret. Instead, he told her the only option was to convince her husband that the baby was his. The child would then benefit from the security of a loving family. He would, of course, discreetly provide financial support as he or she grew up, but their affair could not continue. It was their duty to do the right thing, no matter what they felt for each other. They must sacrifice their own happiness for that of their baby. Petra was heartbroken, but Edmund convinced her he was right. She remembered thinking what a decent and moral man he was. So clear in his thinking and so bound by his parental responsibility to their child. She reluctantly and tearfully agreed to his plan and, after a half-hearted conversation about his time in Europe, they ended the call. They were not to speak again until the child's birth.

'Somehow Petra convinced Sam that the child was his. If he had sat down and worked through the dates, he would have seen the lie but he chose not to. I think he probably fostered a forlorn hope that the new addition to the family might reignite their marriage, just as the birth of Margaret had done thirteen years previously. Maybe he was right, but we will never know.

'As the late afternoon sun continued to beat down, the heat in the spare room became suffocating, but Petra did not seem to notice and continued telling her sad tale in that same monotone, emotionless voice. The only time her voice broke was when she spoke of the night she went into labour and the birth of her child. You see, my dear, it had all been a lie. The baby had not been stillborn that night in 1965, instead it was born a fit and healthy boy, weighing in at 8½lbs.'

Lincoln, Martha and Rosie all stared at Catherine with shock and puzzlement on their faces. 'No way!' exclaimed Rosie.

'Yes, my dear. A stupid and cruel lie.' Catherine reached into her handbag, retrieving a tissue. She dabbed gently at the corner of her eye. 'I'm sorry my dears. It still makes me so angry when I think of it all.'

'It's okay, Catherine. Take your time,' said Martha, gently reaching out her hand and resting it on the wrinkled and pale fingers of her great aunt.

A few moments passed until Catherine felt ready to continue again and complete the sad tale of her sister.

'As soon as Petra had felt the first pangs of labour, she had managed to call Edmund on the emergency number he had previously given to her. He wasn't in the office, but she left a short coded message with his secretary saying that a delivery from Petra was on its way. Even at that time, with Sam dashing around the house, sorting out her overnight bag, dropping off young Margaret at the neighbours and packing the car, she still felt an illicit thrill when she thought she would finally get to speak or maybe even see Edmund again. When they arrived at Ipswich General, they were ushered into a private wing of the hospital. Neither Sam or Petra queried it at the time as they were so focused on the birth. Petra disappeared behind closed doors, as they did in those days, while Sam stayed in the main waiting room, along with half a dozen other anxious looking prospective fathers. The birth presented no problems and the boy was delivered within two hours by a doctor and nurse who were waiting in the room upon Petra's arrival. Following the birth, Petra slipped off to sleep, suddenly overwhelmed with exhaustion, with her newborn son resting peacefully on her breast.

'She awoke an hour later, to find herself alone in the room. No medical staff and no baby. She pressed the buzzer on the side of the bed and called out for the nurse, panic rising in her voice. It was nearly five minutes later when the door opened and in walked Edmund Buller. Petra was aghast. What was he thinking of? She told him he should leave straight away. Sam was in the waiting room and would be coming in to see their son in any minute. But Buller did not leave. He walked to the foot of the bed and instructed Petra to sit up and listen. He had something important to say and he didn't want there to be any misunderstandings. Petra, now totally confused, managed to raise her aching body up to a sitting position, despite the pain from the birth. She remembered looking into Edmund's eyes and seeing nothing. There was no wit. No charm. No feeling. Nothing. Just a void where humanity had once been.

'His tone was clear and precise, as he explained to Petra that Sam had been told one hour ago that the baby had died and had been instructed by the doctor to return home and look after his daughter. Edmund went on to tell her that all records of the birth had been removed from the hospital files. The doctor and the nurse who had helped in the delivery were privately hired and had been amply rewarded for their silence. The baby was fit and well and would be leaving the hospital, with Edmund, immediately. Petra was to never see the baby or Edmund again. If she ever tried to find them, Edmund would tell Sam what had happened between them and would make sure that Petra's reputation would be ruined and she would lose custody of her daughter in any divorce proceedings. In compensation for the inconvenience of the birth, a sum of £500 would be deposited into her account. In addition, the mortgage of the house had been paid off and she could continue living there, rent free, for the rest of her or her daughter's lifetime, whichever was the longest.

'With that, Edmund turned away, closing the door on the screaming protests of the mother of his child, who would never see her new born baby again.'

## CHAPTER 22

'CAN I help at all, Mr Marsh?' asked Emma Coldpepper, the youngest member of Luminosity's Marketing team.

'Please Emma, call me Lincoln.'

'Sorry, yes, of course. Can I help you, Lincoln?'

'I was just wondering how to get the lights in the boardroom to come on. I've tried the switch, but nothing. I was looking for Jilly to see if she can help, but she doesn't seem to be in today.'

'Jilly left last week. We don't have a receptionist at the minute I'm afraid. A load of lights fused a few nights ago and we've been waiting for the electrician to come, but he hasn't turned up yet. I think Sarah said he would be coming today . . . or she might have said tomorrow.'

'Okay. Thanks, Emma. I will have to find somewhere else to sit,' said Lincoln.

'Perhaps you could use one of the spare desks in Marketing? I know it is not ideal, but it has to be better than sitting in the dark,' suggested Emma, smiling and gesturing over to the opposite corner of the open plan space.

'Sure. Why don't I try that.'

Only four of the marketing team were in the office that morning. Emma, one full timer, called Colin, and two temps Lincoln had not met before. He found a desk facing one of the windows and did his best to make himself comfortable. He had never really been a fan of the open plan office environment. He thought all that nonsense about 'the power of collaborative working' and 'breaking down the barriers in the workplace' was all so much bullshit masking what was purely a cost cutting exercise so employers could squeeze more employees into less space. As far as he could see, productivity, creativity and critical thinking all slumped as endeavour gave way to mindless gossip and never-ending coffee rounds.

He had been scheduled to come into Luminosity for his monthly planning meeting with Sarah, but she had been locked away in her office all morning with the door closed. Maybe she had forgotten? Maybe she still hadn't forgiven him for the episode with Adventureland TV? He didn't particularly mind the delay, as it gave him a chance to finish off the spreadsheet he had been working on since his meeting at Plat Principal in Bramfield a few days ago. By the end of the evening, Catherine had been exhausted and, once she had said her goodbyes to Martha and Lincoln, Rosie had escorted her to the car and whisked her away back to her home in Framlingham. Lincoln and Martha had stayed on for a bit in the restaurant's small bar area, finishing their drinks in silence, thinking over all that Catherine had shared with them. It had been a lot for Martha to take in. After a few moments, Lincoln asked if she was okay.

'Yes. I'm fine.' Martha replied, rotating the ring on her finger. 'I just can't stop thinking of Petra and the baby. Nobody should be treated like that.'

Another minute ticked by.

'Blyth fits as the first word of the third line on the saddlebag note by the way,' said Lincoln. 'So the line now reads, *blyth 92 dunnings alley 9 barkham*. Whatever the hell

that means. It sounds like a bloody shipping forecast.'
Martha laughed lightly.
Another moment passed.
'Thanks for being here, Lincoln,' she said. 'I really appreciate it . . . I just can't . . . '
'Oh my God, I think I'm going to be sick!'
An out of breath Rosie was leaning on the side of Martha's chair, bent double and breathing hard. 'I've sprinted back from the car. I lugged this all the way from Grandmother's house and then forgot to give it to you at dinner.' She heaved the large canvas bag onto the table and then put up her hand in front of her. 'Just give me a minute.' Rosie closed her eyes and sucked in some more air, regretting that last piece of cheesecake. She pointed at the bag. 'This is the other stuff that was in the attic. Not sure if it is going to be any use to you, but Catherine wanted you to have it. It's all that is left of Mildred Stone's notes.'

Lincoln had agreed to return to London with the bag and put it all in some kind of order while Martha finished off some bits and pieces she had to attend to at her mother's house. They planned to meet at his flat at the end of the week when she was back in town to see if they could make some sense of it all. Lincoln had been up late, skimming through the aged documents and Mildred Stone's handwritten notes, putting it in order and creating an index. He was re-ordering some of the entires and reformatting the file when he was interrupted by Sarah.

'Sorry I'm a bit late, Lincoln. I have been stuck in my office with Tariq since eight o'clock this morning.' Sarah was wearing a mustard coloured top and some mauve trousers, all set off perfectly by a pair of pink framed spectacles. Around her neck was a long, dark green, silk scarf. Its refined presence jarring with the rest of the expensive but garish outfit. The scarf flapped and fluttered behind her as she walked in to the boardroom, as if trying to wave at passers by to come save it.

'Sure. No problem,' said Lincoln, closing his laptop in

readiness for their meeting.

'That man is driving me mad,' Sarah screamed, gesticulating wildly over towards the far corner where her office was. 'I have never known such a pernickety and worrisome individual. As you know, our accounting year finishes in December and he is flapping as per. Why I have to go through this every year, I simply do not know. Accountants! They sit around saying nothing all year and then, when you actually need them to do some work, everything is a drama and a crisis. Flap. Flap. Flap. Anyway, he wants to talk to you when you have a minute.'

'Me? What does he want to talk to me for?'

'God knows. I stopped listening to him half an hour ago.'

\*

Tariq Shad was hunched over his laptop at the end of the long meeting table in Sarah's large, corner office. He was rhythmically tapping away at the keyboard with his right hand while sliding the index finger of his left down a column of numbers printed on the sheet next to him. Tariq had worked for Sarah for five years now, having moved from a small publishing house based in Ealing. Lincoln had not had a great deal to do with him during his time at Luminosity. Once a year he bumped into him at the Christmas office party and occasionally saw his name on the expense claim cheques he received. Apart from that, their paths did not cross. He was a short man, with a round earnest face and a bald head. He was probably in his early 40s, but in truth it was impossible to tell. He wore wire framed glasses which were one size too large, requiring him to constantly push them back into place on the bridge of his nose, which always somehow made him look busier and more frenetic than he actually was. He finished the last entry and then looked at the screen.

'Oh bollocks and balls.'

'Nice to see you too, Tariq,' said Marsh.

'Oh dear, sorry, Lincoln. It is not you. Sorry.' He gave

the screen of his laptop one more despairing look and then turned his head towards Sarah, who had taken up her seat behind the large, executive desk, strategically positioned so she could see and be seen by all of her team working on the office floor.

'Well, did you ask him?' Tariq said to Sarah.
'I thought you wanted to do that, Tariq.'
'No Sarah, Mr Marsh does not work for me.'
'Sure, but it is your stupid idea, not mine.'
'It is not stupid. It is necessary.'
'Necessarily stupid more like.'
'Hang on you two. If someone has something they want to ask me then go ahead and ask me,' said Lincoln, calling a halt to their spat.

Sarah looked at Tariq pointedly, waving him forward. 'Off you go, Tariq. You heard the man. Ask him.' Sarah looked towards Lincoln, apologetically rolling her eyes and shaking her head, pointing a despairing finger towards the accountant.

Tariq pushed his laptop to one side as Lincoln sat down in one of the black leather chairs at the other end of the meeting table.

'This is all a bit awkward to be honest, Lincoln,' Tariq said, pushing up his glasses. 'I wonder if I . . . sorry, I wonder if WE can ask quite a large favour of you?'

'Sure, fire away.'

'I would not normally do this and you have my . . . sorry, you have OUR absolute word that the delay will be as short as possible, but we were wondering if your quarterly payment could be delayed until . . . lets say . . . February?' he said, wincing painfully at the final word as if he wanted to suck it back deep inside his lungs as soon as he had voiced it.

'Yes, no problem.'

Tariq jolted in his seat. 'Really? Are you sure?'

'Of course. Not a problem. Happy to help.'

A wave of relief washed across Tariq's face. 'That is great. Thank you, Lincoln. That is so good of you.' He beamed at Sarah. 'Everything should be fine then, Sarah. I will include this adjustment in my workings, but fingers crossed, there shouldn't be any further issues.'

'I told you, Tariq. You worry too much. You know he's only nineteen years old, don't you Lincoln.' She said pointing at the accountant. 'It is this constant worrying that has aged him before his time.'

Tariq laughed. 'Oh you can make fun of me all you want, Sarah. I don't mind. But it is you who makes me worry. You never listen to me, then it gets to December and bang. Everybody wants to be paid and panic stations.'

'You just need to have a bit more faith, Tariq. Everything always works out fine.'

'Well, that is not what they taught me when I was doing my accountancy qualifications, I can promise you,' he said, shaking his head.

'Oh bless you. What would I do without you? Thank you, Tariq.'

'It is not me you have to thank, Sarah. It is Mr Marsh,' Tariq said, bowing slightly towards Lincoln as he did so. 'If it wasn't for his kindness in accepting the late payment of his fees and the *Ralph & Hugh* series, then I don't know where we would be.'

Lincoln, who had been absentmindedly enjoying the playful jousting between the CEO and the Chief Accountant suddenly snapped back into consciousness. 'I'm sorry? What? What did you say?'

'Oh do come on Tariq. Can you please let me have my office back,' said Sarah, suddenly animated and bustling the accountant out of his chair. 'You have wasted quite enough of my day already. Come on, come on. Off you go.' Sarah was now on her feet, sweeping Tariq across the room towards the door.

'Okay. Okay. I am going, Sarah. I am going,' Tariq said, clutching his laptop to his chest and leaning back to pick up his pen from the table. When he got to the door he stopped briefly, turning towards Lincoln. 'Thank you again. You really saved our bacon this year.'

'Alright. You can save all that wishy washy stuff for the Christmas party, Tariq. Now, out.' said Sarah, closing the door on him. 'Honestly, I have had quite enough of Mr Shad for one day. Now, Lincoln, darling, how is my favourite screenwriter?'

'What was all that about, Sarah?' Lincoln asked.

'All what?'

'You know very well what. The *Ralph & Hugh* series. What series is that? We haven't even agreed we are going do it yet, let alone who with.'

'Oh don't worry about that, my sweet. It's nothing. Just finance.'

'What do you mean "just finance"?'

Sarah returned to her desk, waving her arms in the direction of the door Tariq had just left from. 'You don't know what he is like sometimes Lincoln, you really don't. Tariq was panicking, as he always does, so I told him about the *Ralph & Hugh* spin off idea.'

'The *Ralph & Hugh* spin off idea that we can't agree on you mean.'

'Yes, but that is only a matter of time, sweetie. We will get there in the end.'

Lincoln raised a sceptical eyebrow. 'I am not sure about that Sarah. Anyway, I don't see how any of that helps Tariq. Why would he be interested in a nonsense new concept that we may or may not launch down the line . . . unless . . . ' a look of concern appeared in Lincoln's eyes as he stared across the desk at the Chief Executive. 'No, Sarah. Tell me you haven't. Please God, you haven't done what I think you've done have you?'

'He was panicking, Lincoln. He just wouldn't leave me alone, so I just exaggerated things a little bit.'

'What did you tell him, Sarah?'

'I just said that the meeting the other day with Adventureland TV had gone well and we had agreed a price and an advance payment was due this month. It was just to stop him going on and on and on at me. Day after day. He can add the numbers into his blessed spreadsheet and then he goes away happy and I can get on with my work.'

'But Sarah, there is no payment.'

'But there will be.'

'There might possibly be sometime in the future. If there is, it won't be paid this December and it certainly won't be coming from Adventureland TV. You cannot declare money you do not have. That's fraud. Christ, you know all this, Sarah. What were you thinking of?'

'Yes, yes, yes. I know, but it is just a cash flow blip. That is all. I am sure everything will be fine in January when we get some payments in. It always is. Tariq was stopping everything. He told me we didn't have the money to recruit anybody so I couldn't fill any vacancies. You can see for yourself that we are slowly descending into darkness. That's because he put a stop on the monthly payments to the maintenance firm. I just need a bit of time so we can get things straight again and I can get on top of things.'

'What about the staff? Are they being paid or have you put them on stop too.'

'Yes of course they are being paid. You know me better than that, Lincoln. I would never default on staff payments.'

'Except mine.'

'And mine, Lincoln. And mine. I haven't taken a salary for three months. But look, I am sure everything will be fine in January. Don't worry about it, my sweet. Honestly. When have I ever let you down. Now, what you need to do is to stop worrying about Tariq and see if you can write a lovely new series called *Ralph & Hugh* so we can pitch it to some studios in the new year. Quick as you like, if you don't mind, my sweet.'

## CHAPTER 23

THE lift shuddered as it made it's faltering way to the third floor of the deserted office building on Marchmont Street. A small, ineffectual bulb oozed out a musty, yellowed light into the cramped confines of the lift cage. In the corner of the lift, there was a drop down seat for the sole use of the extravagantly titled 'lift commissionaire' who accompanied visiting guests on their journey up and down the building in a custom long since assigned to the past. The lift jolted to an unwelcome standstill. The doors hesitantly slid apart, followed by a metal curtain, pulled back and coming to rest with a cushioned clang on one side of the lift exit. In front, was a short corridor with six doors, three on either side, opening onto individual offices. The rooms ached with a disconsolate absence. A lonely stillness had settled on the disused, old-fashioned furniture, still redundantly present throughout. The oversized desks, each with a large blotting pad positioned front and centre, still had various dockets and paperwork arranged in measured piles within metal post trays.

Black bakelite telephones sat prominently on the corner of each desk, next to a pen holder and notepad, ready to take down the commands from a long forgotten past. The rooms were silent, apart from the occasional crack from the building foundations, as they adjusted in readiness for another long day holding up this unwanted pile of brick and timber.

At the end of the corridor was a heavy wooden door, which opened onto a large office, caked in leather and oak. On the right hand side, were two tall windows letting in some shards of reluctant light. The carpet was dark brown and recently laid, still giving a springy release underfoot. The remaining furnishings were in keeping with the offices outside in the corridor and were from another age, untroubled by the communication revolution of the 21st century.

Louisa Willoughby looked despairingly around the room as she made her way to the brown, leather chair next to the windows.

'My God, Anthony, I do not know how you endure this place.'

Anthony Willoughby's gaunt, loveless eyes looked up from his desk and settled on his unwelcome visitor. He spied the familiar profile and straight-backed poise of his sister as she perched on the chair, throned by the light coming in from the window. There was no warmth, no love to connect them. No shared memory of youth, no bond of a familiar upbringing. All had been long forgotten. In both, the child within had long ago withered to nothing, disfigured by age and greed. Unencumbered by love and with too much malign history resting between them, they met not as brother and sister, but as weary adversaries. Willoughby against Willoughby.

'You are early. Marquand will not be here for another ten minutes,' said Anthony Willoughby. 'I've just had the last of the coffee so you will have to do without.'

Louisa made no reply, but turned her head towards the window and waited in motionless silence as her elder brother dealt with an assortment of paperwork. The only sound was the occasional turning of a page or the scratching of Anthony's fountain pen, as he put his mark on various legal authorities. His time at Marchmont House was precious to him, providing sought after moments of lonely reflection where he was able to consider matters of the Estate, refining his plans and priorities. The office had once housed Filby & Sons, a family run fabric and clothing business, first established in 1838 and the first property he had acquired as Head of the Family, shortly after the death of his father in 1964. Willoughby had brought Filby & Sons to it's knees by coercing its suppliers to cease trading with the centuries old business. To this day, he could recall the moment he extracted the lease from the tearful and befuddled Mr Filby, Sr and instructed the cowering employees to clear their desks for the last time and leave the building. The power he held at his command was alluring beyond anything he had felt before. It was a real power, the power to alter lives and create a ripple of consequence that would spread far beyond the four walls of Marchmont House. Despite the goading of his eldest sister, he retained the property within the portfolio of the Willoughby Estate, keeping the interior as it had been over fifty years ago, as a reminder of his first blood. He rarely invited others within its confines, but Louisa obstinately refused to enter his club on Pall Mall, calling it 'a godforsaken mausoleum of misogyny'. Marchmont House was settled upon as a suitable alternative.

James Marquand greeted his patrons with a respectful reserve as he entered the room. He placed his folder and pen on the desk in one flowing movement, sat down and waited, looking towards the Head of the Family for permission to begin proceedings. Unhurried, Willoughby finished reading the document in front of him before moving it to one side and nodding towards the patient family lawyer. The main purpose of the meeting was to review and sign the documents pertaining to the sale of the Homerton land to Easton City Council. As with all of the more substantial family transactions, this required the signatures of two family members. The paperwork was all in order and the sum associated with the sale was acceptable, if slightly under market value.

'And you do not envisage any difficulties, James, with the consecration issues surrounding this site?' asked Louisa, her pen hovering above the sale papers.

'No, Miss Willoughby. I expect the Homerton Complex Planning Commission, under Mr Giltmore's leadership, to recommend the development as outlined. I am confident all Commission members are either on board and able to provide support or incompetent and unable to understand the issues involved. Either way, it will progress unhindered.'

'It is good we have marshalled Mr Giltmore back in line, James, after his shambolic television performance.' Louisa signed the document and handed it back to the lawyer. 'Well, that's that then. Better late than never, I suppose, although disappointing to see the value eroded, but needs must.'

Willoughby ignored the rebuke, taking a sip from his now cold and slightly congealed cup of coffee.

Louisa turned once again towards the lawyer. 'Whilst we have you here, James,' she continued, 'it would be helpful to understand where things sit with the other sensitive sites that were purchased alongside Homerton and, if you can excuse the pun, what other skeletons in the closet we need to contend with.'

'Is there really a need to do this now, Louisa?' interrupted Willoughby, impatiently. 'I do need to get on and I am sure Mr Marquand has other work to occupy him. We do not all have an endless bounty of leisure time at our disposal.'

Louisa turned her head towards her brother. 'If not now Anthony, when exactly? You have forbidden me raising the issues at our family meetings in front of Elizabeth and Andrew, which I quite understand, but it does leave me at a disadvantage. We agreed that you would keep me informed of these matters, but have repeatedly failed to do so.'

It had long been Anthony's policy that the two younger members of the Willoughby clan would not be troubled by any of his more sensitive property and land arrangements. These would be dealt with exclusively by the Head of the Family, although, under duress, he had agreed that Louisa, as Anthony's potential successor, would be kept up to date as required. As the siblings rarely spoke throughout the year outside of the tortuous family meetings at Widford Hall, these updates remained, at best, infrequent.

'Or perhaps, Anthony, you would prefer I add it to the agenda of our Christmas Day meeting?' said Louisa, provokingly. 'I am more than happy to do so. It would be interesting to garner Elizabeth's and Andrew's views on how their interests are currently being managed.'

Anthony Willoughby could feel his anger stir and turned a menacing stare in the direction of his sister. However, Louisa, as she always did on these occasions, had already looked away and was resting her eyes on some ill-defined something or other on the other side of the room, leaving Anthony's look of reprimand to fall harmlessly away. He let out a weary sigh and turned to Marquand. 'Tell her what she needs to know, but keep it brief.'

Marquand nodded, folding his hands in front of him on his lap and pompously leaning back into his chair.

'As you are aware, Miss Willoughby, four similar pieces of land were acquired by your ancestor, Mr Norris Willoughby, between the years 1889 to 1892. It transpired that they were not the most judicious of acquisitions and, for a range of circumstances, all have proved to be challenging in later years. Aldersgate was disposed of in 1905. Homerton we have already discussed and it is pleasing to see the proposed sale nearing completion. The Blyth land is sold and development plans for housing and a memorial site are due to commence within the next two months. The final piece of land, or what's left of it, at Dunnings Alley, we are not able to resolve, although it is a small area and represents a relatively slight financial opportunity.'

'But is there still a risk associated with the Dunnings Alley site?' asked Louisa 'Should the family remain concerned?'

'I do not believe the risk is material,' replied Marquand. 'As you will recall, there are a couple of lines of verse on one of the walls mentioning 'the black ditch', but it is vague and in no way incriminating and should, therefore, not elicit any concern for the family.'

Louisa nodded her head slightly, accepting the advice of the lawyer. 'What about Blyth, James? Remind me how much we had to invest, for want of a better word, in the Blyth memorial?'

Marquand looked at Willoughby, seeking reassurance that he was happy for this figure to be devolved. Willoughby gave him the slightest nod of the head.

'£200,000, to secure the site to the specifications required,' confirmed Marquand. 'This includes the cost of the monument itself, the build and setting, plus a guarantee of its ongoing protected status.'

This was actually a slightly smaller figure than Louisa had envisaged, however she feigned a look of stunned surprise.

'Good Lord. That is an extraordinary sum, James. I hope we are getting our money's worth, Anthony?'

Willoughby remained silent, staring directly ahead and choosing not to rise to his sister's taunt.

'And we are confident, James,' she continued. 'That the land beneath will remain undisturbed during the erection of this stone exorbitance?'

'Completely confident,' assured Marquand. 'Our own people are handling the build. The monument will be in place in the New Year and will be formally opened by the Mayor of Halesworth on the 12th January, the anniversary of the Kennedy crash.'

The oversized memorial was to commemorate a fatal plane crash which took place in the skies above Halesworth and Blyth in 1944. The Americans were testing a BQ 8 remote controlled bomber that would crash into a designated target, carrying twenty one thousand pounds of explosive. The operation required a two-man team to fly the plane to a height of two thousand feet, activate the remote control and parachute to safety. On this particular run a secondary plane, a USAAF F-8 Mosquito, was filming the test flight. All had gone to plan until two minutes after the bomb activation, when the plane exploded prematurely, killing the crew who were still on board. The Mosquito was flying three hundred yards behind the BQ 8 bomber and was hit by the force of the explosion, causing it to make an emergency landing at the small airbase at Halesworth. The debris from the BQ 8 fell onto the towns below, destroying 59 properties. Miraculously nobody on the ground was seriously injured. The pilot of the remote controlled bomber on that fateful day was Lieutenant Joseph P. Kennedy, the elder brother of John F Kennedy, the future President of the United States. The pilot of the Mosquito, who survived the emergency landing was Colonel Elliott Roosevelt, the son of the then current US President, Franklin D Roosevelt. The local population had not given the incident much thought during the intervening seventy years and it was largely forgotten until the Willoughby Blyth project had sparked renewed interest within the great and the good of the local community.

'I can assure you that all has been thought of, Miss Willoughby. The necessary arrangements are all in place,' said Marquand, comfortingly

Louisa looked at the lawyer. 'Well lets hope so, James, lets hope so. We cannot afford the slightest error.'

'Yes, well, thank you for the pointer, Louisa,' interrupted Anthony, unable to contain his annoyance for a moment longer. 'We are acutely aware of the importance of this project and, as Mr Marquand has just informed you, everything has been thought of.'

'I am delighted to hear so, Anthony,' replied Louisa, secreting a narrow, insincere smile in her brother's general direction. 'I shall watch events unfold with interest.' Then, after a slight hesitation, 'What about the business with Buller's house? Has that now been resolved? I must say, I was surprised that we are still the registered owner of that particular property. It always seemed such a foolhardy and unnecessary piece of work. You authorised that acquisition as I recall, did you not, Anthony?'

Indeed it was a still wet behind the ears, Anthony Willoughby, who, in 1965, had been persuaded by Edmund Buller to buy up Manorview so it could be used as payment for Petra Taylor as some recompense for her unwilling involvement in furthering the Buller line. It was an unnecessarily extravagant gesture in retrospect, but Willoughby had just started out as Head of the Family and needed Buller on his side. Besides, his father had always taught him that property acquisition was the key to the Willoughby fortune. Admittedly, his father was probably not referring to a small three bedroom cottage in Suffolk when he made that proclamation, but for the insecure eldest son, it, alongside Marchmont House, served notice that his reign as Head of the Family had started in earnest.

Louisa had noticed a flicker of vulnerability pass across her brother's face. 'Margaret Green's untimely death has created quite a hullabaloo,' she continued. 'What with the police crawling all over the car wreck and then the daughter becoming involved. Who would have thought Petra would have had a policewoman for a granddaughter? That's a rotten bit of luck,' she said, her face cocked in mock sympathy.
'You must feel cursed, Anthony, you poor thing. Although, I am sure you have the constitution to ward off the demons, even as they circle around and about you.'

Willoughby straightened in his chair, firmly placing his hands authoritatively on the desk in front of him in a show of defiance. 'It is all in hand, Louisa. So best to let it drop and leave it to Mr Marquand and myself, and of course Mr Cassidy. We have covered all eventualities.'

'Of course, Anthony,' demurred Louisa. 'As you suggest, I will leave it with you to untangle. I am sure Mr Cassidy has proved an erstwhile cohort throughout these difficult times. Talking of which, do you feel it was quite fair to ask Milton to deal with the Greens, under the circumstance? Two birds with one stone and all that, but it all seems a bit heartless, even by your standards.'

Louisa could see Willoughby's pulse flick through the thin skin covering his temple.

'As I have said already, sister. Leave it with me.'

'Of course, brother. I am sure you know what you are doing.' Louisa picked up her handbag and and made to leave. 'Well, I had better be off. I have an appointment at the Savoy and I do so hate being late. Goodbye James and thank you for your insights. Goodbye Anthony. Do look after yourself and do watch out for those demons. You will keep an eye on him won't you, James?'

Louisa Willoughby had disappeared out of the gloom of her brother's office before Marquand was able to respond.

# CHAPTER 24

LINCOLN had grouped the paperwork under three main headings - Reverend Barkham; Blyth Workhouse; and St Botolphs. It covered most of the kitchen table of his Twickenham flat. Under each heading, he had split the paperwork into two piles. The piles on the right were made up of what he considered to be the key documents. The ones on the left, the taller piles, consisted of extraneous paperwork, general research and many, many pages of Mildred Stone's precise and ordered, handwritten notes. The piles were not uniform in shape and included maps of various descriptions and oversized legal papers, causing several of the them to tilt precariously.

He had been explaining to Martha how the paperwork was organised when his phone rang. It was Stillman who wanted to discuss an offer he had received for his parent's house. Lincoln told him he would call him back later and returned to his explanation, pointing to the Reverend Barkham pile first.

'The bad news is that Mildred hadn't cracked who the killer was,' he said. 'There is nothing of great interest in this lot, to be honest, just some old newspaper cuttings and some interview notes from when she met Rose Harsent's parents. Apart from that, there is just her never-ending notes and this hand-drawn map of the route past Sorrel Cottage, scrawled on some kind of parchment.

'That's disappointing. What about the Blyth pile? Anything there?' Martha asked.

'Once again, nothing very conclusive . There's the original bill of sale from Halesworth & Blyth parish to the Willoughbys. A map of the workhouse itself. A few legal documents and the mandatory reams of notes from the ever diligent Mildred Stone. The only other thing is a story from the local press about a fire on a fishing boat, which took place off the coast of Southwold at the back end of 1902. Unfortunately, Mildred doesn't say what relevance this has, but it must have meant something to her.'

Martha let out a despairing sigh. 'Please tell me the St Botolphs pile tells us something new?'

'Yes. The St Botolphs pile is where it all clicks into place. It is all about workhouses Martha. Blyth in Suffolk, where the Nicholls family disappeared, is a workhouse and down in East London, in the St Botolphs parish, there are three other workhouses. Dunnings Alley, Homerton and Aldersgate. All four were bought up by the Willoughbys, along with eleven others, between 1889 and 1892. The fifteen workhouses seemed to have stayed on the Willoughby family's books until 1896 when they started being sold off, one by one. By 1902, only four remained in Willoughby ownership - Aldersgate, Homerton, Blyth, and Dunnings Alley. Aldersgate was then sold in 1905 and the bulk of Dunnings Alley in 1907. '

Detective Green was standing next to Lincoln, looking down at the mounds of paperwork, tentatively flicking through the faded sheets on the top of the St Botolphs pile. 'But what did they want with fifteen workhouses?'

'From what I can make out,' continued Lincoln. 'The Willoughbys had set up a deal where they could buy up the workhouse buildings and land on the cheap. According to

Mildred's notes, the parishes were trying to close down many of the older workhouses at the end of the 19th century. They wanted to move the inmates to newer, larger buildings that were more economic to run.'

'So the Willoughbys bought up the buildings and the surrounding land once they were empty?'

'No, that's what I thought at the beginning but, according to Mildred, the deal they struck with the parish meant that the Willoughbys took on all liabilities and running costs of the old workhouses until the new ones were built. Once the new, super workhouses were up and running, the inmates would be transferred across and the Willoughbys would then be free to do what they wanted with the old property and surrounding land.'

'But why would the parishes let the Willoughbys run the workhouses? Surely they would want any profit generated for themselves?'

'There were no profits, just costs. Probably, earlier in the century, the local parish could turn a small profit, but they slowly became more and more expensive to run. By the time the Willoughbys took control, they were proving to be a heavy financial burden on the local authorities. In her notes, Mildred writes page after page about the history of workhouses or 'houses of industry' as they used to be called. She goes all the way back to the 1600s when the first workhouse appeared. Initially, they were small units, very cheap to run and for the most part, self funded from the goods produced by the inmates, but over the centuries, more and more workhouses were built and it became increasingly difficult to break even. The final straw was in 1834, when the Poor Law was amended.'

Lincoln flicked open his notebook, where he had jotted down some of the key points from Mildred's research. 'Prior to the Poor Law amendment being introduced, the state or the parish was responsible for providing poor relief to the aged and infirm or the 'deserving poor' as they were known, in the form of something called 'outdoor relief', where those entitled to the handout would continue living in their own dwellings. The Poor Law changed all that and introduced 'indoor relief'. This meant that those needing support would only receive funds if they agreed to enter the local workhouse, causing a significant increase in the numbers being housed.'

'Even so, they must have been cheap places to run. They were still tough places to live in, right?' asked Martha.

'Yes, they were truly appalling. They were deliberately designed to be repugnant to the poor, to dissuade the able-bodied from entering and picking up a handout they were not entitled to. Inmates spent up to fifteen hours a day doing menial and fairly pointless labour and then at night, they slept in the wards, which were just one big room with some scraps of bedding on the floor and a single bucket in the centre for sanitation.'

'So basically, it was just a Victorian prison, but for people whose only crime was being poor or infirm.'

'Pretty much,' confirmed Lincoln.

'I don't get where the escalating expense came from though. A bucket and some rags is not going to cost a lot surely?'

'No, but they did have to feed the inmates, even if it was just gruel, vegetables and the occasional bit of boiled meat. Then there was the staff wages, including medical staff. Remember, one of the purposes of the workhouse was to look after the genuinely ill, so there were the costs of doctors and medicine to consider. Plus, once a man entered the workhouse, then so did his whole family. This meant there were a lot of children in the building who all needed to be fed and looked after. This was one of the ironies of the workhouse system. If you were outside the workhouse and you needed medication or schooling for your children then you had to pay for it yourself or go without, but if you were inside the workhouse, then the parish was compelled by law to provide it. All free of charge.'

'So. the system backfired on them.'

'In many ways, yes. The workhouse population kept

increasing and the costs kept escalating.'

'Why on earth would the Willoughbys want to get involved in something like that?' asked Martha.

'The land. The parish must have offered them a big reduction on the market value at the time. Also, you can see from some of the records that the Willoughbys arrogantly believed they could turn the workhouses from loss making, into profit making enterprises through better management and a more stringent control of costs. Look.' Lincoln reached for two slips of paper from the table. 'You can see what they tried to do from the monthly cost sheet from the Union Road Workhouse in Dover:

Master - Quantity: 1 Cost: £5.4s
Matron - Quantity: 1 Costs: £2.9s
Chaplin - Quantity: 1 Costs: £3.0s
Schoolmaster - Quantity: 2 Costs: £7.0s
Schoolmistress - Quantity: 2 Costs: £3.2S
Medical Officers - Quantity: 2 Costs: £6.2s
Nurse - Quantity: 1 Costs: £1.3s
Cook - Quantity: 1 Costs: £2.0s
Porter - Quantity: 1 Costs: £1.5s
Firemen - Quantity: 1 Costs: £1.8s
Superintendent - Quantity: 1 Costs: £2.6s
of outdoor income

Food & Provisions - £1.8s
Linen - £1.0s
TOTAL - £37.7s

'The only workhouse income came from the tasks the inmates completed during their confinement, which consisted of four main activities:

Laundry - £7.4s
Breaking Stones - £3.0s
Picking Oakum - £12.2s

Bone Crushing - £8.6s
TOTAL - £30.12s

'So, when the Willoughby's took over the running of the workhouse, it was incurring a loss of £6.15s per month. They immediately set about cutting some of the costs by removing the cook, the fireman as well as one schoolmaster, one schoolmistress and one of the medical officers. They also reduced the amount spent on food and linen. By the time they were done, the total costs had reduced from £37.7s to £24.8s but they kept the expected production unchanged so making a monthly profit of £6.4s. £6 back then would be around £700 in today's money. Not a bad return at all. The problem they had was that they couldn't get all fifteen of the sites into profit.' He turned to the second sheet. 'Blyth, tells a completely different story. It looks like the costs were already paired to the bone before they took over and, even though they made still more cuts, they couldn't get it to break even resulting in a monthly loss of £5.2s.

'The same is true for Dunnings Alley, Homerton and Aldersgate. These four workhouses continued to make a loss, no matter what the Willoughbys did.'

Martha had been sliding her finger down the cost sheet, checking the numbers when she suddenly stopped. 'Uh, what the hell is bone crushing?'

Lincoln flipped to another page in his notebook. 'Apparently, each workhouse had a 'bone crushing room' where inmates would spend the whole day smashing the bones of animals into fragments, which could then be used as fertiliser on the surrounding fields. It was outlawed in the end, when a group of inmates at the Andover workhouse caused a mass riot fighting over scraps. They were so hungry they were trying to suck the marrow out of the rotting bones.'

'Charming,' said Martha, wincing. 'What about Oakum? Should I know what that is?'

'I'd never heard of it. You get it from painstakingly picking apart old tarry ropes or the rigging of ships. It was then used to pack the joints of timbers on wooden vessels.'

'Good grief. Those poor people,' she said. 'Bad enough that you had no work and no money, but then you had spend all hours of the day picking at a rope or crushing bones. Meanwhile, the likes of the Willoughbys were trying to make a fast buck out of you by reducing the amount of gruel you got to eat.'

'It was just the times they lived in I suppose,' said Lincoln

'I suppose so.' Martha looked across the table of documents. 'Right, so I get it. The Willoughbys bought up fifteen workhouse sites, later selling eleven of them for a big mark up. The remaining four, that were not sold, were all loss makers.'

'Yes, plus, once we add the word 'aldersgate', all four are mentioned on the saddlebag note.' He handed Martha his notebook, so she could read the completed version.

*aldersgate to homerton*
*blyth 92 dunnings alley 9 barkham*
*providence at peasenhall*
*kill them all*

'I guessed at 'to' in the first line, but it looks right. Can't say I am any the wiser, but at least we have filled it in,' he said, closing his notebook.

'So, where now?' Martha asked, slightly dispirited.

'As I said earlier, it is all about the workhouses,' replied Lincoln. 'Amidst all the notes, maps and certificates of ownership, there were these letters,' he said, holding up a pile of papers. 'The first is from Norris Willoughby to the Master of the Homerton workhouse, agreeing a timescale for the transfer of the inmates from Aldersgate to Homerton. You can see this happened in 1902 and the sale of the then empty Aldersgate site to a manufacturing company followed a few years later in 1905. The second correspondence is similar to the first, confirming the transfer this time of the Dunnings Alley inmates, once again to the extended workhouse at

Homerton. However, the third letter is from Mr Bernard Dreadsmith, the Master of the Homerton workhouse, informing Willoughby that he is happy to accept the eighty seven adults from Dunnings Alley as requested, however, he is not in a position to accept the transfer of any children under the age of twelve, as the children's ward is currently oversubscribed and there is no space. This is in November 1900.' Lincoln pulled out a further stack of letters from the St Botolph pile, bound together with a thick elastic band. 'These are the subsequent letters between Norris Willoughby and Bernard Dreadsmith between January 1901 up until September 1902, at which point they suddenly stop. The letters are all similar in content, with Willoughby asking for the transfer to be authorised and Dreadsmith replying that there is still no room for the children. The tone of Willoughby's letters gets increasingly abrupt and threatening, but this just seems to cause Dreadsmith to harden his resolve and he continues to stubbornly refuse the children's transfer.'

Martha flicked through the pile of correspondence. 'What's the grey sheet attached to each of Willoughby's letters?' she asked.

'That, Detective Sergeant, is a manifest. Now this is where things really start getting interesting.' He went back to the first letter and folded the paper so they could both see the details written on the manifest. 'The list is the names of all the children due to transfer. There are sixteen children in total.' Lincoln then turned to the very last letter on the pile. 'But here, by the time he writes his final request, look, there are only nine names left. I presume the seven missing children either left the workhouse, died or reached the age of twelve and could transfer straight into the adult ward.'

Lincoln waited, looking at the detective in anticipation. 'Do you see, Martha?'

'Yes, yes, I get it,' she replied thoughtfully, continuing to look down at the names and ages of the children listed. 'The children are The Dunnings Alley Nine. Did Mildred Stone reach the same conclusion?'

'Yes, definitely. If you look on the back of the final manifest you can see one of Mildred's neat notations. Her writing is tiny, but it says *'nine children left in Dunnings Alley workhouse in 1902. BD, see map.'*

'BD?' asked Martha.

'Remember what we both saw written on the wall of the Dunnings Alley workhouse.' He flicked through his notebook until he landed on the page he was looking for, turning the book towards Martha. 'Now look at this map.' He spread out the document onto the table. The three East London workhouses were marked on it, written in Mildred's hand - Dunnings Alley, Aldersgate and Homerton. Just to the right of Dunnings Alley was a snaking line, running towards the Thames with the words BD written by it.

'So, what are you thinking, Lincoln?' Martha asked.

He placed his notebook back on the table between them. 'There were nine children at Dunnings Alley according to Willoughby's last letter. We can see from the correspondence from Dreadsmith that they never made it to Homerton. I think Mildred knew where the children ended up. Right there.' he said, pointing to the black line on the map. 'They are there, there in the Black Ditch.'

## CHAPTER 25

THE December sun issued a thin and fragile light as they made their way along the overgrown path that ran parallel to the Black Ditch. They had taken the train and tube from Twickenham across town to Limehouse and had then used Mildred's map to find what was left of the forgotten London river. The original meandering curves were still visible, although it was no more than a narrow stream in most places, the water occasionally collecting in pools, some no more than a puddle and some reaching ten to fifteen feet across. Martha had decided upon the start point for their journey and suggested working north, towards the source, at Holywell Row in Shoreditch. This route would bring them to within a few hundred yards of the site of the Dunnings Alley workhouse. In total, it was no more than a two mile trek, which, under normal circumstances, they would have covered within an hour, but the route was blocked along the way with buildings which had been erected over the last century and large swathes of impenetrable undergrowth, which meant they had to keep taking unwanted diversions and rejoining the route further upstream. They had been walking for nearly three hours and were still a short distance away from Shoreditch. Martha had been moving at pace along the whole route, concentrating on the map and the boggy riverbed, barely making any conversation with her companion. The change in the month from November to December had pressed upon her the unwelcome fact that time was running out. If she found no new evidence, then her hearing would go ahead in February, resulting in her dismissal and conviction. Her eyes scanned each alcove and muddy tributary, looking for God knows what - a sign, a clue, an indication that her investigation was at least heading in the right direction.

'Wait up, Martha,' said a breathless Lincoln, as he scrambled up yet another bank covered in thorny brambles and nettles. 'Slow down, for fuck's sake. You're like a psychotic bloodhound. We don't even know what we're looking for.'

Martha was waiting impatiently, hands on hips, at the top of the bank, breathing hard, mud spattered over her shoes and jeans. 'We've got to keep moving, Lincoln. It's two o'clock already. We only have another couple of hours of daylight left.'

'But you don't know what you are looking for, Martha,' he repeated.

'I know but we have got to keep going. There has to be something here. I will know it when I see it.'

'See what? A child's hand sticking out of the mud? A gravestone? It was over a hundred years ago, Martha. Whatever clues there were, will have long gone by now.'

She looked down angrily. 'Oh for God's sake, Mr Marsh. It was your idea to come here in the first place. If you can't keep up and want to stop then get on the tube and go home. I am not stopping you. I am perfectly happy to carry on without you.'

'"Mr Marsh"? Where the hell did that come from?' he said, laughing and looking up the bank towards Martha. She was staring back towards the path they had just walked along.

He could see the desperation in her eyes, reminding him just how important it was that they found something that would help her in the hearing. He pushed through the undergrowth and made his way towards the top of the bank. 'I'm sorry, Martha. I wasn't trying to piss you off. I know how important this is, but I just think we might do better if we stopped for five minutes to catch our breath and think things through.'

'Sure,' the detective said dismissively, not making eye contact. 'We should be at the source now anyway, according to the map. Holywell Row should be just up here,' she said, pushing some branches out of the way and making her way along the overgrown path.

They sat down on a stone bench in the grounds of the ruins of Holywell Priory. A plaque, erected by the Borough of Hackney, marked the spot where the building had once stood. There wasn't a great deal left on the site now, just a few crumbled walls marking the outline of the building and a small enclosed structure at the far end of the site where the knave had once stood. The priory grounds and path were surprisingly well maintained, as was the low, wooden fence surrounding it. A tall man, in long black overalls and a donkey jacket, was carrying out some repairs at the rear of the ruins.

Lincoln, after two failed attempts to make conversation, had taken refuge in silence, leaving the policewoman to come to terms with her frustration and anger uninterrupted. A cold wind had risen up and was sweeping towards them, carrying a few specks of rain, causing Lincoln to button up his coat and push his hands deep into his pockets. His phone vibrated. It was another text from Stillman asking him to phone him at his office as soon as possible. The lawyer had called on the way over to Limehouse and had left a message saying that Benjamin Marsh had been in touch on a number of occasions during the last forty eight hours and was extremely keen to agree the house sale this week, so they could aim for exchange by Christmas. Apparently his brother had been 'somewhat agitated and truculent' when he had called, urging the lawyer to go ahead with the transaction without waiting for Lincoln's agreement. Stillman had advised Ben that this was not possible as permission from both brothers was required before a sale could proceed, at which point Ben had hung up on the lawyer. Lincoln turned off his phone without replying to the text or returning the call and let out a half-hearted sigh.

'What's up?' asked Martha, breaking the acrimonious silence. 'Is it about the house again?' Lincoln nodded. 'Look, I know it is nothing to do with me,' Martha continued. 'But why don't you just agree and be done with it. I know it was your parent's house, but they are not here now. Just let it go, Lincoln. Time to move on.'

'You are starting to sound just like my brother.'

'Well, maybe he has a point.'

'Sure. The eminently sensible and all-knowing Benjamin Marsh. The absolute banker. You haven't even met him and you're taking his side.'

'That's not what I'm saying, Lincoln, and you know it. Anyway, it's not about sides. I don't know, maybe that's part of the problem. Maybe you're just not thinking straight. Maybe you just don't like being told what to do by your big brother?'

'Maybe. Maybe not.' Lincoln replied. 'But I tell you one thing we can agree on, Martha. You are quite right. It is nothing to do with you.'

The weather had deteriorated since the morning, but exhausted, they continued sitting in silence for a further ten minutes, being blustered by the wind and lightly doused by the thin winter rain.

'Excuse me. I hope you don't mind me asking, but what exactly do you think you are doing?'

They both looked up to see the tall groundsman in front of them. His hands covered in the creosote he had been applying to the fence at the back of the priory. A further dollop of paint had landed on his head, streaking down his tufted, short, grey hair.

'Just sitting down for a few minutes, mate,' replied Lincoln curtly, making it plain that they didn't want to be disturbed.

Martha instinctively reached for her badge, before she remembered she didn't have it with her. 'I'm a policewoman, sir. We are conducting some enquiries in this area. Could I ask you to move along please.'

'You could ask I suppose. I doubt I will comply,' replied the caretaker in a playful but forthright tone. 'It seems a strange way to conduct enquiries officer. Sitting in the middle of a 10th century priory with nobody around. Are you waiting for the criminals to come to you perhaps? If so, I think it unlikely that they will keep their appointments.'

'Yes, very amusing, sir. Please move along and leave us in peace.'

'I bet they are saying the same thing,' replied the man.

'Who is that, sir?'

'Them,' he said, pointing to the bench. 'The people you have been sitting on top of for the last half hour. You do know you're sitting on a grave, officer?'

Lincoln and Martha both sprang up from where they were sitting, turning round to look at the seat.

'Oh, I wouldn't worry, they are quite dead and have been for some time or at least since the year 942,' said the caretaker, with a smile. 'To be honest, I am not sure they were ever in there in the first place. I always believed it was more likely just a memorial than a grave, despite the headstones,' he said, pointing at the stone base. 'You can't make out the words any more. Such a shame. It's the resting place of Stibba, the great Saxon warrior who first travelled up the Thames and settled in this area in the 10th century. He was meant to be over seven feet tall and as strong as an elephant, so the legend goes, and there next to him is . . . what is she called now? . . . what is it?... oh well, Mrs Stibba anyway. Sorry her first name has slipped my mind.' A large gust of wind swept across the exposed graveyard practically knocking the elderly man off his long, thin legs. 'Do you mind if we seek refuge, as it were, in the priory,' he said, pointing toward the knave. 'Come on. Chop chop, or we'll all get drenched.'

\*

Inside the knave, there was a small heater, a teapot, four mugs and a kettle. It reminded Lincoln of his grandfather's old potting shed on his allotment where he had visited as a boy.

'All the home comforts you could wish for,' the caretaker said, removing his coat and his black, paint-splattered overalls. 'I think I even have some biscuits somewhere. Could you have a look behind the teapot young man,' he said, pointing to a small tin just to Lincoln's left. As the caretaker turned back to light the gas hob, having removed his overalls, he revealed the cassock and collar he had been wearing underneath, causing Lincoln to choke slightly.

'You're a vicar.' he exclaimed.

'Am I? How on earth did that happen? Well, I'll be blowed,' the man said, looking at his formal attire with fake puzzlement. 'Well deduced young man. Not much gets past you I can see, but now, come on, your lady friend looks like she is going to fall away with hunger.'

'I can assure I am fine,' replied the detective

'Nonsense. Nonsense. Take a biscuit, before Inspector Poirot here hogs them all.'

The wind outside was now beating against the door, causing it to rattle in it's frame. The light rain had turned to hail, peppering the windows of the knave. The vicar, Father Sandford, bolted the door and clicked the heater on at the wall. They made their introductions and settled down in the warm shelter, protected from the elements.

\*

Ten minutes later, Lincoln finished his tea, placing the cup next to the kettle, where it had come from. He looked around the old, wooden walls, built on top of the stone foundations of the priory. 'What is this place?' he asked.

Father Sandford swept his outstretched arm around the room. 'This young man, is my hideaway, my sanctuary, my shelter from the storm,' he said, grandly. 'It also serves as my shed where I can lock away my tools and materials for safe keeping. It doesn't seem to stop the local thieves, but I like to think that it slows them down a bit.'

'Do people still come here to worship?' asked Lincoln.

'Of course not.' Father Sandford looked at Martha with smiling eyes, shaking his head. 'Oh dear. He's not the brightest candle on the altar is he? I am not vicar of Holywell young man,' he said, turning back to Lincoln. 'The priory hasn't been used for centuries, well, since 1539 to be exact, when Bluff King Hal tore down all things holy across this fine land. My church is St Augustine's down the way. I only come here to keep an eye on the old place and do the occasional odd job. The council gave up providing funds years ago so, if I didn't look after it, nobody would.' He turned to the police woman. 'Would you like another cup?'

'No. Thank you, Father. We need to head back to Twickenham. We may be back this way tomorrow though, if the weather eases.'

'I will look out for you.' Father Sandford said, taking her cup from her and offering her one last biscuit for the return journey. 'You never did tell me what you were doing.'

'We were looking for something,' the detective replied. 'Probably a bit of a wild goose chase. Anyway, we are not going to find anything in this weather.'

'Up here in the priory?' Father Sandford asked.

'Not sure really, Father. There is a lost river running near here and the thing we are looking for is somewhere along that route. Like I say, probably a wild goose chase.'

'Ah, along the mysterious Black Ditch,' he said. 'If you

were looking for the grave site from the Great Plague, that is just north of here, but there is not much to see I'm afraid. If it's the ducking pool, then that is to the east, toward Whitechapel. Fittingly, on Ducking Pond Row.'

'No, neither of those, Father,' replied the detective. 'We were following up a story from a long time ago about some missing workhouse children. We had heard they had disappeared somewhere along the river.'

'Oh, the Dunnings Alley Nine. Where did you hear about that old wives tale?'

Martha looked across at Lincoln and then back towards the vicar. 'You've heard of them?'

'Most definitely, yes. Although I think, Stibba, our friend out there, deserves more credence than the Dunnings Alley Nine. Nothing has ever been proven, you see. Just stories.'

'What stories, Father Sandford? This is important. What stories and where?' she asked, in the probing, aggressive interviewing style Lincoln had experienced on several occasions when they had first met. 'Where, Father, where?'

'Okay my child, okay, calm down. There is not a great deal to tell or at least as far as I know. The story goes that a group of nine workhouse children were crossing the river at low tide near Stonebridge Pond. The pond had been an old watering hole for cattle and horses back in the 16th and 17th century, but became disused and stagnant once the industrial revolution took hold. At low tide the river would drain into the pond meaning that on the right day at the right time, the river bed could be crossed. It's said that some children were making their way across the river bed, but started sinking beneath the mud. There was a pub nearby, the White Horse Inn, where the locals heard the screams of the little ones and ran out to help, but they were too late and could only watch helplessly from the bank. Allegedly, the pub landlady went mad, haunted by the sight of the children slowly sinking beneath the mud, screaming for their mothers.'

'What were they doing there? Why were they crossing?' Martha asked.

'Who knows? Legend has it that there was a tall, shadowy figure on the bank, directing them across the river, encouraging them to walk further and further out until they had no way of making it back to the safety of the riverbank. Some say the mysterious figure was the devil himself, leading them to their death, making the children suffer for the sins of their indolent parents.' He shook his head. 'Pah! All stuff and nonsense, of course.'

'Where is this pub, Father? The White Horse?'

'The White Horse Inn. Well, it was down near Limehouse,' he said, pointing southwards. 'But I don't know that you will find anything there now. It was knocked down some time ago. The whole area is just boggy marshland now. It's all fenced off these days. Some building work or something is going on down there.'

Martha wasn't listening. She was up on her feet, putting on her coat.

'Are you coming?' she said to Lincoln.

He looked at the continuing storm outside the knave. 'Wouldn't we be better off lea . . .' He looked up and saw the look in Martha's eyes. 'No, of course not, silly me. Right, let's go.' He pulled on his still damp coat. 'Thank you for the tea, Father.'

'You are most welcome. But, even if the story is true, I don't know what you expect to find. Don't forget where Limehouse got it's name. The lime in the ground there will have destroyed all signs of any bodies a long time ago.'

But it was no use. He was talking to himself. Detective Sergeant Martha Green and Lincoln Marsh had already walked out into the raging, winter December storm.

## CHAPTER 26

THE wind whipped around the buildings and deserted streets of Limehouse, sending litter and fallen leaves tumbling from one side of the road to the other. Heavy raindrops beat down onto the polycarbonate roof of the bus shelter where Lincoln was standing. He pulled up the collar of his coat, but it provided little protection from the biting, cold gusts sweeping down across southern Britain from the barren and snow covered savannah plains of Eastern Europe. Their taxi was parked up on the side of the road and he could see Detective Green in the back seat, talking to her police contact on her mobile. In the front seat the large, disinterested taxi driver was idly looking at his phone with exhausted and straining eyes. Another long and arduous night at the bidding of impatient commuters, tipsy dinner dates and retching students stretched out wondrously before him. In the meantime, he continued to wait patiently for his passenger to end her call and pay the fare.

'Thank you for getting back to me, sir. I appreciate your time.'

'Not a problem, Martha. You know I want to help as best I can. Are you alone? Can you talk?'

'I am in the back of a taxi, but, yes, I can talk. Did you follow up on Strathdon yet?'

There was a slight muffled laugh on the other end of the line. 'That's the Martha I have come to know over the years. Avoiding any social niceties and getting straight to the point.'

Chief Superintendent Colin McSty had first been introduced to a young Martha Green at one of the Metropolitan Police Accelerated Promotion assessment centres, held annually at the Crime Academy at Hendon. He had been impressed with her overall assessment scores but had witnessed her fail spectacularly in a group exercise designed to assess, amongst other factors, team and social skills. The exercise had started well, but it was clear that the recently graduated Miss Green was quickly losing her patience with her conciliatory and overly polite colleagues. By the end of the exercise she was essentially ostracised by the rest of the group and was working successfully in isolation on the task. The assessors were unanimous in their judgement that Green had failed and would not go forward for selection, only to be overruled by the Chief Superintendent, who insisted that she progress at the cost of a more stable but less eye-catching candidate. Since then, he had followed her career closely, providing advice and mentoring her through the ranks.

'Sorry sir. I just . . . I am struggling to make progress and could do with a break of some kind.'

'No problem, Martha. You don't have to explain to me. I understand. Your impatience has always been one of your finer qualities. I'm still looking into references to Strathdon, but nothing yet of any note. Although,' he added cautiously, 'from what you have shared so far, Martha, it sounds to me that Anthony Willoughby is where you need to focus your attention for now, not Strathdon. If what you are saying is true, and I have never had any reason to doubt you up until now, then he is the one pulling the strings. Maybe a direct approach might work.'

'I am not sure sir. I have no badge, no authority.'

'You might be surprised. You don't need a badge to hide behind, not you. Sometimes the most direct way forward is the best. You may not get any answers, but you may just rattle him a bit. People do funny things when they are under pressure Martha.'

'I'll think about it sir.'

'Sure, I will leave it with you. I hear he uses a place in Pall Mall, the Burgoyne Club, as his main watering hole. But you should know, Martha, that the Directorate of Professional Standards have submitted their initial findings to the Police Complaints Commission and they are confident that the evidence is solid. You know what that lot are like once they get their teeth into one of their own. Make no mistake, they are coming after you, Martha. You need to stop them in their tracks or at least give them pause. I know this is not what you want to hear right now, but you need to know. Time is pressing.'

'I'm doing what I can, sir,' replied Martha, exasperated but determined. 'I know I am running out of time but I am sure I'm close, I just need to join the dots. I have to press on and not lose focus. I'm over in Limehouse this evening, following up a lead. It may be nothing, but I'll let you know if it turns up anything important.'

'Fine. In the meantime, I will keep looking for references to Strathdon in the files but I will have to keep things well below the radar. You know I shouldn't even be talking to you, don't you Martha?'

'Yes, and I appreciate it, sir. Like I said, we just need a break.'

'We?' replied Chief Superintendent McSty, unable to hide the concern in his voice. 'Are you still with that writer chap, the one whose phone you asked me to put a trace on? Be careful who you involve Martha for Christ's sake. You know next to nothing about this character and he is certainly not to know that you have spoken to me. I hope that is understood.'

'He knows I have a contact at the Met who is helping me, but I haven't mentioned you at all, sir. I wouldn't do that. He's okay though honestly, sir. A bit of a reluctant helper and can get in the way at times, but he has proved to be useful. Besides, he is the only ally I've got.'

'You've got me, Detective Sergeant Green. You've always got me.'

'Thank you, sir. That means a lot.'

'Right, I have a meeting in central London. I will be in touch Martha. Be safe and keep going. We will clear up this whole mess soon enough. You wait and see.'

'Thank you, sir. Good night, sir.'

\*

The lightning lit up the landscape, briefly defining the grotesque metal silhouettes that bordered the large and muddy building site. The oversized machinery dwarfed Lincoln and the detective as they made their way towards the site of the Black Ditch. Even with the heavy rainfall, the riverbed remained ill defined and lost beneath the earth, but they continued on to the area where the ground was at the lowest point. Lincoln looked down at the deep gash on the back of his wrist. The blood was flowing down his hand, dripping onto the muddy earth from his fingers. The fresh blood mingled with the rain, making it look like he was wearing an ill-fitting red mitten.

Martha was shouting at the top of her voice to make herself heard over the sound of the storm. 'Here, use this.' She had found a tea towel and two torches in one of the portacabins at the entrance of the site. 'Wrap it round tight to stop the bleeding. Are you okay to carry on?'

'Yes. It's not as bad as it looks,' Lincoln shouted back. 'It's my own stupid fault. Come on, forget about it, lets keep moving.' He had watched Martha scale the barbed wire fence surrounding the building site in one easy movement and had followed suit, but instead of landing neatly on the other side as she had done, his hand had slipped and the flesh on the back of his wrist had caught on one of the barbs, leaving him dumped on the floor in a clumsy pile, but with one hand left hanging in the air, skewered to the fence.

'The river course should be right here,' Martha shouted, pointing to the ground directly in front of her.

A vehicle with wheels as tall as a man was parked to the left of them. On the back of the truck, pointing towards the sky, was what looked like an oversized drill bit, some twenty feet long and 6 feet wide. The slogan *Crossrail: Moving London Forward*, was emblazoned on the side of the machine. There were three holes bored into the ground directly in front of them. The largest hole was square and on a slight angle, sloping into the earth. A heavy, iron padlocked gate lay across the entrance. To the right, were two circular holes, both six feet across and around twenty feet deep. The holes were directly next to each other, less than one foot apart. A short wooden plank had been placed on the sodden earth dividing them. The one on the right was relatively dry, shielded from the rain by a brown canvas awning that had been pegged neatly above it. The one on the left was unprotected and was half full of muddy water and covered by a thin layer of ice. Martha stepped over to the side of the second hole where there was a wooden sign that had fallen forward into the mud.

'What does it say?' Lincoln shouted.

Martha wiped the board with the sleeve of her coat. '*Area controlled by the Museum of London Archeology. Do not enter.* Then there's a contact number.' She took a photo of the board with her phone and let the sign fall back into the mud. The building of the new underground train system had been going on in London for years and she had heard of several incidents where the digging had been suddenly halted when significant historical finds had been unearthed. Teams of archaeologists were then drafted in to sift through the surrounding areas, recording and preserving anything of note. Along with the many vestiges of the past that had been found,

including weapons, coins and household utensils, she had heard of at least two instances of skeletons being discovered.
She loosened the awning and shone her torch down into the large, dry cylindrical hole that had been protected from the rain. She could see string laid out in small grids across the base and a collection of trowels, brushes and picks piled neatly in the centre of the dig. There was no evidence of the archeologists findings, but there was a clipboard pinned to the cylinder wall about five feet from the top of the hole. She laid down on the wet mud and stretched out her hand to retrieve it, but it was just out of her reach.

'Lincoln. See if you can find a ladder.' Lincoln looked back, cupping his ear, trying to block out the sound of the wind and the torrential rain. 'A ladder. I need a ladder.'

Martha lay across the plank, dividing the two holes, her hand gripping the top of the second metal cylinder that was slightly protruding above the earth and reached down. By letting the top half of her body hang over the side, her fingertips could touch the clipboard, but she couldn't get enough purchase to unhook it off the nail that had been driven into the wall of the metal shaft. She pulled herself back up, just as Lincoln returned.

'The ladders are locked away against the wall of one of the cabins,' he shouted, pointing back towards the entrance. 'I can't see a key anywhere.'

'Okay. We will do it without. Hold onto me. Tightly. If I can just get a few more inches lower, then I think I can reach it.'

Lincoln wrapped his arms around her waist and the top half of her legs as she lowered herself over the side. On the third attempt she managed to unhook the board. 'Pull me up Lincoln,' she shouted at the top of her voice. He grabbed the back of her coat and pulled, hoping he was not choking her as he did so. Detective Green heaved herself back onto the plank between the two holes, clutching the clipboard and breathing hard. She manoeuvred herself onto her back and looked up at Lincoln. The rain fell across her face and hair, pushing it back against her head as she laughed in relief. Lincoln smiled back at her, shaking his head.

'That was all a bit hairy,' she said, brandishing the board. 'But I got it.'

Martha pulled herself up and got onto her knees, still on the plank of wood separating the two cylinders. She peeled back the cover of the clipboard so she could see what was recorded in the archeologists record just as a crash of thunder exploded above their heads, followed by a sweeping gust of wind. The force caught Martha unaware and, still slightly disoriented from hanging upside down in the metal shaft, she lost her balance. She called out Lincoln's name and they both stretched out their arms to each other, but her hands were just out of reach and she fell backwards into the second hole, tumbling into the icy water that had collected in the unprotected cylinder about ten feet from the surface. Lincoln swung his torch in Martha's direction and could see her below. She was taking short, shallow breaths, shocked by the fall and the chill of the water. She had dropped her torch and he watched as it snaked down towards the bottom of the cylinder floor, coming to rest next to the submerged clipboard. The beam shone momentarily in the muddy water and then flickered and died.

'Martha. Are you okay? Martha.'

There was a short delay and then Lincoln could see the detective look up towards him. 'Yes. I'm okay. Just get me out of here.' The walls of the cylinder giving her voice a slight echo.

'Thank God. Can you reach the bottom?'

'No. It's too deep. I'm treading water. Can you see the clipboard?'

'Forget the clipboard for God's sake.' Lincoln lay on the muddy ground and reached down into the hole. 'Grab my hand.' The detective pushed herself towards the side and reached up, but she was at least two feet short of Lincoln's outstretched hand. He pushed himself further over the side, desperately trying to reach her, but it was no use. They were too far apart.

'You'll have to get something for me to grab hold of,' Martha shouted, sliding off her coat and letting it fall through the water below. 'Hurry Lincoln, please hurry. There is nothing to hold onto down here.' Lincoln got to his feet, grabbed his torch and went looking for something to help, leaving the detective trying to stay afloat in the pitch black of the hole.

Another crash of thunder echoed overhead as he ran back to the ladders he had seen earlier and pulled on the locks again. They would not move. He turned around, scanning the building site with his torch, looking for something, anything that might help. There was nothing in the main area apart from the drilling machinery and the oversized vehicles. He ran behind the portacabins and saw a pile of scaffolding. He grabbed one of the six foot metal poles, put it on his shoulder and sprinted back. He shone his torch down into the darkness and could see Martha still treading water in the middle of the hole.

'Grab this, Martha.' He heaved the pole over the side just in front of her. Martha reached out for it, clinging to the cold metal. She breathed deeply and rested her forehead against the pole. She looked up at Lincoln who was already struggling with the weight.

'Can you pull yourself up so I can grab you?' he shouted.

Martha summoned all her strength and started pulling herself up the pole, but her hands were numb with the cold and she couldn't get a grip. She tried four times before she gave in.

'I can't do it, Lincoln. It's too wet. My hands keep slipping,' she shouted up to him. 'You are going to have to find something else.' Lincoln looked down. He could see the fear and panic in her eyes and knew she couldn't hold on much longer.

'Hang on, Martha. Hang on. I will get you out of there, I promise,' he said, trying to sound as confident as he could.

'You are going to have to let go of the pole. I am going to let it fall to the bottom.' Martha closed her eyes, clinging onto the security of the pole for a few seconds more, and then pushed herself away and began treading water again. Her aching limbs barely able to generate a wave in the ice cold water.

'Be quick, Lincoln. I don't know how much longer I can do this.'

Lincoln ran back to the area behind the portacabin. Next to the stack of scaffolding poles were two buckets and a pile of earth. He ran back to the other side of the site. Nothing. He tried to block out the image of Martha desperately trying to stay afloat. He shone his torch behind the large drilling machine. There against the fencing was a pile of wooden planks of various sizes. He sprinted across to them, looking for what he needed. There were two long planks right at the bottom of the pile. He threw the shorter ones to one side and hefted the two long planks onto his shoulder. He ran as fast as he could back to the hole, carrying the dead weight of the wood. He made it just as his legs began to buckle, dumping the planks onto the mud. He fell forward onto the ground and shone his torch into the hole. Martha's head was just above water. He called her name, but there was no reply. She didn't even look up. Lincoln heaved the two planks, side by side, over the edge praying that they were long enough to reach the bottom on the far side of the hole. He rested the other end of the planks on the side of the hole nearest to him, about two feet from the top so the planks were wedged, on an angle.

'Grab the plank, Martha. Grab the plank.'

At first she didn't move, her hands paddling slightly below the surface. He shouted again. This time she moved slowly towards the wood. Her white hands gripped onto the side and she was able to rest her aching and frozen body across the surface of the two planks.

'Martha. Look at me.' The detective slowly turned her exhausted eyes towards the surface. 'I need you to pull yourself up the planks so I can reach you.' At first she looked as though she didn't understand what Lincoln had said, but then he saw a familiar look of determination appear on her face. She tightened her grip on the wood and began to slowly pull herself up the incline. She had taken off her jeans and sweater to help her stay afloat and was just clothed in a white t-shirt and her underwear. Her pale flesh visible above the waterline as she pulled her exhausted body up the rough wood. Lincoln stretched out his right arm as far as he could, down towards her.

'Just a bit further, Martha. I have almost got you,' he shouted. 'Just six inches more.'

She rested for a moment and then with one final effort, she wrenched herself up and reached out for Lincoln's hand. He grabbed her and pulled. Her tender skin scraping on the rough wood. He managed to get both his hands under her arms and then pulled her up the last few feet onto the earth. He tore off his coat and wrapped it around the freezing, near naked policewoman. He pulled her towards him, wrapping his soaking arms around her.

'I've got you, Martha.'

She looked up towards him, shivering, her eyes bloodshot, her lips trembling.

'Did you get the clipboard?' she asked.

He looked down, smiling, and brushing her soaking hair off of her face. 'No, Detective Sergeant Green. I did not get the sodding clipboard.' He picked her up in his arms. 'Come on, we need to get you into the warmth.'

## CHAPTER 27

LOUISA Willoughby slowly withdrew her right leg from between her lover's thighs and slid from the king size hotel bed. Her spine poked through the grey, translucent flesh of her back as she rose to put on her silk negligee. The claggy taste of her lover's saliva lingered in her mouth, following their early morning couplings. She looked back towards the bed and noticed a damp patch where she had been laying. Such a sordid epitaph to their endeavours and so inconveniently and thoughtlessly messy, she thought. Her lover grunted and rolled over, revealing his large, white, left buttock, mottled with a mix of grey and black hair. Louisa generally preferred a younger body, but this one was too useful to let go, besides, he had aged well, all things considered. Strong hindquarters, a well ribbed upper frame and mutton withers giving him a deceptively powerful thrust through the core. Despite his muscular croup, he was short at the leg, like a stunted dray. In front of others, he was invariably 'above the bit', sashaying around like he was in charge and on show at all times, but this overcompensation was true of so many men limited in height, particularly those who had been bruised by early hair loss. They clung to the myth that their bald pate and stunted size was a sign of virility and pranced and preened in front of the women, while trying to dominate and ridicule the men. Why did they try so especially hard, as if everybody around them was commenting on their physical shortcomings? If only they knew how invisible they were.

*

Dressed in a dark blue Chanel dress, Louisa crossed the hotel lobby of the Savoy. Her heels clicked on the black and white tiled floor as she made her way past a table flooded with red and white gardenias and entered the Thames Foyer at the rear of the hotel. The head waiter greeted her with a restrained nod and ushered her to one of the corner tables, where James Marquand was already seated. An anodyne watercolour was hanging meekly on the wall to one side of the lawyer, lit up by a green shaded table lamp.

'I trust you had a pleasant night's sleep, Miss Willoughby?' asked the head waiter, gently pulling out the chair from the small round table. 'Could I fetch you some breakfast, some croissants perhaps?'

'Very satisfactory thank you, Jameson. No breakfast. Just an Earl Grey and a glass of water, if you wouldn't mind. Anything for you, Mr Marquand?'

The lawyer ordered a filter coffee and watched as the head waiter glided away to issue his instructions to the kitchen.

'Thank you for making the time to see me, James, so soon after the session at Marchmont House. I take it by your email that you have a response to my enquiries?'

Louisa Willoughby was generally recognised as a patient person. She was seen by many as being steeped in a dignified restraint that made her appear almost completely indifferent to the world that spun meaninglessly around her. Her own mother, Cressida Willoughby, recognised this disengagement with the present, saying to her husband one night after the Christmas festivities had drawn to a close, that it was almost like nanny had not slapped her soft, newborn bottom hard enough when she left the womb and the child was still yet to breath in the air of this mortal world. However, under this aloof reserve, something unpleasant stirred. She felt her brother, as her father before him, increasingly failed to recognise the paucity of intelligent thought in his management of the Estate. He hid behind bloodline and tradition as though a delicate fluke of birth excused his foolishness. When she showed him his errors, he declined to see. When she questioned him, he declined to answer. When she offered help, he declined to accept. She was tired of it. She had been brought up by her mother to accommodate the male line of the family and all it's tedious and emotional shortcomings, but no more.

Marquand unfurled a pack of legal papers onto the table. 'I have considered your comments and reviewed the original will of your father,' he said, tapping the sheets in front of him, while peering over the top of his reading glasses. 'I am afraid there is nothing in the wishes of your father to support your ambition. Indeed,' he stiffened in his chair, 'depending on interpretation, the claims of both brothers may supersede your own.'

There was a pause as Louisa considered the implication of the lawyer's words. 'I beg your pardon, James.'

'As I say, Miss Willoughby, some phrases in the will are open to interpretation, but certainly, given the right counsel, your younger brother, Andrew Willoughby, could feel inclined to progress a claim on the estate and become Head of the Family at such a time that Anthony passes on.' And then adding redundantly. 'I do of course appreciate that this is not what you were hoping to hear, Miss Willoughby, and I am deeply sorry for that.'

The waiter returned and Louisa took a sip of the ice cold water before replying. 'Indeed, James. This is disappointing news.'

Prior to the meeting at Marchmont House, Louisa had written to the lawyer on a confidential basis, trusting that his discretion would be absolute and binding. She sought clarity as to the terms in her father's will relating to the position of 'Head of the Family' and more specifically, under what circumstances could the role be passed on to one of the other siblings. Would a prison term or mental incapacity preclude the current incumbent from continuing in the position? In short, how could she usurp her brother and take over the managing of the Estate?

'You spoke of 'interpretation,' she said. 'Would you care to elucidate?'

'Certainly.' The lawyer sat back in his chair and rested his clasped fingers gently against his bloated epigastrium. 'The wording is peculiar in being specific but ambiguous at the same time. If I draw your attention to. . .' he flicked to the final page of the document and scanned down the addendum to the late Mr Basil Willoughby's will '. . .now where are we. . . yes, here it is . . . *regarding the management and devolution of my estate . . .sole responsibility of my son . . . as long as he is able to write his name.* There you have it, Miss Willoughby. As I say, specific yet ambiguous and, more to boot, damned irregular if I may say so.'

'I'm afraid you may have lost me, James.'

'Well, according to this will and testament, your brother could be imprisoned or incarcerated on mental grounds, but as long as he can scrawl his name at the bottom of the page, he stays put as Head of the Family.'

'Even if he, let's say, is found guilty of murder. . . or worse?'

'He could murder the royal family and be banged up for the rest of his life, Miss Willoughby, it would make not a jot of difference. He would still remain the Head of the Estate and would continue to manage the portfolio how he sees fit.'

'Even if it is to the detriment of the inheritance?'

'Yes, even if he loses the bloody lot. His power when it comes to family matters is absolute. You, your brother and your sister, may advise but you are not able to interfere. In many ways, you are like me, Miss Willoughby, when it comes to family affairs. We are both at your brother's beck and call, summoned to do as he bids, no matter what.'

A deep, gnawing irritation settled in the pit of Louisa's stomach, but she continued to sit with perfect poise, retaining unflinching eye contact with the lawyer. 'You mentioned Andrew, Mr Marquand, and his potential claim to the position in the. . . absence of my brother.'

'Yes, Miss Willoughby. You will have noted the wording *"the responsibility of my son"* in the addendum. There is no reference to a daughter and, if I was to be advising Master Willoughby at the point of his brother's death, then I would certainly be resolute in the assertion that both you and your sister, Elizabeth, are not entitled to take on the position of Head of the Family as long as a male heir is still alive.'

'How very forthright of you, Marquand,' replied Louisa, with a slight timbre of irritation in her voice. 'Then we will have to ensure that you are not the one advising young Andrew when the time comes. Unless of course you want a corrupted gawk to be in charge of the Willoughby Estate and, may I add, your future livelihood.'

The lawyer, realising he may have overstepped the mark, blustered, 'I did not mean to imply, Miss Wi. . . '

'Oh do not fuss, James, I know you were only providing a hypothetical viewpoint. I am sure my brother would fall clean away at the prospect of increasing his family responsibility beyond any level more taxing than fetching the ice for the next round of gin.' Louisa stood up to leave. 'Well, thank you again, James. Most enlightening.' She looked down at the glass of water and the untouched cup of Earl Grey. 'Out of interest, may I ask who has seen the will and the addendum to this point?'

'The lawyers at the time, your brother of course, and myself, Mrs Saunders, the family's housekeeper, who signed as a witness, and of course now you, Miss Willoughby.'

'Nobody else?'

'Nobody else, no.'
'Most helpful. Good day, Mr Marquand.'

*

When Louisa returned to her room on the sixth floor, the Stunted Dray had his back to her at the window, finessing his suit and tie. She moved silently into the bathroom to gather her thoughts. The prospect of attending future family meetings under Anthony's rigid glare, filled her with dread. When had the precocious little boy in ill fitting shorts and a poorly disguised stutter, grown into such an oafish clot, she wondered? His short sighted arrogance and absurd obsession with Cassidy, was all too much to bear and would certainly result in loss and failure for the family. She could not be expected to stand by and watch her inheritance be put in such jeopardy. But what could she do? Louisa looked up at her reflection, tucking her head on one side as she removed one of her amber earrings. There was nothing, simply nothing to be done. She was sentenced to watch from the side as her fool of a brother made mistake after mistake. She held her earring over the fingernail of her left index finger and, without flinching, pushed the stud wire through the thick red nail varnish into the tender flesh below. The right side of her mouth twitched, but her eyes betrayed no pain as a small pool of blood dripped down her finger into the enamel sink. She would suffer and forbear. As she had always done.

Louisa reached behind her back, unzipping her dress and letting it fall to the floor. She looked up and down her body in the mirror. She carried no fat and her hips and stomach, not having been inconvenienced by childbirth, remained reasonably taut. Her breasts, while harnessed in her bra at least, retained some firmness. Her skin, creased at the edges, was still as soft as a woman ten years her junior. But she was getting old. Every day, on it went, the teetering decay of her femininity. She looked back up to her face. A small tear had gathered in the corner of her left eye, not daring to fall.

'*Men may fall when there is no strength in women,*' she said out loud, staring at her rigid reflection. Turning away, she called out from the bathroom. 'Are you off?'

'Yes, I need to get across town to a meeting in Bayswater. Why?'

Louisa stepped back into the room and lay down on the bed. 'It's just that I have a need for distraction,' she said, letting her thin, aged legs fall gently apart.

The Stunted Dray stopped fixing his cufflink. A shot of anxiety coursed through his body. It had only been a couple of hours since their last encounter and he was not a young man any more. Did she really expect a repeat? So soon? He really was too attractive for his own good sometimes. But what to say? What to do?

'Louisa, my dear, I would love to. Of course, you know that. But the meeting is important and I would be missed unfortunately. Besides,' he offered up what he thought to be a coquettish look, 'you might not have me at my best and I would hate to disappoint.'

Louisa looked up at the Dray, opening her legs further apart.

'Improvise.'

## CHAPTER 28

A line of muddy footprints trailed across the floor from the front door to the bedroom of the Twickenham flat. A still wet t-shirt was draped over the radiator in the sitting room next to a pile of damp and dirty clothes. Some loose change was scattered over the kitchen table, along with a £75 receipt for the taxi that ferried Lincoln and Martha from Limehouse across to West London. It was nearly midday and the flat was silent. Outside, the storm had passed, having beaten the south of England into a dizzy submission. Branches and rubbish littered the road along with the occasional stray traffic cone that had lost its moorings and drifted, aimlessly, into the night. A pair of BT vans were parked up on the pavement, outside the flat, next to a huddle of engineers looking up, bemused, at a telephone post that had snapped clean in half during the storm.

Lincoln pulled back the white sheet and reached for a clean pair of jeans that were folded, by the side of the bed. His shoulders ached from the exertions of the night before, although the bruising on his arms and legs from his fall down the well in November had finally disappeared. He gingerly stood up and made his way down the ladder from the mezzanine towards the kitchen to put on some coffee trying not to to wake Detective Green, who was still sleeping in the downstairs bedroom. He didn't usually have sugar in his coffee, but felt in need of a comforting energy boost and pulled the half-full bag out of the eye-level kitchen cupboard, knocking over a tin of hot chocolate that went spiralling to the floor, bursting open and spraying its contents across the kitchen in a brown and sugary puff.

'Oh, fuck off.' Lincoln shouted, immediately slapping a hand across his mouth. He stood motionless for a moment, checking that all was still silent and then quietly looked under the sink for a dustpan and brush. A door slowly opened behind him.

'What was that?' Detective Sergeant Martha Green stood mumbling and half asleep in the doorway of his bedroom, dressed in an extra large, white t-shirt printed with the cover of the first Led Zeppelin album, which just about covered the top of her thighs. She squinted at the light coming in from the kitchen window, pushing her thick auburn hair back from her face. Lincoln temporarily found himself speechless. At that moment, he thought the policewoman was the most disarmingly beautiful sight he had ever seen in his life.

'Was somebody shouting?' she asked, sleepily.

'No, that was just me. I dropped the hot chocolate all over the floor,' he said, flustered, waving his arms in the direction of the powdered mess. 'Can I get you a drink?'

'Of hot chocolate?'

'No, of coffee.'

'I thought you said you were making hot chocolate.'

'No. Just coffee. Although I can make some hot chocolate. If you would prefer. Would you like a cup?'

'Of what? Coffee or hot chocolate?'

'Hot chocolate. Or coffee. Or both. I mean either.'

'You're making my head hurt, Mr Marsh. I'm going to have a shower.' With that, the detective stumbled off towards the bathroom, leaving Lincoln standing alone in the kitchen with a pink dustpan and brush in his hand and a brown dusting of chocolate powder on his chin.

*

An hour later they were both sat at the kitchen table eating toast and drinking tea. Martha had borrowed an old blue jumper and the smallest jeans she could find, which she belted up into a bunch around her waist. She had spent the last twenty minutes cancelling her credit cards and contacting her bank. Her purse, along with her mobile phone, were both lying at the bottom of the cylinder, covered in water and mud and were of no use to her now. She stared at the screen of Lincoln's laptop, scrolling down the mouse pad with one hand and eating a piece of toast with the other.

A comfortable silence settled across the room.

'What do you want to do about the museum? Do you want to head back to the site and get the contact number?' Lincoln asked. 'Or shall we give them a call?'

'It's alright. I took a picture of their details. Should be in the cloud. Let me just order this replacement phone and I will take a look.' Her engagement ring tapped on the keyboards as she typed in her details. She finished her toast and reached for her third slice. 'Of course, we wouldn't have to do any of this if you had only manned up and jumped in to get the clipboard.'

Lincoln looked up affronted. 'But . . . But . . . I was trying to save you . . . you were drowning, Martha . . . I can't believe . . . '

'Calm down, Lincoln,' she said, smiling across the kitchen table. 'I was only joking. Besides we would still have...Shit!'

'What's wrong?'

'My card's been declined. I've just cancelled the lot.'

She put her head in her hands and let out a small scream of frustration. 'What an idiot.'

'Just use mine. Here,' he said, passing over his wallet. 'Take your pick. They're all good.'

Martha opened the wallet and pulled out a Visa card from the neatly arranged array of plastic currency. 'Jeez. Get you. Are you made of money, Lincoln? You know, I've never even seen Eden Castle. Never. Not one episode.'

'Lovely. It's Castle Eden, by the way, but thanks for the feedback. Always good to hear from the public. And no, I'm not made of money. I'm just low maintenance, Martha, just very low maintenance.'

She smiled, twisting the credit card absentmindedly in her fingers. 'Seriously though, thanks Lincoln. For everything. I don't know what I would I do without you?' Her eyes lingered for a moment as she looked at him affectionately across the table. Lincoln felt his pulse quicken as he looked back into her eyes. 'Look Lincoln . . . I probably should tell you that . . . '

The doorbell rang, echoing through the flat and making Lincoln jump, despite its familiarity. At the same time, his phone started vibrating on the table in front of him. Lincoln looked down at the screen.

'Oh great. It's my brother. He must be outside.'

\*

Benjamin Marsh entered the room like he wanted to leave. After giving the detective a cursory glance, he took up a position by the kitchen window, looking back at his brother with a face that was full of spite.

'So, you still haven't agreed to the sale price.'

'Hang on there, Ben, let me get you a coffee. Sit down for goodness' sake.' Lincoln had reflected on the words Martha had said to him when they were sitting in the chapel about letting go and moving on and had reluctantly concluded that she was probably right. It still felt too early to him to sell the house, but maybe it always would and maybe he should just stop fighting the inevitable. Besides, he was tired of falling out with Ben all of the time. They didn't have to like each other, but surely things could be better between them than it had been recently and if it meant that much to him to prove that he knew better how to handle his mother's estate then, so be it.

'How's Astrid?' he asked breezily, while filling up the kettle at the sink. 'She looked great the other day, then again, she always does. We meant to catch up but you high-tailed it to the airport before we had a chance. I would have liked to have talked to her, it seems so long since we spent some time together. We should go out for a meal the next time you are both over. This is Martha by the way. Martha, this is Ben, my brother.'

Martha reached out to shake Ben's hand, but he either didn't see the gesture or just ignored it.

'All you had to do is agree to the price and sign, but you can't even be arsed to do that can you? Same old Lincoln. Always too busy pissing your life away, doing your own thing and sod anybody else.'

Lincoln turned back towards his brother. 'Hang on, Ben. That's a bit strong, mate. Look, lets not fall out again. I'll sign. I just needed some time to think it through, but I'll accept the offer and sign, I'll do it today. Come on, sit down for a minute so we can sort it all out. I'm tired of all this.'

'I don't want to sit down.' Ben moved forward directly in front of Lincoln, confronting him. 'You're 'tired' for fuck's sake. Tired? What on earth have you done to make yourself tired? What have you ever done, Lincoln? Look at your facile and irrelevant life. What have you ever achieved? Sat out here in the arse end of nowhere, fiddling around endlessly with your clever-clever TV script so you can clog up yet another Sunday evening schedule with your banal, pretentious shit. Hiding away in this trendy little cubbyhole you call a flat, with all its gauche designer furnishings and hipster artwork. It's a sham, Lincoln. You're a sham.' Ben was now no more than six inches from Lincoln's face. His eyes bulging. Spit flying from between his teeth as he spoke. 'Mum and

Dad thought the same. You were nothing but a disappointment to them. Dad would always stick up for you, but you could see it in his eyes. He was fed up with you. Fed up with seeing you drift through your life with nothing to show for yourself. You let him down, Lincoln. Time after time. You let him down. And all Mum wanted was to see you settle down, stop shagging around for five minutes and have a few kids, but, no, you couldn't even stump up a couple of grandchildren for her, because you were always 'too tired'. You're pathetic, Lincoln. An embarrassment. You always have been.'

Lincoln felt the blood drain from his face as a mixture of hurt and anger took hold. He was breathing hard, disjointed thoughts flying through his head, but he had no words to say.

'People die, Lincoln. That's what happens. People die every day. And when they die, the rest of the world shrugs and moves on. It doesn't even miss a beat. But you, you can't let go of the house. You know why? Guilt. Guilt for being a hopeless, selfish and downright useless son. You think by hanging on to an empty property you can show the world how much you loved them really and make everything alright? But you can't, Lincoln. It's too late for you to make amends. They are dead. They are gone. It's all too late.'

Ben's lip was trembling with anger as Lincoln pushed him away and then grabbed him by the shoulder, directing him towards the door. 'Right, you'd better leave, Ben.'

Ben tossed his shoulder back, shaking off his brother's grip. 'Get your hands off me, Lincoln.'

Detective Green had been watching open mouthed as Ben had unleashed his verbal attack on Lincoln. She could see the anger between the two brothers and knew that Ben was one small step away from resorting to physical violence. She reached out to touch Lincoln's arm. 'Hang on, Lincoln. I think Ben is going. Just let him leave.'

'And what the fuck has it got to do with you, may I ask?' Ben said, rounding on the detective. 'I presume you're just the latest, dizzy slag from the office. Got a bit tipsy at the

Christmas party did you love and before you knew what was happening, found yourself all ends up in his bed? Don't worry pet, you're not the first and you certainly won't be the last.'

Lincoln tightened the grip on his arm, white anger in his eyes. 'Just get the fuck out, Ben. Now.'

'I said, get your hands off me, Lincoln.' Before Lincoln could defend himself, his brother's fist landed with a hard, metallic thud onto his left cheekbone, making him fall back onto the kitchen table, sending the cups and his laptop flying to the floor. Lincoln could feel his head spin as he tried to get back up. He could hear Martha asking him if he was alright, but he pushed her to one side and flew at his brother, knocking him down to the floor. Too late, Ben tried to protect his head which hit the corner of the table causing him to shout out in pain. Ben tried to get up, but Lincoln was too strong and had him pinned to the ground, his fists raining down on his brother's face. He had landed three blows before Martha could stop him. Screaming at him and putting herself directly between the two brothers. Lincoln looked at her then looked at his brother, lying curled up defensively, blood flowing from his nose and lip. He slowly got back up off the floor and rose to his feet, breathing heavily.

'Get out of my flat, Ben. Get out now!'

His brother staggered up, spitting blood onto the wooden floor and stumbled out of the door and out of Lincoln's life.

## CHAPTER 29

LINCOLN walked the short distance from the Angel tube station to the Museum of London Archeology on Eagle Wharf Road and waited for Detective Green who had stopped off at her Paddington flat to pick up some identification. The miserable prefab facia of the building did nothing to lift his spirits. Nor did the weather. Spiteful shards of ice were being whipped along the pavement, directly into his face and stinging the still sore bruise on his left cheekbone. He huddled behind the rusted blue gates of the Museum, attempting to take shelter as best he could from the hail shower. Martha arrived a few minutes later. Lincoln nodded a subdued greeting and they walked together into the unimposing and unwelcoming building.

A forlorn piece of pink tinsel had come loose from the lack lustre Christmas decorations that adorned the reception area. It swayed to and fro in the gusts of warm air being belched out by the ancient air conditioning unit, above the main desk. The young and distracted receptionist barely looked at the detective's out-of-date identity card, clearly being accustomed to numerous visits from various members of the Metropolitan Police Force. They were told to wait in the lobby where they would find a tea and coffee machine and some water in a jug, if they wanted something to drink. The receptionist warned them that the milk might be a bit 'iffy' as the refrigerator had 'conked out' two days ago. They sat down next to each other on the brown two-seater leather sofa, both staring down at the floor and not speaking. After a few moments, Martha turned her head slightly so she could take a sideways look at the injury on Lincoln's face.

'How are you feeling, Lincoln? I think the swelling has gone down a bit.'

'I'm fine. Thank you.'

'You didn't have to come you know. I can handle this.'

'I wanted to come.'

Another moment passed.

'If you're worried about yesterday, Lincoln, you shouldn't be. You did nothing wrong. Your brother completely deserved all he got.'

'I know, but somehow knowing that doesn't make things better. Look, can we just not talk about it please. I know you are trying to help, but can you leave it. Please.'

They carried on staring at the lobby floor in silence as they waited for the Museum representative. The air conditioning unit thundered away in the background, filling the room with a claustrophobic heat. After a few moments, Lincoln broke the silence.

'One thing I don't get is what you are expecting the archaeologists to have found. You heard what Father Sandford said. Limehouse got its name from the lime in the soil and the quicklime that was manufactured in the area. Surely that means, chances are the bodies and bones will all be dissolved into the earth by now.'

'Quicklime doesn't dissolve corpses,' replied the detective, in a business-like tone.

'Yes it does. You always see it in films when people want to get rid of bodies. In fact, I must have used it at least three times in Castle Eden over the years.'

'Well, I'm afraid that is a common misunderstanding. Quicklime is a chemical compound known as calcium oxide. When it is exposed to $CO_2$ from the air it will react, causing light and heat and, when sprinkled on a corpse, will prevent putrefaction and decay, but it will not dissolve bodies. On the contrary, once hydrated, it acts as a preservative, keeping the body intact rather than destroying it.'

Lincoln stared at the detective. She looked back at him. 'Chemistry A' Level. Sorry.'

'Which one of you is Detective Green?'

A short woman with brown hair, clenched in a swarm of tight curls, walked briskly towards them and shook Martha's hand, once she had identified herself.

'I'm Jane Morrison. The Museum's Chief Operating Officer. What is it that you want and why wasn't I informed of your visit in advance Detective Sergeant Green?'

'Please accept my apologies for that. Somebody back at the station was meant to contact you to let you know we were on our way. I need to know about the Limehouse Crossrail dig and what has been found there?'

'Limehouse? The bodies you mean? But you know all about that. We sent over the details days ago. Really. This is all too much. What is the point of us following protocol if there is no communication at the other end. Sometimes I wonder whether the right hand of the Met knows what the left hand is doing, I really do.'

Martha did not acknowledge Jane Morrison's criticism or show her relief that skeletons had indeed been found on the site. 'Yes, the bodies. I was after any further details you have - age, height etc.'

'What, so you can lose the information in your systems again?'

Detective Green paused, fixing the Museum executive with a humourless stare. 'Can we keep things on a professional footing please, Ms Morrison. It is important case, so I would appreciate your help, not your censure.'

The C.O.O. bridled, crossing her arms in front of her chest. 'Very well detective, but if you have suspicions about the circumstance relating to these skeletons then you should have sent a request for input from our Forensic Archaeology Team, which I can see from our records, you have not done.'

'Point taken, but in the meantime Ms Morrison, is there anybody available who can provide me with some further insight regarding the find?'

Jane Morrison tutted one more time, rolling her eyes in annoyed exasperation. 'You will need to speak to the Osteology department, Detective. Janice,' she said, turning her attention back towards the reception desk, 'get Danny Whitehead down here will you?' With that, she turned her back on her two visitors and retreated into the corridor of offices leading away from the lobby, shouting as she went, 'And Detective, please make sure you make an appointment next time.'

*

Danny Whitehead, Senior Human Osteologist, could not have been more helpful. Partly because his general disposition was to be courteous and pleasant and partly because he was clearly smitten by the tall and beautiful detective.

'It is not altogether an exact science, Detective Green, but we have grouped the nine skeletons into three categories. The three children in the first group are aged between three and six years old. The two in the second group are between six and ten. Then the final four are slightly older, perhaps in their early teens, maybe younger. All are malnourished and show signs of teeth and bone decay. We estimate that the bodies have been underground since the turn of the last century, somewhere between 1895 and 1905. As far as the cause of death is concerned? Well, that's difficult. If I was a betting man, I would say they died from asphyxiation caused by sinking beneath the mud. Quite why they were there, I don't suppose we'll ever know. If you want to know more or you need the cause of death verified, then you really should get in touch with the Forensic Archaeology Team.'

'Yes. That has been mentioned to us and I will follow it up with them in due course,' replied the detective.

'Shall I walk over with you?' Whitehead said, enthusiastically picking his coat off the back of his chair. 'They are just over in the building next door.'

'No. No need, but thanks.'

'Are you sure? It's no problem, Detective. It will only take five minutes.'

'No, honestly. That's very good of you, but I am sure we will be fine. Thank you for the information, Mr Whitehead. You have been very helpful.'

'It's Danny, please,' he said giving the detective a broad and friendly smile. 'No problem, Detective Green. My absolute pleasure. Anytime. Let me know if there is anything else I can do. Anything.'

*

They sat in silence during the tube journey back to central London. Seeing the small, fragile skeletons laid out in a neat row at the Museum had brought home the awful horror of the fate of the Dunnings Alley Nine. It was hard to shake the image of the young workhouse children slowly disappearing into the Black Ditch, desperately clinging to each other and fighting for air as the cold and stinking mud filled their mouths and throats, stifling their screams as they sank below the surface. Lincoln shook his head, trying to dislodge the image from his mind.

'Who do you think the person on the bank was? The shadowy figure, Sandford mentioned. Could it have been one of the Willoughbys?' he asked.

'No. I doubt that,' replied Martha. 'Remember Lincoln, we don't know that there was actually any wrong doing. It could have been just a terrible accident. Nothing to do with the Willoughbys.'

'What about the note. The 'Dunnings Alley Nine'. We've seen them now, with our own eyes. All nine children. Dead. Murdered.'

'Dead, yes, but we don't know they were murdered or at least we don't have any proof and even if we did, we still don't know why. Basically Lincoln, whether we like it or not, we have nothing.'

The tube rattled to a standstill at Tottenham Court Road and they made their way up the escalator and onto Oxford Street, amidst the never-ending flow of tourists and day-trippers, forging their way to Covent Garden and the shopping districts of the West End. Neither Lincoln nor Martha were particularly keen to return alone to their respective flats, so they stepped into one of the nearby hotels on Russell Street, away from the maelstrom of sightseers, where they could try and come to terms with what they had seen at the Museum. The bar downstairs was empty apart from a couple lost in each others eyes, enjoying the electric thrill of a new office romance. The couple sat, hands entwined, in the far corner of the bar taking refuge from inconvenient thoughts of home and partners and the probing eyes of work colleagues.

'I don't agree with you, Martha. We have more than nothing. We have the saddlebag note. The note mentions four workhouses, all of which belong or belonged to the Willoughby family. It also mentions Barkham and The Dunnings Alley Nine and the phrase 'kill them all'. That is a lot more than nothing, Martha. Surely you will concede that?'

'I know we have the note, but for it to be a crime we need more evidence than that. Solid, concrete evidence. We don't even have a motive. If we think the Willoughbys were involved in the murder of The Reverend or the workhouse children, then we need proof and we need to know why.'

The waiter placed their two drinks onto the table, along with a small bowl of stale and dusty crisps. Lincoln had taken the note from his wallet and was staring down at the now familiar words.

'But we do know why they were murdered, Martha. We just don't understand all of the details yet. We know the Willoughbys are all about property, right? We also know they bought a load of workhouses which they operated for a while, but only until they were in a position to sell them on, or at least sell the land on, for redevelopment. By 1902 they had sold them all except these four - Aldersgate, Homerton, Dunnings Alley and Blyth. Why? Because they couldn't. Because there were still inmates there and as long as that was the case they had to keep them open because that is what they had agreed with the local authority.'

He turned the note around so Martha could read it.

*aldersgate to homerton*
*blyth 92 dunnings alley 9 barkham*
*providence at peasenhall*
*kill them all*

'It's all there, Martha, you just need to know where to look and learn how to see.'

Martha looked back, puzzled. 'What on earth does that mean?'

'Nothing. Forget it. It's just something someone once told me. The point is, the note is an instruction, an order to ship out the Aldersgate inmates to Homerton and then kill anybody left in Blyth and Dunnings Alley, along with your tenacious great grandfather. We don't know who the note was to, but we can have a good guess that the original order came from the Willoughbys.'

'Based on what? A hunch?'

'No, based on the note, Martha. Aldersgate, Dunnings Alley and Blyth all belonged to the Willoughby family. They were the only ones to gain by emptying them of inmates and they were the only ones to gain from securing The Reverend's silence. We may not have proof, but we know it was them. It has to be.'

Martha rubbed a hand across her face. 'Maybe Lincoln,

but we still have no evidence to back it up. Besides, do we really think the Willoughbys arranged the drowning of nine innocent children, just so they could sell some land?'

'Why not? It's a perfect way to get rid of them. No witnesses. No bodies. No evidence. All lost, beneath the filthy mud and water of the Black Ditch. Hidden forever, or at least until Crossrail came along wanting to build their tunnels all over East London.'

'You have a theory, Lincoln. That's all. Nothing concrete.' She pointed down at the note. 'What about Blyth? We have nothing on Blyth.'

'Of course we do,' Lincoln retorted. 'We have the missing family The Reverend was trying to track down, the Nicholls family.'

'But even Mildred doesn't mention murder in her notes,' said Martha. 'She just says they were missing. No, Lincoln, sorry, we need evidence and motive and we have neither.'

Lincoln folded the note and put it back into his wallet. He drank what was left of the glass of red wine down in one, not hiding his frustration he was feeling towards the detective.

'So lets go to Blyth, Martha. It's got to be better than sitting here doing nothing. Maybe it will be a waste of time. Maybe there is nothing there, but lets at least go and look.'

Martha had already decided that she would follow the advice of Chief Superintendent McSty and visit Anthony Willoughby at his club tomorrow. She had learnt over the years that Mr McSty was more often than not right and if he thought it was a good idea to try and rattle Willoughby, then she would give it her best shot.

'Sure, Lincoln. You're right. Lets take a look. It can do no harm. I'll meet you at Sorrel Cottage, but not until Friday. There's something I need to do in town tomorrow.'

## CHAPTER 30

ANTHONY Willoughby removed a paper clip from the top left-hand corner of the documents he had been reading and stretched out the metal wire to form a makeshift tooth pick. During lunch, a piece of liver had become lodged in the crevice between his two rear molars, refusing to budge. After his third prod, he felt the meat fall free and slide down the back of his throat. He stared down at the paper clip, which was now smeared with a thin layer of his blood, wiped it on his trousers and pushed it down the side of the armchair he was sitting on, in the main lounge.

'May I get you anything further, sir?' enquired Gulliver, the head waiter at the Burgoyne Club.

'No, Gulliver. I'm fine. I think young Molly is looking after me this lunchtime,' Willoughby said, peering around the large room in search of the waitress. 'Remind her and send her over in this direction, if you will.'

'Very good sir,' replied Gulliver. 'I believe she is just tending to matters in the Thomas Clarkson room, but I will hurry her along.'

Molly James was Anthony Willoughby's current favourite. He had originally strongly opposed the introduction of females onto the Club's waiting staff, but it had worked out surprisingly well, all things considered. It was true that the girls lacked the polish of their male colleagues and sometimes were clearly out of their depth, but they coped as best they could and the more capable actually made quite a fist of it. Indeed, now he had become accustomed to their presence, he found them quite a pleasant distraction. Particularly Molly James.

Molly had joined the staff at the beginning of the year and Willoughby felt they had formed a special bond right from the off. On her first day she was called in at short notice to wait table during a luncheon he had planned with some investors from Germany. After some early nervous mishaps she had coped admirably. At the end of the meal, the generous senior member had passed her a £10 note in the way of a tip for her services and since then, whenever she was on duty she had always gone out of her way to ensure that he was looked after and made comfortable. Willoughby very much enjoyed the attention, even though her comments and manner could be a bit playful at times, some may even have called her brash on occasion. Oh well, no harm done. Besides, he knew how to handle the young and cocksure Miss Molly James

He looked impatiently around the lounge, checking the bar and the other member's tables, but she was nowhere to be seen. Where was she for goodness sake? What was so pressing in the Thomas Clarkson room, he wondered? It really was quite intolerable, particularly when he thought of all the money he had ploughed into the club over the years. Yet, here he was. Waiting to be attended, like a day guest. Who does she think she is, he thought to himself, leaving him here to fend for himself? By God, he would have a word with her when she appeared. Good God yes. . . But then, out of the corner of his eye, he saw her. She walked in through the main door opposite him and by the time she had reached the bar to put down her tray of empty glasses, all had been forgiven. My, she does look lovely, he thought to himself. She's tied her hair back into a ponytail. She knows I like it that way. Typical Molly, always trying her best to please. When nobody was in earshot she would often call him her "Wild Lion", because of his piercing eyes and the way he walked around the Club. Prowling, she would say, always on the hunt, keeping all the new members in check, watching everything. Well, I am watching you today young lady, oh yes, keeping a very beady eye on you, he thought to himself, as his eyes drifted lazily up and down her curves, cushioned beneath her sheer black uniform. And I see everything.

Molly turned towards him and smiled, but rather than walk over to his table as he expected, she raised her index finger, indicating that she would be over in a minute.

Oh, this really is too much, he thought to himself.

It was in fact over five minutes before a breathless Molly James arrived at the side of the senior member.

'I am so sorry, Mr Willoughby. Try as I might, I just couldn't get away. There was just so much to do and there were only three of us looking after the whole room.'

Willoughby looked up at the waitress, a scowl perched on his lips.

'Oh please, sir. Don't be like that. It wasn't my fault, honest. You know I would have been here sooner if I could.' She looked furtively over her shoulder and then whispered. 'Come on my Wild Lion, please forgive me. I am here now. Please don't growl at me.'

He continued scowling, but only for a moment. How could he resist her sweet and delicate manner? An uneven, craggy smile sloped across his face.

'There he is! My brave Lion,' she giggled. 'Now, let me get you your brandy. How about a large one to make up for the wait?'

Willoughby nodded and watched her from behind as she walked back to the bar. What a ray of sunshine she was. Yes, a special bond. No doubt about that.

Once returned, Molly placed the drink on the table in

front of him.

'Well, what an afternoon I've had, Mr Willoughby. I was hoping you would be here so we could have a natter about it. Do you know Lord Chandler?'

'Bill, oh yes, he is a good man. Or was, I should say. You see, my dear, he passed away just recently,' Willoughby informed her, in a sympathetic and respectful tone.

'Not the old one, silly,' she replied. 'I'm hardly likely to waste my time serving soup and salmon en croute to a corpse am I? No, the young one, his son, Gregory Chandler.'

Brash, that's what she was, quite brash, Willoughby thought to himself. 'No, I don't believe I have had the pleasure, Molly, but he comes from good stock so I am sure he is a decent sort.'

'I'll say. What a lovely man. He was so kind to us and didn't mind at all when things started running a bit late. Such a clever thing too and so witty. I tell you, Mr Willoughby, he had them eating out of his hand in there. You know, Mr Willoughby, he is one of those people who just has presence. That's it, presence. When he talks, people listen. It's not just his looks. He is just special. Yes, real presence, I'd say. Some people just have it don't they, sir? I bet you did, once upon a time, Mr Willoughby. You know, when you were younger. Can I get you some peanuts or anything to eat, sir?'

'Uh, no. I will just have my brandy thank you.' Willoughby croaked, taking a large swig of his drink.

'Anyway, right at the end of the meal he starts talking to me. Just turns from the table while everybody is chatting away and talks to me. Asking me my name, where I live, stuff like that. Anyway, turns out he can help me with my degree.'

Willoughby looked up, cradling his brandy in his hands. 'Your degree? I had no idea you were a student, Molly.'

'Oh yes, just finished my second year. Neuroscience at UCL. Boring I know, but I was always good at that stuff at school so why not. Anyway, Gregory, I mean Lord Chandler, knows somebody at The Society of Neuroscience in Washington and says that he might be able to get me an intern job, just temporary of course, over the summer. Which would be just incredible. What do you think of that, Mr Willoughby?'

'Most interesting,' Willoughby blustered. 'You know, my dear, you should have said you were looking for work. I am sure I could have pulled a few strings you know,' he said, tapping the side of his nose.

'Oh, yes, well that's nice of you, sir, it really is, but the SfN. I can't believe it. Anyway, he wants to know more about my course so he can talk to the people in Washington about me so, if it is okay with you, Mr Willoughby, can I go back to sort things out with him.'

'What, now?'

'I know I've only just got here, but you are all sorted for a bit, aren't you? I can get you another brandy before I go if you would like?' She held her hands together, pleading. 'Please, sir. I will make it up to you. I promise.'

His instinct was to say a firm 'No' and Lord Chandler could go to blazes, but the entire conversation had disoriented him. He felt quite hurt and upset about the whole situation. If she didn't want to be here then she could jolly well piss off, he thought, and good riddance. He waved his hand at her, dismissively.

'Oh thank you, sir. You're the best.' With that she turned and walked briskly back to the Thomas Clarkson room, while Anthony Willoughby gulped the last of his large brandy and scowled at the world.

\*

'Mr Willoughby, sir?'

'Ah, Gulliver, I was just about to call for you. I need a word about that waitress, Molly.'

'I am so sorry to interrupt, sir, but there is a young lady to see you. I have advised her to make an appointment, but she is most insistent.'

'Nonsense, Gulliver. What is happening to this place.

Can a man no longer get some peace and quiet in his own club? Send her away. I don't have time for this. Now, look, about that girl, she has got to go, do you hear. . .'

'But, Mr Willoughby,' the head waiter bent his head closer and dropped his voice to little more than a whisper. 'It's the Metropolitan Police, sir.'

'Well, what on earth do they want?' Willoughby said, full of indignation.

'I did not ask, sir, but I took the liberty of directing Detective Sergeant Green to wait in the Bessemer room, which should afford you some privacy.'

'Detective Green did you say?' Willoughby's eyes lit up. Well, this was interesting. So she dared to raise her head did she? And in his lair. Well, that shows pluck if nothing else. Of course, he could just call the police and have her dragged out of the building like a common miscreant. But where would be the fun in that? No, best see what the girl is playing at and maybe have a bit of sport with her along the way.

'The Bessemer room you say.' The head waiter nodded. 'Leave this to me, Gulliver, and Gulliver, please make sure we are not disturbed.'

\*

Martha had told herself that she had to remain controlled and disciplined throughout the interview. There was no proof, whatsoever that Willoughby or anybody connected with the Willoughby family had anything to do with her suspension from the police force, so that was all off limits. There was, after all, little point in lecturing Lincoln about the pitfalls of uncorroborated conjecture if she was going to ignore her own advice. No, she would keep the questioning objective, professional and focussed exclusively on past crimes. The aim was to try and unnerve him, shake him up a bit, make him believe that they had good reason to investigate the Willoughby family's connection with misdemeanours of the past. Control and discipline, she told herself again, control and discipline.

Anthony Willoughby was perhaps slightly shorter than she had envisaged. However, there was a strength and purpose in his stride, a combative manner usually found in a much younger man. He marched towards the centre of the room with menacing authority and stood toe-to-toe with the detective.

'And what should I call you today, I wonder? Is it Detective or plain old Miss Green?' he asked.

'Detective Sergeant Green would be fine, sir. Thank you for agreeing to see me. Shall we get straight to it?,' she asked, not waiting for his response. 'I would like to ask you a few questions relating to some of your current and former properties, Mr Willoughby. Firstly, could you tell me how long you have owned the land and buildings at Blyth in Suffolk?'

Willoughby looked the detective up and down, disparagingly. 'And why would I do that, Detective Sergeant?'

'Because, sir, it is part of a current police enquiry and I need to confirm the ownership of the said property. It would be much easier and more pleasant, I dare say, if you were to provide me with the information today rather than having to visit the station at a later date. Either way, I require you to provide me with answers to my questions, Mr Willoughby.'

'Oh really, you require me to, do you?' Willoughby casually sat down on one of the armchairs in the centre of the room, crossing his legs. 'And on whose authority, Detective Sergeant, if I may ask? It was my understanding that you had experienced some difficulties at work and no longer had a position with the Met. Is that not the case. . . Detective Sergeant?'

'I am afraid you have been misinformed, sir,' Martha replied confidently. 'I am still employed by the London Metropolitan Police Force and maintain the full authority associated with my position. I suggest we go back to the question I asked you, sir.'

'The full authority. Is that right? Well, I am sure you will not mind me checking in with your line manager. Just to make sure today's intervention is all above board and authorised.'

'Check with who you wish, sir. I am at a loss as to why an enquiry about one of your properties requires such circumspection on your part. I can only presume you are trying to hide your family's connection to the wrongdoings discovered during our recent investigations.'

Willoughby rolled his eyes. 'Pah. Wrongdoings. What are you on about?'

'Our investigations indicate that a number of crimes took place in relation to Blyth and several other properties owned or formerly owned by the Willoughby family. These range from abduction to coercion and include at least one count of alleged murder. As head of the Willoughby Estate, you are required to provide us with information and, where appropriate and available, alibis, in relation to these crimes. As well as Blyth, investigations are also ongoing in relation to the Dunnings Alley, Aldersgate and Homerton properties. In addition, the 1902 case concerning the murder of a Reverend Barkham, from the village of Peasenhall, has also been reopened and the Willoughby Estate will be required to answer questions relating to their awareness of and involvement in this crime. You may wish to continue this discussion at the station and indeed, you may think it prudent to have a lawyer present when you do. Today, however, I would be grateful if you would answer my earlier question and tell me how long you have owned the land and buildings at Blyth in Suffolk?'

Detective Green looked directly into Willoughby's eyes, unflinching. She had said more than she had intended, but she couldn't help sensing that she had unnerved the senior member of the Burgoyne Club. She was convinced she saw a flicker of concern, a slight, almost indiscernible beat of doubt in his eyes.

Willoughby had not expected this. He knew that Green

was just chancing her arm, but he was momentarily alarmed that she had connected all four workhouses and the Barkham incident so readily. Cassidy had assured him that this officious bitch had been managed. He had said that he had poisoned her life so completely that she would be subsumed by the internal police investigation and would have time for little else. Yet, here she was. In his club. Accusing him of God knows what. He took a moment before he spoke, steadying his nerves and fixing the detective with a hard and dispassionate stare.

'No, Miss Green. I will not answer your question and that is the end of the matter. However, it strikes me that we are quite alone, which affords me the opportunity to talk candidly to you.' He breathed in deeply, not breaking his stare. 'As far as I am concerned, you are nothing more than a washed-up, pugnacious, drug addled tart. Your career is over, your colleagues have deserted you and you have no authority or power. If I were you I would stop pestering law-abiding citizens like myself and sort out how you are going to make a living once they rip away your badge, which they undoubtedly will do. Looking at those nasty pictures in the newspapers, I would have thought you could make a passable wage whoring yourself out. You're too stringy for my taste, but there will be some less discerning clients out there. Although, you will need to preserve your looks during your stay in prison, which, I should imagine, will not be easy. I am sure there will be quite the welcoming committee for you when they bundle you through the gates of Holloway. In the meantime, you are considerably out of your depth Detective. This is the big boys table where the big boys dine and is not for the likes of you, so kindly stop harassing me with your baseless trumpery and piss off out of my club.' Willoughby's lips curled into a sickening and condescending smile as he waved the policewoman towards the door. 'You're done, Green. Now be a good girl and hurry along.'

Martha could feel hatred and indignation well up inside her. She clenched her jaw and steadied her breathing. Control and discipline, she said to herself. 'I take it, sir, that you are choosing not to answer my questions. Thank you for your time and I will be back in touch shortly to make a formal appointment at the police station. I do advise that. . . '

'Oh do shut up, lassie, and close the door on your way out.' Willoughby reached for the copy of The Field magazine on the table next to him and began, absentmindedly, flicking through the pages.

Green could hear her raised heartbeat and feel her breath shorten. Control and discipline, she said to herself, straightening her back and nodding at Willoughby who continued to disinterestedly look through the magazine. 'Good day, sir, and thank you again for your time.'

She walked stiffly across the room, toward the door, but hesitated when she was directly beside his chair.

Control and discipline be damned, she thought to herself.

'One more thing, sir.' Willoughby looked up lazily at the detective, barely taking his eyes from the magazine. 'As you say, we are alone, so let me be candid also.' She stared down at him, her voice measured and precise. 'I know your family's wealth is built on greed and terror. I know your ancestors committed foul and loathsome crimes and I plan to bring all that evil to your door, Willoughby, and make you account for them. I also know you are responsible for my public disgrace and humiliation and I intend to bear down on you until you and your vile empire are destroyed. I will not waver. I will not falter. And I will not be deterred. My advice to you, Mr Willoughby, is talk to your lawyer and make preparations, because I am coming for you and, be assured, one way or another, I will bring you down.'

*

Willoughby was still seated in the middle of the empty room when, Alastair, one of the club's recent recruits, brought him a jug of iced water some five minutes later. The copy of The Field had fallen to the floor and lay propped up against one leg of the leather armchair. Willoughby's left eye twitched as he contemplated the words of the detective, remembering the look of determination in her eyes. He took a drink of the cool water and tried to collect his thoughts. Of course, he knew she had no proof or evidence, but he would need to call on Marquand to talk through potential scenarios, as a precaution. He would also need to track down Cassidy and hear what he had to say for himself. The young waiter reached down to pick up the magazine and placed it back where it should be. As he straightened the table, Alastair could not help but notice the slight tremor in the hand of the esteemed senior member as he poured himself a second glass of water.

## CHAPTER 31

AT this time of year, the top of the garden did not benefit from the slight warmth offered by the December sun and a thin layer of frost remained permanently in a small area of the lawn, shaded by the two tall coniferous trees that bordered Sorrel Cottage. The cold air was still and a soft and delicate silence descended on the garden, as if it had become unmoored from the present and had drifted apart from the scratchings and interruptions of modern life. Even nature had no voice, apart from the occasional cry of a lone seagull drifting over the cottage on its way towards the nearby coast. Lincoln pushed open the back door and entered the chill of the kitchen. The cold served only to emphasise the unloved emptiness of the house. His parents furniture was still littered around each room, but the tables, chairs and cupboards no longer held any meaning beyond their functional purpose and were now just arrangements of wood and nails, deprived of the life-giving touch of daily use. He stood for a moment in the hall, accepting the aching silence and acclimatising himself to his surroundings. Sorrel Cottage, he thought, this place, this building was no longer home and never would be again.

Martha would not be joining him until the next morning so he had pulled into a farm shop on his way to the house, to buy a small bag of provisions. Just some tea, milk, sausages and beans. He had turned the central heating up to its highest setting and switched on practically every light in the cottage to try and make the rooms slightly more welcoming. The sitting room had a television in the corner, but it had stopped working some years ago and his mother had declined his offer of a new one. "All the programmes are for someone else these days," she had said to him, "I can't tell the difference from what's real and what's make believe." He had persuaded her to let him buy her a digital radio, which she had loved and rarely turned off. Lincoln had not re-tuned it and let the soft and comforting ramblings of Radio 4 spill out into the kitchen and gently meander their way around the other rooms of the house, which were slowly beginning to thaw. Despite it being only late afternoon, he decided to warm the sausages as the long journey and the receding daylight had made him ravenously hungry. He put them on a tray in the oven and sat down at the kitchen table to wait. He had received two messages on his way up to Suffolk, which he had not bothered to listen to until now. The first was from Mr Stillman, the solicitor, telling him that, because of the delay in accepting the offer, the house sale had fallen through. Mr Stillman's main worry wasn't the loss of the sale as such, he was more concerned about who would tell Benjamin Marsh the bad news. The other message was from Tariq Shad, Luminosity's Chief Accountant, asking him to call as soon as was convenient.

\*

'Hello Lincoln, thanks for returning my call.' Tariq had answered on the first ring, giving the impression that he had been waiting impatiently by the phone in expectation of

Lincoln's call. 'Sarah asked me to give you an update regarding your payment. Look, please don't shoot the messenger, Lincoln, but I'm afraid there will be a further delay. The money is definitely coming, I promise you that, but I just need a bit more time to get things straight and restructure the company's costs and cash flow. You will probably want to know when you will be paid, but I'm sorry, I cannot tell you that, at least not now, but it will be soon, as soon as I can, hopefully by spring or definitely by the summer. No later, I promise.' Lincoln could hear Tariq take a deep breath, as if relieved to have got the bad news out of the way.

'So, there you have it. That is where we are. I hope you understand that I am doing all I can to help, but things this end have not been easy. Not been easy at all.'

'Another delay?' Lincoln asked. 'What's going on, Tariq?'

'As I said, I am in the process of restructuring the company's costs and cash flow and a payment will then be forthcoming.'

'Okay, I get that, but what is actually going on. Is Sarah in trouble?'

There was a short pause, then Lincoln could hear Tariq sigh down the other end of the phone. 'I'm guessing she has not spoken to you. No, of course not. She said she would call, but to be honest, I knew she wouldn't. It's all such a mess, Lincoln. A complete and utter mess.' Lincoln could hear the strain in the accountant's voice as he tried to explain the situation. 'You remember the morning you were over at Luminosity, the three of us, in Sarah's office, well that was just the start, things got worse very quickly after that. It took me until the end of the week to figure out that there was no advance coming from Adventureland TV for the new Ralph & Hugh series. Without that, we didn't have a chance. Sarah knew that. I had explained it all to her earlier in the week, laid it all out in black and white, so even a child could understand it. She knew we didn't have the money in the bank and without that we couldn't pay the bills. Not that difficult to understand you would have thought. She had spent all of the company overdraft on that office refurbishment and what a waste of money that was by the way, and now there was nothing left. Nothing. Not a penny. I told her again and again, but you know what she's like, Lincoln, she just would not listen to me, it was all "stop worrying, Tariq", "you are just panicking, Tariq", "have a drink, Tariq". Well, she should have listened to me. She should have listened.'

'Christ, Tariq, take it easy.' He could tell Tariq was on the verge of breaking down. 'What about Sarah? Has Luminosity gone bust then?'

'Yes. No. Well, sort of, but no, not officially.'

'What does that mean, Tariq? Has it gone bust or hasn't it?'

'Well, the Luminosity you know, the company you have worked for over the years, doesn't exist. The fancy offices, the people, the expense account . . . all gone. But the company name still exists. I had always kept a bit back in the accounts for a crisis, you know, just in case, and it's lucky I did. So with that and the money we got when Sarah finally agreed to sell some of her projects to one of the other production companies, Global Reach, we just about managed to avoid bankruptcy. You were the last big client who had an outstanding payment, but we owed you so much, Lincoln, there was no way we could cover it so we extended the payment term. That was what Sarah was meant to talk to you about. I'm sorry, Lincoln, we shouldn't have done it without talking to you first. She did promise she would call you, but, well, that's Sarah.'

Lincoln felt a burgeoning irritation building up inside him. He was less angry about the money, although that was bad enough, it was more that Sarah had not had the decency or guts to call him and explain. Even by her head in the sand standards, this was pretty low. 'What about Sarah? Where is she in all this? Is she okay?'

'She's not good to be honest. Not good at all. She has a

new office, out in Stoke Newington of all places. Not really her style. She is trying to keep things going, but, I don't know, it's all a bit futile. You know what this industry is like. They love it when someone fails. Nobody wants to talk to her. All of her old media friends have suddenly disappeared or don't return her calls. Most of her clients, once they got paid, bailed out and went to join one of the big companies. I can't blame them I suppose, but she was the one who took a chance on a lot of them in the first place when they were starting out and stuck by them, even when their scripts weren't picked up. She still has a couple left, but nothing that will make any money, at least, not in the short term. Last time I spoke to her, she was still trying to put a brave face on it but, deep down, she knows it's hopeless. Try as you might, you cannot work in television if nobody wants to work with you. I think she will try and keep things going for a bit longer, but then, well, that will be that.'

'God. What a mess. What about you, Tariq? What are you going to do?'

Tariq let out a long breath. 'I don't know. I was so cross with her, Lincoln, so cross. It is my reputation too, you know, and we let a lot of people down, a lot of good people. I made sure everybody in the office got paid, but they have no jobs now. What a thing to do to people just before Christmas. They trusted us and we abused that trust. She has behaved so badly. Been so utterly selfish. She should have listened to me, that stupid, stupid woman.' Tariq was silent for a moment, trying to manage his emotions. 'I said I would sort out the outstanding payments and then leave, but, I don't know, I will probably stay until the end I suppose. I don't think I will ever forgive her, but she has been good to me over the years. Besides, she doesn't have anybody else. The whole thing just makes me so sad, Lincoln.'

'Hey, look, you're a good man, Tariq,' said Lincoln. 'You've been a good friend to her. Sarah has been lucky to have you by her side. She knows that, believe me, even if she doesn't say it as much as she should.'

'Maybe, Lincoln, maybe. I just wish I could do more to help to be honest. I hate to think of her stuck in that shabby office all day, waiting for phone calls that never come.'

Lincoln opened the drawer of the kitchen table and pulled out a biro. 'I should give her a call and see how she is. Can you let me have her new details and I'll try and track her down.'

*

Lincoln tried several times during the course of the evening to talk to Sarah, but without success. A glass of whiskey sat on the kitchen table in front of him, next to an ordnance survey map of the local area that he had found in the study, tucked inside a battered, brown briefcase his dad used to take to his office in Norwich. The case also contained an assortment of documents relating to the local archeological digs his dad had been involved with since he had taken early retirement, along with various other odds and sods he had decided to squirrel away from his ever-decluttering wife. Lincoln had marked several red crosses on the map, forming a straight line running on a twenty degree angle, across the landscape, going from Peasenhall in the south, the site of the Reverend's murder, through Sorrel Cottage where the note and the knife were found, then through the location of the Blyth workhouse, and then finally, much further north, there was the site of the Great Yarmouth workhouse where The Reverend had tried and failed to visit the Nicholls family. On the face of it, all separate incidents, but Lincoln was more certain than ever that the events were linked in some way and it was the Willoughby family that somehow joined the dots.

He tapped his biro impatiently on the table, staring down at the map, hoping for some, until now, hidden insight to let itself be known to him. After a few fruitless minutes he pushed the map away and reached for his glass, idly flicking through the other contents from his dad's briefcase that he had spilled out onto the table. Along with the archaeological documents there was a glossy brochure advertising a Volvo estate, not that his dad would have ever shelled out for a new car. There were also some old tickets from various evenings at the local arts theatre and one from a visit to the Norwich Castle Museum, which Lincoln could vaguely remember being dragged along to. In the side pocket, there was a picture of his mum from the year she first met her future husband. She looked young, beautiful and wide-eyed with curious expectation as to what surprises her life with the charming man from the insurance company would hold for her. There was also a family photograph taken one Christmas when Lincoln was eight or nine years old. He could vaguely remember the occasion. It was Boxing Day and his Uncle Bill had come over late in the afternoon, just as his parents had opened their second bottle of wine following a lunch of cold turkey, black peppercorn ham and his dad's bubble and squeak. Uncle Bill was brandishing a new camera that Aunt Jane had bought him following a concerted campaign of hints and suggestions in the weeks running up to Christmas. Bill insisted that the Marsh family have their picture taken to mark the festive occasion. Despite his inexperience, Bill took it all extremely seriously and had a very clear idea of the refined Christmas portrait he wanted to create. He spent five minutes getting the Marsh family into the correct positions, using the window and the darkening sky as a backdrop and then set about fiddling endlessly with the settings, while flicking from one page to another of the user manual. By the time he was finally ready the family, much to Bill's annoyance, had reverted to its normal unkempt and relaxed state. His irritation only served to make his now tipsy relatives more playful, giggling and making faces when they were meant to be looking stoically towards the future in Victorian restraint.

Every now and then, his dad would attempt to rally the family, but each time one of them would start giggling again just as the shutter was about to be pressed. After the fourth failed attempt Bill had had enough and started packing away his camera, despite the pleadings from his brother. It was Mrs

Marsh who eventually convinced Bill to give them one last chance and, as she made her way back to her allotted position by the window, she wagged her fingers at her two sons, mouthing to them to behave. The room fell silent as Bill once again checked his settings and then just when everything was ready, Ben let out a discreet, but audible burp. Lincoln could feel his dad begin to shake behind him in a forlorn effort to contain his laughter. His mum dug her elbow into her husband's ribs, but she was no better and at the very moment the shutter clicked, all four of them had dissolved into a helpless, giggling mess. Bill, now accepting defeat, stomped off home and they didn't see him again until well after the new year when he begrudgingly delivered a copy of the troublesome photograph through the letterbox, without joining them for a cup of tea. Despite Uncle Bill's disappointment, the photo had always been his dad's favourite. "That's the Marsh family at its best and in all its glory," he would say pointing to the image on the mantelpiece and chuckling to himself as he recollected the occasion.

    Lincoln looked down at the photograph, which was beginning to show its age and had faded around the edges. Despite Bill's exactness, the picture was slightly out of focus, but this somehow lent it a warm, natural look. He looked at his mum, red-cheeked from the wine, wrapping both of her hands around her husband's arm, while leaning her head against his shoulder, her face creased with laughter. His dad had his arms outstretched towards Ben, a look of mock indignation on his face. Ben was looking up at his dad, laughing with complete childish abandon, his right hand outstretched and holding onto his brother for balance who was looking back at Ben and barely able to stand up from laughing so hard. Lincoln gazed down at the photograph, smiling, looking from one face to the other. His eyes settled on the face of his brother. His carefree features, in stark contrast to how he had looked when they last met at his flat. Lincoln picked up his phone and scrolled through his contacts to find Ben's number. His finger hovered over the call button for a moment, but then he replaced the mobile back on the table, the number undialed.

## CHAPTER 32

DESPITE it being nearly ten o'clock in the morning and well into the working day, the two floors of the Felicitous cafe, just off Threadneedle Walk, buzzed with business suited industry. A bacon sandwich ordered here, a triple espresso there. The mewling whine of placed food orders filled the air, as the chaff of the London banking and accounting community recovered from another weekend of tedious high jinks. The hours ticked by as infantile anecdotes of greed and debauchery were shared, ad nauseam, over a never-ending feast of caffeine and pastries. Every wasted moment cloaked under the thin disguise of an unattended 'business meeting'. Looking at the throngs of men and women, but mostly men, who infested the infinite cafes of the financial district, it was a wonder that the tall buildings surrounding them, did not stand empty from daybreak to sunset.

In the far corner of the cafe, under a giant mirror, sat a table of middle-aged men, forcing glistening meat-filled rolls into their greasy mouths, while listening in awe to the fatter of the four as he heaved out yet another loquacious dirge of infidelity. The telling of the tale of the fat fool's tits and arse tomfoolery was so spellbinding that they paid no heed to the lone diner on the table next to them, who sat brooding in front of a tepid cappuccino, lost in thoughts that had their source many miles from the tables and chairs of the Felicitous cafe.

Herr Hartmann was motionless. He stared down at the coffee which was now covered with an unpalatable meniscus of froth and milk. He had come straight from his hotel across the river without showering and his blond hair was still greasy from the cabin air of the previous night's flight from Bremen. His blanched skin was covered with a thin layer of day-old sweat, giving his face a spongy, unhealthy texture. His elbows sat squarely on the small cafe table, his shoulders rounded into a spiritless slump. It was only his eyes that retained any form of corrupted animation as they moved incessantly from side to side, seeing images far beyond his immediate surroundings, images locked deep inside his brutalised imagination. He continued to sit and wait, clenched in a helpless and self-defeating anger, as caustic visions of his immediate past were relayed on a never-ending spool in his mind ~ the blood forming an icy pool on the snow ~ the unmarked grave at the end of the garden ~ Lulu's pitiful wail as she awoke from another night terror ~ the appointments with the child therapist ~ his wife's screamed accusations and recriminations ~ the sound of the family car as it pulled away from the drive ~ Hartmann alone in the silent and empty house. Through it all, in the background, like a discordant soundtrack, was Cassidy's voice, repeating, over and over again. *". . . I will always be here Herr Hartmann. I will not go away. . . I will always be here Herr Hartmann. I will not go away. . . I will always be here Herr Hartmann. I will not go away. . ."*

It was ten minutes later that the MP for Easton arrived at Felicitous to meet with the German business man that had contacted Harriet Blackwood, regarding an exciting, new international opportunity. And it was ten minutes after that,

that an alarmed and panicked George Giltmore was wrestling with his coat and heading for the door.

'Sit down, Mr Giltmore. I mean you no harm.'

Giltmore had his right arm safely secured in his jacket, but in his haste he had failed to insert his left arm in the other sleeve on three consecutive occasions and his coat was now hanging off his shoulder, dragging onto the dusty wooden floor.

'No harm? You have got to be bloody joking,' he shouted back at Hartmann. 'Do not contact me again, Herr...oh, whatever your name is. If you do, I will call the police.'

'Sit down and lower your voice.' Hartmann lent towards the flustered politician who had seemingly forgotten how to dress himself, and touched his arm. 'I have a copy of the photographs, Mr Giltmore.'

The MP for Easton froze with his coat still hanging off his back, a look of guilty fear on his face. He then, after a moment's consideration, slowly removed his coat and placed it on the chair next to him and sat back down, looking discreetly around the cafe as he did so. He stared down at the table, not daring to make eye contact with the German businessman sat opposite. His shocked heart was still pumping at an uncomfortable rate from when the man had first introduced himself and told him that it was he who had arranged his hotel guest in Bremen on the night he had been photographed and subsequently framed. Giltmore now realised that Hartmann must have also been responsible for arranging the photographer or, worse still, maybe took the photographs himself.

'As I said, I mean you no harm. In fact, I need your help.'

Giltmore looked up from the table. 'Help? From me? Why would I help you, you little shit. You blackmailed me, you kraut bastard.'

'No, Mr Giltmore. I did not blackmail you. The Willoughbys did that, not me. I just provided the materials they needed.'

'Oh, so that's okay is it? You just set me up with some

German prossy and took the snaps and that lets you off the hook does it?'

'Nobody made you do it Mr Giltmore. You were only too keen to take Simone up to your room, as I recall.' Hartmann raised his hands. 'But you are right, I helped set you up and I apologise. It was a bad thing to do. A bad thing to do to you. I am sorry, Mr Giltmore. Truly I am.'

Giltmore stared back at the German trying to work out if this was another trap. He looked at the deep black rings around his eyes and his puffy face. Hardly the Herrenvolk, he thought to himself. 'You lied to my assistant and got me here under false pretences. Why? What on earth can you want from me now?'

'I need your help. Willoughby has abused and hurt us both and I want to hurt him back, but I can't do it on my own. If I am going to make this happen, then I need us to work together.'

'You want to take on the Willoughbys? Ha! You must be mad. You wont be able to get near them. Not a chance. They are protected, shielded from the likes of you and me. Their money buys them all the security they need, which makes them impenetrable. Give it up, for your own sake, before they make things even worse for you.'

'They couldn't do that. They have already taken everything from me,' Hartmann mumbled. 'I know all about the power of the Willoughbys, but I think, if we are careful and coordinate our actions, then we can get at them. We may not destroy them, but we can definitely hurt them, we just need a plan.'

Although Giltmore did not believe that this German chap could be a success, he found the prospect of a life free of the dark shadow of the Willoughby family too appealing to just dismiss out of hand.

'What plan?' he asked.

A small glint of hope appeared in Hartmann's eyes as he thought that he may have convinced the MP that it could be done. He beckoned Giltmore to lean in a little closer.

'Initially, I thought I could use Simone, the one from the hotel. I tracked her down and spoke to her, and for the right price, I think she would be prepared to put in writing what she did with you that night in Bremen and who paid her to do it.'

A look of terrified panic shot across Giltmore's face. 'What? . . . she would be prepared to do what? . . . for what?'

'Do not worry, Mr Giltmore. I think we can do better. We do not need to involve Simone after all. You have my word.' Giltmore began breathing again. 'No, to really hurt them, we need to get at the family's top people. I am right in thinking that you have come across Milton Cassidy in your dealings with the Willoughbys?' Giltmore nodded. 'He is Willoughby's trusted advisor and second in command,' Hartmann continued. 'We go after him. As you say, we will never get near Anthony Willoughby or any of the other Willoughbys, but we might just be able to get to Cassidy. If we can get him to a location where he feels comfortable, then we may be able to provoke him into talking about Willoughby and his plans. We'll have to get it on tape of course, but that at least is easily done.'

'Absolutely no chance. You'll never get Cassidy to talk. He's far too cute for that.'

'No, I agree. He will never talk to me. I wouldn't be able to get within a hundred metres of him, but he will talk to you.'

'Me? What?'

'Yes, you. He has been working with you on the Homerton project for months, right? As I understand it, all the difficulties have been resolved and you are just waiting for the sale to go though. Correct?'

Giltmore narrowed his eyes. 'How on earth do you know about that?'

'I know a lot of things. Don't worry about it. The point is, if you ask to meet him somewhere to discuss some bogus issue about the sale, then he will not suspect anything and we can get him on tape, or even better, on video.'

'It will never work. Who's going to do all the technical stuff? Besides, I am not going to a meeting with Willoughby's henchman with a cable sticking out of my armpit and, even if I did, he is not just going to confess his sins to me and reel off all his wrongdoings. He's not a fool you know.'

'Yes, I know, believe me, I know. I can take care of anything technical and if we can get him to the right location, then I can set it all up in advance, no wires. I promise. All very discreet. I know exactly what we need to ask him to get him to talk. We don't need everything, just a few facts to give us some leverage so we can go to the police either in the UK or Germany, or both. Trust me, Mr Giltmore. You may not like me, but I do know what I am doing. You don't need to think about a thing. I will handle it all. I will work out the script for you, line by line, if you want. You just need to get him to the right place and ask him a few questions. I will take care of the rest.'

Giltmore looked across at the German, trying to figure out whether he should believe him or not.

'Trust me, Mr Giltmore. If we work together, we can do this.'

\*

As Giltmore walked down Throgmorton Street away from the cafe, he thought through the plan put forward by Herr Hartmann. Despite his earlier reservations, it actually sounded like it might just work. He would have preferred not to have to be there at the meeting with Cassidy, but Hartmann was right, Cassidy would not suspect anything if Giltmore called about some issue or other relating to Homerton and if the German chappie was going to write down what he had to say, then all the better. Ever since he first trod the boards at prep school he had always been good at learning his lines. Besides, realistically, what choice did he have. No choice, that's what. If Hartmann was right and he seemed jolly confident, then the Willoughbys could be out of his life forever. The thought made him want to jump in the air and click his heels, as they did in those old American movies, but acrobatics of that athleticism were way beyond the reach of his portly physique these days, so instead he celebrated by buying a Twix from the newsstand on the corner, which he consumed along the short walk to the Bank tube station.

Back at the cafe, Hartmann remained seated in the corner table. For the first time in weeks, he felt a shiver of relief twist down the taut muscles in his shoulders. The meeting had gone as well as he could have hoped for. There was no doubting that Giltmore was as big a dummkopf as he had appeared in Bremen. Hartmann had gambled that the lure of ridding himself of Willoughby would be too much for Giltmore to resist and he had been proven right. He looked at his watch. It wasn't even midday. He decided to head towards the shops and see if he could lay his hands on some recording equipment, just for show, and at some point he would pull together a bunch of questions that looked relevant and genuine and would provide the quivering MP with some comfort prior to the meeting. Whether Giltmore used them or not was irrelevant. By then he would have served his purpose by luring Milton Cassidy to the pre-determined venue where Hartmann would be ready and waiting to meet him. He allowed himself a brief smile as he imagined the feel of the knife as he pushed it through the tender skin of Cassidy's flank, just below his ribcage. He thought of the pleasure he would savour as he watched him, ever-so-slowly, bleed out onto the floor. What happened after that, Hartmann had given no thought to. There would be no purpose or meaning attached to his life once the gasping lungs of Milton Cassidy had released their last shallow breath and breathed no more.

# CHAPTER 33

A thin, cold drizzle descended on Lincoln Marsh and Detective Sergeant Martha Green as they made their way up the gravel driveway towards the Workhouse at Blyth. A look of brutal determination was on the policewoman's face as she led the way to the imposing red brick building that was perched on top of the hill, some two miles outside the village of Halesworth. They had shared only a few words since they met at the cottage earlier that morning. Lincoln knew the detective well enough to know when she wanted to be left alone and, following her meeting in London the previous day, it was clear that her mood had darkened.

The workhouse building had, for the most part, been left untouched for the last hundred years. An electric fence bordered the perimeter of the unattended gardens, behind which a number of leafless shrubs had taken root, squatting in a disorderly line next to the path, which led to a large sandstone archway in the centre of the building. Several signs were posted around the archway, warning of the repercussions that would be meted out on any unauthorised soul who ventured onto the private land. Next to these signs, were two large boards advertising the building contractors currently employed on site, one specialising in demolition and one a building development company. Martha moved forward and looked cautiously through the archway, which provided access to the workhouse wards and courtyard beyond. She peered through the early morning half-light, looking for signs of any security guards or workmen, in the unlikely event that they would be on site this early on a Saturday morning. Without turning her head in his direction, she gestured to Lincoln and they moved quickly through to the enclosed brick courtyard on the other side of the gated archway.

The workhouse, if viewed from above, was in the shape of a truncated 'H', with the top half of the building containing the Master and Matron's quarters, administration offices and a small lodge for the sole use of the Porter, who would have been responsible for vetting any new arrivals, either turning them away or sending through to the Relieving Room where they would be reviewed and allocated a place on a ward. The bottom half of the complex contained the exercise yard and the various wards and work rooms. Once through the archway, Lincoln had forced open one of the doors leading to the back entrance of the Relieving Room, which was empty apart from two short benches screwed to the wooden floor. The benches had been used by the workhouse officers when interviewing the newcomers and assessing their physical condition. Against the wall, behind the benches, were two rectangle, five foot, metal baths, dug into the ground, where the future inmates were stripped and bathed in cold water before being clothed in an ill-fitting workhouse uniform and directed through to their allotted ward. At the end of the room, at the top of the wall, above the door leading onto the courtyard, was a large engraving, with the words ~

*Be Rid Of Idleness, Ignorance And Vice*
*Or Despair And Be Banished From This Refuge*

Martha and Lincoln walked through the doorway back onto the courtyard from where they could see five entrances. Four of these were to the wards - one for the old and infirm, one for children between the age of two and twelve and one each for able bodied men and women. The fifth door led to the Itch Ward where inmates were sent by the Relieving Officers if they had scabies or any other infectious skin disease. Unlike many workhouses of this period, the inmates shared the same courtyard for exercise, which would have allowed families to be briefly reunited once or twice a day. They made their way across the courtyard, towards the entrance of the Itch Ward where, to the right of the doorway, was a small gold plaque:

*Here listed are the noble and generous Guardians of this Blyth House of Industry, in the year of 1891. We give thanks for their benevolence and christian kindness:*

*Mr Norris Willoughby*
*Mr Ebenezer W Root*
*Mr Donald Squire*
*Mr Jeremiah S Buller*

The detective took a photo of the plaque before following Lincoln into the ward. Four dusty and broken narrow bed frames were still in place at the top of the room, a further two were propped up on their side against one of the damp, mildewed walls. A small black hearth was in the corner, the cracked flagstones, caked in thick charcoal which would have given off a dense, smoky odour, merging with the sour breath of the unwell. At the back of the ward, there were some narrow stairs, with a sign next to them pointing down towards the Bone Crushing Room below. The stairway was completely impassable, obstructed by a locked and bolted cast iron door. They moved, without speaking, back outside and made their way around the wall of the building. An open space, directly above the Bone Crushing Room, had been levelled off and made ready for further building work with small pegs and guide ropes marking out a rectangle onto the flattened earth. In the centre of the cleared area there was a large metal chute, which had been dug into the ground and was poking out of the earth, like a ship's funnel, ready to receive thousands of litres of cement that were scheduled to be pumped into the empty room below. To the rear of the flattened space was a large object, about ten feet high and fifteen feet across with heavy, black tarpaulin draped across it.

Lincoln walked over to the tarpaulin and tried to loosen the ropes securing the object, but could only pull back one of the corners. He bent down onto his knee and looked underneath the covers.

'It looks like some sort of statue or memorial or something,' he said, peering through the hole.

'What of?' asked Green.

'I can't make it out. There's some sort of figure, holding a gun I think, or a stick. I don't know. Whatever it is, it's big.' He looked back to the cleared area. 'I presume they are going to position it there, on top of the Bone Room.'

A large, heavy wooden board was laying on the ground next to the chute. Martha hooked her fingers underneath its edge and pulled it up and out of the way. Underneath was a four foot square grid, with thick rusty bars across the surface. She shone her torch down through the bars and could see the floor of the room, some ten feet further down, covered in what looked like a thick layer of small rocks. Over to the right, she could just about make out the set of stone stairs that ran from the original doorway, leading from the Itch Ward down to the Bone Crushing Room. Lincoln crouched next to her, looking down through the bars.

'This would have been the hatch that they dropped the animal corpses through to the inmates below,' he said. 'Now that is a shitty job. Smashing bones all day long. The stench must have been incredible. Look, you can still see the bone fragments on the floor.'

Martha shone her torch back down the hole, scanning

from one end of the room to the other. What she had thought were rocks were some of the larger, broken bones, from cows, pigs and horses. These rested on the tiny, crumbled fragments of hundreds of animals, smashed into pieces, so small that it had appeared as if a layer of sand was covering the floor.

'I doubt the bones would have even been stripped before they had to deal with them,' Lincoln continued, even though the detective showed no inclination to engage in conversation. 'The main chunks of meat would probably have been removed by the workhouse kitchen or a local butcher, but I would imagine that there was more than enough rotten flesh left on the bones to keep the local rat population interested.' He let out a shallow sigh, peering down into the darkness. 'It makes me sick just to think of it. What sort of life is that? Sat in the dark all day long, smashing bones of dead animals while trying to keep the rats at bay. God, I'd rather take my chances out in the fields, although, I don't know, it was probably just as grim out there if you didn't have any money, especially in winter. No food. Freezing cold. All the work had gravitated to the newly emerged industrial towns back then. There wasn't much going on here in the country, beyond back-breaking work in the fields, but even that was hard to come by. But still.' Lincoln shivered. 'Smashing bones? No, not for me. No thanks.'

They stared down into the room in silence, looking at the crushed bones littered across the floor. Martha bent her head closer to the bars, trying to focus on some of the bigger shapes.

'Those bones, the larger ones,' she said, shining her torch to one of the furthest corners. 'They could be human.'

'Human? Do you think? Impossible to say from up here,' said Lincoln, relieved that Martha had decided to talk to him at last. 'Could be, I suppose.'

Martha continued to look down through the bars. 'The Nicholls family. Maybe they didn't set off on their journey to Great Yarmouth after all? Maybe they ended up here? It would explain why they disappeared all of a sudden and why

The Reverend couldn't find a trace of them. If we now think that Norris Willoughby was so desperate to empty the Dunnings Alley workhouse that he arranged the murder of nine children, then killing another family up here would not be beyond him.'

'Particularly if he had a place as convenient as this to bury the bodies,' Lincoln said, pointing down into the darkness. 'Who is going to bother to look under all of that stuff, particularly back then?'

'We've got to get down there,' Martha said, urgently. She began pulling on the bars, wrenching them up. The two padlocks rattled against the side of the grid, echoing across the courtyard. She pulled again, harder, but they wouldn't move. She jumped to her feet, looking around for something on the ground and picked up a large flint rock from behind the memorial and came back and squatted in front of the grid. She began slamming the rock down on the padlock, hitting it again and again. Smashing it so hard that sparks were flying off from where the stone was hitting the metal.

'Open, damn you,' she shouted.

Lincoln could see the desperation in her eyes and reached across to her. 'Hey, Martha, come on, calm down.'

'Open. Just fucking open.' She smashed the rock down so hard that a large chunk of flint splintered into the palm of her right hand. A thin line of blood dripped down onto her wrist, but she didn't notice, or at least, didn't care, and just kept bringing the rock down onto the lock with all of her force.

'Martha. That's enough. Stop it. For God's sake, it's not going to open. What has got into you?' This time he grabbed her arm tightly, holding her still until she dropped what was left of the flint. Her hands were shaking. She was breathing in short gasps. A look of anger and hatred in her eyes.

'He's going to get away with it. That arrogant bastard is going to get away with it.' She wiped her hand across her face, leaving a smear of mud on her cheek. Lincoln let go of her arm and placed both his hands gently on her shoulders.

'It's going to be alright, Martha. Calm down. You're going to hurt yourself.'

She shook his hands from her shoulders. 'No, it's not alright,' she screamed. 'For fuck's sake, Lincoln, can't you see what's going on? Are you that stupid? Willoughby is going to win. We are scrambling around in this godforsaken place, trying to connect him with the crimes of his ancestors and all the time, he's sat down in London in that fucking club, laughing at us and waiting for the handcuffs to be slapped on my wrists. So, no, Lincoln. It is not going to be alright. Get it? It is not going to be alright.'

Lincoln dropped his hands by his side, looking into the detective's eyes. Behind the anger he could see the fear and dread that was haunting her. He wanted to grab her, hold onto her, protect her, do whatever he could to keep her safe.

'If you're not going to help, then go. It may all be some big game to you. Something to put in your next TV series, but it's my life. I don't need you, Lincoln. I don't even know what you're doing here. You're just getting in the way. I'm better off on my own. Just go.' She was back on her feet, searching for something else to prise off the padlocks, not even looking at Lincoln, who was still kneeling on the floor in front of the metal bars, wondering what he had done to deserve the verbal onslaught from the detective. He was about to answer back, when he heard the sound of a car door slam at the front of the building. He got up and edged around the corner of the wall of the Itch Ward, where he could see a stocky security guard, in a fluorescent yellow vest, walking to the back of his blue transit van. The guard looked half asleep. He dragged his hand across his shaved head and straightened his vest before opening the back of the van and mumbling some words of encouragement to the large Alsatian that leapt down onto the pathway.

Lincoln ran back to Martha, who was still searching pointlessly behind the tarpaulin.

'Come on,' he said. 'We've got to go.' Martha ignored him, pushing him aside. He grabbed her arms and spun her towards him. 'We've got to go, Martha. Now.' She looked back at him, lost, confused, disconnected. 'Martha. Now.' Her eyes seemed to slowly come back into focus.

'What is it?'

'A guard. Out front. If we get caught this time, Willoughby will have you locked up before night fall. We go now, across the fields out back. I can get us to Sorrel Cottage from here, across country. But we go now, Martha, come on.'

*

It took them just over an hour to get back to the cottage. Their shoes, caked in mud, were scattered outside the kitchen door, the falling rain washing the dirt away. No words had been spoken during their trek back, apart from the occasional shouted direction as they trudged their way across the ploughed fields, made ready for sowing. Lincoln pulled off his jacket and tossed it on the kitchen chair. He lent both hands on the kitchen table and looked at Martha expectantly.

'What the fuck was all that about?'

'I know, I know, I'm sorry....'

'"All a big game"?, "something for your TV series"? Who the hell do you think you are, Martha?'

'I know, I said I'm sorry....'

'I know you are under pressure, but talk to me like that again, or put us at risk again by banging around like a spoilt brat, then we are done. Clear?'

'Yes. Clear. I'm sorry, Lincoln. Okay? I'm sorry. I don't know what else to say.'

Lincoln eased his grip on the table and relaxed his shoulders, gently shaking his head. 'What has got into you anyway?' he asked, in a slightly more reserved tone. 'You were fine last week, then this shit. What happened to you on Friday, for Christ's sake?'

Martha could feel the strain of the sleepless night she had spent at her mother's house following her drive up from London late on Friday evening. She'd sat downstairs most of the night, unable to shake off visions of her meeting earlier that day. Her body ached and her eyes felt irritated and strained. She pushed her hand through her hair, letting her fingers come to rest on the back of her neck. 'I had a meeting with Willoughby at his club,' she said, looking back across the table at Lincoln. 'My contact at the Met thought it would be a good idea to shake him up a bit and I think, just seeing him face to face, seeing the arrogance up close, just got under my skin. I'm running out of time, the preliminary hearing is in the first week of February, that's less than seven weeks away and I've got nothing. He knows it. I looked into his eyes, there is no fear there, no doubt, no concern. He doesn't care that we are looking at Dunnings or Blyth. He doesn't care about The Reverend's murder. It's all too long ago to bother about. Caught in the past. It doesn't mean anything to him. He thinks it's funny, amusing and anyway, he knows I can prove nothing, so why should he concern himself?'

Lincoln raised his eyes in surprise. 'Christ, you saw him, face to face. Wow. That takes some balls. At his club? Jesus. And he wasn't phased? Not at all?'

'Couldn't give a damn. Or maybe when I first mentioned all four workhouses and The Reverend, maybe there was something, a brief moment of doubt, but believe me, it didn't last long. I could tell he thinks we are just wasting our time . . . and maybe we are. Maybe I should just be trying to find out who planted the cocaine in my locker and see if I can get them to talk, rather than looking for motive all the time?'

'Do you think you could find the insider?'

Martha thought for a moment, then shook her head. 'No. Not a chance. If he has got someone on the inside getting drugs and planting them on fellow officers, then they will be sewn up tight. No way could I get at them, well, maybe with the full resources of the force, but on my own? No chance.'

'So, keep on looking in the past. You say he was rattled when you mentioned all of the workhouses and maybe that's his weakness. I've no doubt that one incident on it's own is not going worry him, but if we can highlight multiple crimes, then maybe that will be enough to to get the family investigated.'

'Sure, but I know the strength of the evidence they have against me, the drugs, the photos, the forged payments into an account set up with my name. I know the DPS is licking its lips, can't wait to get stuck into me and publicly crucify me as an example of how seriously they take internal police corruption. I know what's coming my way. The crimes we are looking into are a hundred years old for God's sake. Carried out by Norris Willoughby, a man who's been dead for years'

'But the spoils of the crimes,' interrupted Lincoln. 'The financial benefits, the pay off is being cashed in now. By, his grandson, Anthony Willoughby. That makes him as guilty as his ancestor.'

'Maybe, but only if we have proof that he is knowingly covering things up,' replied Martha. 'That he knew that his family murdered the nine Dunnings children, that he knew his family murdered The Reverend, that he knew his family murdered the Nicholls family. Maybe Buller is the connection somehow?'

'Buller? The bloke in Aunt Catherine's story, the one who took the child from your grandmother?'

'Yes, sort of,' replied Martha. 'He was called Edmund Buller, but there was a Jeremiah Buller listed as one of the guardians for Blyth Workhouse. Maybe Edmund Buller's father? Maybe both father and son worked for the Willoughbys? Might be worth looking into? Of course, alternatively, he could have nothing to do with it and it could be yet another blind alley.'

'But worth checking.'

'Sure. Worth checking,' Martha conceded.

'And Strathdon? Anything further from your contact at the Met.'

Green's mobile phone buzzed in her pocket.

'Talk of the devil,' she said, looking at the screen. 'I need to take this. It will give me a chance to update him on Blyth.

Maybe he can help get us access?' She disappeared into the sitting room, leaving Lincoln alone in the kitchen, staring out into the back garden that was now drenched with winter rain. He thought about what Martha had said about Jeremiah and Edmund Buller. Maybe Jeremiah Buller was the man on the bank of the Black Ditch the night the children died and maybe it was him that the saddlebag note was written to? Also, as a Workhouse guardian, he would have had access to the Nicholls family at Blyth, so could have helped with their disappearance. He would also be long dead, thought Lincoln, so would his son, Edmund, most likely, but the boy he took from the hospital, the one stolen from Petra, he could still be out there, alive. Maybe he could help somehow?

Behind him, he heard the door of the sitting room open and turned to Martha, keen to share his thoughts about Edmund Buller's boy. He began explaining, but stopped as soon as he saw the detective's face. The colour had drained from her cheeks. She walked slowly back into the room, looking frail and defeated.

'Martha. What's wrong? What's happened?'

She raised her tired, lifeless eyes towards him.

'They've brought forward the preliminary hearing. I have to report to headquarters on Tuesday morning at ten o'clock.'

## CHAPTER 34

'FUCK!'

'I'm sorry, I can't really hear you, Sam. What was that?'

'Nothing sir, sorry sir.' Sam Wilson had spilt his coffee over his keyboard and work space at Milton Cassidy's Kensington office. A large splash had also landed on his thin, white cotton shirt, scalding his skin. 'Let me press the buzzer, sir. We are on the top floor . . . sorry, you of course know that . . . sorry . . . here . . . the door should be open now.' The ugly moan of the door entry system resounded across the empty office space.

'Fuck! What the fuck! Fuck!' Sam dabbed at the coffee with a napkin with one hand while trying to tidy his desk with the other. He had only met Mr Willoughby face-to-face twice before. Once at a the wedding of his younger sister and once at Willoughby's club, when he had been asked by Cassidy to take over some particularly sensitive paperwork for signing.

They had spoken on the phone on many occasions, but what was he doing here, at the office? Why today of all days, when he was on his own? He dashed around the other desks, putting things in order, although, in reality, not much was out of place. It never was.

It was some five minutes later when Willoughby, red cheeked, walked through the main office door. Sam was there, ready and waiting, doing his best to appear calm and in control and trying to ignore the scalding, limp material that was clinging to his stomach.

'Mr Willoughby, what an unexpected pleasure,' he said, reaching out his hand.

'Sam. Good to see you. You're looking well. How is your father and Marianne? I trust they are keeping healthy.' He paused, trying to catch his breath. 'I presume Felix has scurried off to his hideaway in the Maldives as he always does this time of year, getting some much needed practice on the golf course I shouldn't wonder. If Marianne lets him that is, eh Sam?' Willoughby let out a conspiratorial, laugh that soon descended into a throaty, hacking cough as the strain of the climb up five flights of stairs took its toll.

'Let me get you a glass of water, sir,' said Sam, dashing off to the small kitchen area.

'Thank you,' replied Willoughby, in between coughs. 'Why Cassidy doesn't put in a lift I will never know. I must have told him a dozen times already.' Willoughby swallowed the chilled water in small gulps, passing the glass back to his obliging employee when he was done. He took a moment to get his breath and then walked to the centre of the small office, his eyes crawling over his surroundings.

'It's been some time since I have been here, Sam. All appears shipshape. This one is Cassidy's office isn't it?' he said, walking purposefully to the door at the back of the floor and turning the handle. 'Locked. Quite right. Quite right.' He turned back to Sam who was trailing behind him. 'Anyway , I just thought I would pop in, see how you were getting on, make sure everything is going okay with you. Cassidy treating you well?'

Sam looked momentarily flummoxed by the unexpected civility. 'Uh, yes sir, quite well. You know how it is, sir, always busy, but we keep on top of things.'

'Good. Good.' Willoughby's eyes continued to wander around the office. 'Bremen all closed up?'

'Yes sir. All terminated. The paperwork has all been completed and filed.'

'Great. And Blyth? The developers all ready to go?'

'Yes. All ready. Planning permission is in place. Technical audit complete. We are just waiting on one point regarding the ecological survey, but that will not cause a problem for us, so all good.'

'Remind me, Sam, how many flats are they planning to build?'

'Uh, from memory, I think they hope to convert the existing building into twenty nine residences. I think that's right.' Sam made a motion towards his desk. 'I can check, sir, the exact number, if you would like me to.'

'No, Sam, please don't trouble yourself.' Willoughby put his hands behind his back, looking across at the locked door of Cassidy's office. 'And Homerton? Is the land sale proceeding as planned?'

'All back on track, sir. Mr Cassidy is meeting Harriet Blackwood as we speak, just to iron out the final details, but yes, that should all be done and dusted within the next week or so. I know that Mr Cassidy is pushing hard to get the monies transferred across before the Christmas break.'

Willoughby finally turned his gaze back towards Sam. 'Yes, the transfer. I forget, Sam. How does that work again? The transfer I mean. It's all a bit circuitous as I recall, cloak and dagger stuff, but remind me, if you would be so kind.'

'The transfer? The route back to the Willoughby account you mean, sir?' Wilson said, instinctively dropping the volume of his voice to no more than a raised whisper.

'Yes, that's right, Sam, and Strathdon and all that convoluted nonsense that Cassidy insists upon.'

'It's a bit complicated to explain.' Sam said, reluctantly. 'Mr Cassidy is the expert, maybe you would prefer to wait for his return, sir?'

'Just the top line if you don't mind, Sam.'

Sam bit the side of his lip as he gathered his thoughts. 'Well, I'm not sure of the details of all the placements and layering that goes on, to be honest. Mr Cassidy plays things quite close to his chest, but I believe there are two main transfer routes. You'll be aware that only transactions associated with the Strathdon account are handled this way, such as the forthcoming Homerton sale. All other regular transactions go through the main Willoughby account, or one of its subsidiaries, and are handled by our accountants in the normal way.'

'Yes, fine, fine, Sam. Please. You were saying about the two transfer routes.'

'Sure. Sorry, sir. The first route centres around, or is at least dependent upon, our relationship with the Grande Lin casinos and online gambling business in Macau and Hong Kong. Regular funds derived from one of the major transactions, such as the Blyth sale earlier in the year, are converted into chips, played through the casino or online and then the proceeds, minus Grande Lin's commission, are wire transferred out of the Far East across multiple borders until it ends up in a Trust held out in the Cayman Islands.'

'And the Trust being the Strathdon Trust?'

'No, sir, not Strathdon, not yet anyway. No, the Trust is called the Fontaine Trust which in turn is owned by the Anderson Trust, which has its banking facility in Luxembourg managed by a Swiss Company called Eszett Investments.'

Willoughby looked at Sam with a creeping impatience. 'So, where does the Strathdon Trust come into it?'

'Perhaps I should get to that once I mention the other main transfer route, sir.' Willoughby nodded and waved his hand, encouraging Wilson to get on with it.

'The second route is dependent on the land transactions we complete throughout the year, particularly those in southern Europe. I know Mr Cassidy was keen to acquire some additional land in Germany, before it was decided to close that operation down but, for now, our main focus is

France, Spain and Portugal. This route involves certain suppliers, all hand-picked by Mr Cassidy. We buy goods and services from these suppliers such as site security, building work, conveyancing, that kind of thing. When the company bills us for their services they over-invoice us. Nothing too onerous and certainly not more than a 20% increase on the original invoice. Mr Cassidy is a stickler about that. The companies list the extra expense as an offshore consultant or an exceptional cost of some kind and the over-invoiced sum is then transferred to one of our shell companies, based in Vanuatu. Then, periodically, this money is wire transferred out of the shell companies, once again across multiple borders, until it ends up in another Trust fund, the Imogen Trust, based in the Virgin Islands, which is managed by a Guernsey company called Bailliage Capital Markets.' Sam paused momentarily. 'Is this all making sense, sir?'

Willoughby, who had decided to take a seat at one of the desks, nodded. 'So far so good. Strathdon?'

'Right. Strathdon is the name of the Trust fund in the UK. I have no idea where the name comes from, but it has existed as an account, in one form or another, for many, many years, literally centuries.' Sam pointed to the chair on the opposite side of the desk. 'Do you mind, sir?

'No, of course not, please sit down, Sam.'

'Thank you, sir. Okay. So, throughout the year, the bankers from Eszett Investments and Bailliage Capital Markets deposit small, untraceable sums into this account. The sums are usually no more than $50,000 at a time, and bearing in mind the size of some of the sale transactions involved, you will appreciate that the whole operation is a long, drawn out process lasting many months. Over time, as you will be only too aware, the sum retained in the Strathdon Trust account has grown significantly and this money is then used to buy various items here in the UK, mainly land and properties, but occasionally precious items, works of art, that kind of thing. Nothing too high profile you understand and all selected and acquired personally by Mr Cassidy. After an appropriate time, Strathdon then sells these items on to a branch of Willoughby Trading Limited, theoretically at market price. In reality, the transaction is purely a paper exercise, no cash actually changes hands, but it gets the acquisitions off the Strathdon account and onto the Willoughby books.

Willoughby Trading Limited then either hangs onto the items and treats them as capital assets or sells them and turns the assets into cash, thereby integrating the funds, originally banked in Hong Kong or Vanuatu, back into the UK, cleansed and completely untraceable, and that's basically it, sir.'

Willoughby reflected for a moment on what he had heard, looking across the desk at Sam. 'As you say, a complicated process, but all necessary precautions I suppose. And Mr Cassidy manages all this?'

'Yes, sir. Occasionally I may assist if requested, but his knowledge of all the processes, the contacts in Europe and the Far East and all the properties involved, is well out of my reach. I've got to say, he really is quite formidable in his oversight of the operation. He has an incredible eye for commercial detail and somehow keeps all the plates spinning, as it were. My role is purely to handle the sale of the land and goods from Strathdon to Willoughby Holdings and make sure the audit trail is commensurate with our objectives. The easy bit if I'm honest.'

This is what Willoughby had hoped to hear and indeed, it was exactly what Marquand had told him when they had spoken earlier. 'That's interesting,' said Willoughby, looking pensively at the young protege. 'So, if I understand you correctly, nothing gets credited into the Willoughby account unless you make it happen, Sam. Is that right?'

'That's correct, sir.'

'And how often do these transfers take place?'

'There maybe the odd item that is transferred across during the year but, for the main part, items are transferred from the Strathdon account to the Willoughby account twice a year. Once on the 1st June and once on the last trading day before Christmas. I believe that is a tradition introduced by your grandfather, Norris Willoughby. "The Christmas Bloat", I think he called it. He thought it pleasing to see the Willoughby account balloon at that time of the year. Like a Christmas present to himself and the family I suppose. The new transfers and the account balance would then be announced at the family Christmas dinner, amidst a flourish and a fanfare. I don't know whether that still goes on, sir?'

'Well, to a degree I suppose it does, but to go back to the transfer of goods, Sam, just so I am completely clear. The last major transfer of cleansed funds would have gone through in June?' Sam nodded in confirmation. There followed a brief silence as Willoughby seemed momentarily consumed in his own thoughts.

'Sam,' he said, having reached a decision. 'I think we can forgo the Christmas transfer this year. Just put it on hold, at least for now. I would like to conduct a review, take stock of the whole process. Can you deal with that for me?'

'What? Are you serious, Mr Willoughby?' Sam exclaimed, unable to hide the concern in his voice.

'I think it would be prudent to just confirm that this is indeed the best way of organising ourselves going forward,' replied Willoughby. 'Not a big issue, Sam. Every now and then it is good business practice to take a fresh look at things. Lets just hold the funds in Strathdon for now if you will and please don't worry about Mr Cassidy, I will explain it all to him and I am sure he will concur with me. Best not mention it to him for now though, Sam, not until I have had a chance to catch up with him and talk him through my thinking.'

'But sir, it is not as simple as that,' said Sam, panicking. 'It takes months of planning and things are well underway. I really don't see how I can stop them, not at this late date. Besides, if we stop the transfer it would leave some considerable assets in the Strathdon account. I am not sure Mr Cassidy, as the sole signatory, would feel comfortable with that, what with the Homerton credit coming on board down the line. I'm afraid it might leave the account somewhat exposed, if you don't mind me saying, Mr Willoughby.'

'Your concerns are duly noted, but please carry out my instructions young man and let me worry about Mr Cassidy.' Willoughby raised his voice slightly, just enough to remind Sam that he was in charge of the Willoughby Estate and not Milton Cassidy. 'Just get it done, Sam. Is that understood?'

'Yes, Mr Willoughby.'

'And we keep this just between ourselves for now. Agreed?'

'Yes, sir. Agreed. I will start making arrangements this afternoon.'

\* \*

Meanwhile, across town, Harriet Blackwood was struggling to make sense of her circumstance.

Milton Cassidy had called the previous week to arrange a meeting at his office in Kensington to review some of the finer details of the forthcoming sale of the land at Homerton. Unexpected, but all straight forward enough. Then, at the last minute, without explanation, he changed the venue. So here they sat, in a corner of Scott's restaurant on Mount Street in Mayfair, having ordered their starters and mains from the delightful but expansive menu. Harriet stole a cautious glance across the table. The last time she had spoken to this imposing man was to reprimand him over the thuggish behaviour that was being extended to her boss, George Giltmore, the MP for Easton, and now here they were, dining at an opulent restaurant in an exclusive part of London. At first she thought it was just a tactical relocation following an over-booking at his office, later she decided the lunch served as an apology for their recent misunderstandings but now, she wasn't so sure and was beginning to fear the worst.

'That is a good, well-balanced selection, Harriet. May I call you Harriet?'

'Of course. Yes.'

'A nice blend of dishes. A ceviche to start. Brave,

refreshing, good protein. Followed by Goujons of Cornish Sole That's got a lovely sound to it, hasn't it. "Goujons of Cornish Sole". Makes you hungry just to say it, doesn't it?' Cassidy laughed, awkwardly. 'Yes, a good balance. Well done, Harriet, well done indeed.'

Harriet, not knowing quite how to respond, having never been praised for ordering food from a menu before, replied meekly, 'Thank you, Mr Cassidy. I'm sure your selection will be equally as enjoyable.'

'We can only hope so, Harriet, we can only hope so.'

A stilted silence settled between them. Cassidy looked back down at the menu, in the hope of finding another topic of conversation hidden within the embossed details of meat and fish. But nothing. A furrow appeared across his brow as he tried desperately to think of another suitable conversation starter. What on earth did people find to talk about? Such a ludicrous situation. A man and a woman, with no history and no knowledge of each other, suddenly plonked down in a restaurant and expected to conjure up hours of witty and articulate dialogue. About what for goodness sake? The longer the silence continued, the more irritated he became. He should have planned for this eventuality. That's what he should have done. After all, he would never enter a meeting without proper planning so why would he treat this . . . what was this anyway? . . . this . . . this date . . . any differently. It would not happen again. Next time he would make sure he was satisfactorily prepared for the occasion.

A faint ring emanated from Harriet's bag. Usually, when socialising, she would ignore the interruption and wait for voicemail to kick in, but today she dived into her handbag with the alacrity of a young child delving into their stocking on Christmas morning. She checked the screen and had pressed the answer button before the phone was up to her ear, looking apologetically across to her host.

'I'm so sorry, Mr Cassidy. I need to take this. It's the office.'

A relieved Cassidy waved an accepting hand towards her,

offering her some privacy by averting his eyes back down to the now familiar menu. On the other end of the line, Harriet's sister was finding the businesslike tone of her sibling somewhat disconcerting. Sure, she had only phoned up for a chat, and goodness knows the whole family knew how mightily important her high-flying sister was, but there was no need for this cold, distant tone. If she was busy she should just say so. She could always call back later.

'No! Don't go!' Harriet's voice pierced through the dignified hush of the lunchtime diners. A blush of embarrassment rose on her cheek before she continued her conversation at a more acceptable volume.

Cassidy continued to stare down at the menu. He was uncomfortable. Throughout his life he had learnt to be good at everything he did. His abilities had brought him wealth and power that would be the envy of most men. He could honestly say that there wasn't a situation that he did not feel master of and yet, when it came to women, he remained heavy-handed and gawkish. He did not have an earthly clue as to what was expected of him. It was as if the whole world had attended a seminar on male and female relationships that he had not been invited to. But, now that he had found a suitable mate he would have to be equal to the task if he was to secure the continuance of the Cassidy line. His eyes slowly rose from the comfort of the menu and he took the opportunity offered by Harriet's ongoing distraction invoked by her call, to consider his future partner. There was no denying that she had an outstanding brain. He had felt the brunt of that, first-hand, during their recent contretemps. A bit naive perhaps, but that was charming in its own way. Women were generally more trusting than men in his experience and it would be wrong to hold her to account for the general failings of her sex. A pleasant profile, bit of a snub nose, but any offspring would benefit from the counter-balance of his own distinguished Roman physiognomy. Teeth look strong, white. Hair, full, a pleasing shine. His eyes wandered down to the rest of her body, taking in her narrow waist, smooth arms and full bosom, couched within her silk blouse. He concentrated, trying to summon up some enthusiasm for the flesh on display, willing himself to feel a burgeoning sense of arousal. He could feel his body tense, but nothing stirred under his tightly drawn flies. Not even the slightest flicker. He tried to imagine Harriet naked. The firm flesh on her legs, rising to her rounded buttocks, split by the dark crevice between her cheeks, then round to the pubic mound of her pelvis and finally back up to those swollen breasts. Bulbous handfuls of fatty flesh, like tepid jelly to the touch, designed to satisfy the ravenous appetite of a suckling child until, a decade or so later, they succumb to the worthless droop of middle age. A shudder of nausea coursed through his body. His mouth curved into a sickened sneer of disgust, as he continued to stare down at Harriet's ample cleavage just as she was winding up her call and returning her attention back to her fellow diner.

'Can I help you, Mr Cassidy?' Harriet asked, abruptly. 'Is there something on my shirt?' she said, half-heartedly looking down at her chest. 'No, I thought not.'

She began to slide along the green leather seat, reaching for her bag as she did so, knowing that the time was right to make her escape. 'I'm so sorry, Mr Cassidy, but something has come up at the office that needs my urgent attention. I need to get back.' She waved across at one of the waiters, signalling that she needed her coat. 'Thank you for your time. Please let me know if there are any further queries. Email maybe best. Failing that, we shall press ahead and complete as soon as possible. Please don't get up. Have a good day, Mr Cassidy.' She had reached the exit, grabbing her coat from the waiter as she did so, before Cassidy had a chance to respond. Cassidy rose to his feet just as the waiter appeared next to the table.

'Ceviche, sir?'

\* \*

Willoughby looked out at Hyde Park from the back seat of his Bentley as he took the short trip from Kensington back to Pall Mall. The drizzling rain that had been falling tirelessly on the city for days had at last eased and the dog walkers and joggers of the metropolis were making the most of the change in weather, despite the chill breeze. A group of school children, wrapped in blazers and scarves, were being herded through Queens Gate Lodge towards the entrance of Kensington Palace, revelling in their release from classroom confinement. Willoughby's sallow eyes looked out onto the world with quiet satisfaction. It had been a good day's labour. He would call Marquand and let him know that he had followed his advice and uncoupled the Strathdon account from Willoughby Holdings, at least for now. He would leave Cassidy to find out about the change in due course, confident that he could rely on the discretion of the young Sam Wilson. By that time, matters may well have worked themselves out; the Homerton and Blyth projects would be complete and that tiresome Green woman would be securely housed in one her majesty's prisons. Let's hope so, he thought to himself, then business can resume and the family's financial arrangements can return to the status quo. In all honesty, his sister had been right when she had raised her concerns during the family gathering at Widford Hall. Things had all got a bit out of hand. Cassidy needed to address the outstanding issues and clear up this rotten mess once and for all. If not, then no more can be done for him. Willoughby sunk back into the creaking leather upholstery and rested his eyes. For the first time since becoming the Head of the Willoughby family in 1965, he contemplated a future without the steadying influence of Milton S Cassidy.

## CHAPTER 35

LOUISA Willoughby read the email for a second time as the hostess in the British Airways Concorde lounge at Heathrow, removed her nearly spent glass from the table.

'Could you leave that please?'

The hostess looked down and could see a small splash of tomato juice, barely covering the bottom of the glass. 'I'm sorry, Madam, I thought it was empty.'

'Well then, you were mistaken. Put it back,' corrected Louisa, not taking her eyes from the note she had received less than an hour ago.

The hostess did as she was instructed and then returned to her station in front of the display of exclusive wine and champagne at the side of the room, rolling her eyes with despair at her colleague, who was looking on sympathetically from behind the cream topped bar.

Herr Hartmann's name was familiar to her only though the cursory update provided by her brother regarding his doomed foray into Germany. As she understood it, Hartmann was the family's main contact in the new territory and was responsible for smoothing relationships with the German authorities and providing useful contacts. George Giltmore she knew only too well through the Homerton project. The last time she had seen him was on television, when he had delivered his cack-handed response to the BBC reporter, but she had also met Mr Giltmore face-to-face, at a charity evening where she had sat opposite him on the top table. At close quarters he had struck her as the sort of man best avoided. Partly because he was bereft of anything useful or interesting to say and partly because he had the table manners of a Saddleback hog. The MP for Easton was one of those gentlemen who treated every such occasion, no matter how refined or well intentioned, as nothing more than a glorious 'all you can eat' buffet. His capacity to lay waste all foods placed before him was, quite simply, breathtaking. As a consequence, Louisa Willoughby had not enjoyed her evening sitting across from Mr Giltmore at the Carlton Club, although it could have been worse. She could have been sat next to the corpulent oaf. Giltmore was a diner who liked to share, so while a large proportion of the benefactors feast made it's way down his soft gullet, a generous quantity was speckled on the silk and linen of those within his immediate vicinity.

The two gentlemen certainly struck Louisa as an unlikely pairing, but she now had it on good authority that they were seemingly in league with each other hatching an, as yet, ill defined plan. Her source had confirmed a meeting in the City, followed by the German half of the partnership undertaking a shopping trip involving the purchase of various items of surveillance equipment, some pliers and a large Böker hunting knife. His English counterpart had purchased nothing, but had returned to the office and cleared all appointments from his diary on Thursday, 22$^{nd}$ December. He had then fired off an email to Milton Cassidy.

*Mr Cassidy*

*Unfortunately, some issues have arisen regarding the*

*Homerton sale which will need to be addressed immediately if we are to achieve the agreed, pre-Christmas completion date. The issues, for the main, relate to the consecration concerns, as previously discussed. I do not believe the problems are insurmountable and I am currently preparing a draft version of an addendum that should help us reach a satisfactory resolution. This will need to be signed by the appropriate signatory from your office. That responsibility, I believe, is yours Mr Cassidy.*

*I suggest we meet at 4:00 p.m. Thursday 22nd December at the Edition Hotel, Berners Street, where I am attending a conference. I fly out to Switzerland for a family Christmas break that evening, so if you are unable to attend the date proposed then the transaction will have to be delayed until the new year.*

*Regards*

*George Giltmore*
*Member for Easton*

Louisa looked up towards the bar where a group of Italian businessmen had gathered, talking loudly and gesticulating with impassioned Mediterranean fervour. Once past her thirties, she had found all variants of male bonding and horseplay, whatever the dialect, increasingly tiresome, but she was wise enough to know that any rebuke or reprimand from the opposite sex would only be seen as provocation or, worse still, encouragement. She had spent the previous evening in a small boutique hotel just outside Brighton in the suffocating company of the Dray and felt she had had her fill of the needy inadequacies of man. She muttered an oath under her breath and returned to the matter in hand.

Could these two unlikely cohorts really be conspiring together? If so, to what end? Entrapment? Worse? Surveillance was one thing, but a hunting knife? All very melodramatic. If they were hoping to inflict some revenge on Mr Cassidy then, certainly from what she knew of the man, they would need more than a knife at their disposal and better manpower than a German businessman and a plump politician to constrain his muscular physique. The question was what to do about them? The most prudent option would be to nip it in the bud at the onset and protect the interests of the family and the physical well-being of Anthony's second in command. One word from her and the plans of the two conspirators would be subverted and then expunged, but Louisa was yet to issue the command. Even though their endeavours were certain to fail, she could not help but be enlivened by the prospect of her brother's loyal guardian being roughed-up by these erstwhile confederates. Who knows, maybe the German was more resourceful than she imagined. As a race, they rarely lacked guile and competitive grit. Maybe Hartmann would succeed and draw to a close Cassidy's tenure within the family. If that was to be the case, then it certainly was about time.

She rested her long fingers on the keys of her iPad for a moment and then typed:

*Monitor for now. Do not hinder. Inform me of progress.*

*LW*

## CHAPTER 36

THE air on the overcrowded train to Stoke Newington was thick with the smell of damp coats and bad breath. Lincoln had been lucky to get a seat and was now bolt upright, barely able to breathe, squeezed up against the window, which was dripping with syrupy condensation. He vaguely wondered what human form Transport for London had in mind when designing their seating. Someone of particularly narrow girth and with tiny legs seemingly, like an undernourished Victorian waif. Nevertheless, the absence of space did not faze the young woman next to him who was heroically attempting to make a call at the same time as reading her copy of Grazia, while drinking tea from an over full Starbucks cup. Each time the train juddered, which it did frequently, another slosh of her hot beverage slopped onto the floor, creating a steaming pool next to Lincoln's right shoe. The young woman remained unperturbed and continued her discussion with her partner about what they should eat that night. A lasagne from M&S with a stick of French bread appeared to be the current frontrunner.

They had parted company at Liverpool Street. Martha taking the tube to St James's Park where she would have just a short walk to New Scotland Yard in time for her ten o'clock hearing. She looked the part, dignified, self-assured and immaculately groomed, but they both knew that crisp tailoring and confident body language were no protection for what lay ahead. Lincoln could feel a slight tremor in her arms as he pulled her close and wished her good luck. She did not reply, but smiled and squeezed his hand and then made her way down the steps to the Circle line. He watched her disappear amongst the grey suited commuters, flowing en masse in a silent, one-paced procession to their places of work. She had explained the night before that today was just the preliminary hearing. A chance for the Directorate of Professional Standards to flex their muscles, clarify the charges and outline their preferred timescale for the oncoming proceedings. Martha was certain that, in light of the weight of evidence against her, they would be pushing for an accelerated process meaning that she could be called back for the full hearing as early as the first week of January. If found guilty by the internal panel, then criminal proceedings would follow. Lincoln knew that it wasn't just the disciplinary process and the accompanying threat of a prison sentence that concerned Martha, it was also the vile ignominy, the shameful disgrace of being publicly judged and condemned by her peers and seniors. She didn't say as much, but he got the impression that her contact at the Met would be present at the hearing and the thought of him being walked through allegation after allegation, no matter that they were false, weighed heavily on her mind. They planned to meet up again at Twickenham in the evening to review the day and seek solace in a bottle of wine or something stronger, depending on the outcome. In the meantime, Lincoln was intending to see what he could find out about the mysterious Edmund Buller, once he had managed to catch up with an old friend.

He had still not managed to talk to Sarah, despite having left numerous messages on her voicemail and on her home ansaphone. According to the address Tariq Shad had given him, her new office was in Clissold Building, at Shelford Place, near the centre of Stoke Newington. The outside of the premises was not immediately endearing. The building was split over three floors. On the ground floor, two large wheelie bins were housed near the entrance, a third was lying horizontally on the pavement, like a soldier passed out on parade. The spilt rubbish from the bin was scuttling around the front of the building, being tugged this way and that by the sharp wind that blew along the narrow cul-de-sac. The council must have recently completed a half-hearted attempt at removing some graffiti that had been scrawled onto the adjoining wall, next to the entrance. The words were faded, but were visible enough to remain a meaningless, multicoloured eyesore. Lincoln looked up to the third floor, towards Sarah's office. The two windows at the top of the building were the only ones with the blinds still drawn.

Next to the office door, at the top of the stairs, was a name plate with the words Luminosity Enterprises stencilled onto it. He leaned towards the open door to listen for any activity within. There was none. He gently pushed the door wider onto a small and fairly pointless lobby which housed a solitary rubber plant and a water cooler. The plant was leaning towards the window on the far wall, pining for a warmer climate in a humid land many miles away from the grey skied north London suburb in which it had found itself so cruelly anchored. Three coat hooks were screwed onto the wall next to the door. Two were empty. The third was straining under the weight of a thick, winter coat. The expensive, dark brown wool was further distinguished by some delicate, gold stitching and a fur trimming that ran around the hood and then down the front of the coat. Try as it might, the trimming could not hide the electric green lining that stirred menacingly beneath. He knocked on the closed door next to the coat hooks.

'Hi Sarah? Can I come in?'

There was no reply. He knocked again.

'Sarah. It's me. Lincoln.' Once again, no reply. He waited an instant, then cautiously pushed open the door. It took a moment or two for his eyes to adjust to the muddied light. The only illumination was that bouncing off the laptop screen resting on the desk in front of the television production company Chief Executive as she watched an early morning cookery show on ITV. Sarah remained motionless, her eyes fixed on the screen. A half empty bag of Quavers lay scrunched up next to the laptop, alongside an unopened can of Lilt. A dozen screwed up tissues littered the floor around her chair. Her hair was pushed back under a black band, partly concealing the pair of white earphone leads that were draped down her neck. Lincoln edged forward, creeping apologetically into her eye-line, waving a conciliatory hand.

'Hi Sarah. Sorry. I did knock.'

Sarah's exhausted gaze swung slowly towards the moving shape in the room, her TV addled brain gradually decoding the large, animate object, awkwardly waving its hand in her direction. It took a moment before things suddenly fell into place and then, realising she was no longer alone in her office, she let out a short high-pitched squeal before, inexplicably, grabbing the can of Lilt, opening it and bolting down two large gulps.

'I'm sorry, Sarah. I didn't mean to frighten you,' he said, his palms raised apologetically. 'Are you okay?'

Sarah stared back at him, bug-eyed, speechless, unable to compose herself. A sticky drool of Lilt seeping from the side of her mouth.

'Tell you what, maybe I should put on the lights? Is that alright with you?' He flicked on the switch, the vicious, fluorescent beams snapping Sarah out of her embarrassed, puzzled malaise.

'What the hell are you doing here?' she bellowed, pushing herself away from her desk and shielding her eyes melodramatically with her arm. 'And turn those lights off.'

'But it's pitch black in here for God's sake, Sarah. You can't sit in darkness all day.'

Sarah kept her eyes covered and waved her hand to the right of the desk, pointing to a small round table in the corner. 'Put the lamp on, the lamp, the one over there.'

Once Lincoln had corrected the lighting to Sarah's satisfaction, she slowly lowered her hand, peering over the top of her arm as if to check that it was really him.

'That Tariq,' she snarled. 'He could never keep his mouth shut. I told him, I said I wanted to be left alone, just until I got things back on track, but old blabbermouth couldn't help himself could he.'

'Don't blame Tariq, Sarah. Poor chap. I made him tell me.' He pointed down at the laptop, grinning playfully. 'Besides, it doesn't look like you are doing a great job of sorting things out. Anything tasty on today's show? A nice risotto or beefy cassoulet? Or how about a palate cleansing peach sorbet?'

Sarah slammed the laptop shut. 'Don't take the mickey, Lincoln. I was just recharging the batteries. It has been a bit of a harum-scarum morning, to be honest. The phone just has not stopped. You know what it's like sometimes. We've got some good new shows in the pipeline, as it happens. To be truthful, it has probably been a bit of a blessing, all this business over the last few months. Bit messy sure, but it's given us a chance to regroup, get some new talent in, blow away some of the cobwebs. No offence, Lincoln, but Castle Eden is all a bit old school, not very now, a bit stale for the new us. Sometimes you need to throw out the baggage before you can really start going places. You know, move on as it were.' She started looking for her pen amongst the detritus cluttering up her desk, but came up empty handed so reached for her mobile instead. 'Sorry Lincoln, is there anything I can help you with, as I really do need to get on?'

Lincoln looked puzzled. He knew this was just her pride talking, but he made no comment, not wanting to embarrass her still further. 'Tariq seemed to think the company was still in a bit of a spot. Things not going too well.'

'Really? No, quite the opposite in fact. You know what

Tariq is like,' she said dismissively. 'Glass half empty and all that. No, no, it is all coming together very nicely and don't you worry about your payment, Lincoln. I will chase that up with Tariq and get that over to you just as soon as things settle down, you have my word. I can't have you out of pocket, not now you're moving on.' She picked up her notebook and started flicking through the blank pages as if urgently searching for something. 'I don't mean to be rude, Lincoln, but if you've just come here to gloat or chase down your money there really was no need. Lovely to see you, but now I really *must* get on. I have a conference call scheduled at eleven o'clock, so please, if you don't mind,' she said, pointing towards the door and raising her phone to her ear. 'Lets do lunch sometime when you are in town, perhaps when you have settled into your new production company or whenever suits. I would so hate to lose touch.'

He nodded his head and made as if to leave. 'Sure, I can see you're busy so lets get some time together after Christmas when you have less on, but before I go and just so I am clear, you want me to take Castle Eden to another company?'

Sarah put the phone down and leaned back in her chair, trying her best to look the polished, world-weary executive. She let out an impatient sigh. 'Look, Lincoln, my sweet, we go back a long way, but you must do as you see fit, of course you must. I'm just saying, I understand, sweetie, it's okay. Maybe it's the right time for all of us to move on, you know, for both of us.'

'So you want me to leave Luminosity?'

'Come on, Lincoln. Lets not fall out You want to go your way and I want to go mine. Lets be grown up about this. I respect your decision, so lets try and keep things amicable. We had a good run together and now it's over and that's fine. No problem. Good luck to you, but, Lincoln . . . please . . . sweetie,' she pleaded, pointing to the phone and pad as if to illustrate the extraordinary amount of work she had to contend with.

'What decision?'

Sarah had started dabbing numbers into her mobile. 'You know, your decision to take Castle Eden away to a new production company,' she said disinterestedly.

'When did I make that decision? You are going to have to remind me.'

She carried on tapping in the phone number, which seemed to be of an extraordinarily prodigious length. 'When we didn't pay you . . . twice . . . and when I lied about the Ralph and Hugh thingy . . . and the Americans . . . to Tariq. . . and to you . . . and when we went, sort of . . . bust.'

'I suppose when you put it like that, leaving does sound like the sensible thing to do, but, Sarah . . . *Sarah*. Put that phone down. Where are you calling? Timbuktu?' She looked up, startled at his raised voice, her large round eyes suddenly full of fear and hurt. 'Sarah, we're a team. I'm nothing without you. I'm not going anywhere.'

*

There were tears. Big dollops of tears. Pendulous and heavy. And smiles. Broad, radiant and full of love. And hugs. Short hugs. Long hugs. Lincoln's shirt was wet from Sarah's tear-stained hugs. Just so many tears. It didn't take much for the truth to come out. It exploded from her, like a geyser. The sadness. The pain. The guilt. The day that she had to inform her staff, "my babies", that they had no jobs to return to; locking up the offices for the last time and giving the landlord back his keys; the endless lectures from Tariq but then his unstinting, unquestioning help and support; her colleagues in the industry deserting her, refusing to take her calls or meet for lunch, wanting nothing to do with her; her clients demanding their scripts back and running, literally running, for the door.

'It was awful, Lincoln, awful. I couldn't sleep, I started over-eating, well, you can see that, and the drinking, my God, so much drinking. Anything would do - champagne, wine, whiskey, anything. At least until Tariq put a stop to that.

Then sitting here in this shitty office, day after day, hour after hour, minute after minute. In this never-ending, punishing silence. No calls. No visits. Nothing. People are cruel Lincoln, so needlessly and spitefully cruel.'

Then more tears. Then more smiles. Then more hugs. And then it was over.

Lincoln asked if he could use some of her office space to do some work while he was there. Sarah insisted that he use her desk, logging him into her Mac, and setting herself up in the small, secondary office next door. She was a little peeved when he explained that he was just doing some research and not working on a new Castle Eden episode, but she was still so elated following their recent reunion that she chose not to mention her disappointment. Once she had checked that he didn't need a drink and that the lights were okay and the air conditioning was not too cold and the chair was at the right height, and the air conditioning was not too warm, she finally left him to it, returning an hour later with a cup of unasked for tea and a small, chocolate cup cake.

'You must try this, Lincoln. There is a small bakery on the high street, completely the wrong location, but sells the best cakes and pastries. I was eating a sack full a day when, you know, things were not going well. Simply divine, my sweet, expensive but delicious. Try, go on, try.' Lincoln picked up the cake from the small paper plate in front of him.

'See. I told you. Yummy aren't they?' she said, looking expectantly at Lincoln who was obediently chewing the moist, dark chocolate offering. 'Anyway, enough of that. Back to work, Lincoln. Can you take a look at this, my sweet.' She pulled away the plate and laid a sheet of A4 in front of him on the desk. 'It's just a short press release, announcing our continued partnership, just so everybody knows. I would love to see the faces of some of the witches that blanked me when things all went wrong, you know, when they read this and see that we are back in business. I shall make them suffer. Cold, vile, evil creatures.'

Lincoln, ignoring Sarah's maniacal ramblings, finished

reading the note. 'It says you will be "utilising the Luminosity Talent Fund to invest in new, young writers, in support of fledgling projects". Out of interest, how much do you have in the "Talent Fund"?

Sarah looked down at the plate, speckled with dark brown crumbs. 'To be honest, our celebration cake put a sizeable dent into it, but it will all be fine now, now I have Lincoln Marsh back on board. The offers will soon start flowing back in. Anyway, the press release? Okay?'

'Yes, fine,' he said, handing it back to her. 'You certainly seem to have been more productive than me. I'm getting nowhere. This man Edmund Buller seems to have been a ghost. I can find nothing on him.'

'Yes, he is a bit elusive isn't he,' she said, moving round to his side of the desk and peering at the almost blank page of notes in front of him. 'I did have a little look myself, just out of interest. I managed to find the odd bit.' Sarah flicked over the page of her notepad, revealing a jumble of facts, nearly filling the whole sheet. 'He's a real charmer isn't he,' she said, sarcastically.

Lincoln could not hide the surprise in his voice. 'Where on earth did you get all that? I've been looking for an hour and couldn't find a thing.'

'Sweetie, you forget, I started in legals, looking at copyright and stuff, you know, verifying stories, making sure we were not going to get sued. Do that long enough and you get pretty good at finding out about dead people, believe me.' She lay the notepad onto the desk. 'Do you want to have a shifty at what I've found?'

'Uh, yes please,' replied Lincoln.

'Right, well all pretty hard to find, but this chap, Edmund Buller, was born in 1918 to a Jeremiah and Hattie Buller, and died in 1967, aged 49. According to his death certificate, he died near Edinburgh of a heart attack, but was buried in a village called Widford, down in Hertfordshire. I looked at the military database, nothing there, although I did find the record of the father, Jeremiah Buller. He was shot on the very last day of the First World War, unlucky so-and-so, which, ironically, was also the day his son was born. Jeremiah, Buller senior, had originally been a blacksmith, or, to be completely accurate, a striker, the person who swings the sledgehammer - so I would imagine he was pretty well built, pretty solid. At some point in his early twenties, he seems to have moved down to Hertfordshire from where he was born in Chorley, Lancashire. Between 1875 and 1888, he committed a load of crimes, petty theft, assault, a bit of poaching, that kind of thing. All pretty unsavoury. Then, from 1889, it all goes quiet. Absolutely nothing, right up until his death in 1918.'

'What about the son, Edmund?'

'His record is even more sketchy. I have his birth certificate and death certificate. His name is on a number of property purchases and sales, although he didn't seem to have a fixed address himself. His name also pops up on a companies house search engine, but the companies he was involved in have all long gone or at least I can't track them down. There is no record of him receiving treatment on the NHS, or owning a car. I can't even find a national insurance number. The only thing I did find was the name of the people who paid for his body to be transported down from Scotland to Hertfordshire. I looked up Widford funeral directors. There were only two of any note: J. H. Turner and Sons and Wexford Family Arrangements. The Buller funeral was handled by Wexford's. According to their accounts, the total funeral costs, including the transport of the body was paid for by Willoughby Holdings Ltd. I don't know if that means anything to you.'

Lincoln nodded, 'I think I've heard the name.'

'Apart from that nothing, as I say. No wife. No children. Nothing.'

'No children? Are you sure about that?'

'Pretty sure. Well, as sure as I can be. I could keep searching, but I can't find a birth certificate listing your man as the father.'

Lincoln remembered Great Aunt Catherine's story. The baby wouldn't be registered anywhere, under any name as it had been treated as a stillbirth. The child then taken from the hospital by Buller, in secret.

'What happens if there is a child, but for whatever reason, no birth certificate was issued? Can you still track them down?'

'No birth certificate? Well, that would make things difficult. I would need to do a search for every person called Buller alive between 1918 and 1967 and then see if I can find a link between them and Edmund or Jeremiah Buller.' She winced. 'That would be a big job. We could be lucky and stumble across them early or, more likely, it would take days, weeks of painstaking research and cross referencing. What's all this for, Lincoln? A new episode?'

'A new episode? Sort of, yes, just background. Something to get me started.'

'Sounds nifty. I'll keep looking, but I can't promise anything.' She looked down at the empty plate. 'I've worked up quite an appetite after all that. Don't suppose you fancy coming with me to the high street to help me invest a bit more of that Talent Fund do you?'

# CHAPTER 37

LINCOLN poured another glass of the light and uncomplicated bottle of white wine he had opened when Martha had arrived at his Twickenham flat. The choice of simple grape an indication that the hearing had gone as well as could have been hoped for earlier in the day. The team from the Directorate of Professional Standards had been typically belligerent and intimidating in laying bare the accusations of drug abuse, illicit sex and police corruption before the members of the Police Complaints Commission. The DPS team was led by an unpleasant individual named Inspector Martin Cruickshank, who had taken a particular delight in recounting the various sexual indiscretions Martha had been accused of, lingering on some of the more lurid details and, where photographic evidence was lacking, providing a precise and compelling commentary. In his summary, Cruickshank made it abundantly clear that it was the view of the DPS that public interest was best served by a quick and decisive response to these heinous crimes and the PCC should do all in its power to cut out "this weeping tumour of corruption at its root". Therefore, it was proposed to bring the hearing forward to the first week of January.

The Commission was chaired on this occasion by Deputy Assistant Commissioner Virginia Coulton. A formidable woman, now in her early fifties, who had made her name as a reformer and champion for diversity within the force. Her period of tenure on the Commission had seen her embroiled in some of the most high profile police corruption cases of recent years. She held no quarter when it came to sentencing and had gained a reputation for issuing some of the most stringent and far reaching punishments ever given to members of the Metropolitan constabulary. At the conclusion of Martin Cruickshank's terse summary and accompanying call to action, Virginia Coulton addressed the rest of the panel.

'I am sure we are all grateful to Inspector Cruickshank for providing us with such a detailed overview of the case and, taking into account the strength and depth of evidence presented as well as the torrid nature of the accusations involved, the Chair is minded to agree with the recommendation of the DPS for an early hearing. This would seem apposite under the circumstances, but I am willing to hear any opposing views from the panel if they be forthcoming.'

Two members of the three-man panel, Chief Superintendent Sheila Brough and Superintendent Philip Hardwick, gave a cursory glance at each other and then nodded in unison toward the Chair, indicating their agreement. The third Commission member looked down at the bundle of papers that had been presented to him by the DPS, frowning and gently rubbing his chin.

'Chief Superintendent McSty? Are you in accordance with the rest of the panel?' asked Virginia Coulton with a poorly disguised trace of impatience in her voice.

McSty scratched the bald crown of his head before glancing first at his fellow panel members with a look of disappointment and then turning his attention to Chairperson Coulton.

'I am afraid not, Madam Chair. No. I am not in accordance with my colleagues or indeed yourself.' Towards the back of the room there was a slight rustle as the two members of Human Resources who were in attendance to take notes and advise as appropriate, sensed some intrigue and, eyes peeled, leaned forward ever so slightly in their chairs so as not to miss any of the words spoken by the esteemed members of the Commission.

'And why is that, Chief Superintendent McSty?' asked Coulton, in a voice clearly indicating that his opposition was unwelcome but not unexpected. 'What is it that you are seeing that is beyond the understanding and wit of your peers?' She turned towards the back pages of her pack. 'She is one of yours I believe, this Green. One of your fast tracked proteges we are all hearing so much about. Isn't that right?'

Chief Superintendent McSty bristled both at the inference of favouritism and the side swipe at the development programme he had championed and become associated with over recent years.

'Yes, Detective Sergeant Martha Green did successfully complete the Accelerated Management Programme, but I do not believe that makes her 'one of mine' as you put it Deputy Assistant Commissioner, it just makes her an outstanding and valuable officer. A fact that seems to have escaped the notice of the DPS in their summary.'

'I am sure the DPS and your colleagues on the panel are only too aware of Green's career to date,' replied Coulton. 'But I'm afraid what she has achieved in the past is irrelevant and holds no sway on today's proceedings. A spotless record does not make an officer immune from corruption as, to my disappointment, I have witnessed in the many similar cases I have been asked to preside over in recent years.'

'Point taken, Ma'am, but, with respect, we are not trying previous cases. We are trying Detective Sergeant Martha Green, a loyal and brave member of the Metropolitan Police Force whose industriousness and sound policing has rid our streets of a large number of villains and helped make the community she works within a better, safer place. I do not seek special circumstances for Martha, that is not my intention, but I do insist she is treated in a fashion appropriate for one who has served the public so valiantly.' He turned his gaze towards the leader of the DPS team who was staring distractedly at the floor, a thinly veiled look of contempt on his face. 'I'm afraid I find the rabid hunger for prosecution, exhibited by Inspector Cruickshank and his team, quite frankly, beneath contempt. I would urge him in future to abandon his abeyance to red-top investigative practices so we can consider the unequivocal facts of this case rather than the regurgitated tabloid gossip and satellite news channel dross he has presented to us this morning.' Cruickshank turned, red-faced, to his colleagues, forcing out a supercilious chuckle to mask his discomfort.

McSty's gaze moved back towards the top of the room, where the Deputy Assistant Commissioner sat. 'If Ma'am, Detective Sergeant Green is guilty then no doubt, under your stewardship, this Commission will issue appropriate punitive measures, but to push this case through at double the speed recommended by our very own code of practice for the sake of securing an eye-grabbing headline or some career boosting notoriety would be extremely lamentable and I will use all means at my disposal to oppose this move.' He turned slightly to the right to include his colleagues seated next to him. 'We are seen as the leaders of this force and we must accept the responsibilities that go along with that title. Our intention must be to treat our people, our teams, with the respect, the decency, the fairness that they deserve. Every one of them, including Detective Sergeant Martha Green.'

'What did you do while all this was going on?' asked Lincoln.

'What could I do? I just sat there, straight faced, trying not to laugh out loud or run around the Commission doing high fives. It was crazy.'

'It must have been difficult for that Coulton woman to tolerate? Being admonished by her junior.'

'To be fair, she handled it well. I think she realised that it was a mistake to break the code of practice and bring the case forward. She thanked Colin in the end and gave Cruickshank a bit of an earful when he started protesting about the reversal. It was all a bit surreal. But, you know, nothing has really changed, it just means I have bought myself an extra month at most. Apart from that, I'm still in the exact same place.'

Martha tipped her wine slightly on its side, watching the golden liquid cling to the side of the glass. They were both quiet as they accepted the sobering truth of her situation. A couple of minutes had passed before Lincoln broke the silence.

'Look, I do not mean to pry, but this McSty, that's your contact right? The guy you have been talking to at the Met, the one who has been helping you out now and again. You don't have to tell me if you don't want, but it is him isn't it?'

She raised her eyes, a slightly sheepish look on her face. 'Yes. It's him but you cannot tell anybody. He would kill me if he knew I had told you. He could lose his job, everything.'

'Who am I going to tell for God's sake? Your secret's safe. So, did you talk to him about it all?'

'Yes. I went to his office afterwards. Only for a few minutes. It didn't seem inappropriate. He was my boss once after all and I wanted to thank him for sticking up for me and everything he said during the hearing.'

'That go alright?'

'Yeah, fine. He's a good man, you know, decent and kind. I sometimes think I don't deserve the faith he shows in me.' She looked away, towards the window. Outside the sky was its normal metropolitan half-light, as the soft orange glow of the street lamps bled through the darkness. Lincoln thought he could see a vague hint of a tear in Martha's eye. 'I always feel like I'm going to let him down somehow.'

'You won't let him down, Martha. You won't let anybody down.' He touched her hand across the table. 'Did he have any advice for you? Any help?'

'He's still looking at Strathdon, but not finding much.

Seems like he should get your Sarah on the job from what you've told me. She might have more luck. He was interested in the Bone Room at Blyth, but there is no chance of us getting a warrant or a search there. He says he would need a human bone as proof, but I knew that any way. I told him about my meeting with Willoughby at his club. He thought that was good. Thinks we should keep piling on the pressure, but apart from that, not much else. He wants me to keep in touch and let him know what else we find out and then he just told me again that he believed in me and reminded me that this is what cases are like sometimes. They drift, untethered, rolling nowhere. But it only takes one signal or one gust of wind, to get things back on track. I've been here before, I know what this is like. I remember the first assault case I was ever in charge of. A woman hit from behind. I had nothing, absolutely nothing to go on, but then suddenly, due to a some ridiculous fluke, we got him. It all happened so fast. Nothing, then bam, he was locked up.'

'What happened?' asked Lincoln.

'Oh, it was daft. He hit this woman, well young girl really, over the head when she was walking home. No witnesses. No cameras. Nothing. He emptied out her bag, stole her purse and took her cash, leaving her credit cards, obviously not wanting to risk them being traced. The weeks went by and we were getting nowhere. Then, out of the blue, a constable gets called to the local cinema where some bloke has tried to get in using one of those monthly passes you can get. He thought he would just wave it at the attendant and then wander in to watch a movie, one of those Fast and Furious films I think it was. Anyway, the attendant, new in her job, checked the photo on the back, saw the picture of a woman not a man, and refused entry, calling her supervisor. The bloke, realising he'd made a mistake starts kicking off and a little while later the police are called and there we are. We check the name on the card, see it belongs to the assaulted girl and he's locked away by nightfall. Nothing to do with 'sound policing' or whatever Colin called it. Just luck.

Completely out of nowhere.'

'So, you never know.'

'Nope. You just never know. When the going gets tough, keep going. Something will turn up.'

Lincoln picked up his glass and walked over to the sink. 'I think I'm going to switch to red. Then, do you want to go back over the stuff that Sarah came up with?'

'Mmm, we could do I suppose but you know what, lets not. Just for once I want to switch off. Just tonight. Let's go out to dinner, Lincoln. Somewhere nice, my treat. Lets just have a great night. You and me. What do you think?'

This all caught Lincoln a bit by surprise to be honest. He was just reaching for the wet glass on the draining board so he could give it a quick wipe with a cloth when Martha made her suggestion. So keen was he to accept that he spun round, knocking the wine glass as he did so, sending it tumbling to the wooden floor of the kitchen. At the same time there was a ring of the doorbell.

'Damn. Sorry Martha, would you mind getting that while I clear this up.'

'Sure, no problem,' she said, smiling, and springing up from her seat. 'Just try and not break anything else while I'm gone.'

'I'll try not to, but I can't promise anything.'

Lincoln was bent under the counter, sweeping out the last fragments of glass when Martha returned.

'Lincoln, you've got a visitor.'

He looked up to see his brother walking purposefully across the floor towards him. A look of impatient anger on his face.

## CHAPTER 38

'WE need to talk.'

Lincoln could feel his body instinctively tense. His fists clenched on the wooden breakfast bar that separated the two brothers.

'What do you want, Ben?' he asked, aggressively.

'Just to talk, okay. I need to ask you something.'

'Okay then, fire away. Say what you have got to say and then go. I don't have time for this crap.'

Ben glanced briefly at Martha. 'Can we talk alone?'

Martha made to leave, but Lincoln called her back. 'Stay Martha. This is not going to take long, believe me. Whatever he's got to say, he can say in front of you. Now what is it, Ben? What do you want?'

Ben stared at his brother. His eyes, cold and resentful. His tone, brittle and distant. 'Fine. Whatever, Lincoln.' He moved towards the breakfast bar causing Lincoln to flinch.

'Just say it and go, Ben. I mean it.'

Ben put up his hands. 'I'm not looking for a fight, right, I just . . . I just need some money.'

'What?'

'I need some money okay? About £20,000.'

'What? £20,000? What the hell are you on about?'

'I need some money, that's all. It's not complicated. The way I figure it, if you hadn't pissed about with the house, delaying everything, then the sale would have gone through and I wouldn't be talking to you about this. It's your fault. The whole mess. You should have done what I asked you to do in the first place. If you'd done that, then things would have been fine, but you kept putting things off.'

'No, hang on. Go back a bit. You need some money? You, Ben Marsh, need some money. From me? £20,000? From me? Why would *you* need money from *me*? You're loaded. You may be a prick but you've always been a rich prick. Get your own money, Ben. Leave me out of it. What do you need £20,000 for anyway, for fuck's sake?'

'It doesn't matter what I need it for. A lot of my cash is tied up. I can't get at it. That's all.'

'So, sell one of your cars or one of Astrid's horses or sell that house of yours.'

'I can't sell the house. Look, it's your fault, all this. You should have done what I asked, instead of pissing about. You lost the fucking sale Lincoln, not me. So now you need to put things right. I need some money and you're going to give it to me, at least until the cottage sells. Christ Lincoln, even you must have £20,000.'

'Whether I've got the money or not doesn't matter. Why would I give it to you, just so you can buy into some deal you've caught a sniff of. I presume that's it right? One of your sleazy trader pals has put some dead cert your way and you want a bit of the action. Get a quick markup. Is that it? Am I right? Is that why you've come crawling round her? For a deal? Tell you what, you've got some front, I'll give you that. After what you did. Or have you forgotten what happened last time you were here?'

'I didn't come round here for another argument, Lincoln. Are you going to give me the money or not?

'What's it for?'

'It doesn't matter what it's for?'

'Tell me what it's for and I will see what I can do. So, what's it for?'

'I don't have to tell you why I need it. Are you going to help me or not?

Lincoln met his brother's gaze, looking deep into his eyes. His brother blinked and looked away. Lincoln grinned back at him. 'I knew it. I fucking knew it. It's a deal. That's what it is, isn't it? It's one of your grubby financial deals.' He leaned over the bar, towards his brother. 'No, Ben, I'm not giving you the money. Understand? You will have to get your pocket money elsewhere. Get one of your city buddies to finance you or miss out. Either way, you're not getting anything from me.'

Martha watched as the two brothers stared at each other. Locked in an icy, menacing silence. The only sound, the faint dripping of the tap that Lincoln had neglected to turn off properly after washing his glass. Eventually, Ben took a deep breath and turned away from his brother, brushing past Martha aggressively as he made to leave. When he reached the door, he stopped, his hand resting on the door latch. 'I really need this, Lincoln. I wouldn't ask otherwise.'

Lincoln looked at the back of his brother's head. He couldn't help enjoying the moment after the shit Ben had put him through over the last few weeks.

'Really? Is that right? Tell you what, if you really need the money then do what normal people do, you know, in the real world. Sell something. Remortgage the house or better still, sell the bloody house. There's a few million quid right there.'

'I said, I can't sell the house. She won't let me.'

'I'm sorry? What did you say? She won't let you? Who won't let you?'

Ben remained at the door, his back to Lincoln. He was speaking softly now, defeated by his brother's stubbornness. 'Astrid. Astrid won't let me. Otherwise I would have sold it a long time ago.'

Lincoln, let out a laugh, his hands now resting on his hips. 'Ha! You have got to be kidding me. This coming from you? You, of all people. You, the one who has been berating me for weeks for being too sentimental and too indecisive. You, the one who has marched into my flat and spent the last ten minutes slagging me off for not sorting things out and supposedly losing the sale. And all the time, you're just as bad. You won't sell your house because your wife won't let you and you don't want to upset her. Oh bless. You're a joke, Ben, you really are.'

Martha was standing to the right of the door watching the brothers argue. She could hear Lincoln continue with his taunting, but she was watching Ben. He was still turned towards the door, but from where she was standing, she could just make out the side of his face.

'Lincoln,' she said, trying to interrupt him.

'Aren't you the one who is always slagging me off for not sorting stuff out,' Lincoln continued. 'And all the time, you daren't do anything without permission from your wife. The lovely Astrid. God knows what your city boys would think of that. The big, brave CEO can't even sort out his own finances.'

'Lincoln.' she said, louder.

'The great Benjamin Marsh. Can't even handle a house sale. Instead has to come crawling to his brother for some spending money. It's fucking hysterical. I didn't think I . . . '

'Lincoln. Shut the fuck up.' Martha screamed. Her voice stopping him dead in his tracks. He turned towards her, mid sentence, the remnant of a cruel grin still on his face.

'What? What is it?' Lincoln asked, irritated and confused,

'Your brother,' she said, pointing, 'something is wrong with your brother.'

Martha had been watching Ben, frozen at the doorway. All the aggression, the anger, the fight had slowly drained from him, leaving nothing in its place. His two-day old beard was scraped across his bloodless cheeks. His hair, greased back, unwashed. His lips moving slightly, as if he were muttering to himself. His eyes empty, looking down, fixed to the floor.

Lincoln edged round the breakfast bar, moving slowly towards his brother who remained motionless, his hand still on the door.

'Ben? What's going on? What are you doing?' He thought he heard his brother whisper something. He moved closer. 'What's that? I can't hear. Speak up Ben? Do you want something?'

'It sounded like 'fahrenheit',' Martha said, bending towards him, her ears straining to hear what he was saying. 'Or 'fork and hammer'? Something like that.'

Lincoln could see his brother's face now. He could see his worn and tired features. The thin traces of wrinkles around his eyes. His lips were hardly moving, just making gentle repeated shapes, mouthing out a word over and over again. His voice was so quiet it was barely audible. Lincoln bent his head, close, next to his brother and listened.

'Folkhemmet. He's saying Folkhemmet. It's the name of his house, in Sweden.' He put one hand cautiously on his brother's shoulder and placed the other on the hand still resting on the door and then gently turned him round so they were facing each other. 'What is it, Ben? What's happened? Has something happened to your house? Are you and Astrid okay? What is it, mate?'

Lincoln gently placed his fingers under his brother's chin, raising it so he could see his face. Their eyes locked. Both the same shade of dark, muddy green they had inherited from their mother. There was a moment of recognition. A sudden remembrance of the shared childhood, the history between them, the bonds that tied them.

'I don't know what to do any more, Lincoln. I can't let her go. I just can't let her go.'

'Can't let who go, Ben? Is it Astrid? Is Astrid leaving you?'

Ben looked back, an age of sadness in his eyes. 'My Astrid. My engelchen.' His eyes dropped to the floor once more. 'She's dying, Lincoln. My Astrid is dying.'

## CHAPTER 39

BEN didn't need the money after all.

Not all of it anyway. Just enough to pay the hospice where Astrid had been staying, on and off, over recent months. The rest of the money had been for one last ditch attempt at finding a cure or at least slowing her decline, but that was no longer required. Astrid died two days after Ben had visited Lincoln at his Twickenham flat. When the end came, it came quickly. They were together when it happened, so that was some small comfort for Ben, although the coma Astrid had slipped into the night before meant she was not aware he had made it back from England in time to say goodbye.

The Swedish custom is to wait for two or three weeks before burying the body, but Lincoln had persuaded the church and authorities to circumvent the traditional timeline. He knew his brother wanted to lay Astrid to rest as soon as he could. 'No fuss', she had told him 'just tuck me up and let me sleep.' Her mother and father, who looked surprisingly conservative parents for a child with such a creative force burning within her, arrived from Bavaria on the morning of the funeral. Small in stature, wizened with age and crushed by grief. They clung onto Ben at the graveside, like shipwrecked sailors, fallen into the sea, hanging onto the solitary piece of driftwood that would save them from submerging into the cold depths of the vast ocean. At the end of the service, all three joined hands and stepped hesitantly towards the grave. Each laying one solitary flower on the coffin as it was lowered into the ground. Sankt Clemens church was on the bank of Lake Delsjön, directly opposite Folkhemmet, Ben and Astrid's home, on the other side of the lake. It had been some comfort, when they had become more accustomed to the inevitability of her death, that she would be laid to rest so close to the house she had loved, 'and where I can keep an eye on you and make sure you are not moping about, depressing everyone.'

The money that used to sit untouched and in crisp and bountiful piles in Ben's multiple bank accounts, was all gone. Spent on specialists in London, New York, Paris and Berlin. All to no avail. The Corticobasal Degeneration, or CBD, had relentlessly and progressively worsened. The spaced out look in Astrid's eyes, which Lincoln had dismissed as artistic otherworldliness when they had met some time ago at Sorrel Cottage, was the result of heavy sedation and ongoing cognitive dysfunction. His brother's urgency in leaving the house that day in such a brusk manner, wasn't rudeness or ill manners, but a desire to get his wife home and in bed where she could rest, following yet another failed consultation, this time in Harley Street.

Ben had managed to get through the service without breaking down. He looked frail and alone, standing in the stone alcove of the church in front of the small congregation of close friends and loved ones. His voice had broken only once when he read the words of Jørn, Astrid's favourite Swedish poet.

*You will hear me call, as the snow falls onto the storming sea*
*Your will hear me call, from where the Grey Wolf howls alone*
*You will hear me call, from the mossed granite beneath your feet*
*You will hear me call, calling you to be strong*

*You will hear me call, crying beneath the Graylag's bending wing*
*You will hear me call, when the night sky is cold and long*
*You will hear me call, when the Corncrake beckons in the spring*
*You will hear me call, calling you to carry on*

*It is not a home, that waits at the end of my lonely climb*
*It is not a home, that the hollow voices call me to*
*It is not a home, where I must spend my darkening time*
*It cannot be home, so far away from you*

When the service was over, Lincoln was surprised that it was he who shed the first tears. Sadness for Astrid, but also so much sadness for his brother who had not shared his burden with anybody else, not even his own family. When they were standing in the church waiting for Ben to thank the priest for the service, Martha gently pushed Lincoln, encouraging him to speak to his brother. 'He needs you, Lincoln. Go to him.' A clumsy commiserating handshake was followed by a warm embrace. One supporting the other, both bound in grief. The younger of the two holding firm as the pain of loss shuddered through the crumbling body of his elder brother.

On returning to Folkhemmet, beer, akvavit and small open sandwiches of prawns and salmon were served to the mourners. Astrid's father made a toast to his daughter and thanked his son-in-law for looking after her during the final weeks, raising his glass high against the backdrop of Astrid's paintings and sketches, which adorned the high, white walls of the two-floor, open plan living space. Slowly, the grey afternoon changed from one of sadness to one of celebration for a life well lived and Lincoln could see his brother gradually revive, energised by the anecdotes and kind words of his friends and family. After a while, Lincoln stepped outside onto one of the many wooden terraces that surrounded the large, white building. Thin flakes of snow had begun to circle aimlessly in the cold air of the Swedish night. He looked across the lake and could just make out the dark profile of the church opposite. Its discreet candles in stark contrast to the warm, yellow light gushing from every window of Folkhemmet. Lincoln gazed into the dark water that stretched out beneath him. Despite all that had happened, he was glad that the distance between him and his brother had been bridged and vowed not to let such pointless spite occur again. He looked up towards the half crescent moon, hung in the corner of the sky, just as he heard the sound of the glass living room door slide open behind him.

'Brrr, it's a bit cold for star gazing, Lincoln,' said Martha. 'What are you up to?'

'Just thinking. About Ben, Astrid and stuff.' He looked back into the warmth of the room. 'He's going to be okay isn't he?

'Sure, he'll be fine. It will just take time. I think he's getting a little bit tipsy in there. Anyway, he'll always have you to look out for him.'

'Yeah, guess so,' replied Lincoln, smiling. 'Hey, Martha, I never thanked you for coming out here. It was good of you, with everything else you've got going on.'

'Don't be silly, Lincoln. Besides, I had to come. Someone had to be here to make the arrest if you two started beating each other up again.'

He laughed. 'Good point. But seriously, we have lost a few days, haven't we. I was going to get in touch with Sarah when we get back to England and see if she found out anything more about Edmund Buller. Bit of a long shot, but could be worth a try.'

'Sure, but I was thinking about things again on the flight over. I know we talked about this before, but we are still spending all of our time looking back into the past. Maybe that's our mistake. Maybe we need to see what's going on today. Right now.' She dug her hands into the pockets of her thin black jacket, trying to keep warm. 'When we were at Blyth, we saw the bones on the floor of the Bone Room, which we thought might possibly be human, but without getting down there or getting a warrant, we can't prove it.'

'Correct. Unless you can persuade your man McSty to issue a search warrant,' he said

'Which he won't do without evidence. Chicken and egg. No bones, no warrant.'

'Fine, so we're stuck.'

'Maybe. Maybe not,' said Martha. The moonlight caught the stone of her engagement ring as she raised her hand to brush away a snowflake that had landed on her cheek. 'Listen. You said there was some kind of memorial at the Blyth site, yes? Under the tarpaulin? Then there was the cement chute ready for them to seal up the Bone Room once and for all, before they start converting the rest of the workhouse into a load of apartments.'

'Yes. Well, that's what it looked like anyway,' said Lincoln.

'All seems very convenient, doesn't it? Suddenly they are going to put up a memorial, just as the building work gets started and it just happens to be right on top of the Bone Crushing Room.'

Lincoln nodded. 'Yeah, absolutely. No question about it. Someone is trying to cover their tracks. That place has sat there untouched for over a hundred years. It's never been a problem because it was guarded, completely fenced off, but now the building work is going ahead. . .'

'. . . they daren't risk it anymore.' Martha interrupted, finishing off his sentence. 'So they plan to cover any wrongdoings under ten feet of solid concrete and then stick a ruddy great memorial on top, just to make sure nobody messes with it any time in the future.' She reached for Lincoln's arm, gripping it tightly. 'So, lets find out who is funding that memorial, because whoever it is, seems to me to be doing their damnedest to cover up and destroy one of the only bits of evidence we have.'

'And if the person commissioning the work is Willoughby,' said Lincoln, hopefully, 'then we've got him?'

Martha let go of his arm and turned away toward the lake. 'Well no. Unfortunately not. We need something more substantial than that. But if he is funding it, then that might be enough for me to go back to Mr McSty and try and persuade him to issue the search warrant and then if there are traces of human bones down there . . .'

'. . . then we've got him?' asked Lincoln.

'Well, he would certainly have some explaining to do, yes.'

'Right. So, we fly back tomorrow morning, get up to Suffolk and find out who is behind the memorial.'

'I think we do need to get back to Suffolk, but I have already looked into the memorial,' said Martha. 'I gave the district council a call yesterday when you were sorting out the church. I spoke to a very helpful lady who explained that since the council was part-funding the project, then all of the donors names were in the public domain. She emailed me over the list this morning.'

'Well?' he asked impatiently. 'Is Willoughby funding it?'

'No.'

Lincoln's shoulders slumped, a look of irritation on his face. 'If it's not him, Martha, then who is it for God's sake?'

Martha reached into her pocket, pulling out the email she had been sent from the Halesworth & Blyth council office. 'That's the strange thing. It's not just one person. There are a whole load of different companies listed. Thirteen in total.' She passed the list of names to Lincoln who scanned them for anything that looked vaguely familiar.

'They don't mean anything to me,' said Martha, taking the list back from Lincoln. 'I looked some of them up on the

Companies House website, but nothing. They aren't registered here in the UK, so, no accounts, no directors, no forwarding address. Just the name of the company and the value they have contributed to the President's Kin memorial. That's what it's called by the way. Something to do with the Kennedy and Roosevelt families and something that happened during the Second World War.'

'But these companies, they did definitely provide the funding?' asked Lincoln.

'Yes. Each company contributed up to £16,000. Small amounts, to keep things below the radar, I guess. Just over £200,000 in total. Their details must be out there somewhere but, to be honest, I have no idea how I go about searching for a non UK business. Financial misconduct is not my area of strength, I'm afraid. We need some help, Lincoln. Some expertise.'

Lincoln let out a sigh, his warm breath forming a small white cloud in the cold night air. 'Every time I think we are making progress, we hit a problem. Is there anybody in the Met who could help?'

'I think I have asked enough of Mr McSty for now. There are a few names I could try I suppose, but, to be honest,' she looked up tentatively towards Lincoln. 'I was thinking we might try someone a bit closer to home.'

They felt a warm gust of air as the glass door slid open again.

'Hey, you two. Here you are. You must be freezing. Come back inside, let me get you something to drink and maybe a . . .' Ben stopped talking, feeling suddenly uncomfortable under the focused gaze of his brother and the Detective Sergeant. ' . . . Lincoln . . . Martha . . . why are you both looking at me like that?'

\*

It was five hours later. The friends and relatives had all left apart from Astrid's parents who were staying in the guest wing and had decided to retreat to their rooms for an early night. Ben, Lincoln and Martha were in the study that looked out onto the boathouse and the steam room at the rear of the waterfront property.

'Honestly, don't worry about it, Martha. I'm glad I can help. To be honest, I'm grateful for the distraction.'

'Thanks anyway, Ben. I really do appreciate it.'

He nodded towards the policewoman. 'No problem. It's the least I can do.' He laid out a large sheet of paper on the glass table in the centre of the room. The names of the thirteen companies were listed along with the names of a further four companies not mentioned on the original email. All of the companies had been connected with different coloured arrows.

'So, I had better tell you what I've found,' said Ben, 'I don't know what you've got yourself involved with here, but these people know what they're doing and don't want to be traced. All very impressive. I haven't managed to get right to the bottom of all of it, but even to get this far I've had to call in a load of favours.'

He placed a condescending hand onto his brother's arm. 'Okay, Lincoln, I know you are not very bright, so I will try and keep things *really, really* simple,'

'Very funny. Just get on with it Ben,' Lincoln replied, smiling.

'The trick is to follow the money, no matter where it goes and eventually we should be able to trace it back to its source. We know the funds end up in Halesworth & Blyth council, of all places, but before they arrive there, they bounce between one country and the next, travelling across whole continents, generally staying in US dollars, but occasionally switching currencies. Some of the funds even pass through a gambling syndicate out in Hong Kong at one point. We lost them there for a bit, but managed to pick them up again when they came out the other side.' He took his pen from his pocket and pointed to the sheet in front of them. 'The thirteen companies are subsidiaries of these four larger companies - Ethel &

Millie Ltd, Foulton Enterprises, Lothing Landmark and Henham Holdings.' He drew a circle around Henham Holdings. 'This one, I cannot trace. I got so far, then the trail disappeared in a puff of smoke somewhere in Tokyo. All I know, is the main signatory is someone called Bonzo McGuire. I might be able to track it down again, but the transactions are buried so deep I would need a lot more time and some more resource. So, if it is okay with you, I have ignored it and concentrated on the other three companies.' He looked up at Martha, who nodded back in agreement.

'These three companies are run on a day-to-day basis by two management firms who oversee the whole operation - Eszett Investments and Bailliage Capital Markets. I'd never heard of them before and I can't find much out about them. Eszett and Bailliage have put in place Directors on each of the three Boards. These Directors are not much more than ghosts really. Could be anyone. Nothing to do with who actually owns the money, I'm afraid. I could give you their names but they are more than likely relatively junior and just do as they are told by their bosses in the management companies. To be honest, I doubt they have any idea what they are doing when they sign off payments and transactions.' He looked up and could see the frustration already visible on Martha's face.

'Don't worry, Martha,' he said, smiling and trying to placate her. 'It gets better, I promise.' He reached for a second sheet of paper, which had a long list of names, currencies, and addresses scattered randomly across the page.
'Things got interesting when I started comparing the routes the different pots of money took on their long journey to Blyth. All quite different, some going via Asia, some via Eastern Europe and some via South America and the Caribbean. However, somewhere along the way they all touch two trust funds. One called the Imogen Trust based in the Virgin Island and one called the Strathdon Trust based here in the UK.'

Both Lincoln and Martha visibly jumped at the mention of

Strathdon, staring back at each other across the table.

'I'm guessing that name means something to you,' Ben said looking between both of them.

'Yes,' said Martha. 'Please Ben, go on.'

'Okay. The two Trusts are hidden behind loads of red tape, but after a bit of digging I managed to find out the name of the main Trustee, the person who is actually making the decisions and is not just some phoney baloney finance lackey added on just to make up the numbers. Ben turned over the sheet of paper where he had written someone's name under each of the Trusts. 'Okay, so the name of the main trustee on the Imogen Trust is someone called Alfred Beech. I did a full search on him but came up with nothing. No trace of him anywhere. He could be dead for all I know. The other one, the Strathdon Trust, has a trustee called Milton S Cassidy, birth date 1$^{st}$ February, 1965. Mean anything to you?'

Martha shook her head. 'No. Never heard of him.'

'Okay, well look, Martha, you are going to have to block your ears for this bit. I got somebody to do some special research for me and I'm not about to land a friend of mine in prison.'

She looked back, reassuringly. 'Ben, I'm not about to arrest you or your friend. Honestly.'

He turned to his brother, saying playfully. 'You heard her, Lincoln. You can be my witness when they try and lock me up.' Lincoln smiled but rolled his finger, encouraging Ben to carry on and finish. He hadn't seen his brother so animated for a while. It was like an enormous weight had been lifted off him once the funeral was over. The relief of it all, mixed with a half dozen glasses of akvavit, had sparked some bullish enthusiasm within him. He knew the levity was only temporary, but still it felt good to see him smile again.

'Okay. I could find nothing on Cassidy,' Ben continued. 'No trace anywhere and, believe me, I know how to track down people like this. Like I say, these guys know what they're doing. However, I have a friend, fairly high up in the Inland Revenue who I once helped out in a big way.' He turned briefly to Martha, 'You really don't want to know about that.'

'Understood,' she replied, raising both of her hands.

'My guy in the Revenue, after a bit of persuading, agreed to hunt down any income tax paid by Cassidy over the last, say, twenty or thirty years. Now, get this, there was nothing. No payments whatsoever for someone with that name and date of birth. Absolutely nothing on file. Not even a national insurance record. I mean, these guys are really, really good. However, after I tore into my friend a bit and reminded him of the debts of friendship, he had another go, this time cross referencing his name against a load of different databases and after a while, bingo! As it turns out there's a Milton S Cassidy, born on 1$^{st}$ February, 1965, listed as being in receipt of an annual payment, paid on his birthday, beginning two years after he was born and lasting up until his sixteenth birthday, in 1981. The payment is just an inflation linked nominal sum, a few hundred quid a year. It looks like a living allowance or savings account, probably set up when he was a toddler and then forgotten about.'

Martha leaned forward, 'So, who set up the payment?' she asked.

Ben reached for his pen. 'Well, it was set up by an individual, not a company, some rich uncle perhaps? Here, let me write it down for you.'

He handed the bit of paper to the policewoman. She looked down and then slowly read out the name.

'Mr Anthony Willoughby from Willoughby Holdings Limited.'

## CHAPTER 40

LINCOLN sat in the small seating area of the Espresso House, just opposite Gate 14 of Landvetter airport, minding the bags while Martha went to get some more coffee. The plane back to Stansted had been delayed by two hours. No sensible reason had been given by the chirpy but unhelpful ground staff who had now disappeared behind the scenes to avoid the impatient glares of their marooned passengers.

They had left Folkhemmet just before six in the morning, having said their brief goodbyes to Ben, who was tired and hungover, bracing himself for another difficult day in the house still so fully occupied by the presence of his absent wife. Just before the taxi arrived, Ben took Lincoln aside to thank him one last time.

'Hey, and look after yourself, little brother.'

'I will, Ben. And you.'

'You know what you're doing, yeah? With all this weird business you've got yourself involved in?'

'No,' he laughed. 'But we'll figure it out. At least, I hope so.'

'And you know what you're doing with Martha?'

'Eh? What do you mean?'

'C'mon, Lincoln. You guys seem like good people together, it's sweet, but you've seen the engagement ring, right? You know she's off limits.'

'We're just friends, Ben. Don't worry. There's nothing going on. I just landed myself in this mess and, well, she needs the help. That's all.'

Ben thought about pushing back. It was obvious to him that there was more going on between the two of them than just friendship, but he bit his tongue. Why risk breaking the fragile truce they had so recently established. His brother could look after himself. He would be fine.

At the airport, Martha returned with two cups of coffee and a piece of Christmas Stollen cake on a small paper plate.

'Grab this will you, Lincoln,' she said, nodding at the cake. 'It's past eight o'clock in the UK now, so I'm going to go and try and call Colin. Update him on the Willoughby connection to the memorial and see what he thinks about a warrant. You okay on your own for a bit?'

'Sure, no problem. You go,' he said, waving her away.

She put the drinks on the table, which jogged slightly spilling the coffee onto Lincoln's jeans.

'Oh fuck!' he shouted, causing the passenger seated with her two young children on the table next door to look across, disapprovingly.

'Sorry, Lincoln. You okay?'

'Yeah, sure. It was just a bit hot. Don't worry. Go and talk to McSty and good luck.'

Martha walked away to a corner of the airport that was slightly more private, leaving Lincoln to dab his legs with the now soggy napkin. Not much of the coffee had, in all honesty, landed on his jeans and what had, was only lukewarm. It wasn't the coffee that had made him swear so loudly. It was the sudden memory of Sorrel Cottage and him sitting at the kitchen table, a bit tipsy, sorting through the contents of the wooden box. He remembered the dirty, broken stirrup, rolling on the table and the piece of delicate paper he had retrieved from the knife all those weeks ago. Then he remembered the cup of coffee that had nearly spilt onto the note and him grabbing the muslin that had been wrapped around the saddlebag and shoving it under the wobbly table to avoid any further mishaps. How had he managed to forget about that for all this time? All these weeks of scrambling around, looking for the tiniest bit of evidence and all the while, the cloth that had been wrapped around the murder weapon, was at his parent's house, squeezed under the leg of the kitchen table. How could he have been so stupid?

He decided quickly that he couldn't tell Martha. Not now anyway. It was probably nothing, just some old cloth. Why would it matter? It wouldn't. No, best to sit on it for now rather than make himself look a complete prat in front of her. They were going back to Suffolk anyway. He would get to the house, get the cloth and, once he was certain that it was worthless, he would tell Martha about it. Make a joke of it. It didn't mean anything anyway. Yes, that was what to do.

'You okay Lincoln? You look like you've seen a ghost.'

He jumped slightly, startled at the sound of Martha's voice. 'Just thinking about something. It was nothing. How did it go with McSty?

Martha sat down on the hard, plastic chair opposite him. A look of disappointment on her face. 'Not great. I told him about the funding and the connection to Willoughby, which he thought was good, but not good enough to issue a warrant. His point being that, even though the money trail clearly indicates that the Willoughbys are most likely involved in all sorts of improprieties, it isn't actually illegal to fund a monument, however you go about it. He said he would take a look at the case as it stands later today, but thought it unlikely that he would be able to issue a search warrant at this time without some new and compelling evidence.'

'Brilliant,' said Lincoln. 'I thought this bloke was meant to be on our side.'

'He is Lincoln. He's just doing his job. He's usually right

about these things. The last thing we need is to go public before we're ready. The DPS will tear me apart, say I'm just desperately trying to smear a respectable family to save my own skin. No. He's right. We need something more substantial.'

'Maybe we should just grab Willoughby and stick a gun to his head until he confesses. Would that satisfy Mr McSty?'

'Come on, Lincoln, that's not helpful. Be sensible.' She looked down at the now cold coffee. Considered taking a sip, but thought better of it and pushed the cup away. 'I think I know what I've got to do.'

'To get some evidence?' asked Lincoln.

'Yeah. It's probably not a great plan, but it's the best I've got.'

'Go on,' he said, hesitantly.

'I go back to the Bone Crushing Room at Blyth. Sawing through those bars would make too much noise, with the security guards and dogs around the place, but I was thinking that the chute, the one for the concrete. Maybe I could get down there. It would be tight, but I think I could just squeeze down. Leave a rope tied at the top. Grab some of the bone fragments and climb back up. I'm pretty sure I can sweet talk Danny Whitehead, the guy at the London Archeology Museum, to do some initial checks and then, if it is what we think it is, take it to Mr McSty. He would issue a warrant there and then. What do you think?'

Lincoln was staring open mouthed at her. 'This is you being sensible is it? Jesus, Martha. It sounds like a ridiculous plan. Stupid. Dangerous. Just absurd.'

'Mr McSty liked it,' she said, taking a nibble from the piece of Stollen. 'He said it showed initiative. Don't worry, Lincoln, he has asked me to let him know when I'm planning to go down. Told me to "Take care, that's an order Detective Sergeant Green"' she said in a deep voice, impersonating the low burl of the Chief Superintendent. 'He's going to make sure that there is a patrol car in the area, so if things do go wrong, which I'm sure they won't, then he sends in the cavalry. It will all be fine, Lincoln. Don't worry. Piece of cake.' She looked down at the limp Stollen she still had in her hand. 'Talking of which, you better have this. Don't want to get get stuck halfway down the chute.'

# CHAPTER 41

ANTHONY Willoughby was dining alone in the corner seat of the Crown Room of his club. His table afforded a narrow view of the wet pavement of Pall Mall, now beginning to swell with Christmas shoppers. He prodded the bloody lamb cutlet on the plate in front of him, occasionally pushing the sprigs of broccoli around the dish, unable to summon an appetite. The uncertainty over family matters was beginning to interfere with his usually robust constitution. His eyes, heavy and strained from lack of sleep. His face, pallid and chalky. He had tried to paint a positive picture of the immediate future, but had found it difficult to envisage. His ambition was to attend the family Christmas day dinner in five days time in the knowledge that things were returning to normal, present the annual accounts as was the tradition and relish the look of disappointment on his sister's face as she realised all was in order, despite her previous misgivings. However, for now, he remained out of sorts and jiggered with unease.

It was pretty bad form to keep mobile phones to hand

when dining in the Club, but on this particular damp and miserable lunchtime, he was almost alone in the large, austere room. The only other members present were the Granville brothers, propped up in the opposite corner, who were both so old and forgetful that, in their blurry malaise, they seemed to have quite simply, forgotten to die.

The phone rang twice before Willoughby answered it.

'I am sorry to disturb you, sir. It's Sam. Sam Wilson. You asked me to call if I picked up anything untoward on the wires.'

'Ah Sam. Quite right. What do you have for me, young man?' Despite Willoughby's relaxed tone he felt a soft tightening in his throat as he waited to hear his young employee's news, fearing the worst.

'Well, it is probably not significant,' began Sam, hesitantly, 'but we have recorded some further search enquiries regarding Strathdon, as well as a number of other accounts associated with the Trusts. This happens on occasion. Most often nothing. An over exuberant accountant somewhere who has had their interest peaked. Usually Mr Cassidy would ask me to monitor, but take no action. As I say, usually nothing, but thought that, following our last conversation, you would want to know. The bulk of the activity took place in Sweden by the way. I don't know if that means anything to you sir?'

Willoughby felt some relief that Sam's call mentioned nothing more serious than the onset of inconclusive chatter. He turned his heavy silver plated fork over in his fingertips as he tried to think of a Swedish connection. The family had some other business affairs in Scandinavia, but no property interests to date. 'No, no Sam. Nothing comes to mind.' He skewered a floret of broccoli, sweeping it into the thick gravy resting underneath the cutlet. 'As you say, most likely nothing, Sam. Please monitor and continue to keep me informed if you would.'

'I will sir.' There was a momentary pause on the end of the line before Sam raised the second issue. The one that was giving him more concern than the first. 'One other point, if I may, sir.'

'Of course, Sam,' said Willoughby, happy to delay for a moment his forkful of vegetable. 'Go ahead, young man.'

Sam gently cleared his throat. 'Amidst the general dead-end enquiries was a reference to an account I had not come across before. Just a small sum, so I am sure it is not material, but I thought I should mention it, because in the wrong hands it could illustrate an explicit connection between Mr Cassidy and yourself. I am not sure if this means much to you sir, but do you happen to recall setting up an account in your name, but on behalf of Mr Cassidy. It was many years ago now, in 1967. Like I say, just small sums, but regular, every year on the same day until 1981. I am sure it's nothing, sir, but felt I should mention it for completeness.'

Willoughby's mind drifted back to a hot summer's day nearly fifty years ago, when he was still in his early twenties. He recalled standing in the hall of the family residence alongside his younger brother and two sisters, looking down on the bundle of legs and arms, wrapped in a soft white sheet of Egyptian cotton. The young child lay asleep, his guileless thoughts adrift in an innocent slumber. Despite the lack of blood ties, Willoughby found that the bond of responsibility developed quickly for the young infant, who would spend his youth and formative years cloistered within Widford Hall as he was groomed for service within the family. The setting up of a small fund for the boy was an immature and sentimental act for a man who had recently taken on the role of Head of the Family, but at the time it felt good to enact such a magnanimous gesture. And that was all it had been. A small, pointless gesture. A foolish act of an impetuous man, yet to be hardened by the world he would take residence within. But now that gesture had resurfaced. Spied upon by others. Tangling him with Cassidy, his fallen angel.

He gathered himself and returned his attention to his phone call. 'Thank you for letting me know, Sam, and lets keep this to ourselves for now, there's a good chap.' The willing assistant was voicing his accord on the other end of the line, but Willoughby had already placed his phone back on the table. He glowered down at his meal, replaced his fork and pushed the plate away, conscious of a strange, nauseous fluttering in his stomach. He felt so tired all of a sudden. So helpless. It seemed as if he had relinquished control of his own affairs and could do no more than watch, sidelined, as events played out before him. He raised his eyes to the ever-present Gulliver who made his way towards the senior club member, a decanter of brandy in his hand.

## CHAPTER 42

CASSIDY had tried to call Sam twice on his way to Berners Street to meet with George Giltmore. On both occasions his efforts had been greeted with an engaged tone. Rather than try a third time, he decided to visit the office once he had dealt with the Homerton issue. He needed to get to Blyth by midnight to follow up on a message he had received from the Workhouse security team, but would have time to speak to Sam face-to-face beforehand and find out about the Strathdon account and why several of the large December transfers remained outstanding. He knew Sam well enough to know that he would have a sound reason for the postponement, however, it was not like him to delay payment without first informing Cassidy.
Christmas carols were playing over the speakers in the main foyer of The Edition Hotel as the evening's guests checked in, eager to begin their celebrations in the bars and restaurants of Soho and the West End. The reception staff, although busy with the evening rush, were relaxed and smiling, happy to join in with the festive spirit during the final few days before

Christmas Eve. Giltmore was lurking behind one of the ostentatious marble pillars on the far side of the reception area. He caught Cassidy's eye and directed him over towards the lift.

'I managed to hijack one of the rooms downstairs in the basement where we won't be disturbed,' he said, ushering Cassidy into the waiting lift. Once inside, he took stock of his guest. 'You look well Milton. Nice suit. Smart haircut. Have you been working out?'

Cassidy grunted an acknowledgement, but nothing more. He was unsure why Giltmore suddenly thought they were on first name terms. No mind. The MP was a fool who had come to the end of his usefulness and after today it was very unlikely their paths would cross again. He intended to get the document checked and signed as quickly as possible and then be on his way.

'We're this way. It's like a maze back here, isn't it?' said Giltmore, continuing in his jocular tone. 'Two little rats shuffling along towards the cheese,' he joked. 'Squeak, squeak, eh Milton. Squeak, squeak, squeak'

Giltmore had surprised himself. He thought the meeting with Cassidy would make him a bag of nerves, but once Hartmann had shown him the script and pointed out the discreet recording equipment, he found to his utter astonishment that he was enjoying the drama of it all. The thought that they were going to trap the great Milton Cassidy, get him to inadvertently do the dirty on the whole rotten Willoughby enterprise, was just too delicious. He had to admit, despite being German, this Hartmann was a very impressive chap. He seemed to have it all figured out. All the MP had to do, after some general chit chat about Homerton, was to get Cassidy to reply to the preset questions that the German had put together. That was all there was to it. He then would make sure Cassidy left the building, while Hartmann took the recordings across to his waiting contact over in Scotland Yard and, bob's your uncle, Willoughby, Cassidy and all his cronies, snared. All locked up, just in time for Christmas. And bloody good riddance to the lot of them.

George couldn't help himself. 'Going away for Christmas, Milton?' he asked, smiling as they made their way along a narrow and poorly lit corridor, just off the service area of the hotel.

'No. Where is this room, Giltmore? I have a busy evening ahead of me and want this done quickly,' replied Cassidy, impatiently.

'Relax, Milton, it's just here.' Giltmore walked past the loading bay on the left and opened a door onto a small windowless room. A table and two chairs were positioned in the middle of the floor with a jug of water, two glasses and a vase of hydrangeas, clumsily arranged towards the centre of the table. As Giltmore took his seat he looked knowingly around the room and at the vase of flowers where the surveillance equipment was housed. All looks in order, he thought to himself. He sat down and opened a thin folder of papers he had been carrying under his arm, handing a document entitled Homerton Consecration to Cassidy. He left the folder open in front of him, so he could see the several prompts he had written for himself to make sure he stayed on script.

'Right, let's get started shall we, Milton? I'm afraid there is a bit to read through, but best to be thorough, don't you think?'

Cassidy took the small pack of papers and began sifting through them. There was nothing there he hadn't seen before countless times. He checked his watch. He should still be able to make it back across town for six o'clock to sort out the transfers, all being well. Opposite him, Giltmore was glancing at his pack and was just about to ask the first of Hartmann's cleverly worded questions when there was a knock at the door, followed by the entrance of one of the hotel waiters who backed into the room, pulling a trolley laden with refreshments.

'Tea? Water? Some biscuits, gentlemen?' the waiter asked, in a heavy East European accent, dragging the reluctant trolley behind him, into the narrow room.

'No thank you,' Giltmore said impatiently. 'We don't want tea thank you very much. Please leave us in peace and close the door behind you.'

The waiter continued moving backwards into the room, towards the table.

'New coffee for you? Refresh? Yes?'

Giltmore rolled his eyes at Cassidy. 'No. We don't want coffee either,' he said loudly in an attempt to overcome the language barrier. 'No coffee. No tea. Go. Please.'

By now the waiter was level with Cassidy. Giltmore was about to stand up and position himself in the waiter's eye-line to see if that helped him get his point across, when he heard a strange, muffled cry and looked up to see Cassidy shaking uncontrollably in his chair as a spasm of electricity shot through his body from the taser gun Hartmann had stabbed into his neck. Cassidy's body jolted and then fell into a shuddering heap onto the floor, next to the table. Giltmore could only look on in complete horror as Hartmann pulled off the waiter's jacket and knelt down next to the wide eyed Cassidy who was writhing silently and uncontrollably on the floor. Hartmann grabbed a chunk of Cassidy's hair, pulling his face up towards his. 'Hello my old friend. Happy Christmas you fotze.' The two men's eyes met. Cassidy could barely breathe, his thoughts were scrambled with the pain of the electric charge, but Hartmann could see in his eyes the shocked realisation that some kind of nameless horror was about to be unleashed upon him.

'Hartmann. What are you doing for God's sake?' cried Giltmore. 'You said we were just making some tapes not . . . this,' he said, pointing to Cassidy. He sprang up from his chair. 'I cannot be here. I need to go. I need to go now.'

He made for the door, but it was locked.

'I need to go, Hartmann. I'm an MP in Her Majesty's Parliament, you bloody idiot. I cannot be here.'

Hartmann did not take his eyes off Cassidy's twisting body, a faint smile on his face. 'Sit down, George,' he said quietly.

'No. I need to get out of here.' Giltmore started rattling the handle and banging on the door, shouting for help.

Hartmann turned impatiently to the MP. 'Sit down, Giltmore or you will be next,' he said raising the taser gun towards him.

Giltmore turned the handle one last time and then rested his head on the door as he realised the hopelessness of his situation. After a brief moment, he let go of the door handle and slowly returned to his seat.

'Good boy, George. Now sit. Have a glass of water. Enjoy the show. You will like it,' Hartmann said, trying to relax the MP. 'Then you can go. Run away to your ski trip or whatever, I don't care, but for now, sit and be quiet.'

George looked down at Cassidy, still quivering on the floor.

A sour sweat had begun to soak through poor George's day old shirt. He thought of his wife and kids getting ready back home. Squeezing winter coats and ski trousers into their cases. His two boys arguing about who was going to sit by the window on the plane. His wife, making sure she had packed her husband's Kindle so he had something to read during the flight. He just wanted to go home and be with his family. Get in his car and go. Just for once, he wanted to be the good husband and the good father and look after them all and be there for them. He didn't want to be here. Not here. Anywhere but here.

Hartmann had wrapped some thick silver tape across Cassidy's mouth and around his legs and wrists, which were bound together in front of him. He reached for the jug of water from the table and threw it at Cassidy's face.

'That's it, my friend. Wake up. You need to be nice and alert. After all, we don't want you missing any of the fun.' Cassidy shook his head to get the water out of his eyes and looked up at Hartmann, his body still jerking with the pain of the electric charge.

Hartmann reached back into the trolley and pulled out a bag, unzipping it and removing the pliers, the hunting knife and a plastic rack. He placed the items neatly onto the floor, side by side, next to Cassidy's quivering body.

'To be honest with you, Mr Cassidy, you probably realise now

that things are not going to end well for you. Not well at all. You can see that, yes?' he said, checking that Cassidy was paying attention. 'I will miss you, Cassidy. You know that? In my own way, I will miss you. Are you listening?' He grabbed Cassidy's head and banged it back down onto the floor. 'You must listen, Cassidy, like I listened to you when you did that little house call in Bremen. You are listening, yes? Good. As I was saying, I will miss you old comrade, so I thought I would take a small memento, something to remember you by. In fact ten mementos, if you don't mind.'
He grabbed Cassidy's head again and banged it back down on the floor, this time harder than before, causing a small rivulet of blood to flow down Cassidy's temple. 'Of course you do not mind. You are a generous man. I am always saying to George, what a generous man Mr Cassidy is, aren't I George?' He looked up at the politician who nodded his head, desperately trying to please, a look of puzzled and terrified panic on his face.
'Now we need to do things right. Everything in order you see, Cassidy. It is like when I am cooking a Geflügelragout at home for my girls. Everything in order. First you roast the chicken and then you cut up the bird so you can make the stew.' He reached for the pair of pliers and rested the fulcrum on the flesh of the small finger of Cassidy's left hand, the metal levers closing tightly around the digit. Cassidy tried to pull his hands away, but following the taser charge, the German was far too powerful for him. 'To separate the chicken joints you must break the bones first otherwise the joint will not come away cleanly.' He closed the pliers on Cassidy's finger, squeezing the handle until he heard the dull snap of the bone breaking in two, just beneath the bottom joint. Cassidy let out a loud muffled scream, his eyes bulging with pain. 'There, that is a good clean break, don't you think?' said Hartmann. 'Now we are ready for the next step.'
He laid the pliers gently back in their position on the carpeted floor and reached for the hunting knife. 'Now we can remove the joint cleanly. Please do not struggle, Cassidy. There,' he

said, resting his knee on his chest. 'I have got you. Keep still please.' Hartmann gripped Cassidy's hand to the floor, before taking the jagged blade and cutting through the skin at the bottom of the finger. Cassidy tried to pull his hands free as he looked down in horror, as the knife cut through his flesh and tendons where the finger had been broken in two. Hartmann pressed down hard, cutting, until the finger came away. 'And there we are. See. Not a bad job. Can you see, Cassidy?' He held the amputated finger in front of Cassidy's eyes. 'See. Not so bad. I will put that one just here,' he said, resting the finger in the rack by Cassidy's head. 'Claudia, my wife, you remember Claudia don't you, Cassidy, well, my wife is a science teacher so I borrowed this test tube rack from her laboratory. It works well doesn't it, Cassidy? *Fit for purpose*, you would call it, I think. Yes. Fit for purpose. You see? We can now make a neat line. Ten little fingers, all in a row.'

Behind him, Hartmann heard a choking, gagging sound and then a muted splash as Giltmore threw up onto the carpet of the small meeting room. A waft of warm sick, billowing into the air.

'Oh George, don't spoil things. That is not helpful. Please,' Hartmann pointed to the trolley, 'tissues.'

George wiped his mouth on his sleeve and reached for the box of tissues from the trolley, desperate not to anger his psychotic accomplice. He dabbed pathetically at the small pile of sick, pushing it around the floor. The pungent stink of the vomit soaked tissues mixed with the smell of Cassidy's blood, filling the room with a muggy, moist stench. The heating system blew a waft of the warm fetid air towards Giltmore just as he caught sight of the stub of Cassidy's finger. The starch white bone poking out through the bloody flesh of his fist. He felt a wave of cold sweat swell up his body and wretched once more onto the carpet, on top of the pile of sodden tissues.

'George. Please. Don't make me angry,' Hartmann shouted, before turning back to his agonised victim. 'Now, Mr Cassidy, where were we. Ah yes. So. Everything in order. First we must break the bone.' Cassidy watched in horror as, once again, Hartmann reached for the blood stained pliers.

*       *

The Lisbon flight had landed at Heathrow just after three thirty in the afternoon. Her young, Portuguese lover had proved to be in an inventive and generous mood and Louisa Willoughby felt revitalised and restored following her short sojourn on the continent. So much so, she even felt she could contend with the clumsy and pedestrian grapplings of the Dray. What grubby, prurient torments was he going to offer up at their liaison in Cambridge tonight, she wondered. She crossed her legs in the back seat of the car, muttering softly to herself, "Endure and persist; This pain will turn to good by and by." The phone had started ringing just as her driver turned onto the M25 and she listened carefully to the update, informing her of the recent activities of the resourceful Mr Hartmann and the hapless Giltmore.
'And you say the meeting has been in progress for nearly thirty minutes now?'
'Yes Ma'am. There were sounds of a scuffle of some sort at the onset of the meeting, but since then, nothing.'
Louisa looked out onto the passing motorway at the other cars, packed with families travelling to this place and that for Christmas, busy conducting their strange little lives in their ordinary worlds. 'Okay, I think that's enough, don't you? Would you mind asking your men to step in and please bring Mr Cassidy up to speed.'
She smiled as she replaced the phone back into her bag, amused by her generosity. Well, she thought to herself, it was Christmas after all.

# CHAPTER 43

SHEILA Clarke had slipped a couple of chocolate digestive biscuits onto the tray next to the late afternoon cup of tea she had prepared for her boss, Chief Superintendent McSty. She was aware that he had missed lunch earlier following the meeting of the Ethics Committee, which had finished 45 minutes later than scheduled. Since then, he had been in back-to-back meetings. Having worked for Mr McSty for over three years now, Sheila appreciated how diligent he was and knew he would not have found time to even grab a sandwich during the afternoon, not wanting to let his own needs interfere with the agenda of the department. She gently knocked on the office door and entered with the much needed refreshments.

'Ah Sheila, just the person. Have you seen the Robson file? I was amending it the other day on the train, but I cannot for the life of me remember where I put it,' said Colin McSty, flicking through the neat stack of paperwork in his in-tray.

'The grey filing cabinet, second draw down, under Talent Rationalisation.'

McSty spun his chair around so he could access the filing cabinet, opened the drawer and pulled out the file.

'Sheila Clarke. What would I ever do without you?' he said to his dependable assistant. 'I swear, the whole Metropolitan Police Force would shudder to a standstill if you ever decided to leave us.'

Sheila waved away his compliment, blushing slightly. 'Just doing my job, sir,' she said dismissively, although, in truth, nothing gave her more pleasure than receiving praise from the Chief Superintendent, who she regarded as the best boss she had ever worked with during her fifteen year career as an Executive Assistant. She placed the tray on the desk, turning the handle of the teacup towards her industrious line manager.

'Sorry for the interruption, sir, but I just wanted to remind you that the meeting with the Diversity and Equality Panel has been brought forward to two thirty, tomorrow afternoon. I think Superintendent Ferguson is looking to get away early so she is able to travel down to Cornwall for drinks with her relatives. I've booked you on an eleven o'clock train tomorrow morning, which should give you plenty of time to get to the station following your presentation, which is scheduled to finish at nine thirty. The presentation powerpoint file is saved on the laptop under Action Against Crime Conference and your train tickets and hotel reference are in the folder in your overnight bag,' she said, pointing to the brown holdall positioned next to the door so he wouldn't forget it. 'Your meeting this evening with Gus Reyner from the Communications and PR team is running late so will not start until five o'clock, but that still means you should be fine to get the seven o'clock train from Kings Cross this evening. I have told Jenny to make sure you are out of the door by quarter past six, at the latest.'

'Brilliant Sheila. That should keep me well and truly occupied and out of mischief. Good to see you've got me working as hard as ever,' he said cheerfully, making a mental note to stop off at Fortnum and Masons on his way back to the office tomorrow morning to pick up the small hamper he had bought Sheila for Christmas. 'Actually, I do need to make one more call before I leave this evening, do I have time now do you think?'

'I would have thought so sir, you have ten minutes or so. I will knock on the door when you are due to leave, but I dare say that Mr Reyner could start without you if you needed more time.'

'No, no ten minutes should be fine. The call shouldn't take long,' he said, reaching for his notebook. 'Oh and Sheila, thank you for the biscuits. Just what I needed.'

His PA turned and left the office, making her way back to her workplace, her face warmed with a contented glow.

Chief Superintendent McSty turned the pages of his book to where he had scribbled down some notes during his conversation with Martha Green. As he had promised her, he had reviewed the evidence she had compiled and had regrettably concluded that a search warrant was not attainable at this stage. Martha's unwavering determination never ceased to impress and it appeared that, given time, she could compile some compelling evidence against the Willoughby Estate, however they both knew that time was a resource she was fast running out of. He had decided that he needed to step in and see if he could assist in some way to help her move things forward. It would be foolhardy to mobilise any of his department's resources at this stage, it was too early for that, but a small intervention from himself may just tip the balance in their favour. From what Martha had said previously, her meeting with Willoughby had caused the Head of the Family a brief but notable degree of anxiety and maybe he could make use of the weight of his office to discreetly add to that discomfort. He checked the office door was firmly closed and then dialled the number he had written at the bottom of the page. The phone rang four times before going to voicemail.

'This is a message for Mr Anthony Willoughby. My name is Chief Superintendent McSty and I am calling to arrange some time when you are able to help us with some enquiries regarding an ongoing investigation. I am able to visit you at your place of residence or some other suitable location tomorrow evening. The case in question concerns a number of financial irregularities taking place both here in the United Kingdom and abroad, most notably in Hong Kong, Guernsey and several Eastern European states. The investigation has a particular interest in an account named as the Strathdon Trust which includes an arrangement set up in 1967 between yourself and a Mr Milton Cassidy. This is an urgent matter, Mr Willoughby, requiring your immediate response.'

That should stir things up, he thought to himself. He would tell Sheila that the appointment tomorrow evening was just a drink with some old friends from the police college. There was no need to make anything official just yet. He closed his notebook, picked up his overnight bag and made his way down to the 3rd floor for his meeting with Gus Reyner. In his haste, he had forgotten to eat the biscuits, which remained untouched on the tray next to the half finished cup of Earl Grey tea.

## CHAPTER 44

BY the time the three armed guards forced their way into the back room of the hotel, Hartmann was about to remove the sixth of Cassidy's fingers.
It was a difficult scene to make sense of at first. A fair-haired man was on his knees, hunched over. His blood red hands holding a large hunting knife which had lumps of flesh caught in its serrated edge. The second man, lying on his side, his white shirt soaked with his own blood, was emitting a strange, grunting sound through his covered mouth and squirming on the wet floor like a landed fish, his hands and legs tightly bound with tape. To their right was a third man, this one overweight, bent double, shaking with fear and silently weeping. His tears dripping onto a small mound of wet tissues piled at his feet. The tissues were speckled with lumps of orange and yellow matter, giving off a bitter and rancid smell. On the floor, in easy reach of the blond man, was what looked like a school test tube rack, but rather than being filled with glass vials, the classroom holder contained five sawn off fingers, standing upright in a row of descending size, with the

two smallest fingers from each hand lined up on the right.
The three guards were dressed in black and were brandishing Glock 26 sidearms. The first two entered the room swiftly and almost silently disarmed the man with the knife, pinning him to the floor in one well-rehearsed move. The third man, the leader of the group, knelt down next to Cassidy and removed the silver tape wrapped around his mouth, hands and feet. Once released, he pulled Cassidy up by his shoulders so he was resting against the far wall of the room.
'We have been sent to assist.' He glanced down at Cassidy's two mutilated hands. Thick, dark red blood was still seeping out of the short stumps at the end of his knuckles where his fingers had been removed. The left hand had just two digits remaining, the thumb and the index finger. The right hand had the thumb, the index and the middle finger, although the last had been broken at its base and hung limply from its socket.
'I'm just sorry we could not have got here sooner, Mr Cassidy.'
Cassidy's face was white. There was a thin layer of sweat on his forehead. The nerve endings in his missing fingers were spliced and laid bare and his trembling hands ached with an incessant and agonising throb. The leader of the guards had to lean in close when Cassidy tried to speak. His words barely audible.
'Who sent you?'
'All I know is that the order was originated by someone called Willoughby, sir,' the leader replied. Cassidy nodded, grateful for his employer's intervention.
'We came as soon as we were given the all clear,' continued the guard. 'We have been instructed to resolve conflict and provide assistance.' He looked back down at the bloody remains of Cassidy's hands. 'As I said earlier, it's a shame we were not able to move sooner. Apparently there was a communication problem. The client was on a flight over Europe so she could not be contacted.'
Cassidy's eyes snapped into focus. 'She?'
'Yes, Willoughby, Louisa Willoughby. She was on a flight

from Portugal. She was updated as soon as she left the airport. Just a shame it wasn't sooner.'

The leader briefed Cassidy as best he could in the time available, bringing him up to speed and letting him know who his team of mercenaries were working for. Cassidy tried to process the unexpected information. His eyes darting from left to right as he looked for answers. His frayed mind slowly organising his thoughts. He steadied his breathing and tried to slow his heartbeat to a controlled rhythm. He looked around the room, taking in his gory surroundings. Over by the table, he could see the pathetic MP, head bowed and sobbing into his lap like a cowardly schoolboy. A pool of blood and sinew spread from the middle of the room, staining the carpeted floor. His eyes came to rest on the German, still pinned to the ground by the other two officers who were looking towards their leader, awaiting instruction.

'Get the tape,' Cassidy muttered in a cold, monotone voice, nodding towards the trolley. The guard did as he was asked and returned to a kneeling position by Cassidy's side. Cassidy held up his right hand. 'Wrap my two fingers together.' He made no sound as the guard pulled the limp, broken digit straight and bound it to his index finger.

'That's the best I can do for now sir. We need to get you to a hospital and get that looked at properly,' the guard said, apologetically.

Cassidy looked down at his two hands, slowly flexing his remaining fingers and thumbs, They looked like a pair of grisly crab claws that had been sewn onto the end of his arms. He closed his eyes and took one long deep breath and then slowly rose to his feet, making his way to the table where the taser gun was lying. He picked it up and looked at it carefully, studying it, holding it close to his eyes with his bloody claws.

The taser lay in his left palm, his index finger resting on the trigger, as he took three menacing steps towards Hartmann and placed one leg either side of his prone body, staring deep into the German's eyes as he towered above him. Hartmann let out a desperate cry of protest, first in German, then in broken English. He struggled to free himself, wriggling from side to side, but his captors held him rigid to the floor. Cassidy raised his foot above Hartmann's stomach and then slammed it down onto his unprotected thorax. The force of the blow, causing Hartmann to double up in pain, winded and open-mouthed, gasping for air. Cassidy nodded to the two guards to move away and stretched out his left arm, aiming the taser gun into the German's open mouth, piercing the tender flesh at the back of his throat. Hartmann's body convulsed with a shuddering force. A strange odour rose into the air as his tongue and the flesh on the roof of his mouth began to smoulder and burn. Hartmann was unable to breathe, his eyes frozen wide open, as he failed to cope with the searing pain of the burning electrical charge.

Cassidy dropped to his knees, straddling Hartmann's quivering body. He picked up the hunting knife lying next to one of the guards and turned it over in his hands before wiping it on his trousers, leaving a bloody stain on the tailored cloth of his suit. Hartmann's mouth was opening and closing like a hungry fledgling, his blackened and swollen tongue flapping up and down as he tried in vain to call for some salvation, some relief from the terror and pain. Cassidy grabbed a mop of Hartmann's blond hair in one of his claws, jerking his head back. He then leaned forward, bending down so close to Hartmann that their two faces were almost touching, their breath intermingling. He moved the hunting knife up to Hartmann's right eye, the bloody tip of the blade resting just above the soft surface of the cornea. He could feel Hartmann's whole body shaking uncontrollably with fear as he whispered,

'Frohe Weihnachten Herr Hartmann,' slowly pushing the tip of the blade through the tender anterior chamber of the eye and into the lens. The clear gel of the vitreous humour mixed with a trace of blood, forming a small brown pool of liquid which oozed out from Hartmann's eye and rolled down his cheek.

Hartmann choked on the guttural howl lodged in his throat,

panting a dozen jagged breaths in short succession before Cassidy thrust the blade through the back of his eyeball and the soft tissue of his brain and then out through the back of his skull, skewering him to the floor of the hotel room.

The two guards still laying beside the body of Hartmann looked at each other in speechless horror and then watched as the man with the claw hands stood up and walked slowly back to the table in the centre of the room, taking a short sideways glance at the test tube holder still resplendent with its gory display.

'I need a car.'

The leader of the guards took a moment to respond, still trying to comprehend what he had just witnessed.

'A car,' Cassidy repeated.

The guard turned his gaze away from the twitching body on the floor and back towards Cassidy. 'We have been asked to transport you to a safe house. You will be able to get some medical treatment and . . .'

Cassidy stopped him short. 'I need a car.' He reached out his hand. 'Keys.'

The guard tried once again to explain his orders but Cassidy refused to listen. He did not issue another request just remained standing in front of the guard with his bleeding hand outstretched. The guard paused momentarily and then shrugged his shoulders, reaching into his pocket and placing the keys petulantly onto the table.

'There's a black Range Rover out back in the loading area. We will clear this mess up, but if you get pulled over by some traffic cop or whatever, then you're on your own. Is that understood?'

Cassidy nodded as he picked up the keys and put the tape, knife and taser gun into Hartmann's bag and made to leave.

As Cassidy bore down on him, the cowering MP slunk away to the side of the room like a beaten dog, issuing a slight and high pitched whimper.

'I'm taking this one with me,' said Cassidy, dragging Giltmore behind him towards the exit.

## CHAPTER 45

IT was just after he had replenished his brandy glass for the third time that Anthony Willoughby picked up the message from Chief Superintendent McSty. The deep baritone of the policeman adding an intimidating authority to the enquiry, which despite the warming alcohol, caused Willoughby's curdled blood to run cold through his congested veins. He received the message as a dark augury of defeat. The demons his sister had spoken of during her visit to Marchmont House, were gathering around and about him, circling ever closer, ready to clench their teeth into his mortal flesh and bones. His mind seethed with portents of despair. He could sense his downfall coming remorselessly into view, ready to sweep over him, like a deep and swollen mudslide, laying waste to all he was.
Fearing his own company, he sought refuge in the Seacole room where a particularly grubby crowd of club members, made up of financiers and moneyed elite, would often gather late in the evening, coalescing into a fetid and mean spirited

muster of crowing spite. Their acrid mordancy, first learned from the prep school bullies of their youth then honed during careers in politics, banking and business, was discharged with unrestrained malevolence. Any variant from English, white, wealthy masculinity giving cause for contempt. Colour of skin, political leaning, sexual preference, religious affiliation, an overweight spouse, failings of sons and daughters, a buck tooth, an occasional stammer, a balding head - all gave licence for the Seacole room to berate, ridicule and demean. Each cry, swelling the bilious chorus of privileged malignity into a barking, loud-mouthed jeremiad, lamenting life itself.

It was here that Anthony Willoughby sought refuge from his lot.

Within an hour of entering the room, he had begun to relax, buoyed up by alcohol and the pack mentality of his brothers in arms. He felt protected, secure amongst his own, the fathers, brothers and sons of the rich. Thoughts of family intrigue and forgotten funds slowly receding behind the mighty, solid oak doors of the impregnable Burgoyne Club where all manner of swindlers, shysters and crooks had sheltered over the centuries. The evening swept along with one hoary debate following the next. Willoughby even found himself so enlivened by the derision heaped upon the state of the NHS, that he too joined in the discourse.
'End it now,' he thundered. 'It's the only way. No more handouts. No money, no treatment. All our problems solved overnight. The hangers-on, the wasters, the obese, the work shy, the leaching foreigners, the old and useless, let them all go to Hell. In a few years time, we'll be a fitter, leaner society, you mark my words. The population will be at a sustainable level and the country will be run by and for people who have something valuable to contribute and not for the sole benefit of the grasping wastrels that currently monopolise the liberal conscience of Westminster.'
'Bloody, here, here Anthony old chap,' cried Lord Chadwick.

'First bit of sense I've heard about the health service for ten years. We should get old Willoughby into parliament eh, what?' he laughed, receiving the fulsome support of his fellow kinsmen. Chadwick reached forward and slapped Willoughby on the shoulder. 'Here, old man, have another drink.'
The night wore on with sickening inevitability as the gays, the jews, the hindus, the BBC, the farmers, the nurses, the teachers all fell under the pie-eyed judgement of Willoughby and his cronies. Prejudice and loathing wafted across the room like cigar smoke. Minority group after minority group were shunted out of the Burgoyne Club's new world order, leaving a place rid of those who didn't look, think and sound just like them.

And so the hours passed.

By midnight, the group had reduced in size but not in volume. The six remaining members were huddled in one corner of the room, sprawled across the leather upholstery with Anthony Willoughby holding centre stage discussing the injustices of a progressive tax regime. Glasses refreshed, he turned his enmity towards the increased level of personal tax allowance recently announced by their moronic and dim-witted Prime Minister.
'The poor are never going to learn the value of money if they get it all tax free, subsidised, once again, by yours truly. Why the deuce should I be penalised just because I've had the wit and wisdom to get up off of my backside and do an honest day's labour.'
His colleagues banged the table in a tribal show of support and then Lord Chadwick picked up the baton discharging his views on the inconsistencies of disability allowances. As Chadwick railed and moaned, Willoughby looked around the flushed faces of his fellow members. All good blokes, he concluded, not a bad fellow amongst them. Every one, bloody first rate. What a night it had turned out to be, he reflected. Just what he needed. A chance to blow off some steam

amongst the chaps and forget about all that other nonsense. He would tend to it in the morning. Greet the problems head on with fresh eyes and renewed vigour. Get it all sorted just as he had done many times before. There was always a way. But for now, it could all go hang.

He sighed when he noticed the lights dim, taking it for a sign of last orders. What a shame, he thought to himself, just as things were really getting going. He watched as the lights around the room continued to darken, although his chums hadn't seemed to have noticed and were still deep in animated discussion. He tried to tune back into the debate, but found he couldn't really follow their arguments any more, in fact, he was struggling to make out the words. Out of the corner of his eye, he caught a glimpse of the brandy glass as it slipped from his right hand and fell to the floor, spilling its contents over his polished, leather shoes. He tried to laugh, but could not. He tried to voice an apology, but could not. The lights continued to dim as a dribble of spit curled from the corner of his mouth and drooled down onto his lapel. He could see the faces of his friends now, rosy red, blood vessels cracking beneath their skin. They gathered around him, peering at him, as he slumped further down into his chair. Chadwick was laughing, cackling, pointing at him. He could see their mouths move but could only hear a dull, rolling and continuous drone. His breathing became staccato as the world seemed to close in around him. He could hear the heavy flutter of his heart in his ears. Like a caged jackdaw seeking an escape. The whole world felt off key, out of tune.

Suddenly, he felt so utterly, miserably alone.

Above him, the face of Gulliver, the head waiter, came into his dimmed view. His kind, pale blue eyes looking down on him, a soft glint sparking off his gold framed spectacles. Gulliver reached down and placed a gentle hand onto his shoulder.

'Mr Willoughby, sir. Can you hear me? The medical officers are on their way and will be here shortly. Please try and stay calm. Sir, I believe you are having a stroke.'

## CHAPTER 46

MARTHA approached the workhouse from the field at the back of the yard. It was just after four o'clock in the morning and still pitch black, the only light coming from the lodge at the front of the building where the security guard was taking an extended break, blowing on his recently brewed cup of tea. His Alsatian dog was laying at his feet, curled up and fast asleep. It was the end of the shift and both he and his owner were tired and ready for home.

Martha could hear a steady, rhythmic grinding sound coming from the opposite side of the yard. The closer she moved to the site of the Bone Crushing Room, the louder the sound became. She checked the guard one last time and then bolted across the open space until she reached the grid covered by the rusty iron bars that looked down onto the bone covered floor. The grinding noise was louder than ever. She shone her torch to her right and saw an unmanned grey and red cement lorry parked next to the memorial. Its ten cubic meter barrel rolling in its berth, turning over the cement ready to be funnelled into the workhouse room later that day. She removed the rope from her bag and tied the end to one of the iron bars on the grid. The other end she dropped through the chute. It looked narrower than she remembered. She pushed the bag down through the hole and then slowly slid into the tight passage, feet first. Her hips were pressed tightly against the side of the funnel, slowing her descent and she had to twist her body and gradually work her way down the narrow opening. When her legs and waist had made it through, she raised both her arms above her head and, clutching the torch, dropped to the floor below.

A thick puff of dust blew up around her as she landed, making her cough into her arm to hide the noise. As the dust settled, she turned on her torch, illuminating the damp brick walls and the bone covered floor she had seen from above. The room was larger than she thought it would be. A large metal, water pipe ran along the right wall, about two feet above the ground. The room was empty apart from a broken wooden bench and some metal rods, about nine inches long, with square heads which hooked onto the brick wall above the stairs leading back to the locked door of the Itch Ward. She recognised the metal rods from a picture Lincoln had shown her in Mildred's notebook. He said they were called 'rammers'. The inmates used them to smash the animal bones into pieces small enough to be used as fertiliser. At the other end of the room was a low level wall, about three feet high, which ran across three quarters the width of the floor, dividing the room in two.

Martha shone her torch back down to the floor of crushed bones. Most of them were small, just splinters or fragments, no bigger than short twigs or pebbles, but, scattered amongst the rubble, were larger bones, the humerus, femur and tibia. Some were big jointed and heavy, probably belonging to a horse or cow, but others were slightly smaller and looked the right proportions to be part of a human skeleton. Her instinct and experience told her she had found what she was looking for, but she would not be sure until she had returned to London where they could be checked by Danny Whitehead.

She placed a bundle of the bones into her bag and moved to the other side of the room, stepping over the low wall into the alcove.

At the base of the wall there was a broken rammer rod lying on the floor, snapped in two. At this end of the room, the bones were pushed into piles, like small skeletal cairns. The cold air, undisturbed for countless years, was heavy and stale with age and a thick, musty smell clung to Martha's clothes and hair. She shone her torch onto the piles of bones, stretched out in a row along the wall, and thought she saw a rounded shape towards the bottom of the pile closest to her. She reached down and dislodged one of the large limbs at the base. The disrupted mound crumbled to the floor, tumbling out across the layer of crushed bones at her feet. She looked down at the fractured ribs and broken legs and shoulders. Her blood froze in her veins. Laying on its side, directly in front of her, was a small, round skull of a child. A dark, jagged hole had been smashed into the rear of the head, just above the cervical vertebrae. The grotesque, square-shaped silhouette replicated the square end of the rammer rod. Martha reached down and gently picked it up, holding it close. The skull was so small it could rest comfortably in the palm of her hand. The bone was smooth and cold to the touch. She looked into the darkness of the hollow eye sockets, trying to connect in someway, wanting to let the child know that they had been found at last. She knew she was holding the head of one of the Nicholls children, murdered in greed, her young, soft bones crushed to meaningless fragments and then left here to rot, abandoned in the dark. She placed the skull carefully into her bag. She felt no elation at finding the evidence she had been so desperately searching for. No joy, no celebration, no sense of victory or relief. Just a deep and painful sadness along with a burning, all consuming passion to put things right. Martha shone her torch deeper into the alcove. There were a further seven piles, stacked high against the wall. She moved forward hesitantly towards them.

Martha stopped counting when she reached thirty two. The skulls were lined up in rows at her feet like a macabre tray of oversized eggs. Some belonged to adults, but most were the skulls of children, some so small they would have belonged to infants no more than two or three years of age. She was kneeling on the ground, looking disconsolately at her sickening trove of slaughter, thinking of what to do next when she heard a thick, metallic sound coming from the stairs. The iron door of the Itch Ward thumped open, slamming against the brick wall of the stairway. Thin rays of light from the early morning winter sun broke through the darkness. She could hear a muffled voice, pleading and high-pitched, just audible over the sound of the cement lorry outside. Martha crouched behind the low level wall. She could feel the fear and adrenaline increasing her heart rate as she peered through the half light. At the other end of the room, a corpulent man in handcuffs was pushed down the stairs, landing with a heavy thud on the bone covered floor.

Martha reached for her phone, pressing speed dial. Hoping that Chief Superintendent McSty would be awake and ready to answer her call for help.

## CHAPTER 47

SOME thirty miles away, Louisa Willoughby was having a fitful night's rest. The hotel, for all it's old world, boutique charm, had little to recommend it beyond a passable cellar and some interesting tableware. The staff in particular were singularly bothersome, seemingly unable to comprehend even the most straightforward of instruction. A request for a black tea should result in precisely that, nothing more, so, no milk, no lemon and certainly no pudgy mince pie squeezed onto the saucer, leaving an unsightly sticky paste on the side of the teacup. Dangling a Do Not Disturb sign on the handle of the room should be plain to all, but instead seemed to call forth no end of concerned well-wishers. Would madam like new towels? Would madam like her bed turned down? Would madam like a chocolate on her pillow? And so it went on, until finally Louisa capitulated, abandoning her bid for peace and retired to the small terrace bar on the first floor of the hotel where, unfortunately, the meddlesome prying continued. Would madam like to book a table? Would madam like an olive with her tonic water? Would madam like to see a menu?

The inquisitiveness of the hotel staff knew no bounds. By the time the Dray sashayed into the bar, she felt quite drained. All the gaiety of her Portuguese tryst, melting away like fallen snow on a spring morning.

Supper had been wearisome. The overweening flirting of the Dray with the polite, young waitress was almost too much to bear. He was in a high-spirited, playful mood and engaged the poor young thing in a lengthy discussion concerning the provenance of each item on the menu, like it mattered one jot to him. When the waitress suggested that she ask the chef to come to the table as he knew best, the Dray blustered and backed down, moving with haste to the food order. He was tempted by the steak, but also liked the look of the game pie. In the end he settled for a frightful mess they called The Feast of St Nicholas, which seemed to contain all manner of animal matter. Funny little men and their meat, thought Louisa. Their ordering of the bloodiest, gamiest item on the menu was one of the few ways left for them to mimic the hunter-gatherer credentials of their ancestors. Whilst Louisa picked her way through a rather ordinary Caesar salad, the Dray ate in the only way he knew how and that was to gorge. Big fulsome forkfuls disappeared into his mouth, an occasional drop landing on his pressed, dark blue suit.

'Do take care, you are quidding,' she said pointing to the gravy spot.

'Ah, silly me,' he said dabbing at his lapel and continuing with the debrief. This was what made time spent with the Dray so worthwhile, so fruitful. He knew about things. Lots of things and all in detail. She quizzed him as the main course arrived, teasing the facts out of him. A gentle touch of the hand, reigniting him when the flow of information ebbed. A flirtatious glance, galvanising him to disclose when he felt the need to be circumspect. His careless indiscretion was a delight to behold. One specific anecdote particularly piqued her curiosity. What's more, it gave her the excuse she needed for an early departure the next day. She imagined the gentle breeze of freedom reviving her spirit as the car pulled away up the pebbled drive in the morning. The pleasure of seeing him, posturing and strutting, shrinking in the rear view mirror as she plunged into the depths of the English countryside, unencumbered by the Dray. What a truly sumptuous joy. But that was tomorrow, for now she must giggle, fawn, praise and beguile. Laughing along with him, even when he pointed out with delighted boyish glee, that the dessert menu included a serving of Spotted Dick. Well really, can you imagine!

In their room, much later, she clung to her side of the bed, trying to create some distance between them. She felt smothered by his pugnacious presence having become used to sharing her bed with more slender, more agile creatures than the Dray. A muffled misunderstanding during their lovemaking had left her sore. A pain that would nag at her for days. The discomfort had meant she had slept only in fits and starts and now, just before dawn, as sleep finally came for her, she had been woken by a low humming sound from his side of the bed.

'What was that?'

'Nothing, my love. It is just my phone. Go back to sleep.'

She winced at the term of endearment. So inappropriate in his mouth. She pulled the bedclothes up to her chin and tried one last time to harvest some rest before the day began.

On the other side of the bed, Chief Superintendent McSty let out a heavy, shameful sigh as he saw the name of Martha Green appear on the illuminated screen of his phone. Was this really the man he had become? Was this really all that was left of him? Principle and integrity cast asunder for the sake of a doomed romantic liaison and a bundle of ready cash. He sat on the side of his bed, head in hands, regret and sorrow in his mournful, bleary eyes. He looked one last time at the name of the girl he had prized above all others and then put the phone on silent, gently placing it onto the bedside table, face down.

# CHAPTER 48

CASSIDY stopped at the top of the stairs and looked over to the far corner of the Workhouse room. His deep brown eyes piercing through the darkness. When he pushed Giltmore down to the floor below, he thought he had seen a faint glow of soft light reflected on the wall opposite, but now all he could see was bricks and bones. His tall frame moved down the stairs, stepping over the politician who lay in a crumpled heap amongst the debris of the dead. Martha was laying behind the low wall, hunched over, trying to shield the light of her phone. There was still no answer. Where the fuck was McSty? Cassidy stalked towards her, his long strides kicking up the bone dust from the floor. She felt a sharp pain as he hooked his left claw around her neck, grabbing a thick wad of her hair, and yanked her up from the ground. He looked her slowly up and down, appraising her.

'Martha Green, I presume? I have been expecting you.'

Cassidy was tired and in pain. It had been a long drive up from London. Not helped by the need to stop on several occasions to wipe down the steering wheel, which dripped with the blood from his finger sockets. He had found some aspirins in a small overnight bag in the boot of the mercenaries' car, along with a first aid kit, a spare mobile phone, £200 in cash, a pair of handcuffs and a Glock 17 sidearm. Some kind of emergency provision bag for McSty's men, he guessed. The aspirins had begun to wear off as he dragged Martha over to the side of the room where Giltmore was laying and pushed her down towards the politician.

'Well, seeing you have decided to join us, you had better make yourself useful. Undo his cuffs, then reattach him to that,' he said pointing to the large round water pipe that was bolted to the wall.

Martha didn't move, momentarily taken aback by the sight of his blood encrusted hands.

'Did you hear me? Do it.'

She snapped her attention back to her captor. 'Look, I don't know who you are, but you're making a big mistake. I'm a police officer. You really don't want to do this.'

'I know who you are, Detective Sergeant Martha Green. Now do what I told you.' He pulled out the Glock from his left pocket, gripped tightly by his remaining thumb and forefinger and pushed it hard against her forehead. 'I am not going to ask again,' he said handing her the key with his other bloody hand.

Martha could feel the cold metal of the barrel against her skin. She raised her hands in defeat, trying to placate him, and slowly bent down to undo the cuffs, gently lifting Giltmore to his feet. He looked up at her.

'Are you here to save me?' asked the politician.

'Everything is going to be fine, sir. Help will be here shortly. The police know I'm here and are on their way,' she said, loud enough to make sure Cassidy caught the words above the noise of the cement mixer. 'I just need to get you to sit on the ground, just here. There you go. Now I'm going to clip these back on, just for a bit, before the police arrive.'

Cassidy followed her movements with the gun. 'Give me your phone, Detective and then sit down with your back against the pipe.' He dropped her phone onto the floor before slamming his foot down on top of it. He bent down and reached behind the detective, clumsily wrapping what was left of the silver tape around her wrists and the pipe until she couldn't move her arms. She felt a jagged pain in the palm of her right hand as the diamond from her ring pressed against it, squeezed tight by the binding. Once she was secure, Cassidy put down the gun. He grabbed the broken bench with his right claw and dragged it in front of his two prisoners, perching on the wooden boards. Slowly he began to undo the dressing on his bloody and aching hands. Martha could see the bandage pulling on the shredded skin where it had become encrusted with blood and had stuck to the flesh.

He looked back at Martha and Giltmore, slumped on the floor next to each other, and smiled. Two birds with one stone, he thought. How neat. Carefully, he started wrapping the clean bandage from the first aid kit around his bruised and bloody hands.

'Well this is a nice get together isn't it,' he said. 'The corrupt policewoman and the dodgy politician. What a lovely picture the two of you make.'

Martha looked askance at the dishevelled man, piled in a heap next to her. 'Politician?'

'Yes, Martha. That's right, you haven't met. Please, let me introduce Mr George Giltmore, MP for Easton.' Giltmore slowly raised his head, looked briefly at Martha and began to sob, his shoulders shaking uncontrollably.

She had only seen him on television previously and didn't connect that man with the one seated next to her. 'Don't worry, Mr Giltmore, we will get through this. It will be okay,' she said, doing her best to console him.

Cassidy let out a derisive laugh. 'George. Hey, George. Are you listening, George?' Giltmore looked up at Cassidy through his tear-stained eyes. 'I'm afraid the policewoman is lying to you. No, George. It will not be okay. Not for you. You see, this is what is actually going to happen. There will be no police. No last minute rescue. Later today, my colleague back in London is going to hack into your email account. We will then send a message from you to your darling wife, who I am sure will be wondering where her George is and why he didn't come home last night. Your email will tell her all about your little indiscretion in Bremen with the versatile Simone. You will also confess that you can no longer go on living a lie and have decided to run far away, to another part of the world where you cannot be found and where you and Simone can begin a new life together. Don't worry, George, I will blind copy your Harriet Blackwood so she can help your dear lady with the PR side of things, press announcements etc. Oh, and just for good measure, I will pass a copy or two of the photographs, you know the ones, George, to the tabloids. The photos of you and the lovely Simone, the new Mr or Mrs Giltmore. Not sure which one of you is going to play the part of the husband, but I am sure you lovebirds can sort that out between you. Once everybody knows what's what, you will disappear, never to be seen again. How does that sound, eh George? Look Georgie, don't get upset. The truth is, you will soon be forgotten. Your wife will marry again, the boys will get a new dad and Miss Blackwood will find a new politician to pin her hopes to. You see, nobody will really miss you, will they, Georgie?'

Giltmore looked into Cassidy's smiling, gloating eyes, searching desperately for some sign of mercy. He just saw loathing. He turned away and hung his balding head in a defeated silence.

'Don't listen to him, Mr Giltmore. It will be okay, do you hear?'

'Ah, the beautiful Martha Green.' Cassidy turned his heartless gaze to the policewoman who had triggered wave after wave of destruction and chaos to come crashing through his well ordered life during the past days. 'Ever the optimist. I admire that. I must admit, I had expected you to give up the fight weeks ago, but to be fair, you have some grit, I will give you that. Don't waste your breath on him though, he's not worth it, believe me, besides, he is just missing his family.'

He bent towards her, a cruel smirk on his face. 'Do you miss your family, Martha?

Martha ignored him and carried on attending to the politician, trying to keep him focussed.

'Martha. I said, do you miss your family?'

'My family has nothing to do with you. Whoever the fuck you are,' she spat at him.

He raised an apologetic hand. 'Please forgive me, that's remiss of me. Introductions are called for. My name, Miss Green, is Milton Cassidy, I work for the Willoughby family, although I defy you to ever prove that connection.'

Martha had a moment of recollection, recalling the name of Cassidy from her conversation with Ben out in Sweden. Was this the same Cassidy who was the signatory on the Strathdon Trust? The one who received an annual fund for fourteen years, set up by Anthony Willoughby?

Cassidy noticed the flicker on her face. 'I can see you have heard of me. Very impressive. Well done, Detective Sergeant. Right, now we have got our introductions out of the way, let me go back to my original question. Do you miss your family, Martha Green?'

Martha stared back at him silently, with no trace of emotion on her face.

'I see. It's like that is it? Well, I for one was sorry to hear about your mother. What a tenacious little so and so she was. Who would have thought she was quite such a lush though?'

'Shut the fuck up, Cassidy. You know nothing about her.'

'On the contrary, Miss Green, I know more than you might think.' Martha looked away, disregarding him.

'Please, Detective Sergeant, indulge me for a moment or two and let me paint you a picture.' He paused for dramatic effect, making sure the policewoman was listening. 'Over here, there's a man, a tall man, who is instructed by his employer to make rid of a problem. Whilst over here, there's a woman, brown hair, middle aged. Sound familiar, Martha? The woman is drunk, out of her head, a bottle and a half of cheap vodka inside her, forced down her throat by the tall man. The blonde woman is now propped up in the front seat of her Honda Civic, tucked into a lay-by on the A12, headlights off. It's a quiet night, just before dawn. Nothing on the road apart from, off in the distance, a large lorry, speeding along, fully loaded with the late autumn sugar beet harvest. The tall man, reaches down into the car and releases the handbrake and the car slowly moves out of the lay-by onto the deserted road. Using all of his strength, he pushes the car down the shallow hill, steering it directly into the path of the oncoming lorry, before, just in time, he rolls to the safety of the side of the road . Then, boom. What a mess. I'm afraid not much left for the coroner to look at. Just a ball of twisted metal and human flesh. The police are easily persuaded not to look too hard for cause and effect. The incident gets chalked up as just another drunken driver making their sorry way home after some late night binge somewhere.' He looked deep into Martha's eyes. 'And there it is, Detective. There's nothing more left to say. End of story.'

Martha stared back at him, her breathing hard and fast, anger forcing bitter tears of frustration and sadness from her eyes as she realised she was looking into the face of her mother's killer.

'You fucking bastard, Cassidy. I will hunt you down and I will fucking kill you.' She pulled hard on the pipe, trying to free her hands, but it was fixed solidly to the wall.

'Now, now, Miss Green. Temper temper. That will never do. You will make our George blush with language like that, won't she George.' The politician didn't move, staring at the floor in silence. 'Don't mind me, Miss Green, and my little stories,' continued Cassidy. 'I'm just jealous. You see, Martha, you at least had a mother. Mine didn't even hang around to see me born. Just died, during labour, right there on the hospital bed. That's sad, isn't it, Martha?' Martha was in no mood to hear Cassidy's sob story. She was pulling as hard as she could, trying to loosen the binding so she could get her hands on the cold-hearted bastard in front of her. Oblivious to her efforts, Cassidy continued with his sorry tale.

'My father was not much better,' he said, winding the clean, white bandage around his other hand in a long and gentle stroke. 'Keeled over with a heart attack just before my second birthday. I can't remember one thing about him, I'm afraid. Complete mystery to me. So you see, Martha, you at least had a family. I had nothing. I only bothered to find out my real name a few years ago. My new, well, owners I should call them, the Willoughbys, gave me the name Milton Cassidy. No idea why they landed on that, but there you go. One name is as good as another, I suppose.'

Despite herself, Martha had tuned into his story. Her instincts making her listen. She thought of the house her mother had lived in, bought and paid for by the Willoughby family. She thought of the odious Buller seducing her grandmother just to obtain a son and heir. She thought of the male baby snatched from the hospital. Her brain joining the dots, forming a truth that was almost too revolting, too obscene to contemplate. She looked at Cassidy winding the bandages around his fists. His rugged face, the brown eyes, the auburn hair. It couldn't be, please God, it couldn't be.

Cassidy saw the look of revulsion on her face.

'What, Miss Green? What is it exactly you find quite so appalling? Is it the hands? Well, believe me, they are just as painful as they look.'

'No, it's not that.' She was talking slowly now, piecing the facts together. 'You said your mother died at birth and you can't remember your father?'

'Yes, Miss Green. You heard correctly. Thank you for listening so attentively. I thought you were ignoring me.'

'But you found out your real father's name eventually, a few years ago?'

He nodded 'Yes, what of it? Where's this leading to Detective?'

Martha spoke quietly. Almost not wanting to say the words. 'The name of your father. It was . . . was it Buller? Edmund Buller?'

Cassidy stopped winding the bandages. The arrogant

smile on his face slowly dissolving into a questioning, puzzled look. 'Yes, Miss Green. How clever of you. And may I ask how you know that?'

'You don't know, do you,' she said. 'My God, you really don't know.'

'Know what, Miss Green?'

She looked into his eyes, trying to see beyond the heartless monster he had become. 'Your father, the man you now know was called Edmund Buller, seduced a woman and got her pregnant back in 1964. The woman he seduced was called Petra Taylor. He persuaded her to have the baby, even though Petra was already married, but when the child was born, Buller took the baby boy from Petra and she never saw either Buller or the baby again. The married woman had another child some years previously, a daughter called Margaret. Margaret later married a man called Richard, Richard Green.'

Cassidy was staring back at her, trying to make sense of the facts.

'Don't you get it, Cassidy?' she shouted impatiently. 'Don't you see? The baby boy, the one stolen from the hospital, was you. The other child of your mother's, the little girl, was called Margaret. Margaret Green. Your sister, Cassidy. You murdered your own sister.'

Cassidy's face twitched as he looked for understanding. Searching for some rational sense, a bit of logic he could pin his thoughts to.

'Willoughby, your 'owner' as you called him, bought out Petra's house later on and let her live there, free of charge. Some sort of bribe or guilt trip or something or maybe an attempt to hush things up in case Petra tried to snatch his new prized possession back off him. I don't know. Either way, the house Petra lived in is owned by the Willoughby Estate. Look it up if you don't believe me.' She looked at Cassidy's troubled face. 'Oh dear, the Willoughbys have played you for a fool, Cassidy, haven't they? A worthless, pointless fool.'

At first he could not accept what the policewoman was

saying to him. It made no sense. She was just trying to delay him, put him off to protect her own skin. But slowly her story began to ring true. The facts falling into place. How cold she have possibly known the name of his father? Nobody knew about him. Nobody. If what she said about the house was true, then why would Willoughby, of all people, allow someone to live in one of his properties, rent free. He wouldn't do that. Not Willoughby. Not unless he had good reason. Gradually he started to accept the truth. There was a flicker of remorse for Margaret Green, the woman he had killed, but not much more than that. She was his sister, but he didn't know her and now he never would. She meant nothing to him. It wasn't that which was causing him such pain and anger. It was the fact that the Willoughbys, most particularly Anthony Willoughby, had instructed him to murder Margaret in the full knowledge of what he was asking of him. Willoughby had ordered him to murder his own flesh and blood, just to clear away an inconvenient enquiry that was causing him some concern. But Cassidy knew Willoughby better than that. He knew the devious ways of his mind. Willoughby had seen an opportunity to do a bit of house keeping at the same time as calling short Margaret Green's amateurish investigations. 'Two birds with one stone,' he muttered to himself. It had been a chance too good to miss. An opportunity to wipe away any trace of the Willoughby family's involvement with the Greens and their link with Edmund Buller.

'Cassidy,' Martha shouted. 'Cassidy. You need to let us out of here. I can help you get Willoughby, but you must let me go. You need me.'

Cassidy stood up from the bench and turned slowly towards her. A dark, cold rage in his eyes. He looked down at his pleading relative, his young and beautiful niece. He looked hard into her eyes, those same dark brown eyes that stared back at him from every mirror he had ever looked into. He looked, but he felt nothing. He despised the detective for the trouble she had caused. He despised her for devolving the truth, a truth he wished he had never known. 'No Detective,' he said. 'Blood or no blood. I do not need you.'

He turned and walked away up the stairs, leaving the policewoman and the politician, sitting helplessly on the floor, strapped to the cast iron pipe. He pushed open the workhouse door, taking a deep breath of the cold winter air and walked around to the back of the building towards his car. As he passed the grinding cement mixer, he flicked the valve to *Open*, releasing a torrent of wet cement down the chute and sending it tumbling and splashing onto the floor of the Bone Crushing Room below. He heard a terrified high-pitched scream of a male voice behind him as he walked away into the cold and grey December morning.

## CHAPTER 49

ON the passenger seat was the driver's house keys, phone and holstered revolver, which he hadn't had the time to pack away in his employer's haste to leave the hotel earlier that morning.

'We are driving through Skeilton now, Miss Willoughby.'

Louisa looked out onto the jumble of half-a-dozen cottages, interspersed with the ragged branches of dark and leafless trees. It was still early enough to see the Christmas lights shining in the morning gloom, hung around the simple homes that adorned the narrow road, running through the centre of the village. Irregular illuminated patterns of white and gold festooned the doorways and windows. She wondered if it was a village policy to exclude different coloured bulbs, policed by an officious local, or whether the residents all just fell in line, unthinking, without realising that their little homes looked an exact copy of their neighbours'. Her phone buzzed in her handbag. It was probably just her sister again. She could wait. Elizabeth invariably had nothing to say, even when she initiated the call herself.

The short journey from Cambridgeshire had been tedious

and unsettling, full of meandering curves, bumps and dips, but it did allow her time to reflect on McSty's ramblings of the previous night. Over supper, McSty or the Dray as she preferred to think of him, had confirmed that he had called her brother as she had asked him to, with a view of adding still more pressure onto his poor, sagging shoulders. In addition, she was now up to speed with the sorry end of Herr Hartmann and of his extraordinary venture with George Giltmore. McSty had also informed her of the reported search through the Willoughby trust funds by parties as yet unknown, as well as the endeavours of the policewoman, who seemed intent on scuppering Anthony's plans for his President's Kin memorial at Blyth. The last, Louisa found particularly worrying, but she was comforted by McSty's assurance that Cassidy, despite his physical impediments, had pursued the detective to Suffolk and was in attendance as they were speaking. Louisa gave next to no thought to the portly MP, who she discovered was dragged away, kicking and screaming, by the injured but ever reliable Mr Cassidy. However, it was the TV chap who interested her the most and gave her the excuse to flee the bed chamber at first light. He had not been included in her updates thus far and there was something about his entanglement and the discovery of Jeremiah Buller's dagger that intrigued her. In addition, and on a more practical front, McSty had not been able to determine whether this Marsh individual was a problem that needed to be dealt with or an irritation that could be ignored. Her instinct told her the latter. Besides, Anthony had created quite enough drama to date without her adding to the mess, but seeing that she was in the area, she decided to see the site of the discovery first-hand and then make her decision.

As they pulled up to Sorrel Cottage, the driver noticed a red car parked in front of the house and a thin line of smoke curling from one of the chimneys. It had been the presumption of both he and his employer that the house would be empty following the recent family death, so this discovery was unexpected.

'There seems to be someone in residence, Miss Willoughby. Would you like me to drive on?'

Louisa thought for a moment, gazing at the small lattice windows on the top floor. 'No, pull in please, Woodrow,' she replied. 'Though it might be sensible if you accompanied me into the building, just as a precaution, in case our Mr Marsh is not minded to provide the warm welcome traditionally offered unexpected guests at this time of year.'

\* \*

The cloth that was wrapped around the saddlebag was pinned out on the kitchen table with various items of cutlery holding down the four corners. To touch, it reminded Lincoln of the shammy leather his dad would use to wipe the suds off his Volvo as it dried in the late Saturday afternoon sunshine. The thick, dry material creasing and curling where it had been folded around the shape of the bag many years ago. Lincoln had found it just where he had left it, under one of the legs of the kitchen table. It had first looked blank, but when he rubbed his fingers against the yellowed hide he could feel the slight indentations of some written words. By holding it up to the window on a slant, he could make out a few names listed in a column and the scrawled signature of Jeremiah Buller, but nothing else. It was only when he placed some plain paper on top of the thick parchment and gently rubbed a soft pencil over the page that the rest of the words were revealed, confirming the murderous secrets of the Bone Crushing Room.

It was now eight thirty in the morning and he still hadn't heard from Martha. He impatiently turned off the radio, feeling unable to cope with the Christmas jocularity of the vigorously eager presenter. Martha had told him not to call, promising him that she would ring as soon as she was clear of the workhouse site. For the last hour, he had stared restlessly at his phone. Not able to wait any longer, he dialled her number, but there was no reply. In all the excitement, she had probably forgotten to turn her phone back on, he said to himself, or maybe she was driving and unable to answer, or most likely she just didn't have a signal, the coverage being very patchy in the Blyth and Skeilton area. He was on his feet now, pacing up and down, unconvinced by his own excuses. Finally, he gave in. Even though she had expressly told him not to, he decided he would drive to the workhouse and see if there were any signs that her foolish and stupid exploit had gone badly wrong.

He was just putting on his coat when he heard a gentle tap at the front door.

* *

Martha hadn't expected the cement to feel so cold.

The rough, stony liquid had now risen to the top of her shoulders and had begun to creep up her neck. She could feel the intrusive mix of limestone and clay working its way beneath her clothes and scouring her tender flesh. Next to her, Giltmore was thrashing his kneeling body to and fro in the thickening liquid, screaming for help and trying to pull himself free from the wall. Initially, she had tried to calm him down, fearing that he would dislocate his shoulder or worse, but it was pointless. As she stretched her neck up into the cold air of the Bone Room, trying to keep her mouth free from the cement, she was aware that she too was being overwhelmed by panic and hysteria and felt like screaming into the darkness, just like the politician.

It was getting harder and harder to move her hands below the surface. She could feel the mixture beginning to set around her body. The stone on her engagement ring was cutting into her right palm as she contorted her hands and wrists so she could continue to work the jagged edge against the binding. She could taste chalky splashes of cement as it inexorably rose towards her mouth. Underneath the cold greyness, she felt something give. With all the strength that was left in her body, she pulled her arms apart, feeling the binding begin to tear. She pulled again and fell free of the wall pipe, nearly toppling face first into the mix. Her legs were heavy as if they were already moulded into the building. Her lungs were tightening as the cement began to harden around her chest. She slowly managed to get her right foot onto the ground and pushed up from her kneeling position, rising from the cement like Poseidon surfacing from the depths of the ocean.

She could move her legs, but only just. As every second passed, she was being gradually immobilised by the liquid stone. Giltmore let out a desperate cry.

'Help me, please God, help me.'

She bent towards him and put her hands under his arms and pulled as hard as she could. His head was resting in her neck and she could hear him straining, trying to yank his hands from the metal cuffs. She tried to pull again, but there was no movement. She could feel her legs begin to stiffen and let go of his body.

'I'm sorry, George. . . I can't. . . I'm so sorry.' She could see the terror in his eyes, looking back at her.

'No, you can't leave me here, you can't. No. Keep trying.' The cement was starting to flow into his mouth and he coughed, spitting out a grey mouthful of the mix.

The setting cement was pulling at her, sucking her down like grey quicksand. Martha could barely move her legs and knew that she might not make it across to the stairs leading to the surface. 'I've got to go, George. I'm so sorry. It's too late. There's nothing I can do. I have to go.' He spluttered as another wave of cement washed into his mouth. He screamed at her not to leave, but the detective turned away and dragged herself slowly towards the stairway.

## CHAPTER 50

WHEN Lincoln first opened the door, he took Louisa Willoughby to be a friend of his mother's come round to pay her belated respects, but her eyes did not convey commiseration or care or mindfulness of any description. The unyielding posture, the clothes, the jewellery were not things he associated with the relaxed and homely circle of friends that his mother had always surrounded herself with.

'I am sure you are able to find a few moments of time for me. Please, lets sit shall we?' she replied when he tried to make his excuses and leave.

'I really need to be somewhere else, I'm afraid.'

A large man, carrying a peaked cap, edged into view behind the elegant grande dame. 'Miss Willoughby asked you to sit down, Mr Marsh, lets do as the lady asks,' the driver requested, pointing firmly towards the chair.

Lincoln stepped back inside, slowly replacing his car keys onto the windowsill.

'Willoughby? Miss Willoughby?' A look of puzzled concern on his face.

Louisa stood with her hands clutched in front of her, motionless and serene. 'I can see you have heard the name. Good. That means I have your attention.' She gestured towards the kitchen with a gentle movement of her hand. 'Please, Mr Marsh, be seated.'

Despite the irony of being offered a seat in his own home by a complete stranger, Lincoln did not take issue, feeling he had little choice but to sit back down at the small kitchen table. Louisa Willoughby stepped uncomfortably into the cottage. Her eyes straying over the tattered furnishings and faded wallpaper of the kitchen. Her nose twitching at the smell of damp timber and neglect, causing her to subconsciously raise her hand to her face, resting her index finger on her nose in an attempt to protect her tender senses. She glanced down at the wooden chair opposite Lincoln, pitying its inelegance, and remained standing.

'I thought we should have a conversation, Mr Marsh. I believe we share an acquaintance. Martha Green. You know her?'

'Yes, I know Martha Green. What's it to you?'

Louisa balked at the surliness of his reply, a look of reprimand simmering in her eyes. She took a short breath and began slowly pacing around the table, circling him. Lincoln felt her unsettling presence as she moved behind, out of view. 'In what capacity do you know Miss Green, if you don't mind me asking, Mr Marsh? Lovers? Friends? Colleagues?'

'That is my business, Miss Willoughby and has nothing at all to do with you. I am not obliged to answer your questions and you are most certainly not entitled to come into my house and intimidate me.'

Louisa pulled up with a sudden halt. 'Intimidate you? I have no intention of intimidating you, Mr Marsh. Why on earth would I need to?' She resumed her slow, circular patrol around the room. 'No, on the contrary, I am trying to help you, but to do so I would be obliged if you could aid me in my understanding as to why you are involving yourself in my family's affairs. Are you a private investigator perhaps?'

He glanced down at his phone. Martha had still not called. 'No, look, I am just helping out a friend,' he said impatiently, 'that's all, now I need you to leave.' He stood up and took a step towards the door, but Woodrow moved in front of him, blocking his way, pushing him back to his seat.

As Louisa moved around the table she traced her fingers along its worn edge, ignoring Lincoln's attempt to curtail their conversation. 'A friend. I see, just a friend. How touching. You must miss her,' she said playfully, wondering what cruel misery had befallen the detective once Cassidy had tracked her down to Blyth. The parchment that remained stretched out on the table caught her eye and she turned it slightly so she could look at the faded sheet. 'I am sure you make a fine pair, you and Miss Green. All industry and endeavour no doubt. Long, dark evenings huddled together, reviewing your findings and plotting and scheming your next steps. But you know what they say, Mr Marsh. "Beware the barrenness of a busy life". Your toil may not reward you as you hoped. Take care, Mr Marsh. My brother, alas, does not count patience amongst his many fine qualities and can be quite uncharitable with those who vex him.' She picked up the piece of white paper lying on top of the parchment, her eyes scanning down the list of names that Lincoln had revealed, noting the signatures at the bottom of the page. 'Ah, I see you have come across the labours of the repellent Jeremiah Buller.'

'Could you put that back please,' Lincoln asked firmly, unable to hide the agitation in his voice.

'This?' She said dismissively, holding the corner of the page by her thumb and forefinger and raising it into the air. 'And what exactly do you think you have here, Mr Marsh? Some evidence so revealing that it will shift the very axis of our world, sending us all hurtling towards Hell's Gate? I doubt a list of forgotten country folk and the signature of a reprobate will get you very far.' She replaced the sheet onto the table. 'It was all such a long time ago, I'm afraid, Mr Marsh, and all so very inconsequential.'

Lincoln could feel his anger rising. 'Who the hell are you

people? What nefarious moral code do you live your lives by? Inconsequential? How can the lives of over thirty women and children be inconsequential?'

She looked up from the paper for a moment, taking in Lincoln's words, before slowly returning her gaze to the document and sliding her slender finger down the list of names. 'Oh, I see. That's interesting. This list is just the women and children.' She paused slightly, noticing Lincoln's confusion. 'Would you like to know what happened to the men, Mr Marsh?' Lincoln looked up into her into her dispassionate, blue eyes. 'Yes,' she said, 'I can see you would.'

She remained standing, her back straight and strong. 'I am told that you and your companion found your way to the remnants of the workhouse in Dunnings Alley, shortly followed by a visit to Limehouse, so I presume you came across Buller's handiwork there. So heartless of the rogue to herd that clutch of little ones towards their muddy end. Quite ingenious though, I suppose, in its own brutal way. And that Reverend, stabbed in the back in his own drawing room? I imagine that is old news for you and the tenacious Miss Green. But all that pales into insignificance in comparison to the goings-on at Blyth.'

She pointed back to the table. 'Listed here are the names of the workhouse wives and children who Buller despatched early one September morning when the menfolk were in the fields flint clearing, in preparation for the following year's crops. The Willoughby family was trapped in an agreement they could not get out of and the Workhouse was losing money hand over fist. The agreement to buy Blyth was the worst deal ever done in the name of Willoughby, according to my father, and finally Norris, the then Head of the Family, ran out of patience and demanded that Buller remove all the remaining inmates. Jeremiah Buller was a Blacksmith's son, a 'striker' by trade. A big and powerful man, by all accounts, with a greed and a temper unmatched by his peers. Smashing the skulls and bones of half-starved mothers and their offspring would present little challenge to such a boorish individual, although it wasn't until the following morning that the work was complete. When he finally emerged, so the story goes, he was caked in the blood, flesh and bones of his quarry whose remains were now mixed with animal carcasses and left underground to be stripped clean by the rats and vermin of Blyth. I recall wondering, when I was first told of this barbarous tale, what words of comfort the mothers whispered to their trembling children when it was clear what fate awaited them all.

'The men, however met an altogether different fate. When my father, Basil Willoughby, told me, my sister and two brothers this tale, he took us out to the East Coast where it all took place so we could picture it clearly. He was determined to instil it into our young, impressionable minds. To brand us with the memory. It was a bitterly cold day and I remember clasping Andrew, my baby brother, close to me to protect him from the biting wind as it whipped off the North Sea. My father had to pull us in towards him so we could hear his words above the crashing waves. He told us about the Master of Blyth Workhouse, I forget his name...'

'Caton,' said Lincoln, remembering the evening with Aunt Catherine at Plat Principal.

'Caton. Yes, that's right, Mr Marsh. Well done. Alfred Caton. Another objectionable man,' she said, closing her eyes with revulsion. 'The male inmates woke the morning after their families had been led down to the Bone Crushing Room, to find an empty courtyard. Angrily, they demanded to know where their wives and children were. It was Caton who assured them, with a great show of authority, that they had been transported to the newly built Great Yarmouth workhouse and were now waiting for their husbands to join them. The sixty men were bitter and sceptical having become accustomed to the deceit of the Master, but when a fleet of four open-top carriages arrived, each with a large cask of cider attached to the front bench, the mood of the men changed. They set off to the coast that evening in high spirits, looking forward to seeing their loved ones and happy to see the back of Caton and his miserable workhouse.

'A fishing trawler had been chartered to ferry them up the coast from Southwold to the port at Great Yarmouth. The men were herded by the small, five-man crew into a long, narrow metal cage that had been rigged up on the deck in place of the usual fishing nets. Jeremiah Buller, who was overseeing the transfer, laughed and joked with the men, passing a final cask of cider through the open door of the cage. The winds had risen earlier that day and the seas were now unruly, buffeting the men from one side of the cage to the other as they left the harbour. The boat continued on its course northwards towards Great Yarmouth, hugging the coast as it went. It wasn't until they had travelled six miles and were halfway between Southwold and Lowestoft that the anchor was lowered and Buller pulled the cage door to a close, locking it with the iron key he had hanging around his neck. He and the crew, each armed with a Boarding Knife, circled the imprisoned and confused inmates. Buller had acquired the oversized weapons from one of the visiting Norwegian whaling boats who used them to remove blubber from their catch, but he decided that, at four feet in length, including a sharp two foot dual-edged blade, they would perfectly meet the requirements of his bloody deed.

'Led by Buller, the crew plunged the boarding knives mercilessly into the cages, slicing and maiming the screaming inmates. At first, the terrified men did their best to sidestep the razor-sharp blades, clinging to each other for balance as they slipped on the bloody deck, but slowly, one by one, the men fell to the floor, some dead but most injured and too weak to stand. When he believed that every inmate had been cut or slain, Buller gave the order to lift the cage from the deck by the net hoist. Blood dripped onto the rigging and the heads of the crew as the cage swung over the sea and was lowered into the waves. From the deck, Buller could see those men who were still alive, climbing over the dead towards the vanishing skies, using their last sorrowful breaths to plead for mercy.'

In the silence, Lincoln could hear the sound of Louisa Willoughby gently scratching the dry skin on her left palm. She was looking straight ahead, across the table and into the frozen garden outside the window. 'I have often wondered,' she said 'why my father went to such lengths to tell us the details of that miserable tale. He never thought to explain himself or point us towards a conclusion. Perhaps it was a warning about the brutal nature of unchecked violence or maybe it was an example of good management by our ancestors who recognised an issue and ruthlessly dealt with it or maybe he wanted us to understand the benefit of having people with unquestioning loyalty around us who were able to conduct evil on our behalf. Who knows? I suppose each of the four of us took from it what we wanted and drew our own life lesson. For my part, Mr Marsh, I learnt not to leave loose ends, so, as innocuous as this is, I think I will be taking it with me.' She picked up the sheet of paper along with the parchment and rolled them both together. Lincoln moved to retrieve them, but the full framed Woodrow, once again, blocked his path.

'Please, don't get up,' Louisa said. 'I will slip away now and leave you in peace to enjoy the oncoming festivities.' She looked down at the seated Lincoln with a patronising gaze. 'You strike me as a man with little stomach for the fight, if you don't mind me saying. You have absentmindedly drifted into the path of people best avoided and I am sure you will take this opportunity to step aside and move on with your life and with that in mind, Mr Marsh, I wish you good day.'

Woodrow opened the door for his employer. She stepped gracefully across the mat and into the winter air only to immediately reverse, with faltering steps, back into the room. The black barrel of the gun from Woodrow's passenger seat pointing at her powdered white and startled head.

## CHAPTER 51

MARTHA pushed Louisa Willoughby back into the kitchen with a heavy shove.

A grey smear ran the length of the barrel of the revolver, matching the colour of the thick coating of cement that clung to Martha's clothes, like molten sugar. Heavy lumps of dark brown earth crumbled from her shoes onto the tiled floor, following her walk across the ploughed fields from Blyth. As she arrived at the cottage, shivering and still in a state of shock from her ordeal in the Bone Crushing Room, she noticed the expensive saloon car and then saw Lincoln through the side window. It was clear that he was in trouble. Although she had never seen a picture of Louisa Willoughby, she knew from her profile that the woman peering down at Lincoln, had to be a member of that loathsome family.

'Put that down,' she said, pointing to the rolled sheet Louisa was clutching in her hands.

The affronted Miss Willoughby shifted her gaze from the end of the loaded gun a few inches from her face, to the eyes of the sodden and shaking policewoman. Louisa raised her left eyebrow in a show of impatient disdain. 'I really don't think that will be necessary, Miss Green.' She looked Martha up and down. 'Do you have any idea how ridiculous you look, waving that gun all over the place and making such a mess of Mr Marsh's charming kitchen floor. Woodrow, please can you find Miss Green a towel and Detective, please remove that gun from my eye-line.'

Martha shuffled closer, keeping the barrel pointing directly at her head. 'Stay where you are, Woodrow. I said, Miss Willoughby, put it down.'

Louisa pinched the top of her nose, a savagely patronising smile on her face. 'Detective Green, this posturing may appear effective in the works of fantasy you see down at your local film theatre on a Saturday night, but in the real world it is invariably quite without worth. You are not going to shoot me, you silly girl, so please lower your gun and move out of my way.' She waved a dismissive hand towards the revolver, like she was batting away a wasp and stepped briskly towards the door. In an instant, Martha swung the gun to the other side of the room, so it was pointing directly at Woodrow and then with her other hand hooked her fingers around Louisa's slender neck and slammed her weightless body against the wall.

'I said put it down, you poisonous witch.'

Martha caught a trace of movement out of the corner of her eye as Woodrow forged his bulky frame towards her. 'I wouldn't do that, Woodrow,' she said training the end of the gun between his eyes. 'Back up.' Lincoln was on his feet now, with his hand pushing against the chest of the burly driver, who begrudgingly retreated one step, breathing heavily, barely able to contain his anger.

Martha's fingers were turning white as they gripped the thin, sinewy neck of the eldest Willoughby sister, who still clung doggedly onto the rolled up parchment. Martha tightened her grip still further, watching Louisa's eyes begin to bulge, the exposed veins expanding in the white of the sclera. She pushed Louisa once more, hard against the brick wall until she began to choke. Finally, the parchment tumbled out of her hand, rolling underneath the kitchen table, next to where Lincoln had retrieved it some hours earlier. Martha kept her grip on Louisa's neck for a moment longer. 'Thank you, Miss Willoughby, you see, not so hard,' she said and then unclenched her hand, watching as the aged heiress collapsed onto the tiled floor, choking and clutching her throat.

Woodrow, overcome with concern, pushed Lincoln's arm from his chest and bent down next to his employer, checking she was okay. After a couple of minutes, he slowly and carefully helped her to her feet. All the time, under Martha's watchful gaze, who kept the gun aimed at the two of them throughout.

'Pick up your cap, Woodrow,' Martha said, 'and get that wizened creature from Hell out of this house.'

The driver could hold back no longer and tried to grab the detective, who just managed to move out of his reach in time.

'No, Woodrow. Leave them,' Louisa Willoughby said sternly, her voice cracking. 'She is toying with you. Pay her no heed. We don't want to make matters any worse than they already are.' She dusted down the front of her jacket and straightened her hair, trying to compose herself, but her disquiet was there for all to see. A wary, hunted look was in her eyes. Her features, not used to defeat, failed to find their accustomed poise. 'We need to go,' she said brusquely, taking hold of Woodrow's arm for support.

Martha and Lincoln remained motionless in the kitchen, not speaking. Martha was still clutching the gun tightly in her hand as Lincoln looked down at the rolled parchment, rocking back and forth, beneath the table. Out of the window, Martha could see the large frame of the driver, bent over, slowly easing the bruised and shaken Louisa Willoughby into the back seat of the saloon car. Finally they both breathed a sigh of relief as they heard the soft purr of the engine as it pulled out of the drive and travelled north, towards Widford Hall, far away from the small Suffolk village of Skeilton.

## CHAPTER 52

THE lights in the sitting room of Spring Cottage gave off a warm orange glow. Great Aunt Catherine was seated in her favourite armchair, transfixed as she listened to Martha recount her recent exploits. Two bottles of red wine sat on the table, one empty, one nearly so. Lincoln and Martha sat on the cushioned sofa opposite, side by side. Rosie was cross-legged on the floor, a look of wonder on her face.

'But how did you cut through the tape in time?' she asked, breathlessly.

'It was the ring,' she exclaimed. 'That stupid ring. I will have to give Thomas a call and thank him for buying me an engagement ring so ridiculously tight that I couldn't remove it from my finger, even when he dumped me for that floozy from his publishing firm. I never would have escaped without it and. . .what's even better,' she said, holding her left hand triumphantly aloft '. . . it finally came off!'

As the laughter receded, Lincoln leaned towards the detective and quietly asked, 'So you're not actually engaged then?'

'No, of course not, silly,' replied Martha, hitting him playfully on the shoulder. As Rosie poured the last of the wine, Aunt Catherine smiled as she noticed a look of relief wash across Lincoln's face, like sun chasing clouds across a meadow on a windy day.

It had been Martha's idea to retreat to the home of her great aunt. Louisa Willoughby's presence at Sorrel Cottage had tainted it, at least for now, and her mother's house had too many bleak memories to be a place for celebration. She hadn't mentioned the fate of George Giltmore to Lincoln yet, but would bring him up to speed tomorrow morning. They were planning to drive over to Manorview and lay out all of the evidence and go through it one last time before they travelled down to London for an arranged meeting with Colin McSty. The Chief Superintendent knew about the politician's sad end and had told Martha he would initiate the retrieval of the body this evening, once he had completed the painful duty of contacting the relatives. The rest, he told her, would keep until the morning.

She looked over at Lincoln who was, once again, flirting outrageously with young Rosie. That wonky but loveable smile lighting up his face. He looked relaxed and happy for the first time since they met all those weeks ago. He was a special man, she thought to herself. He deserved to be happy, although she couldn't hide her exasperation earlier when he finally told her where the forgotten parchment had been all of this time. She hadn't realised the document's full significance when she had forced Louisa Willoughby to return it, but now she had read it, she realised why the Willoughby family would be so keen to have it destroyed. The sheet detailing the names of the inmates had been written by Jeremiah Buller, serving as an invoice for payment, five shillings for each body. Down on the bottom right hand corner of the document there was another signature alongside Buller's, that of Norris Willoughby, dated 1902. Next to the date was a line, written in capitals and underlined, 'DUE SUM PAID IN FULL'.

It was getting late and Rosie started collecting the glasses and clearing the plates form the table, all under the close supervision of Aunt Catherine, leaving Lincoln and Martha to themselves. They were still seated at either end of the sofa, their feet resting on the low level table in front of them.

'What are you thinking?' Lincoln asked.

'Nothing. It's just it feels a bit strange to be laughing and celebrating when so many people have died.' It wasn't just the inmates Martha was thinking of when she said this. She knew the sound of George Giltmore's terrified screams would echo in her ears for the rest of her life.

Lincoln nodded, thinking of the children beneath the Black Ditch. 'We have enough now don't we Martha, to stop them?'

'Yes, I believe we do. We can go through it all tomorrow at my mother's house. Just give me some time, first thing, to get it all in order, but, top line, we can prove categorically that the Willoughby family were responsible for killing the thirty nine women and children listed on the invoice and we can prove categorically that the modern day Willoughby family have taken steps to knowingly conceal that crime. The rest - the murder of Reverend Barkham; the Dunnings Alley Nine; the men murdered off the coast of Southwold; my mother's murder; my defamation, well, that will all come in time. I have little doubt that when things start to unravel, Anthony and Louisa Willoughby, along with the whole miserable clan, will be implicated in full.'

'Wow,' Lincoln said, puffing out his cheeks. 'So, once we have it all pulled together we take it down to London, what, and give it to your boss, McSty?'

'My ex boss, Lincoln, and his name is either Colin, Mr McSty or Chief Superintendent McSty,' she said, affably. 'To be honest, I'm tempted to take the whole lot and dump it onto the desk of Cruickshank at the DPS.'

'You mean, Inspector Cruickshank,' said Lincoln.

'Very good, Lincoln, you are quite right, Inspector Cruickshank. But no, I will pass it over to Colin, he will know how best to handle it.'

They both sat in silence, gently warmed by the fire and staring up at the beamed ceiling of the cottage. There was an occasional faint murmur of good humoured conversation coming from the kitchen, where Catherine and Rosie were tidying away the dishes.

'They will be held to account at last,' Martha said eventually. 'The House of Willoughby will fall.'

Lincoln turned towards her, 'You did it, Martha.'

'We did it, Lincoln,' she said, resting her hand on his. 'We did it.'

## CHAPTER 53

LINCOLN woke late. By the time he made his dishevelled way downstairs, Catherine and Rosie were already on their second batch of baking. They were due at a small Christmas Eve gathering at the old rectory later and had promised to provide cakes and mince pies. Catherine seemed the picture of calm, her apron neatly tied and unblemished, her work station clear apart from a small tray of deep-filled mince pies patiently awaiting their pastry toppings. On the other side of the kitchen, there was a frantic blur of activity. Rosie looked like she had been dipped, head first, into a bag of flour. A small speck of mincemeat had found its way onto her flushed cheeks and the bow of her apron had come undone, leaving it to hang loose like a long, striped napkin pinned to her front.

'Happy Christmas, my dear,' said Catherine, enveloping Lincoln in a warm, motherly embrace.

'Yes, Happy Christmas, Lincoln,' joined in Rosie amidst a blizzard of flour and sugar. She came across to embrace him, but noticed the concerned look on his face as she approached.

'Oh, yes, sorry,' she said looking down at her apron. 'Christmas hugs will have to keep until later.'

'Probably for the best,' Lincoln agreed.

'There's a note pinned on the board for you, Lincoln,' Catherine said, pointing to the wall as she returned to her pristine cooking area.

The note was from Martha. She had driven to her mother's house, wanting to make an early start on the paperwork so everything was organised for their meeting later today with Colin McSty. She had added a final line, 'Don't be long sleepyhead, I need you. There will be mince pies!!! M' Her initial was accompanied by two large crosses, written with an affectionate flourish.

'I'd better go,' he said.

'You better had,' replied Aunt Catherine, looking over her reading glasses with a knowing smile.

The snow began to fall when he had travelled no more than three miles from Catherine's house. Not heavy snow by any means, just a light dusting, covering the roads and countryside in a thin layer of frosty white. The roads twisted and curved through the fields and villages of Suffolk, all frozen in the delicate stillness of a Christmas morning. Overhead, in a seamless blanket of white cloud, a flock of crows laboured their way above the woodlands, envious of the long-departed swallow's migratory release to a warmer climate. The conifer trees swayed by the side of the road, their snow-speckled, evergreen branches providing some definition and structure to the leafless countryside. Lincoln muttered a line from a poem he had learnt from school and thought long forgotten "Life is good and joy runs high, between English earth and sky."

Manorview was tucked away off the side of the road. A thatched retreat, surrounded by woodland and fields. When Lincoln looked up, he could see a thin line of smoke trailing from the small chimney, that was perched next to the weather vane, pointing, as ever, steadfastly eastwards. Even though Martha had left the door on the latch, Lincoln knocked lightly and called her name over the warm lilt of Christmas music coming from the sitting room. Not hearing a reply, he carried on into the house. The smell of Aunt Catherine's mince pies being warmed in the Aga drifted through the cottage, reminding Lincoln that he had missed breakfast. He could already see the dishevelled piles of paper, scattered around the sitting room, waiting to be filed and boxed ready for their trip to London. Martha was sitting on the floor in front of her mother's coffee table, her left hand, no longer troubled by an engagement ring, resting on Buller's leather saddlebag.

'Catherine's mince pies smell incredible. You should see it back there, it's like she's cooking for the whole of the county,' he said, stepping carefully through the piles of paper, doing his best not to disturb them. Martha remained an image of concentration, staring down at the documents in front of her. Lincoln moved to the other side of the table where he could see her. A wisp of her thick auburn hair had come loose from behind her ear and was hanging playfully across her face, obscuring the beautiful deep brown of her eyes. On the table was a half-finished mug of hot chocolate, next to a small plate of mince pies, barely touched. A white dusting of what looked like icing sugar was speckled on the top line of her full and red lips.

'Hello,' Lincoln said, waving his hand in front of her, 'earth calling Martha.'

It was then he saw the narrow line of blood seeping from her right nostril, leaving a thin red trail across the white powder beneath. Her mouth was slightly open and faint cracks were already beginning to appear on her drying lips. Martha's eyes were fixed in a cold, unfocused stare, looking rigidly straight ahead, but seeing nothing. The glass-topped table appeared to be covered in small piles of white talcum powder. In front of her, lying on top of the dusty surface, was a crooked and unfinished line of cocaine. In her right hand, pinched between her stiffening thumb and index finger,

Martha held her warrant card, sprinkled liberally with the narcotic powder. Lincoln Marsh looked deep into Martha's vacant, staring eyes, searching desperately for the woman he had fallen in love with, but she was no longer there. His heart breaking, he stumbled forward and fell to his knees, reaching out his hands towards her across the table and howling her name into the stillness of the winter's morning.

Five miles away, a black car carrying four men, one with heavily bandaged hands, turned right onto the A12 and joined the Christmas traffic heading south towards London.

## CHAPTER 54

IT would have been inappropriate to return to the house that was the scene of Martha's death, so Lincoln had offered Sorrel Cottage as the venue for friends and family to meet after the funeral. The small village church had been no more than half full with only a few colleagues from work prepared to make the journey from London. Not altogether surprising, given the circumstances. Martha had no immediate family, but there were a scattering of aunts and uncles and their offspring in attendance, including of course, Great Aunt Catherine and Rosie, her granddaughter. Lincoln had always sensed that there was a special bond between Catherine and Martha and the elderly relative had taken the news very badly, suddenly looking tired and worn out by age. Rosie was permanently at Catherine's side these days, looking after her as best she could. Since Christmas Eve, she had been staying over at Spring Cottage most nights of the week, trying to help her aged relative through the difficult evenings, when her thoughts were plagued by sadness.

Ben had been staying with Lincoln for the last two days. It had been good to have him around to lean on, just like Lincoln had been there for his brother when he was needed. Lincoln had decided to buy Ben's share of Sorrel Cottage, not wanting, after all, to see his family home go to new owners, besides, he no longer felt that he belonged in London.

Once he had taken care of the mourners, Lincoln slipped out through the kitchen door and into the garden. He sat on the small brick wall at the edge of the patio, needing a few moments alone. The air was cold, but the sun was shining with a clear, sharp brightness, cutting through the mists of winter. It would have been good to share the change of seasons with Martha, he thought. He missed her very much. He had hoped that the funeral would give him some sense of closure, and maybe it would given time, but for now, the feelings of loss felt more vivid than ever.

The service had been a simple affair, just a few words of comfort and remembrance from the local vicar. Colin McSty had travelled up and had volunteered to speak, which was good of him. Martha would have appreciated that, thought Lincoln. The Chief Superintendent had glossed over the circumstances of her death, referring to it simply as a "tragic end to a beautiful life". If only the press had been so forgiving. The tabloids had descended on the story with a feverish appetite. A tale of a beautiful but flawed police detective who had finally been undone by her own sordid addictions, was just too juicy to resist and so much better than the endless stories about the weather and bank holiday road chaos that usually competed for column inches at that time of year. Martha's story stayed on the front page throughout the final week of December, vying for prominence with some equally salacious headlines regarding the love life of a medium ranked politician. For the most part, the tabloids gave Martha little sympathy, speaking of 'ironic misadventure' and 'poetic justice'. Several carried the photograph of Deputy Assistant Commissioner Virginia Coulton who had taken it upon herself to release a statement, highlighting the episode as a "salutary lesson for any police officer who has lost their way".

Nobody wanted to listen to Lincoln's claims of murder and revenge. Any valuable evidence had been removed by the time he had arrived at the murder scene on Christmas Eve and he was just left with empty accusations. When Chief Superintendent McSty stopped taking his calls there was nobody left to tell. In the end, it was Ben who told him he should let it go.

'Here you are my sweet love,' Sarah said, lowering herself onto the wall next to him. Her jet black, full length fur coat providing plentiful protection against the cold January air. 'I've brought you a cuppa and a chocolate bikky.'

'Thanks, just what I needed,' he said, placing the cup and saucer on the wall, where it would remain untouched. Sarah had taken care of all the funeral arrangements when she realised that Lincoln was not up to it and that there were no immediate family members left to organise things. The flowers, the headstone, the service had all been quietly and tastefully dealt with by his oldest and dearest friend. 'I meant to say thank you earlier, you know, for coming up here and everything. I appreciate it, Sarah.'

She smiled at him, and picked up his arm, wrapping it under her own. He felt the comforting warmth of the fur as she held him tight.

'You don't have to thank me, Lincoln. I will always be here for you my sweetest love. Always.'

They sat side by side, looking out onto the frosted lawn as the sun slowly arched towards the west. A robin bounced along the hedgerow to their right, coming to rest on the handle of a spade, propped up against the shed at the end of the garden. He perched there for an instant, looking at the broken torch lying on the pile of earth and brambles in front of him, cocked his head to one side, momentarily curious, and then flew off into the fields behind.

\*     \*

Nobody ever came looking for George.

The story Sam Wilson emailed to Giltmore's wife was accepted by all, even the brilliant Harriet Blackwood, who had recently resigned her position, giving up on her short career in politics. Forty eight hours after her resignation, she had taken a post with a well known private equity company where she intended to stay for the next few years, or at least until something better turned up.

It had been a difficult Christmas and New Year for the Giltmore family, but they had got through the worst of it. The invasive photographers had disappeared from the front of the house, so it seemed that the tabloids had finally begun to lose interest. The boys had stopped asking Mrs Giltmore awkward questions and appeared to be coming to terms with the absence of their father. For her part, Mrs Giltmore, now that the gossip and scandal had waned, was feeling increasingly optimistic about the future and could already sense that the memories of her unfaithful and perverted husband were slowly drifting from the back of her mind.

Deep underground and entombed in stone, George was forgotten. His features forever frozen in a sorrowful portrait of feeble remorse.

\* \*

The Willoughby family gathering at Widford Hall had been postponed until the new year, giving time for Elizabeth, Andrew and Louisa to come to terms with their brother's sudden and debilitating illness. Anthony Willoughby had been transferred to an expensive private hospital on the outskirts of Warwick where he was able to receive twenty four hour care. The family lawyer, James Marquand, had visited the hospital, along with Louisa, when the power held by the Head of the Family was formally relinquished and passed onto his eldest sister. The image of Louisa peering down at her dribbling and semi-conscious brother would linger in his mind for some time.

'They tell me things are still whirring around in there,' she had said leaning close to the face of the dying man and prodding his head with the end of her finger, 'but I can't say I'm inclined to believe them.' She wiped her hand on the bed linen before turning to the lawyer. 'Mr Marquand, please do the honours and then lets be on our way.'

Louisa's meeting with Milton Cassidy had gone well. Although clearly still in a great deal of discomfort, he had behaved impeccably and listened attentively to the apology she offered on behalf of the family for the thoughtless mistreatment he had received at the hands of her brother. She hoped he could find it within himself to forgive. Despite Louisa's constant baiting of Anthony regarding, what she saw as the endless Strathdon chicanery and his ongoing dependency on Cassidy, she knew that the management of the Willoughby Estate, at least for now, depended on the continuance of the existing arrangements. Securing Cassidy's loyalty, whatever the cost, was a matter of urgency. As it turned out, Cassidy was easily persuaded. He required no financial incentive and no new terms and conditions of employment. He was content to offer his services to Louisa, as Head of the Family, just as he had done with her predecessor. What else was he going to do? He knew no other life.

As the main course was cleared from the table at Widford Hall, Louisa completed her summary of the Willoughby family's business interests. She was delighted to report that, now some bothersome loose ends had been tidied away, all appeared to be in satisfactory order. She raised her glass, offering a belated Christmas greeting to her brother and sister, who smiled and returned the toast, both wishing to convey pleasure at her recent advancement. Louisa noted that Elizabeth had less to drink before lunch than was usual and, even at this late hour of the afternoon, remained reasonably lucid. She appreciated her sister's efforts although feared this state of relative sobriety was unlikely to be maintained. Her brother's dinner jacket looked uncomfortably tight following his extended break in the south west of France. Paunched and pampered, he looked quite fit to burst, although Louisa had noticed a sharpness in his eyes and a new found confidence in his manner. He was clearly not missing being constantly upbraided by his elder brother and was perhaps hoping to prosper in his new found freedom. Louisa would need to keep her eye on young Andrew's ambitions, applying a swift crack to the flank if they proved ungovernable.

'Before we move on to Any Other Business, I believe you have an update for us, Andrew, on the Henham Development Project,' Louisa said, looking across the linen covered table. 'Just the financials and key highlights if you would, we do not wish to hear any of the lurid details of your undertakings. I am mindful that we are yet to finish our lunch.'

Andrew began his summary as desserts were being served. A small, individual bowl of Black Forest trifle with a single cherry perched on top was placed in front of the three family members. Louisa looked down disparagingly at the sugary treat before her and, after a brief moment, pushed the crystal dessert bowl away, towards the centre of the table and continued listening to the update from her eager brother. The sun had begun to set over the lawns of Widford Hall and she could see the tall elms at the end of the grounds, lit up by the deep orange glow, blazing like winter torches. She breathed a gentle sigh of contentment and let her fingers wander back to the dessert bowl, plucking the cherry by its green stem from the top of the trifle before crunching, delicately, into the soft skin of the purple fruit. A shiver of delight stirred behind the pale lifeless blue of her eyes as she felt the warm kirsch slip gently down her slender throat.

**THE END**